On the Contrary

ANDRÉ BRINK was born in South Africa in 1935.
He is the author of ten novels, including *Looking
on Darkness* (1974), *An Instant in the Wind* (1976),
Rumours of Rain (1978), *A Dry White Season*
(1979), *A Chain of Voices* (1982), *An Act of Terror*
(1991) and *The First Life of Adamastor* (1993). He
has won the most important South African liter-
ary prize, the CNA Award, three times and his
novels have twice been shortlisted for the
Booker Prize, in 1976 and in 1978. In 1980 he
received the Martin Luther King Prize, and in
France the Prix Médicis Étranger. In 1982 he
was made a Chevalier of the Légion d'Honneur
and in 1987 was named Officier de l'Ordre des
Arts et des Lettres.

André Brink is Professor of English at the
University of Cape Town. He has three sons
and a daughter.

ANDRÉ BRINK

[*On the Contrary*]

BEING THE LIFE OF A FAMOUS REBEL,

SOLDIER, TRAVELLER, EXPLORER, READER,

BUILDER, SCRIBE, LATINIST,

LOVER AND

LIAR

Minerva

*This one is dedicated
to Anton, to Gustav, to Danie,
and to Sonja*

A Minerva Paperback
ON THE CONTRARY

First published in Great Britain 1993
by Secker & Warburg Ltd
This Minerva edition published 1994
by Mandarin Paperbacks
an imprint of Reed Consumer Books Ltd
Michelin House, 81 Fulham Road, London SW3 6RB
and Auckland, Melbourne, Singapore and Toronto

Copyright © André Brink 1993
The author has asserted his moral rights

A CIP catalogue record for this title
is available from the British Library
ISBN 0 7493 9798 5

Printed and bound in Great Britain
by Cox & Wyman Ltd, Reading, Berks

On the contrary

– Henrik Ibsen's last words

Those who speak the truth find no shelter in this land

– Estienne Barbier

Contents

[*Part the First*]

· *I* ·

I am dead: you cannot read: this will (therefore) not have been a letter.

I have written so many letters these last few years: to the people of Africa, to Governor Hendrik Swellengrebel, to the Lords Seventeen, to those scum, those wretched dogs, the crooked powerful swindler Fiscal Daniel van den Henghel and the pious thief Lieutenant Allemann and the unmitigated swine Landdrost Pieter Lourens of Stellenbosch, to the Council of Policy and the Council of Justice, and many others besides. My whole life has gone into writing. And what has come of it? No one has paid the slightest attention. To all of them I, Estienne Barbier, am a traitor and a rebel, now condemned of high treason, and awaiting (for how long already? time has no meaning here), in this stinking Dark Hole of the Castle, the end.

Bound to a cross, the verdict said, *his right hand and his head severed from the body, subsequently to be drawn and quartered, the head and hand to be placed on a stake in the Roodezands Kloof, and the four remaining quarters to be displayed in four different places alongside the most frequented highways of the Settlement as prey to the air and the birds from heaven.*

And this is why, in this ultimate letter, this quite impossible letter – I have neither pen nor paper and it is too dark in here to see – I address myself, Rosette, to you.

There is a weird and terrible freedom in this. At last, at least,

3

I can offer you my life – with whatever it contains of rage and dreams and what others would think madness – as a story: in exchange for the inventions with which you teased me so long ago, in that ignominious and shining night, before I understood a word of it.

· 2 ·

No, I have given up trying to explain either others or myself. This is just a story. I am not even sure that I am telling it. In this final darkness where smell – and God, what stench – has replaced the sense of sight, I cannot trust my own presence. When I clutch myself in the cold to cherish what meagre warmth a body fabricates, what I feel is alien. I have already taken my distance from it. When I try to find reassurance or brief release in tearing at that obtuse member that used to be the source of most of the pleasure and so much of the misery in my life, nothing happens. Once the centre of my body and the key to its functions, now a mere appendage, a futile and dangerous supplement. I am absent from myself. I am absence. All I have, think I may have had, is this story. Multiplying, in the telling, into a host of others. And even that may be illusory. Perhaps already I am told as much as telling. Perhaps my very attempt to imagine what has happened to myself (and groping for a spurt of the imagination is as desperate as that other urgent fumbling), is no more than the effect of someone else, in another place, another time, fifty years, a century, two hundred and fifty years from now, who knows, God knows, trying to imagine me. Let me not – no longer – presume.

· 3 ·

– affirming amazement Acc: denies all allegations, because Littera scripta manet, but for reasons of Consequence Hêroïce must seek to defend himself,

4

*and should those who persecute him persist in their jure: by reason of the
vera illata against him: negative; in which case the Acc: will be forced
in summo gradu to employ in his ultimate defence neither chimerica nor
fantastica: as the Prosecution argues in inmaginativus jurista: but in
rerum natura verefacta, alleging Contingentia —*

· 4 ·

I do not even know by what name to call you. Who in God's
abused name first called you 'Rosette'? Some mistress trying to
invoke through it her own sense of that status, real or imaginary,
which in this colony at the edge of the known world counts for
so much? Or was it forced on you by a master eager to bestow
on you the name of a European flower to make you more
acceptable, perhaps more desirable? Or was it simply some
clerk entering into his official register the first 'civilised' name
that came to mind? Perhaps it doesn't matter. I myself was not
concerned at the time to find out your real name. Do you *have* a
real name? I cannot stand 'Rosette'. Yet I have nothing else to
call you by. (Why should it matter – and so much – in this
timeless darkness?)

· 5 ·

No less a luminary than the governor, His Excellency Jan de la
Fontaine, came out to our ship in a rowing boat to welcome me
in person when we anchored in Table Bay on Sunday morning
31 October in the year of Our Lord 1734. You must appreciate
that I was a very important person, having been dispatched as
their personal representative by the Lords Seventeen in the
Netherlands to inspect and improve the fortifications at Cabo
and to report on the actions and attitudes of the top functionaries. It was a secret mission (I myself had not been informed

of its true nature beforehand, and the full truth was only communicated to me by Jeanne after we had boarded the good bottom *'t Huys te Rijnsburg*) and I surmised that apart from Mijnheer de la Fontaine no one else in the colony had been alerted to the matter.

I took to de la Fontaine immediately – a tall, spare, affable man ill at ease in his finery. Seated between his two tame lions of state (awkwardly squashed into the small rocking boat which, I should remind you, also carried a band playing at full blast and a guard of honour doing their damnedest to remain standing to attention) he made an impression more of a seedy châtelain than of a governor; and in fact he was soon to invite me to call him *Oom* rather than *Your Excellency*. But of course it wasn't long before I discovered the real reason for his congeniality, namely a gauche attempt at concealing from me the depths of his corruption: not as bad as that of his luckless predecessor, or – all too soon afterwards – the monstrous van den Henghel, but a bad apple all the same.

We had but a brief conversation before I gave him leave to go. I was very ill from the effects of the voyage, and Jeanne had recommended that I be taken to hospital without delay. But not wanting to disappoint the poor fool I did first accompany him, dragging my emaciated frame up the steps by the railings, to the deck where, swaying and gasping in the tangy breeze, I stood to attention as the overloaded boat rowed back to shore. Two of the guardsmen, who had the misfortune to lose their balance, fell overboard, promptly to be devoured by the largest sharks I have ever seen.

The backdrop, that august mountain rising straight from the sea and the sprinkling of whitewashed green-roofed houses at its foot to the clouds on its famous table top, was most stately.

The light. It is the first thing that strikes one in this place. The light, which makes everything look different. In Europe the light was attenuated, *tamisée*. Here it is direct, uncompromising, aggressive, blinding.

I am, Rosette (and through you, with your permission, I am addressing myself to Jeanne as well) responsible to the future for the otherwise unremembered past.

The first journey into the interior: how unlike the two that followed! On those I was to be a fugitive, the last time with a price on my head; what propelled me then was the urge to reach you, beyond the Great River, amid that motley crowd of outlaws – the disillusioned and the dispossessed, slaves, burghers, hottentots, halfbreeds, hunters, smugglers, you name it – who nurse their fabulous dreams of revenge in a land beyond the calculations of date and time, everything reduced to mere space, hard-baked earth and scrub under the unblinking eye of the sun. But the first journey, 15 February to 24 May 1735 (nothing wrong with my memory), was so different; undertaken officially, as you know, 'to visit the East India Company's victualling posts along the West Coast, and then to venture withal into the less well charted regions beyond in order to explore the feasibility of extending these stations and establishing permanent points of contact with the natives of the deep interior.' There is nothing about it you don't know yourself,

7

you were there, all the way, all the time, and already inventing stories: but allow me to tell it to you again. There is always a new discovery in the retelling.

· 9 ·

At 9 o'clock on the morning of 15 February I departed from the Fort of Good Hope in the name of God. We were, officially, 39 strong: the leader, Lieutenant Rudolf Siegfried Allemann and his wife; the lieutenant's young friend Otto Mentzel; sergeant Godfried Kok from the Castle garrison; three corporals including myself (who had the additional function of scribe assigned to me); a drummer; an undersurgeon; and 30 soldiers. We had with us five wagons, a small and rather ornate one, painted green, for the Allemanns (chosen by Madame Abbetje herself to outdo the blue one the Fiscal's wife had recently imported, in several parts, from Batavia) and four baggage wagons, each provided with 21 draught oxen and a complement of hottentot labourers for each; the Allemanns also took with them 3 slaves, 2 male and one female.

· 10 ·

To these I suppose I should add Jeanne, who naturally accompanied me. But her presence was never officially acknowledged: and in any case she came disguised as a boy, as had been her wont on so many previous occasions. She'd always been boyish of build, diminutive and somewhat *costaud*, her breasts obscured behind the folds of her shirt, her hair worn short; and even if the others had paid attention there could hardly have been objections to the presence of a young *knecht* in my company after I'd so spectacularly – if I say so myself – passed the test of building the new redoubt at the Salt River.

There was only that one occasion, and that was already on the way back, near the Piquet Berg, when things nearly went wrong. In the process of assisting with the skinning of a Camelopard she'd split her breeches without realising it. The first I myself became aware of it was after supper that night when I found myself, with Kok and the two other corporals, opposite her, the fire between us. (The Allemanns had already retired; we could hear the steady drone of Madame Abbetje's complaining voice, like the high whine of a mosquito, from their wagon fifteen yards away.) She was squatting deeply and comfortably on her haunches, absently twirling a twig she'd lit in the flames; and as, inevitably – I am a man – my eyes descended to the open fork of her thighs I could not but notice, in a surge both of desire and of horror, in the deceptive flickering of firelight in her crotch, the split in the seam of her breeches replicating the cleft flesh below. Before I could motion to her I realised that Kok had perceived it too, and was in fact peering at her crotch in disbelief. After a long moment, lighting his pipe very meticulously with trembling hands, his eyes still staring fixedly at what no one could have imagined there, he cleared his throat, shifted stiffly on his haunches, and said, 'Young man, never in my life have I seen such a long arsehole on a man.'

I turned very sharply to him and snapped, 'What the hell are you talking about?'

The others, mercifully, seemed altogether unaware of what was going on.

'I . . . I – ' Godfried Kok blew out a huge cloud of smoke and became convulsed in a fit of coughing. By the time he'd finished Jeanne had already flickered, like a shadow, out of sight; she might never have been there.

Kok said no more; but from the way he stared at me with his small red eyes I could tell that he would never forget – neither what he believed he had seen, nor my interruption of his vision.

9

He retired soon afterwards, without another word, to his bundle of blankets beside the second fire.

In the background Madame Abbetje was still whining away.

· II ·

Indeed, a journey of this kind is not for women. And I knew – everybody on that expedition did – that the lieutenant himself had done all he could to dissuade his wife from what was clearly not only an unprecedented but a highly irregular enterprise; all the more so since she undertook it not from any conviction or a desire for adventure but only to gain a point in her unremitting duel with Madame van den Henghel. A born Afrikaner, she evidently lacked the finesse of her Prussian husband, whose own running battle with the Fiscal was no less intense than hers but who knew how to camouflage it to his own advantage. Herr Allemann is a past master at ingratiating himself with whoever is in power. When the late unlamented Governor van Noodt arrived at Cabo, they say, he immediately took such a dislike to Allemann that he found reason to imprison the man: yet within a month the then sergeant managed to have van Noodt eating from his hand and soon he was promoted to lieutenant and a position of confidence; I've heard that it was van Nocdt himself who arranged the match between Allemann and Abbetje Meijboom and then, through a series of enviable contracts, ensured that the man became the richest military officer in the colony. Then, all of a sudden, van Noodt died – in rather suspicious circumstances, as far as I could make out – and the indulgent old Jan de la Fontaine took over. Once again Allemann was faced with a governor he couldn't stand and whom he'd previously openly ridiculed: yet once again, within months, he'd wheedled himself into a position of trust. Then van den Henghel arrived from Batavia as the new Fiscal Independent and soon – But why rehearse the whole dreary business? (I'm prejudiced, everyone will tell you. But will *you* believe them?)

Once Madame had persuaded the governor to let her go, convincing him that her native knowledge of the land was not only indispensable to such an enterprise but *ad maiorem gloriam* of de la Fontaine himself, we were stuck with her.

Yet if she hadn't come, you too would have remained behind. And then, what would have happened, or not happened? Was that not the decisive event?

You did not even have a choice. You will come along, said Madame. You came.

· *12* ·

I, on the other hand, was free to choose. In fact, it took some manoeuvring to persuade the lieutenant, who had initially selected one of his favourites for the position, Corporal Frederik Courthym, known at the Castle mainly for bowing and scraping.

Why was it so important to me? It was more than the adventure, believe me, although that in itself, I admit, was an attraction. But there was, behind it, the old dream, kept constantly alive by Jeanne's urging, of getting involved in something worthwhile, something great. During all those years in France after the death of the old king – a despot and a *scélérat*, true, but a man who nevertheless made it possible for one to believe in greatness – I'd been waiting for something to happen, a sign perhaps, something resplendent that would shine through the misery and the confusion and the pettiness of the time. But France, even my favourite town of Orléans, had nothing to offer but turmoil and bickering. It was like being a child caught in the middle of a crowd, everybody jostling and pushing: one couldn't see over the heads, you had no sense of moving anywhere, it was only a great flood thrashing and churning this way and that. What I wanted – *needed*, as urgently as water, food, air to breathe – was a horizon: space, distance, direction, clarity, light. And so in the end Jeanne persuaded me (although it was even more painful to herself) that we had no choice but to leave France. A matter of survival, an escape from being smothered in ordinariness.

Wandering this way and that, coming to rest at last (God knows why!) in Middelburg in Zeeland. And then the gradual shaping of the final choice: to leave the last frontier of the familiar world where everything already had a name and betake us to the terra incognita of the colonies. But which?

It was not really a matter of choosing; the question had been decided for me years before in my home village, the muddy little Bazoches, by the first girl I had ever loved, *la fille du Cap de Bonne-Espérance*. It was she, la belle Héloïse, who had first kindled this fierce irrational longing in my guts and implanted that magic name in my mind, a fire no reason could put out.

· *13* ·

And by now I'd been there for nearly four months. Not very long, admittedly; but patience has never been one of my virtues. I'd built my small redoubt, yes indeed; against all the odds, the scepticism, the hostility, the attempts (even by the Fiscal himself) to undermine the project. But what, ultimately, did a small squat stone building on the shore amount to? I hadn't come to the end of the known world to spend my days in the cramped little house assigned to me inside the walls of the redoubt I'd built myself. Behind it all was the need to see more, venture farther, conquer, break into the land, a continent. Monomotapa: that was the magic name, and all the more so since three quarters of a century of exploration still had not discovered it. Most adventurers, I know, had long abandoned it as illusion and mirage. But I knew it must be there. I could be party to finding it.

But Corporal Frederik Courthijm had been chosen, had already received word that he should start packing.

What won the day for me was the revelation of my considerable experience of matters military, prior to my journey to Cabo, first as a scribe to a general of Louis XV, and subsequently as a member of the cavalry in the service of His Majesty King Friedrich Wilhelm of Prussia. Quite an achievement for a born Frenchman, wouldn't you agree? Allemann, of course, had had the same Prussian background – except, as I learned soon after my arrival at Cabo, having discovered that he'd been 'slandered to the king', he'd been forced to desert in order to avoid arrest. It goes without saying that he was impressed by my credentials, especially when I let it be known that I unconditionally believed in his innocence in that little contretemps with the Prussian king. Which, admittedly, had to be taken *cum grano salis* as I really knew nothing about that incident from his past; and actually I'd never met any general of Louis XV, nor set foot in Prussia. But I have no doubt that by accepting me rather than Courthijm in the end the lieutenant himself largely benefited from his choice. Nothing like a journey into the interior of a savage land to separate the true from the false. And at that time, I assure you, I was still irreproachably loyal to Herr Allemann.

Courthijm, understandably but regrettably, was furious.

'The man cannot even speak Dutch properly!' he ranted in the rear courtyard of the Castle, in front of the coach house, pointing a shaky hand at me. 'With due respect, Lieutenant, how can you take Barbier along, let alone appoint him the scribe of your expedition?'

'I shall be the judge of that,' said Allemann curtly, striking as imperious an attitude as he could with his short and rather plump body.

And so I was instructed to load my meagre possessions on one of the wagons (the simple carved chest of Burmese teak containing a few nondescript items of clothing, and my father's chainless gold watch, and his large leather-bound book of chivalric adventure that had accompanied me on all my wanderings); and on that dazzling morning of Tuesday 15 February we set out from the forecourt of the Castle, to the sound of thirteen cannon, a full band playing, the whole garrison cheering and the governor himself waving from the balcony of his residence. And that evening I diligently recorded in a green journal on my knees our first day's uneventful trek, across the Salt River to Rietvlei where we'd halted until 3 o'clock after midday, and thence to the farm of the colonist Joost Myburgh behind the Blauwberg.

· *15* ·

Uneventful, too, most of the days and weeks that follow. Page after page of my journal is filled with the account of our progress: from the Blauwberg to the Groenekloof to the Berg River to the Piquet Berg to the Sonquas Kloof and the Verlooren Vlei, to the so-called Heerenlogement that still bears the incised names of our more intrepid predecessors, Captain Olof Bergh (anno 1682) and Governor Simon van der Stel (anno 1685) and Ensign Rhenius (anno 1721) and others; and thence into ever more arid territory, towards the Oliphants River, and still further.

Everywhere we find traces of our predecessors. Even in remote tracts with almost no sign of human life, small bands of hottentots display items of clothing, copper or beads bartered from earlier travellers; here and there we pass the grave of a previous explorer or farmer, the inscription on the weathered stone barely legible. What I yearn for is the discovery of something *new*, not yet named, not readily nameable; something not witnessed by human eyes before, earth not yet imprinted by human traces. And then, ultimately, Monomotapa.

One day, I know, that fabled city of gold will invade our sight: on the horizon, in the unabating late-summer glare, shimmering with distance and heat, like a mirage, but only too real, my God, *real*.

Meticulously I record in my journal the observation of our daily progress, of latitudes and longitudes measured by our under-surgeon, of topographical features of concern to future travellers and to the administrators in Cabo (hills, plains, watering-places), of farms visited and the families settled on them, of specific animals killed (*Camelopard: adult male: length of head: 1 foot 8 inches; height from forehoof upwards to the shoulders 10 feet; from shoulder up to head 7 feet; length from shoulder to crupper 5 feet 6 inches; from crupper to tail 1 foot 6 inches; height from rear hoof up to crupper 8 feet 5 inches*), such manner of things.

I do not, as one might be tempted to think, find it a dreary occupation. Apart from exercising my Dutch, I draw satisfaction from contributing in my small way to the accumulation of knowledge about what was, a mere eighty years ago, a savage waste and is now beginning to be tamed. Each tract traversed, each page inscribed, extends our occupation of the known. And even if I know, inspired by Jeanne, that my true business is the *un*known, I accept that it is necessary first to define the known. Monomotapa is waiting. I am on my way there; and attention to detail is the price it demands.

· *18* ·

At the official outposts of the Company where we outspan from time to time we are invariably received by the farmers with great demonstrations of goodwill and an alacrity to be of service – none more so than Jan Cruywagen, a peasant potentate of small stature, hoarse voice, and huge hippopotamus whip, on whose farm in the vicinity of the Verlooren Vlei we outspan for fully seven days. 'Here you must all be on your best behaviour,' the Lieutenant warns us beforehand, 'because Mijnheer Cruywagen is a good friend of the governor.' The effects of this relationship, I confess, are readily visible. Cruywagen's property covers what must be a surface equal to at least a dozen ordinary farms; and cattle, sheep and all manner of game abound on the endless plains on which we are entertained to a stupendous hunt that lasts three days and leaves in our wake more dead animals than I have ever seen alive.

Cruywagen strikes me as a small, vicious man; though I may be prejudiced as a result of a small incident when he finds me milking a cow some distance behind his house and promptly sets to belabouring me with his long whip which he handles with diabolical skill. It takes a considerable effort to catch hold of the whiplash (nearly flaying my hand in the process); with it I jerk him off balance. He begins to shout abuse at me. I am on the point of attacking the ranting runt – I tell you, I'm in such a rage I can kill him – when it occurs to me to adopt a different approach. 'I'm sure Lieutenant Allemann will not take kindly to the news that you appear to deny him the milk he has sent me for,' I say. The transformation is amazing. 'Was it the Lieutenant who sent you?' he asks in a tone of consternation and cajolery. 'Of course,' I reply, 'why else should I be here?' Whereupon he invites me into the house, offers me a whole pail of milk for my commanding officer and another for myself, and even presses upon me, from a small leather pouch tied around his waist, several rix dollars in coins, more than a whole month's wages. 'You had better not breathe anything about this to the Lieutenant,' I warn him. 'He is sure to take it personally. He may even report it to Governor de la Fontaine.' With a choking sound he presents me with even more money, which this time I proudly refuse; and I leave him behind cowering like a beaten cur.

· *19* ·

The other colonists in charge of the Company's posts are less actively obnoxious, less extreme in their subservience; yet their preternatural deference remains offensive to me. There is something devious and sly in this eagerness to please, to help pitch our tents and feed our oxen and provide meat and milk and produce like pumpkins or wheat for our sustenance, their sole motivation the rewards offered by Allemann: tobacco and brandy, and promises of favours from Cabo.

At least their ingratiating manner is less of a menace than the reception we are given by those individuals on loan farms who, having been born in the colony, call themselves Afrikaners and appear invested with a profound distrust of anyone or anything emanating from Cabo. Without exception they confirm the negative opinion I first formed of them during the single brief expedition I was sent on, in the district of Stellenbosch, barely a month before this journey. And the further we proceed the more intractable and less helpful they become. Whatever we require must be bought, at exorbitant prices and with considerable haggling. Relying, it seems, almost exclusively on slaves and hottentots for whatever work is to be done on their farms, they spend their time eating, drinking, breeding and bickering.

Enquiries about their situation often provoke a hostile reaction, no doubt due to the fact, Allemann informs me, that few of them pay the annual rent on their farms, which means that their occupation of those places is strictly speaking illegal. On several occasions we meet with such a stern reception that it seems wise rather to proceed than to stay over; at least once, as we approach what Sergeant Kok tells me is the farm of a man called Hendrik Kruger, near the Paleisheuwel, our approach is actually halted by gunfire from the miserable little wattle-and-daub dwelling known in these parts as an *opstal*. Whereupon Sergeant Kok immediately proposes a military assault on the place – this Kruger being, Kok assures us, a notorious fellow with a previous record of unruly behaviour – but the lieutenant countermands his order, arguing that the presence of a woman in our company renders such action unwise.

It is obvious to me that the colony, and the more remote parts especially, is in need of strong control. There is something depressing, if not offensive, about witnessing the signs of European civilisation gradually dissipating as one moves further away from Cabo. It is a savage region still; and the most distressing aspect of it is the depravity of those members of our own European race who in these parts appear to care little for the very law and order they are presumed to represent.

We are truly – this little expedition, with our wagons and soldiers, our drummer and surgeon, our strict routine, my daily recording of events – a precarious yet invincible trickle of civilisation and noble aspirations moving through a dark interior, rewarding it with conscience and history.

Beyond the Piquet Berg. Advanced only 2 miles today owing to unexpectedly inclement weather. Forced to outspan on the farm of one Matthys Willemsz, who appears to have lost a child and all his possessions in the storm.

No need, said Allemann, to dwell on detail; in the larger scheme of governmental affairs it did not concern the smooth running of the colony. For the first time I felt a twinge of resentment at being instructed to suppress what had touched me. That wretched man.

The storm, consisting not so much of rain or hail as of wind, but of such a savage fury as I had never experienced before, not even at sea, had unfurled upon our expedition what must have been the mere tip of one of its wings (and even that was bad enough to blow terror into the less sophisticated among us). But it had descended in its fullest force on the farm of Matthys Willemsz on a largely exposed plain in the crook of a small river. His house, little more in fact than a mud hovel, had partially caved in, killing under the falling stones and rafters his sole child, a mere baby at his mother's breast, and injuring the wife. The wall of the kraal had been blown over, as a result of which (we learned later from a fearful, chattering hottentot servant) all the animals had fled. The farmer himself, this Matthys Willemsz, we found some distance away in a small orchard stripped quite bare by the awe-inspiring violence of the tempest. Bruised and broken fruit and leaves lay scattered about among the torn branches.

'What has happened here?' Allemann enquired of him (rather unnecessarily, it seemed to me).

The man was evidently in too parlous a state to speak coherently.

Looking up with wild eyes he could offer us at first no more than gestures in reply. When at last he spoke, all he could say, in a stuttering and gasping manner, was, 'The wind was blow.'

The next morning we moved on, after assisting him with the burial of his child. Apart from that single portentous sentence he had not spoken to us another word.

· *21* ·

Many of the entries in my Journal are concerned with the hottentots we encounter – individuals or small groups on their way to or from Cabo to barter; tribes wandering in search of pasture for their fat-tailed sheep, their skinny long-horned cattle. I take pride in recording with great accuracy the reported location of their ever-temporary settlements, the borders of their territories: the Kochaquas beyond the Blauw Berg, the Suffiquas and Cochoquas in the environs of Saldanha Bay, followed by the Odiquas (also known as the Udiquas), the Chirigriquas in the valleys of the Oliphants River, the Greater and Lesser Namaquas in the stern expanse beyond that river, the Damroquas even further to the north, on the banks of the Great River which these natives call the Gariep and which is the *limes* of the colony.

If there is one impression all of these convey it is that of being pressed by strange belligerent tribes from the deep interior who assail and plunder them increasingly. One alarming consequence of this is that the relatively tame hottentots tend more and more to undertake raids in the colonised region, disturbing the peace of our settlements. Another is a reluctance on their part to enter into any kind of bartering. In fact, in many instances we find on our approach no more than a handful of very old and useless sheep or cattle; from our own hottentots we learn that upon being alerted to our approach (how?) these people had their herders drive away the bulk of their flocks to remote places in the barren mountains of Bushmanland or

Namaqualand, for fear that we are robbers intent on sequestrating the same. It would seem that this has happened so often in the recent past that they are no longer prepared to put any trust in Europeans. More than once we have the distinct impression – which the Lieutenant, however, decides should be better left unrecorded – of animosities mounting against all colonists at the Cape.

Still, these contacts are not entirely unfruitful. I am particularly interested by the accounts those tribes give us about other peoples, beyond the Gariep where almost no European has yet ventured. Of Monomotapa itself they do not seem to have the faintest intelligence; or if they do they take great pains not to divulge anything to us. But I am prepared to wait patiently until we can discover more for ourselves by approaching ever more closely that Great Beyond. (At this stage, you must understand, I am still confident that Allemann will be true to his early promise and lead us across the ultimate established frontier of the colony: this is why I am here. Only later will disillusion dawn.)

There are alarming rumours of groups of bandits massing on the far banks of the river: escaped convicts, free blacks, runaway slaves, robbers with prices on their heads, white hunters, unruly halfbloods, all manner of outlaws. Other tales, about strange peoples with weird customs, enthral us. From the Lesser Namaquas, for example, we learn of a nation called the Tamaquas, who are blacker than any other people of the continent, yet have long hair and are hairy-chested, with incised slashes on their faces painted in several colours; and of a white nation even further away, with green hair and clothing of dried reeds and spun cotton, and ornaments of blue glass and gold. (Surely this must be a sign of Monomotapa?)

Truly, Africa is a continent of prodigies. For beyond this nation, I learn, live the Cobonas, a race of anthropophagi, who tame lions to pull their sledges; and still further, in a region where trees grow upside down, the inhabitants, too, perambulate in an inverted position, hopping about on their hard heads, their useless little feet dangling in the air.

And then the most remarkable of all, a confidence which I buy from a Damroqua herdsman a day's journey beyond the Oliphants, at the price of a full half-aum of brandy, many spans of tobacco, and three ells of copper wire, concerning peoples far beyond the great thirstland that begins at the Great River: nations of mutes who have no language and converse only in signs: some, it would appear, have no tongue, so cannot speak; still others have hardly a mouth, only a small cavity below the nostrils through which, with a thin hollow reed, they sip up water or grains of wild wheat.

This information makes perfect sense to me, given the various circles of spoken languages I have encountered in this colony. In the centre is the town of Cabo, stamped by a more or less civilised tongue, Dutch (even if of course it bears no comparison, in terms of sophistication, to my native French): but this is itself spoken with different degrees of fluency, considering the motley assortment of Europeans who over the years have drifted down to this outpost of the civilised world, and the many aboriginals and imported slaves (from Madagascar, from Angola, from the East Indies) whose survival in more than one sense depends on their ability to express themselves in Dutch. Then there are the outlying districts where free burghers and natives in a state of cultural promiscuity have developed a *patois* just about comprehensible to a European. And as one distances oneself from the centre the hottentot tongue becomes, as far as I can make out, less and less human in sound and in grammar. It may indeed, I think, be pretty justly considered as a monster among languages, and the pronunciation depends upon such collisions or clashings of the tongue against the palate, and upon such strange vibrations and inflections of that member, as a stranger cannot easily imitate, and neither they themselves nor hardly any else can describe. Hence it is, that they are looked upon as whole nations of stammerers.

It is on this account that it would seem perfectly logical that, at one further remove, one should encounter creatures altogether unable, or biologically unequipped, to speak a human tongue.

· 22 ·

Do you understand now why I wanted to see, hear, find out for myself? There was a thirst in me. And it was thwarted.

· 23 ·

As we proceed I also record particulars of animals we encounter along the way.

Item: THE LION. This animal being often shown in Europe, I shall not dwell on particulars, except to record that my own first sight of a lion did not prepare me for encountering it in the wild. I was then still a child, my tall one-legged father and my mother, a small plump *poule de Bresse*, had taken me from Bazoches, where we lived, to market for an Easter Festival in Orléans; large crowds were drawn to the small stinking cage on the Place du Châtelet and the wretched mangy beast that cowered in it, toothless and almost motionless, pelted and prodded from all sides by jeering children, while its owner stood by to exhort them and his wife did the rounds collecting our *sols*.

I cannot now help but recall that curiously disquieting episode in the book that has accompanied me on all my travels, even on this voyage, where the Knight of the Doleful Countenance has the gate to a lion's cage opened and challenges the beast to a duel, whereupon more from sleepiness than contempt the lion turns his back and drowses off into sleep. (Which, of course – this is important – is no reflection on the courage of his challenger who has had no way of predicting the lethargic outcome.)

On this journey I have had occasion to observe lions as they really are, at least until they were killed, set upon by our many dogs, riddled with shot from our guns, clubbed and speared by our hottentots.

From such experiences I can record that when he comes up with his prey, he knocks it dead down, and never bites till he has given it the mortal blow, and the blow he generally accompanies with a terrible roar. When the lion is wroth, or pinched with hunger, he erects and shakes his mane, and thwacks his back and sides very briskly with his tail. When he is in this action, it's certain death to come in his way; and as he generally lurks 'for his prey behind bushes, and travellers sometimes discover not the motion of the tail until it is too late, a man now and then falls into his paws, as happened to Klaas Duyker, the driver of our first wagon, soon after we had left our camping spot at the place known as Vogel Klip.

What is not generally known is that the lion has a horror of the pudenda of a woman and that the mere sight of them causes him to take flight. I should have wished to put this to the test myself, but regrettably there were no women among our hottentots to employ in this regard, and I was reluctant to borrow Madame Abbetje's female slave lest the experiment fail. (The lady herself might certainly have served the purpose, but then I suspect the view of her nether parts might have sent most animals galloping, not only lions.)

Item: THE ELEPHANT. The Cape elephants are much larger than the elephants of any other country, and their strength is proportionately greater, but the female is much less than the male. What is interesting to observe, and I pride myself on being undoubtedly one of the very few Europeans who have done so (in a thicket near the ford where we crossed the Oliphants River), is that the male and female retire, for the consummation of their loves, to some unfrequented part where they lie down and embrace in the manner of the human species; and that they shun and dread a discovery in the tender article as much as the modestest part of mankind, as was evident from the fury with which I was pursued when the snapping of a twig below my foot, in the act of eager observation, alerted the great bull to my presence. Had I not scrambled up a vast tree in the nick of time – where, I may add, I was detained for full twenty hours until a search party from our group discovered me and its members shot and killed the animals – this might have been the end of me.

Item: THE PORCUPINE. He is no rarity in the Cape countries, about two foot high and three long, his whole body armed with a sort of quills, partly black and partly white, very sharp at the outpoints, and not much unlike goose-quills stripped of the feathers. The most remarkable aspect of the beast, which I have personally witnessed, is that when set upon by a human being, he will wait with bristling quills until his enemy is about ten or twelve paces from him, whereupon he will dart a quill with amazing accuracy, and so effectually that it sticks in the flesh and causes a great pain and inflammation.

Item: THE RHINOCEROS. The colour of the rhinoceros is a dark ash, approaching to a black, and his skin, entirely without hair, is so covered with numberless scars and scratches that at a distance it appears as if fenced with scales. Upon his snout grows a horn of a dark grey, somewhat bent in the manner of a ploughshare and about two foot in length. With this horn, when he is angry, he tears up the ground and flings stones over his head with so great a force that they are heard to bounce and trundle upon the ground with a mighty clattering. Not far from the Brakke Fonteyn, early in the month of April, shortly before Lieutenant Allemann made the regrettable decision to turn back, a hunting party from our expedition came upon a solitary beast of this species. It is known that in normal conditions a rhinoceros will not attack a man. But on this particular occasion the Lieutenant was wearing a red coat, which immediately acted as a flame to the beast's destructive urges, provoking him into a charge, rending and destroying everything in his way. To the great fortune of Herr Allemann we had some of the hottentot drivers in the group and heeding their advice he hurriedly whipped a few paces aside to avoid the furious advance of the monster (it being known that a rhinoceros sees, and consequently charges, only right forward, ever in a straight line) and then divested himself of the red coat before the animal, with a great deal of trouble, could bring his thundering charge to a halt. The rhinoceros then attacked the coat, throwing it over his head with great force and tearing it to shreds with his horn. We were informed by the hottentots that had Herr Allemann still been inside the coat the beast would have fed upon him by licking, with his rough and prickly tongue, the flesh from the broken bones.

It should be added that the breeches of our Lieutenant were in a sorry condition by the time we returned to the camp, defiled as they were with the unsavoury secretions, both fluid and solid, of his affrighted state; and a hottentot had to be sent out ahead to collect another set from the main wagon, without however divulging to Madame Allemann the particulars of the event.

The less delicate part of the incident, needless to say, was not included in my official record of the day.

· *24* ·

The test for the recording of any observation in my official journal was the sanction of our leader; was what was judged acceptable to ulterior readers at the Cape and possibly Batavia and Amsterdam; was ultimately, too, what my cautious – and, I must confess, often halting – Dutch was capable of. Certainly any sign, the merest hint, of the personal disposition of the journalist was *a priori* excluded. Perhaps justifiably. Upon the ignorance and knavery of writers I have nothing to add to what has been said over and over, and is known almost to every one upon those heads. All ages, since writing has been known in the world, have produced as does the present, and as doubtless will every one to come, swarms of the ignorant and the designing to plague the world with mutilated fact and historical fiction. Few people apprehend how truth may be injured by the Melancholic, the Phlegmatic, the Choleric, and the Sanguine tempers of the individual writers. Few have any notions of the wounds, the tarnishes and false beauties the truth may and does often receive from the reigning humour in the author. For my own part I think that it does not little contribute to the discovery of truth in a history to know the temperament of the man who wrote it. It is not difficult to show that the constitution of a man frequently betrays him into a falsehood. And yet the curious thing is that were it not for this latitude allowed the author, this permissibility of falsehood in the individual, no apprehension of the truth may be imaginable at all. It is only by allowing the possibility of the lie that we can grope, as I am groping in this dark hole, towards what really happened, is happening, may yet happen.

· 25 ·

But the conditions imposed on me as the expedition's scribe ensured that merely personal observation, and all suggestion of the man behind the words, be excluded. Which is why I was, after probing discussion, permitted to write what I have written about the Lion, the Elephant, the Porcupine, the Rhinoceros, et caetera, but not a word about the Unicorn or the Hippo-gryph. Yet I saw them with my own eyes; and had a witness for the second! But they were not part of the accepted or acceptable truth of the Cape of Good Hope.

On Sunday 10 April, two days beyond the Oliphants River,

in the late afternoon, as I turn back, on horseback, from the solitary expedition on which I have been sent to explore the possibilities of water and grazing in that fearsome region of barrenness the trek is preparing to enter, I face the setting sun, resting huge and miraculous, unwieldy, like the bladder of a gigantic beast pendulous with blood, on the low undulations of the land towards the blue-black blur of the sea. And I see the Unicorn. It appears, heraldic, flat against the sun, standing in alert pose, head erect, taller than the gazelles of these parts, and shaped somewhat like a horse, a maned creature, pure white in colour – that much can be discerned against the fiery disk – its tall single horn rising like a scimitar from its forehead. I slide from my horse, and load my gun, ensuring despite my trembling hands that powder and lead and plug are rammed securely into place, go down upon my knees to rest the barrel on one of the many pointed boulders scattered in that place, take aim, and fire. There is no need to load again; I am a mean shot. In an almost gentle rolling motion the animal slumps to the earth. A single bright red patch above its dark moist eyes, below its unique horn. I run to the place and stand there for a long time, stunned by the creature's beauty.

It is a curious emotion that overwhelms me: not so much elation at having in one shot introduced a creature of myth into the domain of the possible, *voire* the real, as sorrow. I am standing at some desolate frontier, and no one can tell what lies beyond.

However, there is practical business to attend to. Before the night comes down I must skin the unicorn and sever its head to take the trophy back, in sad triumph, to the camp which lies a good hour's ride to the south. It is only then, as I turn to retrieve my knife from my saddlebag, that I discover my horse has bolted and is nowhere to be seen. Frantically I run this way and that, calling its name, shouting at the top of my voice, hurling both solicitations and imprecations against the descending night. But there is only silence to meet me, and the rushing of a newly risen wind that will increase throughout the night.

I huddle beside the dead unicorn. There is no moon. Yet, as the night increases, a curious pale luminosity seems to emanate from that beautiful corpse. In the distance are the sounds of Africa – the cackling of jackals, the whoops of a hyena drawn like exclamation marks in the void. And then, in the deepest darkest hollow of the night, the sound of a lion, not a roar, only a rumbling low rhythmic growl uttered in fading series, falling silent, then starting up again, ever more closely it seems. The very earth seems to reverberate. Never in my entire life have I been so terrified; never have I been so utterly alone. (Not even Jeanne is near.) It is not simply the proximity of the night's predators that petrify me so – although God knows that is bad enough – but the unreasonable feeling that, somehow, it is not my presence, or that of the carcass, that has summoned them, but the very nature of the deed I have committed.

And there is nothing I can do. There is no firewood in the vicinity, and even if there were it is too dark to look for it. I cannot even pray, lest closing my eyes invite a quicker end.

All night long I remain sitting there, shivering, shot with a terror beyond anything the mind can imagine, delivered to whatever is preparing to avenge the killing of the unicorn. And all night long the prowling predators circle and circle me where I crouch by the dead fabled animal.

At last the dawn comes, wrapped in a white fog from the far sea. The howls and whoops and growlings begin to fade away. When it is light enough I can see their tracks in a near-perfect circle of which I am the centre, its radius no more than twenty paces.

The unicorn lies motionless, stiffened in death, pure white, with the now blackened spot on its forehead, right below the single horn, where the ball struck it.

I know I have to get away from here. There is only terror in this desolate place.

In breathless hurry I build a cairn of rocks over the body to keep it from the sun and what predators may come, and turn to hasten back on foot in the direction of the camp. Three hours later some outriders from the wagons meet me. I can hardly speak – from fatigue, naturally, but also from the unspeakable fear the event has instilled in me.

They offer me a draught of water from a hip-flask, and a length of *biltong*, and take me back, seated in front of the slightest man among them, on his horse. The following day I lead the expedition to the spot, still marked exactly by the cairn. But of the unicorn there is no sign, although the stones are still in place as I stacked them, with no evidence of marauders of any kind around.

A travelling band of hottentots perhaps? What does it matter. It is gone. And no one will believe me.

Except, I should record, the drummer Nic Wijs, a consummate artist on his instrument but otherwise a reticent man who prefers to keep his own company, and who, unasked, when the others have returned to their business, assures me briefly, almost gruffly, that he knows I speak the truth. 'I can say this,' he says, 'because I myself have seen some sights in this land.' He is not prepared to say more, but for me it is enough.

· *26* ·

And then the Hippogryph. I shall be brief this time.

It is again at sunset, only a few days before we are to turn back from the ultimate point of our journey. As I come through a small thicket, carrying on my shoulders a small duiker I have shot, it is suddenly there, not fifty paces ahead of me, in a clearing. The body of a horse; topped with the angry head of an inordinately large bird of prey. I can clearly see, as it turns briefly to stare at me, the fierce glare of its yellow eyes, the mighty beak tipped with red. There is a hint of folded wings. I have, of course, as always, my gun with me but this time I do not even consider raising it. In any case it lasts but an instant; then the animal is gone. There is no sound of hooves, no sound at all. But it was there. I have seen it.

I am cold all over.

Behind me I sense a presence, and I turn. I half-expect it to be Jeanne. But it is another woman, tall and lean, proud in spite of her faded multicoloured rags, her dirty horned bare feet; Madame Allemann's female slave, Rosette, you.

'Have you seen – ?' I whisper.

You say, 'I have.'

'No one must know about it,' I say.

You make no reply. Not even a gesture to accept complicity.

· *27* ·

Of all this, you will say, no trace, no trace; yet here it is, now that, at last, I can write it in my unbounded mind, to find out what I saw, have seen.

After our common fleeting glimpse of the hippogryph I turned to go back to the camp where I had night-time duties to perform; but stopped halfway and looked round, and seeing you still motionless, returned some distance. I had remarked you before, of course, but in the way one notices, and does not notice, a slave. There was, now, having shared this brief miraculous vision with you, something about your erectness which touched me, barefoot and dirty as you were. In a sense you seemed perfectly in place, as natural among the trees and rocks of that spot as the hippogryph had been; yet in the shape of your black eyes, the light copper of your skin, the length of your rippling coarse black hair, you were clearly an exotic.

'How did you get here?' I asked.

'My mistress brought me.'

'In this colony, I mean,' I said, impatient.

'It does not matter.'

'I want to know.'

'I was caught in the forest where I hid when I was only a child without breasts.'

'In what place?'

'They tell me Bengal.'

'Your family?'

'My parents, my three brothers, my two sisters all got away. Not I. There is nothing to tell.'

'They caught you?'

'A band of men with guns and ropes and switches of water-buffalo hide.'

'Did they hurt you?'

'They caught me and laughed when I struggled to break free. They dragged me to their camp and put all those they caught in bamboo cages. In the night I forced myself through the bamboo slats. I was small enough. But the watchman heard and they caught me and beat me. Every day they beat me. And when I refused to eat the men came to force me.'

'You didn't try to run away again?'

'All the time. But then they tied me up and kept me like that, day and night. Even when the men came to hurt me they never untied me. They knew I'd scratch and bite them.'

'For how long did they keep you like that?'

'Until they had caught enough of us. Then a ship came and we were shoved inside. It was black there, and it got very hot, and we had little to eat, and many died, and were left like that for days, in the chains among us. Only once in ten days or so we were taken out to the deck where the sun hurt our eyes, and splashed with sea-water and vinegar water to clean us of the filth, and to be used by the sailors, and then we were thrown back into the belly of the ship.'

'But your life is better now?'

You shrugged.

'The Allemanns use you well?'

Your eyes narrowed, but that was all.

'Will you tell me if they don't?'

Another shrug.

I did not know what else to say. It was getting dark. I returned to the camp; this time you followed, but at a distance, as if you had nothing to do with me.

When I came back among the wagons Madame Allemann called me. 'Corporal Barbier!'

'Madame?'

'Where have you been?'

'I have shot a duiker for supper.'

'What was your business with my slave girl?'

'Madame, I don't know your slave girl.'

She snorted. Then looked past me and called sternly, 'Rosette, come here!'

· 28 ·

It is about a week later – we have already turned back from the unimpressive muddy trickle where Allemann (prompted undoubtedly by his wife) announced his decision to turn back, leaving behind all dreams unfulfilled, empty names ringing – that I come upon Madame Allemann chastising her slave. These sturdy Afrikaner women do not wait for men to perform menial tasks that demand exertion or strength; she even derives, I have come to suspect, a repulsive satisfaction from this particular chore. It has happened before; it will happen again.

I have set my detachment of soldiers with their hottentots working, beyond the fountain that has determined our halt, to gather wood for the night's fires and construct a temporary shelter for our oxen and the small flock of dumb sheep we have accumulated on the journey (last night three lions set upon them and dragged off an ox); on my way back to replace a broken axe I come past the two women. They are behind the

Allemanns' green wagon, which no longer looks as pristine as when we left Cabo two months ago. Abbetje is wielding her hippopotamus-hide sjambok, and screaming: it is a sound everyone in the camp has become accustomed to (as to the shrill of cicadas or the lowing of a cow that has lost her calf), but today it is shriller than ever, a high-pitched stream of abuse that doesn't let up for a moment, her large face purple with rage, her pale eyes burning. The slave woman stands in front of her, naked to the waist (a wretched bundle of rags beside the wheel suggest that they have been torn and stripped away in rage): she doesn't cringe or cower, but stands erect, bearing almost in silence the lashes that smack down on her shoulders, her back, even her breasts.

I have witnessed corporal punishment before, and incomparably worse than this – aboard ship; in the correction chamber of the Castle; at the stake in front of the entrance – so I don't know why I should react with such unpremeditated vehemence today: but before I properly know what I'm doing I lunge forward and snatch the sjambok from Abbetje's hand. She stops in mid-scream, then turns on me, her face contorting, and in an instant I know that my whole future can be decided now.

'Madame,' I stammer recklessly, 'let me.'

Her mouth open, she frowns in rage and disbelief.

What may have issued, I don't know and hesitate to think; but at that moment Lieutenant Allemann comes round the wagon to find us.

Abbetje, too furious to speak, points a trembling finger at me. 'That man,' she gasps, 'that man – that man – '

'Your good lady has overexerted herself,' I tell him. 'I beg leave to finish this thrashing myself and save Madame the trouble.'

He puts a plump arm around the hefty shoulders. 'Come, my dear. An excellent idea.'

'That man,' she repeats, 'that man – '

'He will do it soundly, I'm sure,' he says.

As they disappear round the wagon I strike out with the sjambok on the high rear wheel; and again, and many more times.

It gives me a profound satisfaction to wear myself out in this manner until my breath comes gasping through my open mouth and I am conscious of perspiration soaking through my clothes.

Only then do I notice the woman still standing there as she stood, looking on, the only suggestion of an expression on her rigid face one, perhaps, of bemusement. She has made no attempt at all to retrieve her clothing and hide her nakedness. And it is, unreasonably, I who feel shame. At what I have just done, even if it were in defence of her; at seeing her exposed like that, the delicate brown of her upper body marked with darker weals that curve, as she stands facing me, across her shoulders and her woman's breasts. A woman's indeed, not a slave's. This is what most disturbs me. Pale ochre globes, rounded and complete, the pointed nipples dark as cinnamon.

'You are shameless!' I snarl at her. 'Put on your clothes!'

She says nothing, no word of gratitude; if anything, she seems to mock me as, unhurried, she stoops to pick up the sad torn clothes and, still making no move to cover herself, strides off barefoot – that exquisite trembling, bobbing motion of breasts as a woman moves – towards the tangle of bushes that mark the course of the fountain stream.

· 29 ·

That night, seated at a distance from the others, I wrote in my Journal: *Camping beside a small fountain to let the oxen rest. Weather cloudy and becoming cooler. Acacia trees and rhinoceros bushes in profusion. Lat. 28.5 here, Long. 37.41. We have advanced only 1.5 miles today.*

This, always: below the dull grammar of the daily account, a different course of consciousness. Intimate truths, discoveries, many questions. I pass through a vast uncharted land, unnamed spaces, with scrub and trees and stones for which no words exist in the languages I know: from time to time I see vultures in an openness of sky, black specks upon white, intimations of something, of *something there*, terrible truths happening out of sight, beyond my reach; then night descends. What lies further and deeper must remain undisturbed. The only disturbance is *in here*, in myself. I write my stilted, stunted words. I read – if I have time, if I am not too tired, or not too obsessed with an image of woman's breasts – in my scuffed, much-thumbed book, the exploits of the narrow gentleman from La Mancha, taking arms against giants and Saracens, defending the honour of his Lady Dulcinea, broken but undefeated in battle; a fool; mad to the world.

I lie awake staring at the stars, thinking of the long way I have travelled to this colony at the tip of Africa, near the rim of the earth, I remember the dreams that startled and inspired me, that kept me alive when I thought I would die of fever on the ship. And I ask myself: What have I found, where am I now, where shall I yet go? Has all of that been madness too?

When I know none in the camp is awake to hear, to see, I turn to Jeanne and converse with her. She is the only one who knows, who never fails to understand.

'Go on,' she urges in the dead of the night, so close that her whole presence is contained in her voice, right in my ear: 'Go on, Estienne. You'll be a fool to give up now. Dream on. Be patient. Be impatient. Go on.'

And I believe her.

Camping at the Backeley Plaats. This is all you will find, would have found, in my Journal. In the hand of Herr Otto Mentzel, the new scribe; liar and turd.

Sergeant Godfried Kok had never been an easy man, always eager to pick a quarrel, hard on his men, even more so on the hottentots. Yet no one could have expected him to go so far. True, he had been sulking for a few days; we all knew better than to get into his way. Even so . . .

Only afterwards, when I took a deposition from the dying hottentot driver Ruyter, did I learn that it had begun on the day after Kok's presumed discovery of Jeanne's sex through the rent in her breeches. He'd gone behind some bushes while we were halting for the midday meal, ostensibly to relieve himself; the driver Ruyter, in search of a strayed ox and unaware of Kok's presence in the bushes, had come upon him in the process of inducing another kind of relief. As the ultimate period of rapture had seized him, he'd cried out; and Ruyter, unable to restrain himself, had burst out laughing. It was too late for Kok to undo his business; his member, taking on, it seemed, a life of itself, rearing in unruly fashion, started spurting hugely, Kok staggering in its wake, trying frantically to clutch and contain it. Ruyter was folded double in mirth when Kok, his nether half still exposed to the elements, fell upon him with such blows of fists and feet that the poor hottentot was half-dazed. He managed to scamper off just before the sergeant could pull a knife on him.

For three days Kok sulked (no one except Ruyter as yet knowing the cause), glowering at Ruyter whenever he moved into sight. Several of us, including Allemann, spoke to him, but he was incorrigible. Then, on the third day, at the above mentioned Backeley Plaats (how aptly named: *Place of Strife*), as Kok was seated beside the fire with his recently drained coffee *bol*, he called out to Ruyter to refill his vessel. Now Ruyter was at that moment some hundred paces away, milking one of the goats, while the coffee-pot was almost within reach of Kok himself, from which it is evident how unreasonable the command was.

'I'm busy!' Ruyter called.

No one was expecting such an instantaneous response from Kok: even before we had properly heard what Ruyter had said, the sergeant was on his feet and brandishing his gun. I can remember jumping up myself, shouting something, attempting to strike the gun from his hand; he seemed quite demented. But it was too late. The shot rang out, deafening me; and as I staggered back I could see Ruyter half-rising to his feet, stumbling, and toppling over. The goat he had been milking kicked over the bucket and scampered off in fear.

Three, four, five or more of us immediately set upon Kok to disarm and subdue him, while the under-surgeon and Allemann ran to the writhing and moaning Ruyter. He had a serious chest wound, bleeding profusely, but was still alive. In fact, after some treatment from the under-surgeon to staunch the blood, and esoteric ministrations with herbs and foul-smelling powders from the other hottentots, it seemed within an hour or so that Ruyter might yet survive.

However, soon after that brief semblance of revival, Ruyter had a relapse and began to writhe again in agony, his forces clearly fading rapidly. That was when the lieutenant instructed me – why me? – to take a deposition from the dying driver. From which I learned what has already been divulged above.

I was, that night, too much disturbed to make the customary entry into the Journal; but the following night – the hottentots having buried Ruyter in the morning, marking the shallow grave with a cairn of stones to invoke, they said, the benevolence of their Hunter God; whereupon we had moved on, placing as many miles as possible between us and that unhappy place – the following night, I say, I entered an extensive account of the event into the Journal. While I was working on it, the lieutenant came to me.

'I trust,' he said, 'you will be prudent in your record of these last few days.'

'I am just now in the process of setting it down,' I said.

'Some things are better left unsaid, Corporal Barbier. We should like the authorities to see upon our return that the journey has been successful in every respect. I think we are agreed on that?'

'But surely there are things one cannot supress. You yourself have conveyed to me the Governor's instructions: *to make a daily entry of all that is remarkable.*'

'Remarkable only inasmuch as it affects the Company's interests.'

'Lieutenant, don't you think a death affects the Company's interests?'

'A hottentot's death, Corporal.'

'Granted. But nevertheless killed by a soldier in the employ of the Company.'

He peered at me as if he was observing me across a great distance. His plump face was very white, even in the deep orange glow of the lantern in whose light I had been writing.

'We are all implicated in this, Barbier.'

'All the more reason, Lieutenant, to record as precisely as one can what really happened. Otherwise more than Sergeant Kok may have to pay the price.' (Prophetic words!)

'No one need pay a price,' he said.

Uncomprehending, I stared at him.

Allemann put out his hand. 'Let me see what you have written.'

I had no choice but to obey, watching intently as he read. I could hear his breath coming unevenly.

'Barbier,' he said at last, 'this is serious.'

'Then we are agreed,' I said.

'This account cannot be submitted to the Governor.'

'But it is the truth!'

'Who knows the truth?' he asked. There was a flickering of a small muscle in his jaw.

'But . . .'

'It cannot stand like this.'

'Lieutenant, you cannot tear the page out. It will be visible. The Governor will see it, he will demand the reason. That will be even worse.'

'No one will see it,' he said. 'Let me think . . .' he looked round anxiously, studying the men in the firelight some distance away. His face lit up. 'My friend Otto Mentzel,' he said. 'He's an astute man, Prussian like myself, a teacher, he knows how not to give offence. He shall take over as scribe.' Nervously, with twitching hands, he began to flick over the pages, scanning passages. 'Look,' he said, striking on an opened page with his flat hand. 'Look! All these mistakes of grammar and spelling. You should never have done it in the first place. I should have known better than to appoint a Frenchman.'

I really could think of nothing to say; nothing that would make sense, that is.

'I have virgin books in my wagon,' he continued, getting more and more excited. 'Mentzel can inscribe one of them. He can copy your early pages to cover our progress thus far, correcting whatever mistakes he encounters. We shall submit to the Governor a narrative both correct and gratifying. Every page in this one, as he progresses, he shall dispose of.' He turned away, having seemingly dismissed all thought of me. He called, 'Otto!'

And so my book was progressively destroyed. Day by day, as we proceeded, I watched, in a strange fascination, how Mentzel, that cringing silly man, tore out my densely inscribed pages and burnt them, one by one, in a cold germanic passion, substituting for each his own, the correct and proper truth, geographical, topographical and otherwise, about this particular exploration of the famous and (all things considered) remarkable African Cape of Good Hope.

The strangest sensation of all was that as my initial dismay subsided, I began to feel almost content at being relieved of the Journal; no longer did I have to bear responsibility for official truths. I was free at last to pursue my own, and in my own way.

· *32* ·

Beware of the land where the clocks are struck by hand. This I heard so often in Europe, even in France before I set out for Zeeland, whenever there was talk (and there was, always, in all places) of the colonies; of the Cape of Good Hope.

It is true, of course, that life here is regulated by the bell struck ponderously night and day. (You know even better than I do, don't you; you spoke about it that night; 'Even in my dreams I hear them,' you said, 'that is why I must leave this place.') Owing to the wild winds that often rage here no clock can be put up in the open, that is why the hours must be struck by hand upon the great bell from Amsterdam suspended in the turret over the Castle gate.

Let me remind you of the routine to which I was subjected for so long. (I am a soldier, Rosette: I can hold no long discourse without returning from time to time to matters military; moreover, recalling that regularity helps to demarcate the timeless space of this black hole.)

There are always two soldiers – *rondegangers* as they are called – stationed in the guard-house to see to the ringing of the bell; they know the time by the hour-glass which they take it in turns to watch and to reverse. The glass itself is regulated by the sundial on the *Kat* wall in the Castle.

At 4 o'clock in the morning the corporal of the guard, accompanied by the two *rondegangers*, goes out to make the daybreak round. They waken the adjutant, the sergeants in charge of the companies, the drummer whose turn it is that day to go on duty, the piper, and the six other guards. After striking the bell in the tower the patrol returns to the guardhouse where it is challenged; the corporal gives the password and is dismissed. The two trumpeters sound the morning call.

At 5 o'clock the adjutant and seven *rondegangers* go to the governor's house in the Castle to collect the keys of the gate.

At 6 the bell is sounded again, this time for the slaves and artisans to go to their work.

At 7 the drummers (the one going off duty as well as the one for the new day) post themselves in readiness, with the piper, and on the last stroke of the bell they sound the assembly.

At 8 the guard is relieved by its replacement to the beating of the drum and the playing of the hautbois. At the same time all the officials, merchants, bookkeepers and assistants, hasten to their posts and anyone desiring an interview with the governor comes to his house and requests an audience.

When 9 o'clock has been struck the *rondeganger* rings the bell to announce the assembly of the Council, whether for judicial or political business.

The striking of the 11 o'clock bell is the signal for the slaves and the artisans and the officials and clerks to cease work for the midday recess. The 12 o'clock bell is timed by the sundial (except in cloudy weather), after which the officer of the guard goes to his dinner, either with the governor or at his lodgings. At 1 o'clock the bell recalls to their labours the workmen and slaves, while the civic officials do not return until 2. Moreoever, they lay their pens down again at 4 except when there is special pressure of work owing to the imminent departure of a home-ward-bound fleet.

At 6 o'clock the labourers and slaves desist from work, and the six hautbois players assemble in front of the barracks and play, first an evensong and then various other pieces, for half an hour, after which the drummer whose turn it will be to go on night duty stands on the Leerdam Bastion of the Castle and beats the *Appel* until seven. After the 7 o'clock bell the roll is read and any man who gets back late catches it with the long cane from the corporal in charge.

8 o'clock – 9 o'clock – 10 o'clock (from half-past nine until ten the bell is rung continuously, which is the signal for anyone who lives in the castle to present himself there, and woe betide the man who is absent overnight).

At 11 o'clock the sergeant of the guard goes round and gives the password to the officer when he returns. If, as sometimes happens, the officer is not in the guardhouse, one of the *rondegangers* gives the password to the corporal of the guard. At midnight and every hour thereafter unil 4 o'clock, the two *rondegangers* set out to patrol the Castle by themselves; they always go before they strike the hour, their object being to surprise any sentry who may happen to have gone to sleep on duty.

At 4 o'clock the new day's rounds begin.

· *33* ·

Even so, the Cape of Good Hope is indisputably the best place in the whole of the East Indies for military service. At the other stations – Batavia, Banda, Ceylon, Bengal, Amboine and the rest – the conditions are far worse, and the soldier is held in far lower estimation than at the Cape. But one is easily misled in one's expectations of a place. In my youth in France – those eager imaginings of la belle Héloïse! – and even in the time I spent in Zeeland, the Cape beckoned, to a poor man of action, as the image of Heaven on earth.

This you do not know about me yet: we had so little time to talk (and what time there was I spoiled). But I was married there, you should know, to a sweet and dutiful Dutch girl who had saved me in Amsterdam, where hunger had driven me to steal a loaf of bread, the punishment for which was execution by hanging. Neeltje was selling flowers on the corner: it was spring, the crocuses were out, and I'd impulsively given her my last stuyver for a bunch (simply because I'd found her such a pretty girl) before slipping into the bakery. When she heard the baker raise the alarm and saw the armed market guards prepare to give chase, she ran to the baker and paid him everything she had earned that morning, persuading him that I was her husband – although she was barely fourteen herself – and had arranged with her to pay for the loaf. So I went free; and seeing her distress at what her father would do if she returned home empty-handed, I offered on the spur of the moment to marry her. We told her father that I was a merchant, awaiting a rich consignment of spices from the East, and he, being far gone with gin, was only too willing to palm her off in exchange for a promise of untold riches.

We did not wait for the ship to materialise, but set out without delay and came to rest in Middelburg, where she had distant relatives. She fell pregnant. I joined her uncle's building business. She lost the child, but soon fell pregnant again. This one lived, a sickly boy; the next one was also ailing, whining and wheezing day and night. Just before her eighteenth birthday, in March 1734, Neeltje became pregnant for the fourth time.

Do not judge me too severely, Rosette! I know it was *lâche* of me to leave her and our young family in the lurch like that. But my marriage itself had been a betrayal of Jeanne who'd so persistently bided her time with me; and I assure you, my plight now was really worse than when I'd stolen that loaf in Amsterdam. In fact, there were times when I resented (and told her so) what Neeltje had done to save me from hanging. For this life was but another, and more drawn-out, form of execution. *This* could not be what I had left my beloved Orléans for.

In that more distant past, too, I had foresaken others, and wounded their expectations of me. My father, the carpenter who'd brought me up to take over his trade; my mother, whose only hope I was; Ghislaine, my fiancée, to whom I'd pledged my troth – I confess it all today, everything must be said, including the worst, and God knows I'm not proud of it – with the sole purpose of being allowed prematurely to take my pleasure of her. (And what pleasure it was!) But I ask you, Rosette, how *could* I resign myself to an existence like theirs? I knew, had always known, that I was intended for greatness of some kind. I remember that even as a small boy I would sometimes, in great earnest, confront my mother to ask her,

'Maman, tell me the truth, am I your child?'

'*Mais mon chéri, mais mon chéri . . .!*' She would be overcome with consternation. How could I doubt that she and Papa were my parents?

'I *know*,' I would insist, going into a rage, beating the table with my furious little fists. 'When you had your baby, the *nourrice* stole it and replaced it with another, me. *My* parents are rich, my papa is a landlord and a general, my maman a lady with fine clothes and shoes. They are great and powerful people. I *know* it because I know I don't belong here in this little hovel!'

Poor thing, it drove her to distraction; perhaps it hastened her death. And that was when I decided I should go – after all those years of postponing and hesitation, after Héloïse, after Jeanne had first accosted me on the bridge in Orléans. If I didn't do it *then*, I would be trapped forever. Like them. I spent a last long night with Ghislaine, driving her to the last spasm our thrashing bodies were capable of; and then, as she slept, spent and totally beautiful, sprawling on the wreckage of the bed where the early sun was stealing gently across a sticky thigh and setting alight the dark thicket surrounding her much-used *bijou*, I gathered my clothes and tiptoed to the window, to clamber naked down a vine and dress myself in the gravelled courtyard in the thrilling cold.

Jeanne was already waiting, patiently.

I am not trying to apportion blame. There *is* no blame. The decision was mine and it was based not only on the fear that Ghislaine might soon get wind of my other liaisons. No, it was Jeanne who had made me see, beside my mother's sad and sour death-bed, what had at last become inevitable. Truly inevitable: a fate prepared for me. I could but follow where she pointed. Ever since she'd first entered my life – that grey misty morning on the bridge, after the dance – she was the one who made me see the real misery of my frustrated life, the confining horizon contracting around me like a hungry man's belt.

'If this is what you can be happy with,' she said at my mother's bedside, 'then stay. Otherwise you must go. *Now*, before it is too late.'

'But Ghislaine . . .?'

'She will be heartbroken for a while. And then find someone else. A girl like her cannot be without a man for too long.'

'My poor father . . .'

'He is content to be a carpenter, is he not? You aren't. Your life awaits you. Out there. If you don't reach out *now* – '

'I can never do it on my own. You know that.'

'I thought you were strong. I believe in you, Estienne.'

'But I need you close to me.' I was silent for a long time. 'And you can't leave this place. You're tied to it, for ever.'

'I told you that first day I'd go with you if you want me to. Even if it would be better for you to do it on your own.'

'I need you, Jeanne!'

'Then I'll come.'

I took the great book from which my father had always read me stories; and I removed his watch, his most treasured possession, from my mother's dead hands where he'd left it when he'd gone out to call the priest; and without once looking back at her ashen face on the bed, went out through the back door. And Jeanne with me.

Jeanne: the one constant passion of my life.

But do not misunderstand me, Rosette! If Ghislaine and her contemporaries were all voluptuousness and sexual exuberance and new discovery, Jeanne is cool and chaste; a maid, truly. She has been sisterly to me, not even that; I think of her, as her appearance has constantly encouraged me to do, as a young comrade-in-arms, an inseparable companion, a boy. One of the only occasions in my whole life when the mere thought of her body possessed me, momentarily, was that night on the journey when I imagined her with split breeches, the drunken Kok leering at her *conin*. But I have suffered because of that vision. It is time to be forgiven, even by myself, for that fleeting aberration. My passion for her is a fever of the mind.

And so I left my home, my father's watch burning in my pocket; and Jeanne, carrying the heavy book, with me. First on that long farewell journey through France – her only condition – and then to the Low Countries. Amsterdam; the three interminable years in Middelburg; and all the time she was willing to stay in the background, to discover what it was I really wanted. Only when she saw I could find no happiness with Neeltje did she come back to me. In vulnerable moments, when I was alone in the carpentry shop, or walking about on my own in the long twilight under the low grey skies, or at night; more and more often at night, while Neeltje was snoring uneasily and the children wheezed and simpered in their stuffy cubicles.

'Estienne, Estienne, this is not what you were born for. This is no life for a man of dreams and anger.'

Again I left behind whatever I had accumulated; again there was the glimmering of freedom.

And again . . .?

Every time someone asked my father about how he had lost his leg he would regale us with a different story. (He could always be counted upon, to my mother's chagrin, to interrupt his work on an armoire or a chair or a table for the spinning of a tale.) So I never found out what had really happened. And I couldn't care less. He provided me with the only riches he ever had (apart from the watch, apart from the leather-bound book) to bestow on me: an *inépuisable* stock of stories about wars and cataclysms and disasters and encounters with enemies and robbers and wild animals, hippogryphs and winged horses and dragons and sphinxes and unicorns.

It is not easy to be recruited by the East India Company; there is a constant throng of desperate men streaming into Amsterdam to find asylum and try their luck. And there is a whole breed of unscrupulous men, known as *Kattenhonde* or Catdogs, who hang around the city gate and near the canal turnpikes, to prey on the unwary. But Jeanne had gone ahead and found us cheap but decent lodgings in a hostelry off the Kalverstraat; and before I presented myself at the East India House she first went herself, for two days running, to find out what would be the best way to set about it, so I was well prepared.

Knowing beforehand how great the crowd would be, jostling in the courtyard from which the doorkeepers would allow only batches of twelve to fifteen to enter at a time, I avoided the throng at the great front door (where sometimes, Jeanne had warned me, people would be crushed to death). Instead, arriving early, I moved to one side of the building and there clambered up a tough vine (I had much experience of this from my wooing of Ghislaine and concurrent *amours*); on the ledge of the upper storey I cautiously moved to a grilled balcony above the main entrance. There, suspended from the iron grating, I hung, unnoticed, for what must have been half an hour, until I heard from the tumultuous milling of the crowd below that the door had been opened. I landed on the heads of the men jostling about the entrance and thus was borne into the house.

On the floor of the bare room in which we found ourselves was a musket; and each of the men in turn was instructed by the officials (seated in a row of high-backed chairs behind a long table covered with a heavy oriental cloth) to pick it up and perform certain exercises with it at the word of command. Those of us who performed to the satisfaction of the commissioners were accepted; the name and birthplace of each were entered into a big ledger. Jeanne had seen to it that I was furnished with letters of recommendation from a general in Magdeburg (I have no idea how she came by them, and have a good suspicion that they'd been forged). As a result, I was immediately taken on, not as a common soldier, but as an *adelborst* or midshipman, which entitled me not only to a payment of 10 guilders a month, instead of the usual 9, but also to a rather sizeable chest of Burmese teak in which to stow my belongings aboard the ship. The allowance of such a larger chest (the normal size of which is three-and-a-half feet long, one and a half high, and one-and-a-half wide) was most important, as it made it possible for me to smuggle Jeanne on board. Otherwise we would have been hard put to solve that delicate problem: and had she not been able to accompany me I doubt that I would ever have left Europe alone.

Two months' pay was advanced to each of the new recruits; but this was hardly sufficient to cover the cost of the chest (4 guilders 10 cents) and the prescribed provisions, consisting of one cloth coat and a pair of trousers, two striped linen doublets and two pairs of breeches to match, two blue shirts, a pair of shoes and a pair of woollen stockings, a small barrel of gin and a metal tube with which to draw the spirit, six pounds of tobacco, a couple of dozen bad pipes, a hammock of hempen canvas, with two iron hooks at the ends, a canvas mattress stuffed with cow-hair, a metal spoon, a pewter mug, an earthenware waterbottle, and a knife – at a cost of some 40 guilders. This meant signing a letter of debt to the Company, allowing them to deduct a monthly amount from my pay. Even so, compared to some of the others who had signed transport letters or *maand celen* for amounts of hundreds of guilders, effectively contracting them into slave labour for countless years, I suppose I was lucky. (Of course, soon after my arrival in Cabo I discovered that a soldier's pay never quite covers all the required expenses, as a result of which I, too, was to find myself on the dreary treadmill of ever-increasing debt.)

On Tuesday 8 June 1734 *'t Huys te Rijnsburg* left the harbour and sailed past the three barrels anchored in the Texel that mark the official start of the journey. Jeanne was still below, huddled inside the chest, waiting for nightfall; I stood on the deck to watch old Europe draw back from me – with difficulty, the way one tries to undo a cobweb from one's fingers.

There was a strange elation in my solitude. At last everything that had restrained me was now stripped away from me. Maman, Papa (in my pocket his watch ticking like a heart); Ghislaine and my tumble of other loves; Neeltje and the boys; carpentry; building; mediocrity; misery.

'Estienne, Estienne,' I could hear Maman's voice in the wind, 'why must you always be so contrary?'

I did not bother to reply.

She had never understood. Jeanne did.

· 37 ·

I was on my way to the Governor's residence in the Castle when the woman accosted me in the dark. It was the evening of

Thursday 20 October 1735. No doubt at all about the date. It is the fixed date of one of the Governor's two annual entertainments (the first being in February, when the homeward-bound fleet prepares to sail). More importantly, it is the one date – inasmuch as anything can ultimately be tied to a date – to which everything that has conspired to land me in this end-place, dateless, can be traced. You will know. You were the woman.

I was alone. I was hurrying along the uneven as yet unpaved road ill-lit by the slave's flambeau that alternately flared and crouched low in the wind (the South-easter had sprung up uncommonly early that year, you will recall). I was late.

After a week of enervating exercises with the burgher mounted and infantry forces, the manoeuvres had drawn, just before sunset, to their customary conclusion, with all the burgher companies assembling in front of the barred Castle gate, each company firing three musketry salvos. These had been duly answered by cannon shots from inside the Castle, whereupon the ranks had been disbanded until the following October. I had to hurry back to the small fortress known grandiloquently as the Water Castle, where I was stationed at the time, to get dressed for the evening reception.

It was five months after our expedition's return from the interior. There had been some interesting developments. We hadn't been back for more than a week when one morning, just after the 8 o'clock inspection, Lieutenant Allemann arrived at the humble quarters inside the redoubt I had built.

'Sergeant Barbier!' he called.

I came to attention, but could not help looking at him curiously. 'Excuse me, Lieutenant,' I said, 'I am only a corporal.'

'You were a corporal until last night,' he said, his round face beaming. 'I've had a little talk to the Governor and as from today you're a sergeant. You remain in Cochius' company, of course.'

'But how . . .' For a moment I was quite overcome.

'I recognise a good man when I see him, Barbier,' said Allemann, rubbing his small soft hands in evident satisfaction. 'There may be further advancements along the way, if . . .'

He stopped. I waited for him to continue, but he made no attempt to finish his sentence.

'If?' I asked after some time.

He raised his head to look at me, quizzical. 'If what?' Then seemed to remember what he'd been saying. 'Oh. Yes indeed. I'm sure you get my meaning, Sergeant?' Another smile. 'I rather enjoyed your company on our expedition, Barbier. We should see more of each other.' He made to turn away, then bethought himself. 'By the way, you have no ill feelings about the journal of our venture, I trust?'

'It was for you to decide,' I said guardedly.

He studied me closely. Behind the benevolence of his fleshy face there was something else which vaguely disquieted me.

'I trust the Governor was happy with the final account,' I said. His eyes appeared to narrow; but otherwise there was no change in his expression. 'As a matter of fact,' he said, 'the Governor was bored by it. He intimated that it wouldn't even be forwarded either to Batavia or to the Lords Seventeen. Nothing new, nothing noteworthy. In the circumstances I think that is by far the best that could have happened. Don't you agree?'

'It was an interesting journey,' I said.

Somewhat to my surprise he beamed again. 'Indeed, indeed,' he said. 'But there are kinds of interest that are best kept to those who shared it, not so?'

At least, then, I had benefited (if unexpectedly, both in manner and in timing) from the enterprise. The same day I was transferred to a new station in the Water Castle as overseer of the *bandieten*, the prisoners of the Company. And for the time being that was that; Allemann gave no further sign of any particular interest in me.

But that night in October – even though it was not immediately evident at all – turned out to be the moment of change.

· 38 ·

'Seur,' said the woman in the dark.

There was a movement – no sound; bare feet on stone leave no impression on the ear – as she came from the side of the fortress to touch my arm. I started and drew my sword, then realised it was a woman's voice and asked the slave accompanying me to approach the torch. He held it high. She stood tall in the flaring light.

For a moment I stared; the flame huddled low on its wick in a sudden gust, then leaped in a frenzy; there was a heavy smell of oil. And then I recognised her. And remembered.

'What are you doing here?'

'You must help me.'

Across her cheek, from the corner of the jaw below the left ear, curving across the nose, a dark weal seemed to be oozing blood.

'What has happened?'

She looked at the slave holding the torch aloft. 'I must speak to you.'

I motioned him to withdraw. He seemed reluctant, as intrigued perhaps by her as I was, but after a moment he stood back.

She waited until he was out of earshot, his back turned. Then said in a low urgent voice, 'I am going away, you must help me.'

'You have your place at Madame Allemann's.'

'I am never going back.'

'You know what is done to runaway slaves.'

'I know. I have tried once before.'

'The second time is worse.'

'That is why you must help me. You are the only one.'

'But what can *I* do?'

She said nothing; in the dull light of the torch ten steps away I could make out, from the position of her head, that she was staring at me: quietly, confidently.

I remembered more than I should.

'If you get caught – if I get caught . . .'

'I have waited here for you. You helped me once.'

I knew I was doing a contrary thing. But suddenly I could no longer care. I quickly went up to my slave, nearly stumbling in a pothole, and snatched the torch from him. 'Wait here,' I said. And led her, hurrying, back to the gate of the building where I called out at the soldier on sentry duty. She instinctively withdrew into the obscurity behind me when he presented himself. 'I need another flambeau in this wind,' I told him. 'Go get it from the guardroom.' And as soon as he'd gone I took her by the arm and hurried across the short distance of the courtyard to the door of my small abode, where I thrust her inside. 'I shall be back later.'

I had barely reached the gate again before the soldier returned with a new torch. Holding both, I went back to where my slave was waiting, and handed him one. 'The woman brought a message from Lieutenant Cochius,' I told him, although surely no explanation was necessary, not to a slave.

Together we set off again for the Castle.

I arrived just in time; old Jan de la Fontaine, in his simplicity of mind, may be an easy man but tardiness annoys him. Barely a minute after I had joined the already raucous assembly of burgher commanders and officers of the garrison and insufferably pompous local illuminati (whatever that may mean in this place), the Governor and his second-in-command, Secunde van Kervel, made their joint entrance, announced by the drummer and four hautbois players. There must have been at least sixty men there – no occasion for women, this – and the folding doors between two large reception rooms had been thrown open to accommodate them; a large table ran right through the opening without interruption, the entire length of the two salons.

It was, of course, my first experience of the kind (having, through the departure of our expedition, missed the February occasion) and one might believe that I was overawed by it; yet to tell you the truth – and only the truth is appropriate in my present circumstances – I was barely conscious of the event. Uproarious conversation, shouting, laughter; music and speeches and music again, of various kinds; singing by the men; and trains of slaves in oriental clothing and European wigs – the strongest men and most comely women chosen from the Company Lodge – moving about on whispering bare feet, carrying endless trays and platters and étagères of food. There was much wine too, from my mother country and from the East, and flasks of sweet Constantia, and goblets of arrack and gin and brandywine.

My mind was not contained within that splendid space. Across the open parade in front of the dark Castle (where on holidays criminals were broken on the wheel, or crucified, or hanged from gallows, or drawn and quartered, according to the gravity of their misdemeanours), across cobbled and earthen streets, beyond the houses of solid burghers and the small square stables of artisan slaves, far below the louring hulk of the mountain, near the hissing sea, enclosed within the walls of the Water Castle, my thoughts found her. That dusky woman who had begun to trouble me on our inland expedition; and even more in many an uneasy dream since then.

I ate little; I drank too much.

You were waiting for me in my small enclave.

You must help me.

What did you really want from me?

With a tinge of guilt I thought of Jeanne. But already the fumes of the plentiful drink were obscuring such thoughts. All I could clearly visualise was the outline of your shape; and your voice.

For months I had suppressed all thought of you. Now, all of a sudden, it all came back. Our shared moment of vision. The unsettling story you had told me of your origins. That flogging at the hands of Madame Allemann, where I had intervened. The erectness of your bearing. The defiance of your pride. Your breasts. All of it bound up with the unfulfilled dreams of that journey (that ridiculous little stream dividing forever the known from the unknown). You had been then the property of the Allemanns; I dared not even entertain the thought of you. Now, out of the night, unbidden, you were back. For some unfathomable reason you had sought me out.

I knew I could do anything to you I wished.

I called for more drink; and more.

Some time in the course of the night I found myself outside in the black wind again. Had I been ignominiously thrown out? Tactfully helped out? Why did I seem to recall Allemann talking, in a low voice, in my ear? And what had he said?

No matter. I was outside. Where was the slave? What had happened to my two flambeaux?

No matter.

It was difficult to pick my way home through those streets. Not even a moon overhead; it was a foggy night.

I walked, and staggered, and sang. Sometimes, as I recall, I was on all fours. I vomited. It felt as if all my insides were spilling out. I sang again, and hammered on locked doors, and serenaded dark windows. People shouted abuse at me, and one man opened a window overhead and emptied on me the contents of a chamber-pot. Still I sang. I know now that I was really scared, more scared than I had been when on that inland journey I had come unarmed upon a lion. (Did I tell you about it? I cannot remember now. But it happened. Beside the carcass of a wildebeest. I challenged him with my bare hands. But, sated, he turned his back on me and fell asleep.) More scared than I'd been on the ship in the storm off the Gold Coast that had almost been the end of Jeanne and me. More scared than . . . And why? At the prospect of that woman awaiting me in my cabin? What would I do with her? What would become of me?

The first I would say to her, that much I knew, would be, 'Take off your clothes.' She couldn't expect me not to make use of what she offered me in exchange for her freedom. Her life was at stake, wasn't it? Your life.

Then why was I so scared of going home?

I believe a night patrol discovered me, far off my course – near the Hospital, opposite the Company's Gardens, in fact – and fortunately two of the men, Constable Willem Willemse and Harmen Croon, recognised me and escorted me to my safe little fortress.

At last I was alone with her. With you. I was trembling.

'Take off your clothes,' I said.

· *39* ·

And now I have to die. The bastards. The turds. The dogs. The swine.

· *40* ·

One of my very first duties at the Cape was to attend an execution. The impression it made on me must, at least in part, be explained by my extreme frailty after the six weeks of my convalescence in the hospital. This was the result of the desperate illness with which I had been struck on board (an affliction so severe that I had passed into a coma, as a consequence of which I was not even aware of our arrival in Table Bay, an occasion usually regarded as so momentous, and a sight so nonpareil, that few travellers can refrain from speaking about it for the rest of their natural lives).

Seven runaway slaves, two of them women, had been apprehended in the mountains behind the town after absconding and setting fire to the bushes, as a result of which much of the vegetation was destroyed, to within a hundred paces or so of the nearest dwellings.

At 8 o'clock on the Saturday morning after they had been sentenced the entire garrison, including the so-called *pasgangers* (those with permission of absence to perform temporary private work in various capacities in the colony), was mustered on the parade ground in front of the Castle. By that time two of our companies had already put up a large tent on the place of execution, to which the entire Council of Justice was escorted by the Governor's guard. First came the Sergeant with six grenadiers; then the Messenger of the Court, bearing in his hand a long wand made of thorn bush and tipped with silver, and carrying his hat under his arm. Next came the members of the Council, two by two; followed by the Corporal of the guard with six grenadiers. As they took their appointed places on the chairs provided in the shade of the tent – it was a particularly hot December day – the entire populace of the town, freemen and slaves alike, thronged around the place in great excitement; many had brought with them large picnic-baskets from which they constantly partook of refreshments throughout the spectacle, several of them until after sunset.

Meanwhile the condemned were hauled from the Dark Hole (I was part of that detachment), brought to the double flight of steps that lead up to the Governor's house – I'm trying to recall every detail; it is my only way of keeping a hold on the world outside, you see – where the sentence, together with an account of their offence, was read out to them. And from there we escorted them to the parade ground. (One of the males soiled his breeches most abominably along the way.)

The bell in the turret over the gate was struck continuously for an hour while the spectacle was performed with all due ceremony. I am not a squeamish man, although I confess an aversion to physical suffering; I have witnessed punishments in my time, and even a burning at the stake in Orléans; but to witness this event, attended by the exuberant crowd, was enough to strike me cold on such a hot day. I even, for a moment, sympathised with the slaves.

They were all, men and women, first stripped naked and tied to stakes, then flogged lengthily, and with great demonstrations of both skill and force, by the Fiscal's *geweldenaars* (as the executioners are here called) until the crowd grew bored and began shouting for some other diversion. Finally, two of the men were impaled, and three were broken on the wheel, that is to say each arm and leg was twice beaten with an iron club in two, and then they were bound living on the wheel; the two women had morsels of their breasts torn out by tongs, where-upon they were strangled one after the other while one of the *geweldenaars* waved a burning bundle of reeds about their faces and before their eyes to make breathing difficult.

When I passed by the place again two days later, one of the slaves on the wheel still moaned, and stirred.

· *41* ·

It was not simply a matter of turning a blind eye to the escape of a slave woman. The loss of any female in this Settlement is indeed a severe blow to the future of all the inhabitants, there being so few women, compared to the number of men, in the place.

It is widely known that the European women at the Cape are generally modest, but no flinchers from conjugal delights. They are excellent breeders, as witness the six to a dozen or more children swarming in most houses; brave lads and lasses, with limbs and countenances strongly declarative of the ardour with which they were begotten.

As for those in bondage, they are very lascivious creatures, as they are excused from working, and indulge in an idle life, for about six weeks before and six weeks after travail; they are the most intemperate wretches upon earth in the article and greedily swallow, and enflame themselves with, all the provocatives they can come at till they are got with child. The provocative they mostly take is one of their own preparing, consisting of milk, wine, eggs, sugar, saffron and cinnamon.

The Slave Lodge swarms with children.

· 42 ·

There was no need for me to order her to remove her clothes. She was already naked when I came, and smelled of cinnamon. There was an oil lamp burning on the table. My wooden bed was too small for our purpose; we disported ourselves on the *paillasse* and the bedclothes spread out on the floor. The lamp sat burning and smoking on the flagstones close to us. I remember the huge shadow we cast, throughout the night, on the walls and the ceiling. I do not know what the time was when I came in, but the sun was out when she milked from me the last moisture my sated aching body had to yield.

And in that light of a new day, unforgiving and crude, I was overcome by rage at what I had allowed to be done to me. It was humiliating. She had used her female sorcery to subject me, to ride me like a horse or some dumb animal, denying my higher nature, insulting my pride, turning me, the master, into an object of shame in my own eyes. The triumph with which she rose from me. She stood astride me, looking down as I stared up at her. A woman with no shame at all, it seemed, about herself. I saw the high silhouette of her breasts; I saw, nested in the juncture of her legs, the wet beak that had defeated me; more obtrusive than anything else, as my eyes travelled down her limbs, was the broad black iron band clamped so tightly to her leg above the ankle that it appeared to bite into the flesh, marking it with a festering ring. The sign of her earlier attempt to flee, and her recapture; yet what her attitude said, her bold eyes studying me in contempt, was that *she* was the victor, I the abject slave. And for the first time I knew why Madame Allemann could not suffer her. She was a witch, an object of darkness.

When I finally staggered to my feet, supporting myself against the wall – her eyes cool and unwavering looking me over from head to toe, despising me – I heard behind me the sound of a smothered voice coming from the door which had somehow been opened; and as I turned to face it I realised that it was Jeanne standing there, observing us. Perhaps she had been there from the very beginning. Her silence was even more unbearable than the scorn of the slave woman who had humiliated me.

In the madness that beset me then there was only one way, it seemed to me, to avenge myself, to redeem my manhood and my pride.

Without stopping to allow the slave woman to cover herself, I dragged her outside to the cage where the criminals were kept like animals. I unlocked the gate and shoved her inside. As a cynical afterthought I hurled her bundle of dirty clothes after her.

Half-starved, inflamed with suffering, deprived for God knows how long of females on which to vent their lust and fury, they set upon her like a pack of dogs.

For a day and a night I left her in the cage with them.

In their frenzy, in the soiling and breaking of her once-proud body, I cleansed myself.

· *43* ·

I am not really sure that it was like that. I hurled you into the cage with them, yes. That happened. That I shall remember, blindingly, to the day I die, which must be soon. But not, I think, the night of lust. That was, perhaps, what I saw in my feverish impotence as I thrashed about on my bed during the night while you ministered to me, washing my face with cold water after each spasm of vomiting, sponging my body when I pissed and soiled myself in the uncontrollable aftermath of all that drinking. But I did not touch you, did not lay a finger on you.

When at last I calmed down, shivering under the blankets you had piled on me, you began to tell me stories. And that was how you spent the night with me. That was the shame I had to purge. So help me God.

· *44* ·

I know that in my alcoholic dreams I was confused, believing myself to be still aboard the ship, tossed by the storm, listening to the creaking and groaning of timber, the shouts and despairing screams of the sailors, great thuds and booms of waves, streaming rain. There was no hope of surviving such a storm; we were all going to die.

And how ironical. I'd boarded the ship as a stowaway, crouching under the tarpaulin covering a collection of barrels and crates, miserably conscious of the proximity of death. (But what else could I do? I was already under sentence of death, having killed in a duel the man who had dared to make a pass at a mistress in whose arms I'd sought solace from the whining of my wife and children. I did not mean to kill him. But I had no choice. So I fled to Amsterdam and boarded the first ship I could find, *'t Huys te Rijnsburg*.) And then, slipping from my hideaway one night in search of food, and having secured a ham and a keg of fresh water, it so happened that as I scuttled past the captain's cabin I heard shouts inside; and curiosity getting the better of me, opened the door to find two men doing battle with that good man. I knocked one down with the water keg, which gave the captain time to take care of the other.

So all came out, I had to confess my status (although for the sake of propriety I declined to give the reason behind my stowing away in his ship); still expecting to be sentenced, if not to death, at least to several hundred lashes, I could not believe it when he called an assembly of all the men on board to announce, in their company, my full pardon. Not only that, but even promotion to the rank of *adelborst*.

And there we were, barely three weeks later, caught in a storm that heralded our dismal and collective end.

But this was no storm: I was in my own cabin in the Water Castle built on the rocks to protect the Cape from attackers. There was my familiar lamp on the table, there the woman. The woman?

I recognised you again.

'Rosette?'

'Don't talk,' you said. 'You'll be all right again.'

'But I thought . . .'

'Hush,' you said. 'Have a sip of water. Not too much.'

And you told me stories.

· 45 ·

Once upon a time in a far country in the heart of Africa there was a great hunter who protected all his people against predators and provided them with food from the animals he killed. There was no animal so swift or shy or sly or fierce or great that he did not succumb to the mastery of that man. With spear and assegai, poison-arrow and knob-kierie, with musket and pistol, sometimes with only the skill and power of his bare hands, he overcame his prey and brought it home.

And everybody said, Such a man must have a son so that,

when he grows too old to hunt, there will be a young man in his place to protect and provide for the people.

The great hunter took many women to his bed. They came from far and wide, attracted by his prowess, each of them eager to become mother to the son who would follow in that hunter's footsteps. His repute as a lover soon began to rival his great fame as a hunter. It was said that a woman who once slept with him would never be content to draw another man into her secret self. Yet no child was ever born to him. And slowly, slowly, through the years, the people's admiration changed into derision. As he failed to beget a child he lost his nerve; the member that used to rear so proudly at the approach of a new woman, began to droop, and even strong provocatives and medicines now failed to restore his manhood. As his confidence faltered he also began to lose his prowess as a hunter. Once he was nearly trampled by an elephant, once he was gored by a wounded buffalo, once struck by the paw of a lion that was killed just in time by someone else. When he fired at antelope or gazelle, he would now merely wound or stun them; more and more often he missed altogether.

And the people, too, suffered, because he could no longer provide for them.

In desperation he turned to trapping. It was an ignominious occupation, a pastime of boys and youngsters, not grown men; yet through his skill as a digger of holes and a twister of thongs and ropes he did impose a measure of respect on his followers. And then a great drought came on the land, the last animals moved away in great stampedes, and the people were left to die. All the man could still catch in his snares and traps were small duikers or steenbuck or hares, sometimes reed-rats, or mere mice. And even they became scarce.

When there was nothing left to catch at all the people rose up in anger and threatened to drive their hunter away. But he pleaded with them. Give me one last chance, he said, and I shall prepare a snare so skilful and potent that it will catch what no human being in the whole world has ever caught.

For three days and three nights he toiled on his secret work, plaiting rushes and tough grasses, filing lengths of iron, fabricating a wondrous snare such as nobody had ever seen before.

He set it up in the sacred forest near the village of his people.

For two days in succession he set out in the early morning, followed at a safe distance by all the people, men, women and children; and for two days they all turned back empty-handed.

And then, on the morning of the third day, when they reached the sacred place, they saw immediately that something had been caught in the snare.

They surrounded the spot, huddling close together, peering over each other's shoulders to see.

It was a large egg.

The people gazed in amazement and awe as the hunter gently, ever so gently, undid the egg from the teeth and coils of the snare, taking the greatest care not to harm the thin, thin shell.

He carried it home with him, the others following; and in the middle of his hut he made a fire, and placed the egg within the flames. Everybody waited, and no one said a word or made a sound.

As the flames died down there came the sound of cracking. They saw the perfect egg break open. And from it was hatched a girl-child who, as they looked on in wonder, began to grow and grow until she was the most beautiful woman the world had ever witnessed.

And as they all kept looking, the old hunter took the woman to his body, and laid her down, and lay with her as a man lies with a woman; and what had been dead so long in him began to stir again, and revived, and he entered her, and night came down upon them to hide from the curious eyes the many wondrous postures they assumed.

And as the new day broke the woman gave birth to a boy,

who promptly began to grow and grow. As he grew, the rain came down; and the grass sprouted out, and the trees began to blossom once again, and all the animals returned to those parts.

The following night the old man died and his daughter-wife buried him in the house and made a new fire on the grave. Then her son took the long-discarded weapons of the dead man and in the early morning of the new day set out for the hunting-fields. He brought back many, many animals, enough to feed all the people. And he took to wife the woman who had given birth to him, and they were happy together and had innumerable children. And the people were never without food or sustenance again.

· 46 ·

—Concluding from the above as has been argued, that a drunken mouth speaks from the bottom of the heart, in vino veritas, and exhibitum in juditio—

· 47 ·

You may wish to know (yet, on the other hand, why should you?) where I learned the Latin which enabled me to communicate on an equal footing with the Council of Justice – even if the 'equal footing' refers more to a common propensity to error. The answer is that the village priest in Bazoches took an interest in my education. Mistaking, I fear, my father's carpentry as a sign that I was destined for higher things, the dedicated old man tried for several years to direct my general eagerness for life into a more specific dedication to *agricola, agricolae, amo, amare, amavi, amatum,* and *nihil humanum* something *mihi est* (or whatever); gradually, though, it dawned on me that our Latin sessions were only a pretext, as they revealed more and more an expectation on his behalf of certain manual ministrations from me. Initially, I confess, the activity excited my curiosity, then began to bore me, and in the end annoyed me – all the more so as my own proclivities began to engage more enthusiastically the female half of our parish. As the curé persisted, I was prompted to start devising small schemes of revenge, culminating in my deft attachment, in one of his moments of transport, of a heavy brass padlock from my father's workplace to the holy man's less holy parts. That brought him back to earth. It also brought our lessons to an abrupt end. From the change in the curé's gait – from an energetic stride to a rather painful waddle – during the years the Good Lord still saw fit to keep him in our midst, I deduced that the lock had remained firmly in place and probably accompanied him to the grave. Hopefully Saint Peter would have a key to fit.

Strange that it should have been the image of that crude action that returned to me on the night I saw the iron band clamped so securely round the slave woman's ankle.

After the curé came Jeanne. Hers, as far as I could judge, and that admittedly wasn't very far, was a vulgar Latin, but vivid as stained glass; and it was so much part of the story she brought with her that I found it irresistible. There wasn't much grammar to it, but it had – if that doesn't sound too exaggerated – a spark of divine inspiration.

During my first incarceration in this hellish place, when I was on bread and water for twenty days, she arranged – how, I have no way of knowing – to come to me on Christmas Day. This time she was more than a voice in the dark: she was a presence too, a visual delight. Not allowed to bring me anything, she'd wrapped herself in cloths of many colours, of the kind one finds in contraband Malay shops, and stuck flowers in all the folds, in her hair, even in her ears; she was a walking Maypole, a feast for eyes that had by then come to expect only darkness. 'I thought,' she whispered, 'in this place you see no colour, so I decided to bring you something to look at.' And

67

then, turning with great energy so that all the bright cloths swung out like an extravagant rainbow, she said, '*Nil desperandum.*' Which was the most exalting Latin I'd ever heard.

My third instructor in the dead language was Christian Petzold. A practical man, a poor man, a good man. And now a dead man. They saw to that.

Exhibitum in juditio.

· *48* ·

Never before in my life had I seen the likes of what awaited me in the predawn of that morning when I unlocked the gate of the prisoners' cage. I'd lain awake all night, battling with myself about whether to release her or not. But it was, I decided, already too late. There were thirty-seven *bandieten* locked up in there.

When the three o'clock bell rang out from the Castle over the silent town awash with the sound of the sea, I could stand it no longer. Barefoot, with my bunch of keys and a smoking oil lamp, I left my stuffy little room, itself no more than a cell, and went to the cage of the damned. I turned the key in the lock – a lock as heavy as any that ever enclosed a priest's balls – fully expecting the worst. Even if slaves had a greater resistance to pain than the free, as everybody in Cabo confidently believed, she could not have survived twenty-four hours in that lions' den without being torn to pieces.

But as I raised my lamp I saw her, in that unreal light, sitting on a box against the far wall of the cage, fully clothed, erect as always, surrounded by convicts seated or sprawling on the uneven flagstones. She was, and had been, telling them stories.

I gaped in silence. Even the wind had died down in the night; it was such a silence as one hears only on the high seas, at midnight, when the ocean sighs as it turns in its sleep.

I could not speak. Dumbfounded, I vaguely beckoned.

An angry murmur came from the men.

'Let me finish,' she called at me. And took her time to bring to a conclusion the tale she'd been telling. Only then, and still quite unhurried, she rose and came through the flotsam and jetsam of that filthy crowd, ambling calmly with those improbably tall legs; and involuntarily I stood aside to let her stride past me towards the light. As she crossed the high threshold she raised, with a kind of grace that did not go with her standing, her long dirty skirts, revealing once again in the light of my smoking lamp that incongruous shackle and its ring-shaped suppurating wound.

I locked the gate. In the darkness behind us the cage exploded in a din of shouts and roars and screams, a flood of obscenities aimed at me, not her.

'What have they done to you?' I asked, quite unnecessarily, back in my room.

'Nothing.'

'You told them stories.'

'Yes.'

'But they are animals, not men.'

'They listened. They wanted more, all the time.'

'What are you going to do now?'

'It is for you to tell me. I came to you.'

'You must go back.'

'Is that all you can tell me?'

'Are you scared of what will happen to you?'

'There is nothing they can do to me which has not already been done. That is what you don't understand.'

'Look, I'll speak to Lieutenant Allemann. And his wife.'

'They won't listen. Already they have sold me to another man. His name is Sollier. He treated me worse than the Allemanns so I tried to go back to them, but they wouldn't have me.'

'If I had money I could try to buy your freedom, but I'm in debt with the Company.'

'I can be free without your money.'

'But where will you go to?'

'Into the land. Where we travelled. And beyond that. In the end I shall reach my people.'

'You said you came from Bengal.'

'I come from Africa.'

'You don't look like an African.'

'I come from the House of Slaves on the island of Gorée. They caught me with my two brothers and my sister. My sister was killed when too many men raped her. One of my brothers hit the merchant who caught us, so he was killed. The other jumped into the sea when they loaded us on a ship. The sharks ate him.'

'That's not what you first told me.'

'What does it matter what I told you?'

'Rosette, there is no way you can escape from this place.'

'Many slaves run away. All the time. There's a whole colony of them beyond the Great River where we never came.'

'How do you know?'

'I have heard stories about them.'

'You can't believe stories!'

'What else can I believe?'

'And if they catch you?'

'Then I die. But then I've tried to be free. Not to try is worse.'

'But how the hell can I help you?'

'You have already helped me by keeping me here. All I need now is some food for the road.'

I gave her more. I gave her the horse assigned to me in the Water Castle. And I gave her a letter to Madame Louise Cellier, the Frenchwoman in Drakenstein who, apart from my putative cousin Charles Marais, was my only link in this remote colony with the place of my birth. In the letter I explained that Rosette was a free slave, previously my property, and that she should be given any assistance she might require to visit her relatives inland. I knew that if she managed to proceed beyond the immediate proximity of Cabo, she might elude whoever was sent in search of her. I also knew what would happen to me if she were caught. And maybe I was reckless in the unreality of that night lit only by my lamp and some candles: but I was prepared to run that risk. The important thing was for her to be free.

Why? To strike back, obliquely, at Allemann for having disappointed my most fervent hopes in turning back from that expedition before attaining its *but*, a *coitus interruptus*? Or for humiliating me by taking my journal from me? But this was much too private and indirect an action for that. What then? To exorcise, somehow, the horror I felt in myself for what I had done to you, the enormity of which I could not even grasp yet? Did I have any idea, however darkly, how that night was yet to haunt me and dominate my life in the years to come? There are no easy answers. All I think I sensed in that precarious pre-dawn, in a way I did not even try to explain myself, was that my own freedom had become involved with yours.

There was one last service to perform. The most difficult. To prise that monstrous iron from your leg. It took more time than was really safe; and I think I must have hurt you terribly as I wrenched and hacked and sawed away. Yet you uttered no sound; in fact, I believe I caught a glimpse of detached amusement on your face as, aloof, you looked on.

'Why are you doing this?' you asked, unexpectedly; and, I should have thought, unnecessarily.

'I want you to be free.'

'I am free.'

'This is a sign of bondage.'

There was no way in which I could anticipate your next move. In a twisting, complicated gesture – but you made it seem very easy – you shook the top half of your clothing from your shoulders; it fell down to your hips. You put a finger to your navel.

'This is the sign of my freedom,' you said. 'When they cut me from my mother I was free.'

I looked at you. But what I felt was different from desire; more than desire.

'Cover yourself,' I said.

You did so, with that infuriating half-smile on your lips.

I bent forward again to finish my task. A few last tugs and wrenches – there was blood on my fingers afterwards, but still you uttered no sound – and the iron was detached.

'We must do something about the wound,' I said, revolted by its now unhampered sight.

'That is nothing,' you said with what sounded like contempt. 'It will heal.'

Yes, I thought; you are right. That other wound, your navel, that is the one that cannot heal.

But words could no longer restrain you. You had already detached yourself from me and from that place. Without another sound, you left into the ominously greying dawn.

For days I waited, expecting at any moment to receive intelligence of your capture. Weeks passed. But no news came. And thinking back, I could no longer be sure that you had ever been there with me: the evening in the dark wind, the fever-dream of that night, your sojourn among the wild animals in the cage. It could not possibly have happened.

But there was, in the chest under my bed, the twisted remains of the shackle from your leg. There was also Jeanne's voice, reminding me.

· 49 ·

Is it reasonable to assume that the difference between a free person and a slave is only an iron band around the leg? That would suggest that in my present condition my only problem is a closed door; or a lack of light.

72

There was no need for me in Europe to ponder such things. Slaves belonged to another world. At least, that was what I thought. If there was a specific moment in which the shift was registered (yet such things tend to penetrate the consciousness only *afterwards*, so isolating a given moment is presumptuous; but then, we live, do we not, on presumption) it may have been that storm off the hump of Africa. I was convinced, I have said it before, of my imminent death, and the loss of the whole bottom.

We were all summoned to the deck where we stood, holding on to anything that seemed secure, staggering about and gasping for breath in the torrents of water that seemed to engulf us. The only hope, said the captain, was to lighten the load. Whatever could conceivably be parted with was thrown overboard. Many of the men lugged to the deck the wooden chests they had indebted themselves to buy, containing all their life's possessions. What would happen if they requisitioned mine? Where would I then stow Jeanne? She *was* my life.

The captain had so recently spared me for coming to his aid; but how could I impose on him to ask the same for her? Already there were murmurings among the shipmen about some of the favours bestowed on me. A ship is such a small cramped world; one cannot be too careful in one's dealings with others.

But sacrifice Jeanne? I'd rather go overboard myself.

I cannot say if it is true that in the moments preceding death one sees one's life unroll. In my case there was no order in the unfolding, no chronology (as little as there is in this my last account): everything was happening simultaneously, a babble of voices in my head, a confusion of images. All the women I had left behind. My many many loves, a snail's trail of them wherever I had been, a blur and smudge on the mind: individual once-cherished faces, fondled feet, cascading hair, sucked nipples, despoiled entrances to the deepest recesses of the body, all folded into one. The shouts of cheated lovers and cuckolded husbands wielding clubs, sticks, chairs, muskets, all in pursuit of me – leaving behind girls with dresses still rucked up, limbs spreadeagled, hair tossed about. For that, if you must know, was why I had fled Europe, to save my life from the complications of too many angry men attached to too many ravished women: girls, wenches, ladies, brides, mourning widows left behind by messy wars. The ship a haven, offered by Captain Janssens, an old accomplice in amorous affairs, who'd smuggled me aboard and then invented a convoluted tale of how I'd saved his life from a knife-wielding cook. But here, in this storm-tossed night, my Jonah presence finally seemed to have touched its limit.

More and more of the freight was sacrificed to the waves. Still it was not enough.

There was one final measure to be taken. In the hold we had, apart from bales of wool and flax and great coils of copper wire and kegs of powder and lead and crates of manufactured goods (most of which had by now already been shoved overboard), a consignment of some sixty slaves, loaded at Gorée for distribution in the colonies. And when nothing more turned out to be available the captain gave order to disencumber the ship of the slaves who were, by then, no more than dangerous ballast.

I shall never forget the cries of those men and women (some children too) hauled to the deck in their long chains, trying to cling to masts and railings, and in their ferocious final struggles carrying with them into the sea three of our sailors too, good and true men, hard workers, who had left their families behind in hopes of future prosperity.

The miraculous thing was that hardly had the last of the slaves been hurled overboard than the waves became strangely becalmed, as if a spirit had moved across them. There was only the soughing of the water, a wet rippling of crestfallen sails, a creaking of masts. And perhaps, but that might have been imagination, faint final cries from the distance. Otherwise it was all deadly quiet.

For some reason we all avoided one another's eyes. We went

74

our several ways, each to his appointed task; and later to our hammocks and bunks, as the case might be.

In the dark I huddled close to Jeanne. For once even her voice could not soothe me. And when she whispered I continued to hear those other lost voices in the wind.

· *50* ·

It must have been about a month after you had disappeared into the land – I seem to think it was early in December of that year, 1735 – that old Lieutenant Cochius, who had been my commanding officer all along even if (mainly because of his age and frailty) I'd hardly ever seen him, sent for me one evening after the roll had been read. I was to be relieved of my present duties at the Water Castle, he informed me, and transferred to the Castle proper. He gave no specific reason. (Even if *he* had been given a reason from higher up he would probably have forgotten it before he could convey the message.) But he did say something that caused me some disquiet.

'I suppose,' he said, 'they can keep a better eye on you here.' Then he broke into a fit of coughing.

'Why should they want to do that?' I asked.

Recovering at last from his coughing he stared at me vacantly through his red-rimmed septuagenarian eyes, and it was clear he had no idea of what I was trying to find out.

'Just you obey orders, my boy,' he said kindly. 'You'll go a long way yet.'

I returned, for the last time, to my small cabin now imbued with precarious memories; but could not sleep, and as Jeanne was not in a mood to speak, spent most of the night reading to bolster my anxious spirits.

There is one episode from my *vade mecum* that is particularly dear to me. If I remember correctly (in this place imagination is more real than memory) it occurs in the first part, where the Knight of the Doleful Countenance, wearing only his nightshirt, which must have made him look like a great stick-insect, withdraws into the remote reaches of the Sierra Morena. He sends Sancho to inform the noble lady Dulcinea del Toboso of the penance he is doing for the sake of her love.

But that is madness, says Sancho. Why should anyone do penance for the sake of a lady who has done no wrong?

That is the point, says the Knight. What merit is there in turning mad for a reason? The virtue lies in doing it *without* any reason.

But there isn't even anyone by the name of Dulcinea del Toboso in that village, protests Sancho.

Her real name, the knight confides in him, is Aldonza Lorenzo.

Sancho is astounded. He knows this peasant girl only too well: a brawny lass, well built and tall and sturdy, with a voice one can hear bellowing a good two miles away, a smell of garlic on her breath, and a mean hand at dressing flax or threshing in the barn.

To all these objections Don Quixote merely shrugs. 'I am more than happy,' he says (or words to that effect), 'to believe that Aldonza Lorenzo is beautiful and virtuous. For me she is the greatest princess in the world, because in my mind I can draw her exactly as I wish her to be.'

I was not only born to the wrong parents; it often seemed to me that I belonged to another age too, a more glorious age, of quests and jousts, of rescuing the imperilled and celebrating the good and the just. Perhaps it was partly in search of this that I had embarked on the voyage so many would have regarded as the height of folly. And then to find myself sick unto death, and abandoned to my lot, upon arrival at a Cape so ironically linked to the notion of Good Hope, seemed grossly unjust, a malicious quirk of fate.

During the first weeks of my convalescence in the hospital, I was in constant worry about Jeanne, not knowing whether we had been parted for ever. I saw in it a sign that I was meant to die. The idea was repugnant to me: how could one travel to the frontier of the familiar world, surviving the ordeals of that four-month voyage, that night of apocalyptic storm, only to die in this place! And so I raged against the weakness that threatened to transport me, and battled to hold on to life. Then, one night, after the comforter of the sick had left and the guards on duty were asleep, she was there again. It was very dark, but I immediately recognised her voice.

'Where have you been?' I asked, so overcome that I felt close to tears.

'I was trying to find you. This is such a strange place. I thought I'd lost you.'

'Now you're here again. All will be well.'

How she continued to evade the officials and servants in the hospital, I could not say; perhaps she hid in the adjacent Company Gardens by day. Perhaps she'd even pretended to be sick herself in order to be admitted as a patient: when I asked her about it, she would merely laugh and say, 'It doesn't matter. I'm here. I am all right.'

In the smallest interval she would be there, to talk to me, to exhort me, and keep alive my new resolve to live.

The hospital was not, on the whole, an unpleasant place. It is cruciform in shape like a church (it also faces the real church), and is surrounded by a wall seven or eight feet high; it is not divided into separate rooms (which made Jeanne's visits more hazardous), but consists of one long and one cross passageway. Along the walls are wooden benches similar to those in the guardrooms, and upon these lie the patients who are not very ill. Bedsteads stand in the middle space and are occupied by the really serious cases.

As my condition improved I would be allowed to spend more time in the Company Gardens adjacent to the hospital; this made Jeanne's visits easier, and we would while away many hours in that place. I am apt to think these Gardens are among the most remarkable curiosities in all Africa. And I question whether there is a garden in Europe so rich and multifarious in its productions as the local one, which is said to be provided with almost everything the vegetable world produces by way of fruit and flower. The Gardens are not laid out and divided as are many in Europe, notably in the country of my birth. Nor are there seen in them any considerable works of embellishment: nature has little or nothing to set her off there beside her own charms and the hand of the gardener, with whom I spent many a rewarding hour in conversation. He pointed out to me the different trees and shrubs, and informed me of their provenance; and indeed it seemed there was no place on earth too secret or remote to be represented here.

These conversations strengthened my resolve to learn more about the continent on which I now found myself. So much awaited discovery, both about me and within. But after the inauspicious start, how could I realise it all? It seemed too daunting; I dared not confess, not even to Jeanne, my dread that the dream would never be fulfilled.

And then, one late afternoon, as we returned to the hospital,

Jeanne and I, my eyes fell for the first time on the gold lettering of the Latin inscription above the main entrance:

EXCIPIT HOSPITIO FRACTOS MORBISQUE VIISQUE
HAEC DOMUS ET MEDICA LARGA MINISTRAT OPEM
BELGA TUUM NOMEN POPULIS FATALE DOMANDIS
HORREAT ET LEGES AFRICA TERRA TUAS.

I stopped to spell it out in furious concentration. It was an exceedingly difficult passage for one with my scant knowledge of that alien tongue. 'It receives with hospitality – what then? – the broken, with diseases – and with something else.' I shook my head. The *viisque* was beyond me.

She took over. 'This house and hospital – presuming that is what *medica* means – ministers assistance bountifully. Does that make sense?'

'And then? What is *Belga*?'

'Holland, perhaps?'

Together, we stumbled from word to word: 'Holland, your name something-something to the conquered peoples living here – and the last line? – The African earth shudders at your laws . . .'

Perhaps we were off the mark. But it hardly mattered. Something in that shining pretentious inscription resonated in my mind. It seemed to lend shape, exquisitely and affirmatively, to that unformulated urge which had brought me here. To discover what was strange, to tame the wilderness, to name the as yet unnamed, to impose order and sense on this periphery of the civilised world.

· 53 ·

This was also, I now believe, the conviction that informed my building of the redoubt on the beach. As soon as I had been discharged from the hospital I betook myself to the Governor's house in the Castle. The usual time for audiences with His Excellency, as you know, was 8 o'clock in the morning; but my business was urgent, and even if it meant calling him away from his dinner I asked one of the guards in front of the double staircase to announce my presence. It was unfortunate that he saw fit to provoke me with a supercilious negative response, as it meant I had to draw my sword on him; but after I had dispatched him and kicked the bleeding body down the stairs his companion showed commendable alacrity to do my bidding.

The Governor, evidently happy to see me recovered after our previous meeting on the ship, dismissed all his other guests, including Secunde van Kervel (which was regrettable, as I soon found van Kervel to be the only truly astute man among all the dignitaries at Cabo); flanked only by his two large tame lions, he proceeded with a profuse show of bonhomie, to enquire after my business.

'Oom Jan,' I said, preferring to avoid unnecessary preliminaries and embellishments, 'on my way from the hospital I made a brief tour of inspection around the town, as instructed by the Lords Seventeen. And I must say I am appalled by the inadequacy of the fortifications.'

'We have nothing to fear from Africa,' he said quickly.

'But you are wholly vulnerable to attack from the sea.'

'Who will attack us?' he asked. 'Europe is at peace at the moment.'

'For how long do you expect it to last?'

He was absently passing a joint of venison to the lion on his right, to the visible agitation of the one on the left.

'What do you propose?' he asked.

'We must be prepared,' I said. 'At any moment there may be another war. Between France and Prussia, for example. The Low Countries will inevitably take sides. Which will once again expose the sea route to India. What we need is at least one redoubt on the shore. Preferably several.'

'Who can design and build such a thing?'

'I will. That is my mission.'

'But what experience do you have?'

'I was involved in extending the fortifications of La Rochelle,' I said laconically. 'And before I left France I designed a new fortress for Orléans.'

'Do you have any documents to substantiate your case?'

'What do you require?'

'Preferably a letter from the Lords Seventeen.'

'You have my word.'

The Governor appeared agitated. Which might explain why he fed another joint to the lion on his right.

This led to an unexpected turbulence, as the lion on the left, clearly driven to desperation by either jealousy or hunger or both, uttered the most fearsome roar, leaped from his seat onto the table, and grabbed the poor old governor by the shoulder. The mauling could well have turned into tragedy had I not lurched forward, drawing my sword (still sticky with the blood of the guard at the front entrance) and given the beast an almighty broadside blow across the rump with it. As it swung round, snarling, to face me, I thrust a whole golden pheasant from the nearest dish into its open maw. In an instant the lion's rage subsided and, masticating contentedly, he returned to his seat.

Jan de la Fontaine, still dazed by the experience, was rubbing his shoulder where fortunately no great harm had been done. He took a large gulp from a pewter goblet. This evidently had a reassuring effect.

'My dear Barbier,' he said, not even bothering to wipe his mouth, 'you have saved my life. You may build the redoubt.'

Who would have thought that the construction of a simple square stone enclosure with provision for six cannon could invite so many problems and so much intrigue and animosity?

The trouble lay not with the enterprise itself, not with finding builders and artisans capable of undertaking it: any journeyman mason could have done the job. Having made preliminary enquiries among the soldiers in my barracks in the Castle, especially those who had been at Cabo for several years already and had spent some time as *pasgangers*, I soon established that the most highly skilled workers were to be found among Malay slaves or free blacks; and intelligent scouting led me to Yusuf, a manumitted slave who had previously been involved in the construction of fortifications in Malabar. With his aid I soon assembled a crew of builders capable of work much more demanding and intricate than that presently required of them. The which was of course indispensable to my purpose, I myself having absolutely no experience of building and no knowledge of fortifications.

The problem came in the unexpected politicking surrounding the enterprise.

The Council of Policy having decided on the need for a redoubt at the mouth of the Salt River even before I had set foot in the colony (that much I gleaned from a soldier suffering from dysentery on the bed next to mine in the hospital), one would have thought that everything would now proceed smoothly. Unfortunately various persons in the settlement had their own reasons for wishing to secure a stake in the project themselves. Some were small fry, and could (at the time) be dismissed as of no consequence. Among these were Constable Willem Willemse and Corporal Frans Hagen, both of whom had had solid building experience – Willemse during a year as *pasganger* in Stellenbosch; Hagen, even more impressively, in a battery and on the dikes at Alkmaar in the Netherlands. Getting involved in the new project would almost certainly have meant advancement from the lowly ranks they held at the time. More than an increase in pay was involved. You see, an ordinary soldier is at the mercy of all his superiors; the smallest infraction of draconian rules can be met with outrageous punishment; any favour dearly bought – the only way to survive, for most – means additional years of contract service to pay off the debts incurred. (Hagen, in fact, had been a sergeant before, but after a brawl had been demoted to corporal, although he continued for years afterwards to protest his innocence, bearing a grudge against the world at large.)

Through Lieutenant Allemann – whom at that time I had not yet met – both these men had lodged applications to be placed in charge of the operation; but when Allemann discovered that I was favoured by the governor himself he had no hesitation in promising me his full support. And that was how I effectively first made his acquaintance.

Daniel van den Henghel, the Fiscal Independent, was a different matter. Perhaps for the very reason that de la Fontaine had appointed me this powerful man attempted to frustrate the appointment, even though, legally, he had no direct say in the matter. The murky truth was that van den Henghel desired the post for his wife's younger brother, newly arrived from Batavia.

But old Jan de la Fontaine was a stubborn man and, having awarded me the contract, stood by his decision. He was supported by Secunde van Kervel, especially after I'd chanced to find myself in the forecourt of the Castle during a sudden *averse* one afternoon, which presented me with the opportunity of offering my only good jacket to the disturbingly beautiful Mademoiselle van Kervel, his daughter, universally regarded as the belle of Africa.

Van den Henghel asked the Council of Policy to reconsider the matter. It was widely rumoured that considerable amounts of money changed hands; and the voting was very close indeed. But the Governor's decision was confirmed.

In the normal course of events this should have been the end of the affair. But late in December, mere days before the project was to go into operation, I was summoned one evening to the Fiscal's residence in the *Kat* wing of the Castle. An armed guard escorted me, which gave me the uncomfortable impression of being under arrest.

Van den Henghel, as you know, is a large and powerfully built man; but the upper half of his body is rather too long for his legs which, by contrast, though sturdy enough, appear somehow deformed. His face is very smooth and pale; my prejudice would show if I termed it porcine, yet this is how I've always thought of him: one of those great boars, pinkish white in colour, with small colourless eyes, heavy jowls, and – when he removed his great powdered wig, as was the case on this occasion – sparse bristling hair through which his rosy scalp is visible.

'Monsieur Barbier,' he said, standing beside a black carved desk in his front room, a glass in his hand, the very image of the benign seigneur. 'Can I offer you a glass of arrack, or do you prefer our good Dutch gin?'

'I am on guard duty tonight, Mijnheer.'

His attempt to smile was not very reassuring. He looked at the four men of the guard who were still standing just inside the threshold. They withdrew immediately, closing the door behind them, but I could hear them taking up position outside.

'You are a man of experience, I hear,' he said.

I realised that the merest hint of flinching would undo me. 'I am indeed, Mijnheer,' I said.

'You worked on fortifications in France?'

'That is so. In La Rochelle and Orléans.'

'Exactly when was that?'

'Some years ago. Before I left my fatherland.'

'The month, the year?'

For the moment I was taken aback; but it was as if, at the crucial moment, I could hear Jeanne's voice in my ear. I followed her promptings.

'In 1724 and 1725 in La Rochelle, from May in the first to July in the second. Then I returned to Orléans; my birthplace is Bazoches. My work on the fortress was from March to October of 1728.'

'Who was your overseer?'

'There were several.'

'In the beginning, in the end.'

(Jeanne? Help!) 'I began under François du Bois.' It was the name of my mother's cousin. 'He died when a tower collapsed. That was when General Lavigny asked me for a report, as I'd been an eyewitness. In the report I also indicated what I thought had been the reasons for the collapse of the tower. I made certain recommendations, and was then put in charge of the new operations. But as my mother was ill I asked to be relieved of the command, because I needed to be free to come and go as she required me. The new overseer was Guillaume de Puyfontaine.' (This, I should tell you, was the name of the man I'd killed in a duel.)

There was a very, very long silence. Van den Henghel rang a bell to summon a slave whom he instructed to refill his glass from a stone bottle on the desk right beside him.

'Well,' he said after the slave had left again. He seemed deeply discontented. 'No doubt you have documents to prove all this?'

'I submitted all my documents to His Excellency,' I said, meeting his stare.

It was a gamble; but I believed that if de la Fontaine were challenged by the Fiscal the Governor would feel sufficiently affronted to corroborate my account: how could he confess that he'd appointed me without any credentials?

'I have friends in France,' said van den Henghel, trying it seemed to look right through me. 'I shall make enquiries.'

'I shall be most obliged, Mijnheer,' I said. 'You may also, if you care to take the trouble, enquire at the same time from the Lords Seventeen about the nature of the mission on which they sent me to the Cape.'

His face became flushed with a deeper pink. He drained his glass in a single gulp and rang again for the slave.

'You may go, Monsieur Barbier,' he said when we were once more left alone. 'But you can be sure I shall keep an eye on everything you do. Not only in the building.'

'I am honoured by your interest, Mijnheer. As, I'm sure, will be the Lords Seventeen.'

'One wrong step – do you follow me? – *one wrong step* . . .' He stopped, took a sip from his refilled glass, then put it down brusquely. 'We may meet again,' he said, and it sounded much more like a threat than a greeting.

'It will always be a pleasure to see you, Mijnheer van den Henghel.'

'That would depend on the circumstances, wouldn't it, Barbier?'

He went to the door, and jerked it open, and motioned to the armed men to return me to my quarters.

· 55 ·

On the day after the redoubt was finished, in the late afternoon, when Yusuf and his workmen had left and the governor's committee of inspection had come and gone, Jeanne and I were alone on the beach. Not a very attractive stretch of beach, littered as it was with kelp and disfigured by piles of blackened shells burnt for building lime. But in the sunset the unsightly aspects were attenuated, and the outlines of the fortress stood black and suddenly disappointingly small against the spectacle of the skies. Never, nowhere, have I seen such sunsets as in these southern climes. There is in them a savage splendour unmatched by anything else in my experience.

And Jeanne said (I can still hear the strangely timorous tone of her voice), 'Perhaps this whole country is no more than a beautiful sunset.'

'How can you say that?' I protested. 'It is so young, it has just begun, the whole of its future still lies ahead, and who knows what greatness may yet be in store for it?'

'You have now built this shelter,' she said. 'But so much more remains to be achieved. And unless you *do* something . . .'

'But what?' I asked, assailed by fear I could not define.

She seemed not even to have heard me, as if oblivious of my very presence as she stared at the rapidly deepening, darkening colours.

'A beautiful sunset,' she repeated under her breath, and the night wind came up.

· *56* ·

There was, as we turned back, another figure visible on the empty beach, in the distance; contemplating us as we had contemplated my handiwork. As we approached it moved on. It was the bulky figure of a man whose body seemed somehow too large for its legs, but this might have been the effect of the distance or the falling night.

Had van den Henghel really been serious when he'd promised to 'keep an eye' on me?

This, frankly, was one of the reasons why, when word came only weeks later of the imminent departure of an expedition into the interior, it was so important for me to join it.

It was also one of the reasons why, a year later, soon after my promotion to the rank of sergeant and my transfer from the safety and the comparative remoteness of the small prison fortress in which I had been stationed to the presence and surveillance of the Castle, I put in a request to become a *pasganger*. It would be the first step towards independence; for if matters worked out as I hoped they would, I might soon be in a position to buy myself out of the Company's service. Because this occupation, it was already too evident, was a cul-de-sac.

· 57

There is so much darkness in the people of this land. Can it be that the light is too hard for them, forcing each to retreat into himself?

· *58* ·

I have already intimated that those soldiers who know a trade, and are able to earn more through it than they could get by standing sentry, can arrange to be excused from military service provided they pay their company, in exchange for this privilege, nine guilders and twelve stuyvers monthly. These men are called *pasgangers*, and the fee they pay is known as *dienstgeld* or 'service money'. In their new employment their earnings are arranged between themselves and their employers, invariably well in excess of the military pay. The *dienstgeld* is divided equally among the soldiers who actually perform military service, each man thereby augmenting the pittance he normally receives, the final amount depending of course on the overall number of *pasgangers* in that company.

This avenue was customarily, and for obvious reasons, reserved for the unranked soldiers only; and I was now a sergeant. But there was by now so much animosity against me within the Castle walls that I thought it wise to avail myself of any means temporarily to put some distance between myself and them. There was my fellow-sergeant Godfried Kok, whose misdeed I had witnessed on the inland journey, and Corporal Frederik Courthijm in whose place I had been chosen to go; there were Constable Willemse and Corporal Frans Hagen whose aspirations to build the redoubt had been thwarted; there was Lieutenant Allemann himself of whom I had been very wary since the time of our expedition, and even more so since he'd claimed responsibility for my promotion; above all, looming in the background, was the powerful brooding vengeful figure of the Fiscal Independent himself. Some time of absence from their daily visibility should benefit us all.

At least some of these men might well have attempted to prevent my initiative had they in the least anticipated it; but I moved swiftly, arranging everything personally with the senior Lieutenant, the benevolent asthmatic old dodderer Cochius who had from the beginning taken a particular liking to me (partly because I'd made it my business to provide him, unasked, with small comforts and pleasures in the line of liquor and tobacco from the Company stores, an extra blanket in winter – which he could easily have procured himself but was too absentminded to – and once a young slave girl smuggled from the Lodge). After an initial hesitation, due to his concern that the status of *pasganger* would be unbecoming for a soldier of some rank, he was persuaded to let me go. And towards the end of January 1736 I left Cabo and set out for the farm of the widow Louise Cellier at Drakenstein in the district of Stellenbosch.

· 59 ·

It had been Jeanne's idea that I first present myself to the widow. Blood is thicker than water. Not that she was any relative; but she was a link – tenuous, no doubt, but a link nevertheless – with the village of my birth. Let me explain. It must have been shortly after my birth, thirty-six years before, that Louise and her brother Paul Couvret had left France for the far-flung Cape. The Couvrets themselves had not been natives of Bazoches, but of Orléans; and Paul, a travelling merchant, had chosen his wife from our village: Anne, Anne Falleté, daughter of our smith and reputed far and wide as the most beautiful girl in the whole district, the object of the wet dreams of all the young men of her generation. That Anne Falleté should be snatched away by a stranger, even a man as handsome as Paul Couvret, was momentous enough; that they should then depart from our parts for a place as near-mythical in its remoteness as Cabo de Bonne-Espérance, was an event of such magnitude in our small community that for years and years it remained a *point de repère* for our calculation of dates and coincidences: *It was the year Anne Falleté went to the Cape – Three years before – Seven years after –*

I was thirteen when Paul and Anne Couvret returned to Bazoches, somehow disillusioned with that remote stain on the map. Anne was still barely thirty, but after seven children in rapid succession (only three of whom, two boys and a girl, had survived) had lost her bloom; and both she and her husband were disappointingly evasive about their adventures at the tip of Africa. But their eldest son, only a year older than I, was much more forthcoming than his parents, and as we more or less grew up together Henri was responsible, initially at least, for provoking in my imagination a thirst for that Ultima Thule.

As we grew older my interest in the Couvret offspring gradually shifted from Henri to Héloïse who was budding into a beauty as striking as her mother was reputed to have been a generation earlier, and when she was thirteen, I fourteen, we began to arrange eager breathless trysts, usually in the vestry of our village church where I would linger after the increasingly frustrating Latin lessons with the curé. It was the total experience of first love. Precipitate confidences and gushings, tongue-tied solemn silences, an intensity of stares, sighs, shared laughter, boyish showing-off, girlish gigglings, furtive whisperings, clumsy offerings of untidy bunches of half-crushed flowers or the first wild strawberries of spring; a holding of hands, and once, only once, the smudge of a kiss.

To me, Héloïse was not merely a girl: she was *la fille du Cap de Bonne-Espérance*. And what Henri had first stirred up in me she kindled into a veritable fire. The desire for the Beyond was as fierce as the lust of the flesh. For years, in fact – perhaps for good? – the two were not only linked but were identical. It began with Henri who, putting to his best advantage the year he was older than I, first initiated me into the arts of arousing myself (*'Tu sais pourquoi ça s'appelle un vit? – Parce qu'il vit'*), while listening to his inventions and embroideries on the theme of that fantastic Cape where, if he were to be believed, he had witnessed the most extraordinary practices; while Héloïse – well, in her mere presence, in her smell of bruised grass, in her eyes bright with all the mysteries she had seen of the beyond, Héloïse embodied the very notion of a crossing of boundaries, a venturing into the unknown. It is still with me, with the quick ache of that first revelation.

Perhaps the craving for the impossible would have subsided, would have folded into normality, had it been allowed to run its course, an ordinary adolescent rage that dissipates itself through its own excesses. But her father had other, grander designs for his daughter and to put her beyond my reach she was packed off to a nunnery in Orléans. I was inconsolable. But I suppose I could count myself fortunate to have escaped the fate of my predecessor with that other Héloïse.

· *60* ·

Paul Couvret's sister had not returned to France with his family. She'd met and married another Frenchman at the Cape, Pierre Cellier, who'd emigrated there as a young boy with the Huguenots. From the then Governor Simon van der Stel he had received a farm at Drakenstein. It was first named *La Bastide*; but after his marriage to Louise Couvret she insisted on renaming it *Orléans*.

Back home we all knew about it, although there never was any direct contact. Henri had told me about the aunt who'd stayed behind in that savage place; and so had Héloïse, with whom I'd planned to elope one day to join the aunt. We'd go from Orléans to *Orléans*, cross all the boundaries in between, live there in adventurous bliss for ever after.

Pierre Cellier was trampled by an elephant on a hunting expedition along the south-east coast of Africa, beyond Mossel Bay. This must have happened not many years after Paul Couvrier had taken his family back to Bazoches; but in Europe no one knew. I only found out about it when I first visited the widow. This happened quite soon after my arrival at Cabo, just before building on the redoubt commenced. I was dispatched with a small company of soldiers to the Stellenbosch district to round up recalcitrants reported by the Landdrost of that place for not having paid their annual rent.

It was with a particular sense of fulfilling my destiny that I rode out with my company. At last I could begin to execute the noble injunction implicit in the gilt inscription above the hospital door, and bring the light of law and order to the unruly outlying regions of the colony.

Once we'd reached the small town of Stellenbosch, no more than a sprinkling of thatched white houses among oaks and vineyards, the Landdrost commandeered a burgher councillor or *heemraad*, Charles Marais, to accompany us to the various outlying farms. It was purely by coincidence that we discovered, in the course of our conversations (I was naturally curious to find out all I could about the place and its inhabitants) that he was in fact a distant – very distant – relation of my mother's, from a branch of the family that had settled in the Plessis region before emigrating; she had sometimes spoken vaguely about them, but we'd never had any contact, and although it was known (or rumoured, to be more accurate) that some of them had also drifted to Cabo, it had never been impressed on our minds in any way comparable to the experience of the Couvrets from our immediate neighbourhood.

Charles was a few years older than I; we soon came to like each other, and I found him indispensable as an interpreter of the situation in the colony. My reaction, I may say, was largely one of surprise and indignation at what he revealed to me (and at what I saw for myself during the week of our mission) about the unruly nature of the colonists and their blatant attempts to enrich themselves at the expense of the Company which, after all, was responsible for allowing them to settle there in the first place. The general attitude of these colonists, many of them quite prosperous, was that the Company existed for their benefit, rather than the other way round. And as a soldier in the service of the Company I found this most offensive. The Governor would be well advised, it seemed to me, to take a much firmer line in his future dealings with these ingrates. What made them even more obnoxious to my mind was their almost total lack of refinement. Unlike the burghers of Cabo, most of these creatures appeared to be ill-mannered and indolent (much like those specimens I was soon to encounter on my journey with Allemann). Relying on slaves and hotten- tots for all the work on their farms, they themselves showed interest only in indulging in extravagant meals, interminable *sopies* and incessant smoking of very strong tobacco.

Most of them treated us with a marked lack of courtesy; on two farms attempts were even made, the moment the farmers dicovered who we were, to shoot at us, which necessitated the arrest of the offenders and their delivery to the Landdrost of Stellenbosch.

The only truly pleasant experience of the excursion, apart from the happy coincidence of meeting a (possible) relative, was my brief visit to the widow's farm.

There was no real need for this detour in Drakenstein, as the

93

widow Cellier was reputed to be a model citizen and prompt in the payment of all her rents and taxes. But I insisted. Sending the rest of my detachment, still accompanied by the *heemraad* Charles Marais, to the next farm on our official itinerary, I steered my own horse towards *Orléans*.

After all these years of fantasy the last remaining member of the Couvret family in Africa would now at last materialise. My eagerness to meet her was infused with my recollections of Henri's youthful inventions; above all with my memories of Héloïse whom, all of a sudden, I could see, and hear, and smell again. (That very last smudgy kiss, when I drew back from following her on the last journey.) In a wholly irrational way I must have expected Louise Cellier to be a mature version of my first ecstatic love.

· *61* ·

But the widow Cellier (*née* Couvret) was nothing like my little Héloïse at all. She was not only a mature woman, but decidedly old. Nearly sixty, as I calculated, but looking even older. Her childless life, the loss of her husband, the years she'd managed her estate on her own with gallic determination, had not been kind to her. The face was weatherbeaten and tanned to tough leather by the sun; the hands seemed rough and gnarled. But her grey hair was impressive both in hue and *coiffe*, drawn back severely in a bun, and her dress was of the very best cloth and cut. Entering the house, after I'd explained, somewhat sheepishly, the nature of my mission, was like stepping back into a France of years ago. The furnishings, the drapes on the walls, the carpets, the exquisite porcelain from which we sipped our tea, signalled an era before the death of the old king. Only the light that fell in through the small-paned windows was unmistakably that of this austral clime, severe and strong, penetrating, merciless.

'So you knew my brother's family after they went home again?'

I told her, too precipitately, some random facts; suddenly uneasy lest she disapprove of the nature of my early involvement with her niece. But she seemed oblivious to what surrounded the clutch of memories I offered her; and gradually a kind of passion began to possess her as she demanded, in the way of an almost famished person grasping for crumbs of food, more and more, the merest trifle of information appearing to give her delight.

She also, in turn, told me about her husband and the time they had been together; but when she came to his death she seemed inhibited.

'This land,' was all she said, 'this land . . .'

'Yet you have stayed here,' I ventured.

She looked hard at me (her eyesight, I soon discovered, was bad) and for a while it was impossible to tell whether she was amused or provoked. Then she said, 'What was there for me to go back to?'

'But your brother – his family – you must have had friends – '

'We came here in 1700,' she said flatly. 'There's nothing back there for me. And here . . .' Another silence. From outside, in that dazzling space, came sounds of labourers' voices, bird calls, a drone of bees. 'This land,' she said again 'it gains a hold on one, even if one comes to hate or fear it. You cannot leave, for it will not leave you.'

She asked about myself: my family, my life in Europe, what had brought me here.

Then out of the blue, à propos of nothing I could trace, she asked, 'When is your birthday?'

'The seventeenth of April,' I said, surprised. 'Why?'

'That is the sign of the Steer,' said the old lady, appearing curiously content with the information, as if it had been an accomplishment of my own volition rather than the fortuitous outcome of an unpredictable moment of passion in my parents. 'A good sign for a man. There is an innocence that hangs over you, to soften the anger and impatience of your nature.'

'I'm afraid I have no time for superstition,' I said.

'This is not superstition, *mon petit*. It is reading the signs *le bon Dieu* himself placed up there for us to heed.'

'Then what else do they have to say about me?' I asked, more to humour her than from any true curiosity.

'They say you have no fear at all and would face the devil himself. Yet you cannot stand physical pain. Is that true?'

I shrugged, feeling uncomfortable. How did she know this about me?

'You were born to be a soldier.'

'It was the only way I could come to the Cape, that's all.'

'But your best battlefield is inside your head. Don't you ever forget that. *D'accord?*' She turned her weak eyes towards me. (The light: it must have been the glaring light of this clime that had impaired her sight.) 'Are you happy in your position?'

'I'm not sure what you mean by "happy",' I said. 'But yes, I suppose I am. I have many plans. I am going to build a redoubt on the shore. One day I may go in search of Monomotapa.'

'You sound like my husband,' she said, but whether it was with approval or censure I could not discover. 'You really believe there is such a place?'

'Of course. There have been so many reports of it.'

'The fantasies of seafarers and adventurers.'

'I have seen maps.'

'Who drew them? People who have been there?'

'People who have recorded all the stories.'

She smiled. 'It is in your stars, you know,' she said. 'I mean, to believe in miracles. And if they do not happen by themselves you will *make* them happen.'

I found it a good moment to get up. 'It is getting late,' I said. 'I'm afraid I must go.'

She rose too, with a hint of reluctance. 'Remember,' she said, 'if you ever need work, there will always be something for you at *Orléans*.' A wistful sigh. 'But will I ever see you again?'

'I'll come back, I promise.'

'Do you mean what you say?'

'Of course!' I said, indignant. 'Don't you believe me then?'

'Your stars tell me that you are no stranger to fantasy and lies.' A wise little smile. 'Come, give me a *bise*. I shall wait for you anyway. Perhaps you will defy the stars.'

· *62* ·

Now I was on my way back to her. This journey promised to be more tedious then the previous as I had to proceed on foot, and alone, unaccompanied even by Jeanne, who had said, somewhat petulantly, 'The widow is from Orléans, you won't need another companion from that place'.

It had been quite an argument. In a calm accusing tone she'd said, 'You're running away from what awaits you, Estienne. You did not come to Africa to hide behind a woman's skirts.'

'I am not hiding! I need to earn money to buy my freedom. Surely you understand that?'

'And when you come back?'

'There will be less pressure then. We can plan more clearly what to do.'

'If I'm still here.'

'You can't possibly . . .'

'I shall not wait indefinitely, Estienne.'

'Promise me you'll wait.'

'I won't promise. But if you really need me I'll be here.'

I came close to changing my mind; but in the end I left, weighed down with misgivings. All I took with me, in a folded cloth, was a small provision of food and clothing; and my only indispensable possessions, my father's engraved watch, and the scuffed leather-bound book, to while away the tedium and shield me from the more obnoxious assaults of the world.

I was fortunate in being overtaken, before I had gone more than a mile or so across the wasteland of the Cape Flats, by a farmer and some slaves on a wagon. They were on their way back to the man's place in the Roodezands Kloof, having successfully negotiated the sale of his wares to some visiting English ships in the Bay.

· 63 ·

In this manner I arrived in the Drakenstein valley several days sooner than I had expected. This suited me well. I could not wait to see the widow Cellier again. Not only because I was now ready to take her up on her word and begin to acquire a greater independence for myself, but because at last, Rosette, I could begin to trace your steps into the interior. It was now three months since I had so laboriously relieved you of the iron band that had cut into your leg. If you had presented the widow with the letter I'd given you there would be hope of your survival. There was even the possibility – but surely this was too much to expect! – that she might have prevailed on you to stay with her; here on the farm you would be safe. We might complete some kind of circle here.

But this was the first disappointment. Louise Cellier quickly brushed aside my discreet enquiries. She knew nothing of your whereabouts, had never set eyes upon you.

Was it really unexpected? I should have known better. You were too independent to resort to such methods as I had placed at your disposition. I could but imagine you travelling through the vast interior, trading stories for proviand as you proceeded on your occult course. You were gone for good, had left no trace. Now I would never be free of you.

Almond. It wasn't cinnamon your body tasted of that distant night. It was bitter almond.

The farmer on the wagon was Hendrik Ras. Relieved as I was to accept his offer of a ride rather than continuing on foot, I was also diffident about getting more closely acquainted with one of his aberrant race. And his unkempt appearance – dirty broad-brimmed hat, breeches and jacket apparently homemade from badly cured skins, tousled beard stained with tobacco juice – did nothing to change my apprehension. However, I was cautious to show no sign of disapproval as this Ras was clearly not a man to provoke: a head taller than myself, irascible, built like a bull.

But how significantly did my opinion of the colonist change in the course of that three-day journey! I still thought him, at the end of it, uncouth and brusque; yet I had by then discovered something curiously endearing about him as well, something I hesitate to call innocence, yet I can think of no other word to describe the boyish exuberance of the man, his *joie de vivre*, his sense of wonder, the unexpected revelations of tenderness in someone so tough and strong.

When I asked him about the business that had taken him to Cabo he was, initially, morose. It had not been a good trip, he said. And yet, I pointed out, he'd sold all his produce? There was nothing in the wagon except what he had bought in town.

'You should have seen what I took with me,' he said, stuffing his deep-bowled pipe with angry intricate movements of his huge hands. 'Eggs of chickens and ostriches, fat, honey, soap, fruit and vegetables, all kinds of meat fresh and dried, the skins of all the animals you can think of, feathers, brandy, even ivory, a whole heap of tusks. By rights I should have been a happy man today.' He looked worried. 'My wife will kill me dead if she sees this is all I'm bringing back.' I imagined the great mountain of a woman it should take to strike fear in a man like him. It was only months later that I met her: a tiny wisp of a female person; yet he was truly in dread of her – and utterly devoted to her.

Hendrik Ras turned eagerly to me. 'You want to see what I got here?'

I wasn't allowed much choice. He shifted his huge body sideways on the back of the wagon where we'd been sitting, and reached for the few bundles and a trunk piled in a small heap. There were the groceries to be expected, boxes of seeds, a few rolls of wire, a keg of powder and a quantity of lead, several lengths of material for his wife, as well as a precious packet of needles and a fancy oriental hairpin. ('Can you imagine what Hannie will look like with this in her hair? Man, man . . .!') Last of all he produced, from a carefully wrapped cloth parcel, an exquisitely dressed porcelain doll.

'This is for Marietjie,' he said, holding the small fragile thing out to me in his two great paws, his voice almost down to a whisper. 'She's eight years old, and she's always been sickly. Something wrong with her legs. The days are very long for her, you see. So this is for her.'

I looked on in silence as he wrapped up the doll again and stowed his meagre acquisitions.

'Not much, hey?' he said. 'If you saw what I had to sell for it.' Followed by an unexpected coarse gesture, raising one of his huge buttocks and smacking his backside. 'It's that van den Henghel.'

'The Fiscal?' I asked, pricking up my ears.

'Since that big turd has come to this colony life is a mess.'

'How does he come into it?'

He roared with unpleasant laughter. 'He's in everything,

man. Don't you know then? When the ships come in he and his cronies get the first chance to trade. Only after they've done we farmers are allowed in. And then he claims a percentage of everything we get.'

'But I heard that was stopped thirty years ago when the Lords Seventeen got rid of that bastard Governor van der Stel?'

'You must be a stranger to this place,' he sneered. 'I was a youngster in van der Stel's time, but I know all about what happened then. My own father was thrown into the Black Hole because he signed the petition against the Governor. But I tell you, what is happening today is much much worse. In those times it was a handful of van der Stel's cronies. Now it's everybody. I tell you. Everybody. You can't trust a single one of them further than you can fart.'

'But can't the Governor put an end to it?'

He looked at me in obvious disbelief. 'How can he put an end to it? He's into it up to his neck himself.'

'I – I thought he was a good man,' I stammered.

'Of course Jan de la Fontaine is a good man,' Ras laughed. 'He's in the Groote Kerk with the rest of them every Sunday. But the problem is that graft and blackmail and favours and scheming are so commonplace that no one even thinks of it as wrong any more.'

'Then someone ought to warn the Lords Seventeen about it,' I exclaimed.

He looked at me, shaking his head. 'If you ask me the whole Dutch East India Company is shot through with it, man. All the way from top to bottom. Corruption is its life blood.'

'That I refuse to believe!' I said heatedly.

'It still makes no difference, does it?'

The conversation was interrupted by a sudden jolt of the wagon as it trundled through a ditch. We both jumped off to discover that a rear wheel had come loose. Fortunately, although skew, it still precariously supported the axle. Without a moment's hesitation Ras performed a feat I would not have thought possible. Half-crouching with his massive body under the rear of the wagon, he heaved the whole thing up on his right shoulder and held it in position while the slaves and I secured the wheel again.

His subsequent chastisement of the slave allegedly responsible for not having properly fitted the wheel in the first place I prefer not to repeat to you.

· 66 ·

Tante Louise is unabashedly pleased to see me. Even if 'see' is not the right word: in the year since my last visit her eyesight has deteriorated further, I find; she is now nearly blind. Yet her pleasure at my arrival is undimmed. Not only because there is so much to do on the farm since she dismissed her previous *knecht* several months ago for pilfering, but because she craves company. And in the absence of blood relations the tenuous link of the Couvret/Falleté family serves us well enough for her to treat me as a long-lost nephew.

By day, from dawn to dusk, I work outside. A new barn must be built; the roof of the house needs rethatching; parts of the long wall that encloses the farmyard have caved in; the old cattle kraal is in a bad shape. The slaves, spoiled by having had the run of the place for too long, are in need of discipline. Farming is not my vocation – I still believe I am intended for greater things – but there is a certain satisfaction in taxing the endurance of the body for hours at a stretch in the summer heat, until even the slaves complain; then to immerse myself in the fearsome cold of the amber stream in the kloof behind the house.

But it is a lonely existence; what drives me through the days is not just the contentment of physical exertion but the need to keep myself so busy that there is as little occasion as possible for thought. Yet in the hollow of the night, after spending some hours in conversation with the old widow, I am vulnerable.

Sometimes, to fend off thinking, to slake the searing need of the body that, though aching with fatigue, refuses to come to rest, I make use of a slave woman. But there is little pleasure in it, and often revulsion. After a few weeks I give it up and try to procure my own relief; but this brings with it the image of the frantic Sergeant Kok disporting himself in the wilderness, and of Ruyter. So everything I have tried to evade returns, and ever more urgently.

Questions: What am I doing here? What have I done in the many months since my arrival? What do I hope to do?

Images: Of you; obsessively of you. What has become of you? Where have you gone? Who *are* you? I know almost nothing about you.

I desperately miss the reassuring sound of Jeanne's voice. This is the time of day she has always been closest to me: now I am alone. I feel bewildered and lost.

· 67 ·

Do you realise: Jeanne was only nineteen when she died.

· 68 ·

In the long evenings after our shared meal the half-blind old woman and I sit talking in the gloomy *voorhuis*, the glimmer from the single low-burning oil lamp caressing, here and there, high dark beams, the patina of the floor smeared with cowdung and blood, the anomalous intricacies of furniture from another place, another age.

She asks, interminably, about my early life, my friendship with the Couvret children, my wanderings after I left Bazoches, first through France, then the years I spent in Holland and Zeeland, my voyage to the Cape. After a few weeks there is nothing new to tell, so I start composing new versions of each episode; and she smiles and nods with satisfaction, accepting with great eagerness whatever stories I choose to fabricate. Now I am allowed – encouraged – to talk about Monomotapa, to remake my journey into the interior with Herr Allemann and his eternally bickering wife, to spin fabulous accounts of tribes beyond the frontier of the colony, and unicorns and hippogryphs.

My whole life I reinvent for her; and alternately she chuckles with glee or sheds tears from her eyes with their whitish-blue film of pearls.

Of you I decline to speak: that is still too quick to the touch of words. But once, in a desperation of loneliness, I dare to mention Jeanne and find that she reacts with extraordinary enthusiasm. She seems to see nothing amiss in our relationship; it is only to be understood, sympathised with, applauded. It reassures her not only about my past but about my future as she sees it spelled out in stars. Jeanne's stars, too, she scrutinises: 6 January – the Goat – feet firmly on the ground – ambitious – invincible – the rest I cannot remember. (And it is obvious that she does not know Jeanne as I know her. The stars, too, are to be taken with a pinch of salt.)

'With someone like Jeanne you're safe,' she repeats many times. 'Just do what she says, go where she tells you. You can't go wrong.' Then, occasionally, a sigh. 'I'm old before my time. How fortunate she was to die so young. And then to live for ever.' She pats my hand. 'Tell me all about her.'

'But you know everything.'

'I want to hear *you* tell it.'

And like so many other times I tell her about the peasant girl of Domrémy, and about her voices; the dogged perseverance with which she wore down the resistance of her uncle until he escorted her to Vaucouleurs; and the courage and obstinacy it required to persuade the wicked, manipulating Robert de Baudricourt to take her to Chinon, where she met the Dauphin with his bulbous nose and watery red eyes and hairless brows, and the trust she put in him, bolstering the poor young man's faith in the possibility that he might indeed become king; and how at last, a *pucelle* of seventeen, she was put in charge of a small group of soldiers with whom she broke the siege of Orléans, and led them to victory in another battle at Patay; and then the terrible decline: defeat outside the walls of Paris when her own allies withdrew their support; capture by the Bourguignons below the walls of Compiègne, the despicable dealings of the one-eyed Jean de Luxembourg who sold her to the English; the trial at the tribunal of the unscrupulous bishop of Beauvais, that mountainous man with the thundering voice, Pierre Cauchon (whom in an uncharacteristic demonstration of malice she preferred to call Cochon); and on the penultimate day of May 1431, the burning at the stake in the Old Market Square of Rouen.

Alone in this nightest of places. No Jeanne, no voices. No you.

Back in Cabo, if only for a day or two. Let me fill you in. I couldn't stay with the widow for too long; already I'd been at *Orléans* for three months. On rare visits other farmers – once my distant cousin Charles Marais – had talked to Tante Louise, to me; had inspected my building and the signs of my industry; and had made offers of work on their own farms. An outbuilding here, a paved furrow there, the frame of a roof elsewhere. But my first obligation was to Hendrik Ras who'd taken the trouble on that initial journey of making a half-day detour to deposit me at the widow's door before he'd moved on to his wife, his four sons, his puny daughter in the Roodezands Kloof.

I'd worked there for three weeks, the hardest work I'd ever done in my life. And then he'd asked me to take a wagonload of firewood and bark to a friend of his in Cabo, the tanner Willem Meyer. More important were the twelve huge tusks of ivory concealed under the wood; those were for a retired trader from Batavia who conducted a prolific smuggling operation from his house at the Ronde Bosschje, with the help of unidentified Muslim dealers, and a whole network of agents scattered across the Orient.

I had misgivings about the ivory, the spoils of a hunting trip Hendrik and two of his sons had undertaken along the southeast coast. 'It's illegal, Hendrik,' I said. 'If you get caught – what will happen to me?'

'What are you? A mouse? In this goddamned place we survive by our wits. It's them or us.'

'What was that word you said?' asked his diminutive wife who had entered, quiet as a whisper, from the kitchen.

'I'm sorry, Hannie.' The huge man was genuinely contrite.

'No cursing in my house,' she said, unforgiving. 'If I hear you going on like that again we'll have dinner without you.'

'I promise, Hannie.'

'All right then.' She turned to go back to the kitchen, drying a tin plate with a cloth; behind her head the neat bun was held in place by a mother-of-pearl pin which I recognised. 'And I'll be needing meat for tonight.'

'I'll tell Booi.'

'I'm asking you,' she said pointedly.

Without a word he rose and picked up the puny girl-child who had been sitting quietly on her little chair, solemnly clutching her doll to her thin rib-cage. In one easy movement he swung her on his shoulders, where she remained, holding on tightly like a baby monkey. Wherever he went on the farm, and whatever his business, that was her perch. On this day, too, she remained in place while he calmly and efficiently went about the business of selecting a *hamel* from the small group of sheep kept in an enclosure at the back of the house, and carrying it to the slaughter-block where he deftly up-ended the animal, with one hand stretched the head back until the throat was taut, while with the other he drew a swift knife-blade across it, holding the kicking, jerking animal in place until its spasms subsided. The legs of his trousers were sprayed with blood. But he was used to it. Kneeling beside the carcass, the little monkey-girl still wedged tightly on his massive shoulders with her sinewy arms, her useless thin legs dangling, as she watched without the flicker of a pale eyelid, he proceeded to gut and flay the sheep in quick, long, even strokes.

'Well, there's another skin for you,' he said as he rose and picked up the carcass in one hand to take it to the kitchen. 'You can drop this and the others in the shed off at Willem Meyer's place too.'

And two days later I was in Cabo. There was a sudden lump in my throat as, approaching across the dreary Flats, I saw the outline of the mountain turning steadily a deeper blue. I had forgotten how beautiful the place was.

Dumping the ivory proved easier than I had anticipated. The problem came when, close to nightfall, I found my way to

Willem Meyer's place (the smell proved a more trustworthy indicator than the directions Hendrik had given me). Instead of showing gratitude for the load, he seemed uncommonly agitated.

'I'm sorry,' he said, running his fingers through his unkempt hair, 'But you can't offload the stuff here. I'll be in trouble.'

I stared, uncomprehending, at the man: straight as a plank, his arms bare and stained from working in the tannery behind the house, his hair caked with grease and dirt.

'Don't you need the bark for your tannery?' I asked.

'I have enough,' he said, casting furtive glances this way and that. But the wide street was deserted at this hour.

'But Hendrik Ras said . . .'

'I'm sorry.' He took me by the arm and led me to the back of the house where he seemed to feel more confident. 'Look, Hendrik has always helped me out in the past. But now I have a contract. And I'm not allowed to buy wood from others any more.'

'What kind of contract is that?' I asked.

'It's a military man,' he said. 'His slaves collect the wood from the Company's posts inland, and I'm obliged to buy.' He hesitated and approached even more closely. 'I have to pay him more than I used to pay before. But that's how it is. I've got a family, I can't afford to take chances.'

'But a military man has no right to trade,' I said.

'You tell me.'

'Who is this man?'

He seemed reluctant to reply; but after a while, drawing courage, I presume, from the increasing dusk, he said, 'Lieutenant Allemann from the Castle.'

Willem Meyer agreed to let me spend the night in his house, as Ras had more or less instructed him in the letter (written by Hannie) I'd brought with me – but only after I'd removed the wagon to the Boeren Plein where I left it in the care of the driver. And although he and his wife really did their best to make me comfortable (even if I had to share a room with their three eldest sons), you will readily understand that I found it difficult to sleep.

Yet this experience was only the beginning of a deeply unsettling visit.

In the morning Meyer – who appeared as bleary-eyed and crusty from lack of sleep as I felt – proposed that, as there was little sense in returning all the way to Roodezand with my load, I should visit other likely buyers in the town. And so I spent most of the day going from one to the other – Jan Bengel the shoemaker, Hans Roos the cabinetmaker, Jan de Waal the baker, Jacob Steyn, Hendrik Booysen – only to hear the same response from all. No private citizen was allowed to sell wood in Cabo any more; it was now the self-imposed monopoly of Lieutenant Rudolf Siegfried Allemann.

With the scant consolation of having at least concluded the sale of my contraband ivory, I had no choice but to drive the wagon all the way back to Stellenbosch, where I finally succeeded in finding a buyer for the wood, at one-fifth the price it should have fetched in Cabo.

There is, in the road, an egg. The largest egg I have seen in my life. It is on the last stretch of the way to the Roodezands Kloof, as the sun is going down, the hour of miracles, when the world we know merges with the unknown. This was the hour when Jeanne first heard her voices, when I found the unicorn, when you and I saw the hippogryph, when she and I spoke on the beach about the redoubt and the doubtful future. *This land, a beautiful sunset*.

I am alone. The slave who usually drives the wagon has gone into the bushes to shit. But there is no need to bring the oxen to a halt: they, too, have seen the object in the rutted tracks in front of them, shimmering with a pale opalescent gleam as if it does not merely reflect the dying daylight but glows from within.

A world, I know, can hatch from an egg; and sitting serenely still on the *wakis*, the long rhinoceros-hide whip idle by my side, I lean forward to watch as if prompted in advance to expect something momentous.

And it happens, the moment the last rim of the sun disappears (which I sense rather than see, as it sets directly behind me). Without any warning the shell breaks in two and a woman emerges, fullgrown, beautiful beyond words, glistening with the wetness of birth. It is you.

I slide from the *wakis* and off the wagon; but as I give the first step towards you, there is nothing. You have not run away: you have simply dissolved in what remains of light.

The slave Apollo comes from the bushes, still tying the thong that holds his breeches.

'Why have you halted the wagon?' he asks.

I do not bother to explain.

Then, as he approaches, he suddenly stops to stare. And asks, 'What is this thing?' Pointing towards the two perfect halves of the huge broken egg.

'I don't know,' I say, avoiding his look. 'It was there when we came. The oxen stopped by themselves.'

'It's a pity you were too late,' he says, reaching out to take the whip and urge the oxen on again. 'These eggs usually hatch women. And the man who sleeps with them' – he uses the crude word *kwekwa*, which one hears among the hottentots – 'is protected by the spirits for as long as he lives.' He cracks the long whip; the wagon lumbers into motion. Under the wheels the fragile shell, thinner than any I have seen, is crushed.

· 74 ·

No. No. I must restrain myself. The shell was there, and the circumstances were as I described. But nothing hatched from it. The oxen had stopped in their tracks and stubbornly refused to move; and in what may have been superstitious fear I led them in a wide detour around it and proceeded without daring to look back; and the slave, coming running from the bushes at last to catch up with us, did not see it.

There was no need to wait and watch. I knew it was a sign that I would see you again, as surely as if you'd hatched from that perfect thing.

· 75 ·

In the beginning of the winter, which set in early that year, I moved to the farm of my distant cousin Charles Marais about half an hour outside Stellenbosch, on the Paarl side. The visit had been arranged previously; and he'd already come over to Hendrik Ras's place a couple of times to prod me. The move was not entirely unwelcome, as Ras was in no position to pay me much for my services; some months he had no cash at all, and my *dienstgeld* for the garrison in Cabo had to be debited against my already alarming loan account.

What with the rain and the cold (the mountains were often flecked with a dandruff of snow) this was no time for outdoor work, but what Charles needed me for was to help with the education of his four children. You see, I'd told him, somewhat rashly, that I'd been a teacher in Orléans years ago and as education is not a commodity readily available at the Cape he was eager to let his offspring (three daughters of fourteen, eleven and nine years old, and a son of twelve) profit from whatever I could offer them. Fortunately their requirements were very basic. As a second-generation Huguenot Charles himself could no longer speak French fluently but believed, and I concurred, that learning the language would have a civilising effect on his daughters; for the rest, he was content to let me teach them some elementary arithmetic, reading from the Dutch State Bible (the exaggerated devotion of my Dutch wife Neeltje stood me in a good stead here), and a smattering of history. The last subject was by far the most enthusiastically received, and I believe I invented a whole new past for our race. Putting into sometimes startling new perspective what Jeanne had told me about herself and her age, and my own peregrinations (for the sake of interest I included Prussia, Italy, Russia and Hibernia in the territories covered), I was able to hold all four children spellbound for hours on end. I even considered throwing in some Latin for free, but I restrained myself, not wishing to take too much advantage of a relative, however distant, or his wife, a staunch locally-bred female called Catarina, who clearly brooked no nonsense.

· 76 ·

Apart from my cousin's interest in furthering the education of his brood, I had my own special reason for wanting to spend some time with him. As a *heemraad* or district councillor he seemed to me well placed to advise me about my more disquieting discoveries of recent times. Another disappointment. When, having carefully chosen my moment (the two of us alone with a carafe of wine in the spacious high-ceilinged *voorhuis*), I broached my experience with my load of wood in

Cabo, amplified with other accounts Ras himself had given me, he didn't seem at all surprised.

'My dear Estienne,' he said, stretching his neck momentarily better to survey through the window the rain-drenched scene outside, dotted with slaves and hottentots digging trenches, cutting vines, working manure into the soggy soil, 'what else do you expect? They're only reaping the fruits that go with power and high office. It's human nature.'

'It deprives the ordinary colonists of their livelihood.'

'I'm an ordinary colonist.'

'No Charles, you're not. You're a *heemraad*. You're a rich man.'

'I still depend on favours.'

I looked at him, nonplussed.

Charles gave a brief smile. 'How do you think I got this farm?'

'I'm afraid I don't understand.'

'I gave Jan de la Fontaine a hundred sheep.'

'I don't believe it!'

'How else does anybody get a good place like this? It may be different in the more remote parts of the colony where one can stake off any piece of land as long as you pay your annual rent. But farms in these parts are valuable property, Estienne.'

'And you approve of the way it's done?'

'I don't ask questions. I want to make a living. Preferably a good one.'

'You side with the criminals?'

'No! I'm a colonist. And I understand their problems. But there's no point in making life difficult for myself or my family. I've got children, man. I'll do anything to make sure they inherit something worthwhile one day.'

'Anything?'

'Have some more wine,' he said, getting up to pour. Then looked through the window again, pushed it open – thin driving rain washed across the broad stoep into our faces – and

bellowed at the slaves to bloody well get moving, they didn't
have all day.

· 77 ·

Sometimes of an afternoon when Catarina and the children
were away (the proximity of the farm to its neighbours and to
the village favoured constant visiting) Charles would offer me
the use of the kitchen to disport myself with a slave woman
while he entertained, in the master bedroom, his long-standing
favourite Anna of Macassar, on whom he had already fathered
three children. This was, he told me, a sound investment as the
children, once they were grown up, would also be slaves.

· 78 ·

Often I wake up in the night believing I have heard Jeanne
whispering in my ear; but she is never there, and for hours I lie
sleepless listening to the small intricate sounds of the rain. The
absence of her voice is like a void inside myself, a physical ache.
In passionate self-reproach I remember my cavorting with
slaves, and resolve forthwith to purify myself and do penance
for her sake. To my even greater shame I recall the night on the
journey with Herr Allemann when I stared into the flames and
imagined in their flickering Jeanne herself take shape, a girl in
boy's clothing, the breeches split at the seam (ah happy seam,
favoured above all others); and how furious I was when I
imagined that poor bastard Kok staring with me at her revealed
intimacy. Oh my *pucelle*, my *pucelle*, I am not a man of the spirit.

History was my undoing. I was holding forth to the children that late August morning when the end came so abruptly. On this occasion, as on some others, all seven children were with me in the kitchen, Catarina's four around the yellowwood working table, the slave woman's three hunched on the floor. (Charles believed – although Catarina made no secret of her disapproval – that the 'others' could also benefit from some education, provided it did not interfere with their work on the farm.) I was telling them about Jeanne's betrayal, and her trial, and her death at the stake. Without intending any historical distortion, and really only in an endeavour to portray that scandalous drama as vividly as possible (in the course of which, admittedly, I became rather more transported by the account than normally), I presented the event on the Old Market Square in Rouen as if I had personally witnessed it. And in my enthusiasm I suppose I went too far, narrating – and demonstrating – to them how I had tried to intervene but was prevented; and how I had then called upon two valiant friends, the Spaniard Don Quixote de la Mancha and the Moor Cidi Hamete Benengeli, with whose energetic assistance I routed the English. But all too late, as the maid had already been burnt to a cinder. At least our action had prevented the cannibal English from eating her charred flesh.

That was when Catarina interrupted the telling; I had not been aware of her presence as she treacherously lurked behind the middle door. It was not so much my personal intervention in history that outraged her, I learned, as the discovery that her tender brood had been exposed to tales involving Spaniards, the immemorial enemies of the Dutch, and – even worse – an antichristian Moor.

Charles was sympathetic to my case, and most reluctant to take his leave of a relative, an accomplice in carnal delights, and a teacher, all at once. But Catarina, like some of the other Dutch women in these climes, proved to be quite formidable once roused. And in the end there was no choice but once more to pack my possessions into a leather shoulder-bag Hendrik Ras had presented me with for services rendered, and leave.

· 80 ·

I was back at *Orléans*. Along the way I had stopped for a few weeks to supervise the building of a shed on the farm of Petrus de Wet, a morose man who had the unsettling habit of coming right up to one, only inches away, and then staring fixedly at one's left shoulder without saying a word. Charles Marais had arranged the work for me, as a favour; but I would have preferred to have done without it, as the man's silence soon disheartened me. Fortunately, after three weeks his mother-in-law sent word from her neighbouring farm that she and her daughter required 'a responsible man, not a slave' to drive them to Drakenstein; and I offered to take them provided I could afterwards proceed to *Orléans*. As it turned out, this Elizabeth Joubert knew Tante Louise quite well and she was more than pleased with my company. I, in turn, was particularly taken with her daughter Liesbet, the recalcitrant wife of poor Petrus, whom she apparently had the habit of deserting every few months.

On the way I enquired about that enigmatic character. Neither woman had anything good to say about the man; all I could make out was that his silence had some connection with the death of a child, years ago, for which he'd somehow blamed himself. The ladies were more concerned with the fact of his taciturnity than with its origins.

'Can you imagine what it is like to have a man like that in your house and in your bed?' asked Liesbet. Her mother glanced disapprovingly at her; Liesbet glanced approvingly at me. 'I'm a woman in the prime of my life.'

For the sake of propriety (I guessed) the mother changed the subject. 'He doesn't even have the courage to raise his voice, let alone a finger, when his mother-in-law, a poor defenceless woman like myself, is shamelessly robbed in broad daylight.'

It was such a pointed remark that I had to press for more particulars, which the poor defenceless woman proved only too ready to provide.

No less a person than a sergeant from the Castle in Cabo, it transpired, had arrived on the widow's farm as a *pasganger* in the employ of her mealy-mouthed son-in-law Petrus de Wet (who at the time had been farming at the Breede River). On the instructions – allegedly – of his employer the sergeant had bought sixteen sheep from her, at four *guldens* a head, promising to deliver the money within a week, and then had disappeared. When afterwards she'd confronted her son-in-law (the scene was only too easily conjured up) he'd protested that he had sent the sixty-four *guldens* with the sergeant on the day of the transaction. By this time the shameless swine had already returned to Cabo. Was that not, she demanded, downright theft? The widow, both taller and wider than I, stared peremptorily at me.

I made further enquiries. When had it happened? A good five years ago, she informed me, and she still hadn't seen a stuyver. And did she by any chance remember the name of the culprit? Indeed she did. He was called Sergeant Godfried Kok.

'Mother never forgets a thing,' Lisbet said proudly.

'Neither the good nor the bad,' confirmed the widow.

'*You* are a very helpful man,' said the daughter, as if this was crucial to the whole affair.

And so I returned for some time to the caring company of Tante Louise. After depositing the full widow Elizabeth Joubert and the grass widow Liesbet de Wet at their destination (the farm of Elizabeth's sister and her husband) I was allowed to proceed to *Orléans*, accompanied only by a slave to drive the wagon back. There was a last encouraging look from Liesbet as her hand lingered in mine before she was swept away by her imperious mother.

But I did not dwell on that look; I was too preoccupied with the welter of new thoughts that had been shaping in my mind over the last eight months. What I needed more than anything was a conversation with Jeanne. But she remained distressingly out of reach. The only person I could unburden myself to was Tante Louise.

'What am I doing in this colony?' I asked her the very first night after the house slaves had cleared away the remains of the meal and we were left alone in the dusky *voorhuis*, the lamp turned down low. (Since she couldn't see well anyway she didn't care for unnecessary light.) 'The more I hear about my superiors in Cabo the more despondent I become.'

'What would you *want* to do in the colony?' she threw the question back at me – much in the way I knew Jeanne would have done.

'When I leave one day I want it to be a different place from the one I came to,' I said. (In that deep dusk it was easy to speak strongly.) 'I want the Cape to know that I've been here.'

A slow smile changed the pattern of wrinkles on her face. The light explored the informal embroidered cap she wore indoors, the lace fichu covering the daring *décolletée* – it was, really, a dress for a much younger woman – and played around the deep folds in the heavy damask of her bronze-coloured skirt. She played absently with her small fan. She said nothing.

'Do you think it's presumptuous of me?' I asked, unnerved by her silence.

'Yes,' she said calmly. 'But perhaps that's why I'm so fond of you. If you want something worth while, *mon garçon*, your dreams must be even greater. *D'ailleurs*, I've already seen it in your stars. You will seek out opposition to fight for what you regard as just. It's the boy in you.'

'I'm not a boy,' I reminded her. 'Another three years and I'll be forty.'

'You *act* like a boy,' she replied. '*Tant mieux*. I can't stand middle-aged people. This place is like an unruly horse. Only the young and the bold can bring the saddle to its back.'

'Sometimes *I* feel saddled,' I said. Adding more gloomily, 'Or shackled.'

I had still not told her more about you, Rosette; about that night. And I did not intend to either. It was the one thing, I could sense, she would neither pardon nor understand. But there were more weighty reasons for my silence: in a way, who knows, I had betrayed Jeanne by discussing her with Tante Louise (was that why she was so stubbornly keeping away from me even while she could not but know I needed her?); I could not bring you into it too.

'Sometimes one spends so much time taming the horse that when it's done it is no longer worth the effort.' She peered intently at me in the gloom; I had the feeling that she saw much more than her weak eyes permitted.

'What do you mean?' I demanded.

'Going back to Cabo,' she said. 'What sense is there really in that? You can only feel frustrated, stunted, threatened all the time.'

'What else can I do? My year as a *pasganger* is nearly up. I have no choice.'

Soon it would be a year since that windy night.

'One of these days I'll be quite blind,' she said. The fan was resting motionless in her lap now. 'I can't remain here on my own. Whereas *you* can make something of the farm. Why don't you buy yourself out of the Company's service and come and live with me? You can have the run of the place. You already have. And if things work out, maybe you can take over when I die.'

'I don't have the money to cancel my contract,' I said.

'I do.'

'Why should you . . .'

'Why not? My only relatives are Paul and his family in France.'

(It was painful to be reminded of Héloïse. That day on the steeple.)

'They have given me up. My husband's few remaining relatives are a thankless lot, I never see them. *You* are the closest to a relative I have. Why shouldn't I offer you a man's place on the farm? *Orléans* is in need of a man.'

'I can't just give up everything else.'

'From what you've told me you did just that several times before this.'

'That's why. I can't give up this time. I've got to make it work.'

'Rising through the ranks, cultivating the powerful and the rich, following in the footsteps of your friend Allemann, making it to the top one day, perhaps even commander of the Castle garrison?'

'That's something.'

'Estienne, that's riding a pack mule, not a steed.'

'And what would it mean to accept your offer? Learning the tricks of farming, becoming prosperous, a *heemraad* perhaps like my cousin Charles? That's not it either, *ma tante*. Don't you realise? It's something altogether *different* I want.'

'At least you'll be your own master, take your own decisions.'

'It'll be an escape, not a fulfilment.'

'Who knows in what way fulfilment comes?'

'I can't tell you beforehand. I'll only know when it happens.'

'Is it still Monomotapa you're looking for?'

'The name is not important,' I said impatiently. 'As long as you or I can name it it is not enough. What I want lies beyond. Even beyond names.'

She rose with a rustling of her magnificent dress. Even in that rustling I briefly thought I heard the voice of my long-lost Jeanne, whispering, whispering so seductively. 'Don't be in too much of a hurry to make up your mind, Estienne,' said Louise Cellier. 'Tomorrow is another day.'

· *82* ·

You will readily understand that this was another night with little hope of sleep. I was tired enough, but my thoughts would not lie down with my body and I lay in the dark considering my conversation with the two women on the wagon and what they had told me about Godfried Kok (and that led me back to the night on the journey when Jeanne teased me from the fire; and to Kok's quarrel with Ruyter and the killing of the hottentot; and my journal, and Allemann and Mentzel; and the unicorn and the hippogryph; and to you); I remembered the lingering last look Liesbet de Wet had given me; and most of all I revisited what I'd been trying to exclude, the dialogue with Tante Louise, which again brought back everything else.

In the end I rose from the bed and lit the candle again, and took my soothsaying book from its wraps and, like innumerable other nights, fell to reading. I had developed a habit of reading it as some other people confess to reading the Bible: holding the book on its spine and allowing it to fall open by chance, reading whatever page presented itself to my perusal.

That night, I remember so well, it was the chapter on the knight's encounter with the gang of galley slaves in the mountains. First there is his conversation with the condemned men, each in turn; and I was struck, like many times before, by the way in which each slave tries to put the aspect of a story on his life's history. One narrates that he has been sentenced for falling in love. How can that be, the knight asks, horrified. It turns out that what he fell in love with was a basketful of white linen. Another recounts how he had been sentenced for singing. But the singing, of course, was really his confession on the rack. Yet another, a student, finds himself in chains for having disported himself too extravagantly with two girl cousins of his (how I sympathised with him!), and this too is presented as if it were a mere peccadillo, an escapade more amusing than serious.

The most dangerous criminal in the gang, the most heavily shackled of them all (known as Ginesillo de Parapilla, although that is not his real name), has already turned his whole life into a story, recording everything he has ever experienced in a book; which means that the book can never be finished before his life itself comes to an end. In fact, one comes to suspect that his book *is* his life; or in other words, all that matters about his life is what has been written down.

· *83* ·

How much there was, is, to ponder in those pages. Why does one read the accounts of the convicts as lies, but Don Quixote's inventions as something altogether different?

· *84* ·

There is something deeply disturbing about the end of the particular episode I read that night. (Outside, from time to time, in the oppressive stillness, a nightjar shrieked. Once there was a woman's cry from the slave quarters far behind the house. But whether it was lust or pain was impossible to say; perhaps there is no difference.) With his customary grandiloquence Don Quixote announces that he will demonstrate on the prisoners the purpose for which God has sent him into the world, fulfilling his chivalric vow to succour the needy and those who are oppressed by the strong. When the sergeant refuses to set the men free, the knight falls upon him and his guards and frees the whole chain of slaves. But instead of them proceeding to the village of El Toboso to do homage to the beauteous Lady Dulcinea as they have been instructed to do, the newly freed men turn upon the knight and his servant, knocking down Rocinante, pelting them with stones, beating them black and blue, robbing them of all their possessions, and leaving them behind for dead.

Indeed, there is risk involved in unshackling the condemned.

· *85* ·

I was working long days on the widow's farm. As the good weather returned I toiled on, redressing the ravages of the winter months, building, digging, patching, repairing. Everywhere the world was bursting from its seams with fertility and new life. There were clusters of white arum lilies in all the *vleis*, and wild flowers of every description in the new green grass. The sky was thick with flocks of birds returning from faraway places: swallows, storks, pink flamingos.

I had no way of knowing that this would be my last carefree spring in the colony: the following September I was to be involved in that outrageous, senseless trial, followed by two years as a fugitive. But even if I was not conscious of it, there was something I could sense behind the reckless beauty of the season: an uneasiness, a deep disquiet, a knowledge in the guts that this could not last, that something was gathering, if not around me, then within myself. I had not yet given Tante Louise any answer to her proposal. But it could not be postponed indefinitely.

The turning-point came in a way I could not have expected.

I had spent the day in the kloof behind the farmhouse, working with the slaves and some casually employed hottentots on clearing away a mass of driftwood and fallen trees that had blocked the stream. When I returned it was already dusk. The widow stood waiting outside the kitchen door in a state of agitation.

'What's the matter, Tante Louise?'

'Estienne, I think you are in trouble.'

'Why?'

'Some men came to look for you.'

'Who were they?'

'They wouldn't say, and I couldn't make out their faces. But they're not from Cabo. At least I think not. They speak like the people from here, not like the Dutch.'

'But what did they say?'

'They just said they wanted to see you. When I told them you weren't here, they wouldn't believe me. They pushed me aside – I nearly fell, and grazed my elbow, look – and went through the whole house, turning everything upside down.' She was so agitated she burst into tears, and I had to comfort her.

I took her inside, and made her sit down, poured her some wine.

'A band of ruffians,' she said. 'I was afraid for you. And they said they'd be back.'

'When?'

'I don't know. Perhaps they were just trying to scare me.'

'It looks serious enough.'

The house really was a shambles: furniture overturned, bedclothes strewn over the floors, some cups and glasses broken. They must have known, or guessed, which room was mine, because it was in greater confusion than the rest. Everything lay piled up in a heap in the middle of the floor; and on top of it someone had defecated. They had even torn some pages from my book – although, *Dieu merci*, this vandalism had been abandoned before the damage had gone too far. Even so, the sight of my disfigured cherished book enraged me more than anything else – including the discovery that they had taken all my money, every stuyver I'd earned during the last seven months. (What good fortune that I always kept my father's watch on my body.)

'Looks like an ordinary band of robbers to me,' I said.

'But they kept asking about *you*, Estienne.'

I could find absolutely no explanation. All I knew – and I realised there was no logic in this, it was simply the acknowledgement of something that had become irreversible – was that my time as *pasganger* was up. Whatever lay behind this senseless invasion, and whoever had been responsible, it was time for me to go back. Jeanne had been right: this existence in the margin of the colony was escape; was indulgence. I had exiled myself from the main current of my own life; *that* was why she'd refused to come with me. Now it was time to return, back to where I belonged. I had no idea of what I would be going back to: but it was all I could conceive of doing.

· *86* ·

I pitied the proud, generous, kindhearted woman who would now be left alone on the farm to wander through the rooms of her rambling house like an unfinished thought; but it was time to take my own life in hand.

All she said was, 'Estienne, this is contrary to sense.'

'Perhaps that is why I choose to do it,' I replied.

· *87* ·

If anything had ever been contrary to sense it was my leave-taking from Héloïse in the summer of my fourtenth year. I owe it to you, Rosette, to tell you that she did not become a nun after all. When she came to me the last time to tell me that her father had decided to send her off to Orléans, I cried in despair, 'But how can we stop it? What must we do?'

'There is only one thing,' she said, deadly quiet; she was paler than I'd ever seen her. 'We must run away. But far. Far.'

'To Cabo de Bonne-Espérance!' I said.

'No, even that I think will not be far enough.'

'Nothing can be farther than that place.'

'Come,' she said, with a touch of impatience, 'I'll show you.'

She took me to our village church. We went up in the belfry, all the way to where the big bell hung, a bell like the one suspended above the entrance to the Castle. She was unnaturally calm. I was, inexplicably, terrified. Perhaps, without knowing, I sensed what lay behind her stark serenity. At the very top of the belfry she leaned over the parapet and pointed at the undulating green, green landscape with dark fingers and patches of forest in the folds.

'See?' she said.

'What?'

'That is where we're going. No one will ever follow us there.' She leaned over, swiftly, clumsily, and kissed me on the mouth, the first time, that fatal kiss, a brush of moth wings against my lips. And said, 'Come, Estienne. Come with me.' And grabbed my hand. And jumped.

But I pulled back. I could not jump, Rosette. I was too paralysed with terror. She went on that ultimate journey all alone. I had failed her, utterly. But of one thing I was sure. There was no reason, no sense at all in it: but I knew that for her sake, one day, I would go to Cabo de Bonne-Espérance. Do you understand that?

And do you understand that, for Héloïse's sake too, I could not hide away at *Orléans* any longer but had to face whatever awaited me at Cabo?

I was barely an hour or two away from *Orléans*, three days later, on the wagon track to Stellenbosch, when the mystery was resolved in an unexpected and violent way. A large band of armed men on horseback – forty or fifty of them to my reckoning – appeared round a bend a hundred paces ahead of me, galloping towards me. The track was running through a dense copse right there and as it was rather narrow I scrambled up the incline on my left to make way for the horsemen.

Suddenly there came cries of recognition from them.

'That's him!' 'Estienne Barbier!'

The cries became a bellowing of rage.

Bemused, I stopped to watch their approach. To my amazement they reined in their careering horses, and jumped off. There were wild shouts of, 'Don't let him get away!' 'Kill the bastard!' And suddenly they began to fire at me. There was no mistaking the action, the small puffs of smoke forming in front of their guns, then the loud reports. I waited no longer. There was, I hope, no ignominy in turning to run from them, scrambling in among the high trees.

And then I was hit. I knew it immediately, as the blow struck me on the shoulderblade from behind and sent me sprawling. The ball had entirely traversed my body, emerging from my left nipple like a drop of molten lead. I was bleeding profusely.

And I was still spreadeagled there among the trees, wondering whether I was dead or not, when with warlike whoops those savages caught up with me and hurled themselves upon my prostrate form, kicking and beating. I tried to prevent them as best I could, to discover at least the reason for the unprovoked attack. But when I realised this was useless, I instinctively called on Jeanne to inspire me, and forthwith began to defend myself vigorously. A ferocious battle raged, in which I was hopelessly outnumbered; and unarmed – except I found a new jawbone of an ass and put forth my hand, and took it, and began to strike out in all directions. I can tell you that at least thirty of them lay dead or dying among the trembling trees by the time the rest withdrew, ashamed and demoralised.

· 89 ·

Not quite. I apologise, Rosette; I have been carried away. One needs the sustenance of all one's faculties in a time, a place like this.

It did not happen quite like that. To start with, the band of assailants was much smaller than I have led you to believe. Four or five at most. Still, they were armed; and they had caught me by surprise. That first ball had indeed struck me on the shoulder from behind, but something in the nature of a minor miracle had averted death. You see, I'd been carrying my leather bag over my shoulder; and the ball had been deflected by the heavy much-read tome stowed in it. Don Quixote had saved my life.

Before I could scramble to my feet again the men were on me. I defended myself as robustly as I could, and I am happy to record that I did lay out two of them; but by the time these two were dragged off by their companions – which was the last I was conscious of – I myself was close to expiring.

And why, you may well ask?

That became clear the moment they caught up with me. They were the farmers I'd visited almost two years before with my detachment of soldiers to collect outstanding rent; two of them, Jan la Grange and Koos Jansen, had been arrested at the time for resisting us. Word had reached them that I was now in the neighbourhood, and *voilà*. As banal as that.

If anything, this was reason for me to return to *Orléans*; going to Cabo would seem like retreat, acknowledgement of defeat. And indeed my pride resisted. But in the end I knew that within the larger framework of my life I had no choice but to resume to my occupation. Did I already sense that the greater menace lurked in Cabo, not here? And to avoid that would indeed be cowardly.

· 90 ·

Not that I was in any state to reason thus right then. I had lost consciousness in fact; and when I came to I was on a small rickety one-horse cart belonging to a Malay, an uncommunicative soul who told me his name was Baderoun and then fell silent again. I was not in a mood for talk either, so it was a day or two before I learned that he was a free-black, a tinker on his way back to Cabo after doing his rounds in this far-flung district. Apart from the small box on which he sat to steer the horse the rest of the cart was built into a large cage, from the slats of which rattled and tinkled innumerable welded and mended pots and pans and cans and other containers in pewter, brass or copper. In addition it housed a collection of live chickens and ducks which he had accumulated in part-payment for his services; and these, either for lack of space or from a sense of superiority, had no qualms about perching all over my battered prostrate body as we drove relentlessly on, jolting and swaying, and I dozed, more dead than alive, in a cacophony of metallic sounds worse than anything the author of I Corinthians xiii could ever have thought up.

· 91 ·

Once again I found myself in the hospital opposite the Company Gardens. It is always a sign of warning, I think, when events begin to repeat themselves. Our sense lies in going on, not in returning to beginnings. But this sojourn was shorter, a matter of days only.

It was only when I was back in my cubicle in the Katzenellenbogen Bastion of the Castle that Jeanne returned to me. In the deep of the night she was there; she came in a dream, and when I woke up, she was there. Her voice so close I could imagine the warmth of her breath.

'Why did you abandon me?' I asked, furious with myself that what I meant as an exclamation of almost unbearable joy sounded so much like reproach.

'You needed the time on your own. There are things only you can decide.'

'What if I'd stayed there? Tante Louise invited me to take over the farm.'

'I knew all along you'd be back.'

'What am I going to do now?'

'Bide your time. You should know soon. If you ask me Herr Allemann isn't going to make life easy for you.'

· *92* ·

He set about it in such a roundabout way, his manner seemed so friendly and conspiratorial, that it was difficult to read his real design. But I knew it was there, behind the smoothness of his manner and his voice, the easy gestures of his small soft hands.

It was one evening towards the end of October that he came, after his inspection round, when he handed over to me the control of the company for the night. (Being a lieutenant he did not live in the castle but spent his nights at home, near the Boeren Plein, in the company of his delectable wife.)

'Well, Sergeant Barbier,' he said, pretending to inspect my humble quarters but keeping a peeled eye on me, 'have your wanderings come to an end for a while?'

'I have not been wandering, Lieutenant,' I said. 'I've been working very hard as a *pasganger*.'

'We have had good reports of you,' he said, although it didn't sound very sincere to me. 'I hope we can expect the same now that you are back.'

'I'll try to serve the interests of the Lords Seventeen to the letter.'

He offered me a quizzical frown. 'I hope the two of us can work well together.'

'I belong to Lieutenant Cochius's company,' I reminded him.

'The poor old man is not well at all. One hardly sees him around. Which is why I usually keep an eye on his men as well. People tend to get out of hand if their commander is not visible.'

'Do you have any special instructions for me, Lieutenant?' I asked him point blank.

'No, no. Not at all.' A pause. 'Not at the moment. I just wanted to make sure that I can count on your loyalty.'

I gave no answer.

'It *was* I who arranged for your promotion to sergeant,' he said calmly.

'And for my transfer to the Castle,' I said. Adding after a moment, 'I am deeply *reconnaissant*.'

He turned as if to go. But at the door, with his back still turned to me, he suddenly asked, as if it had just occurred to him, 'You didn't happen to track down that slave woman Rosette who ran away?'

Then this was what he'd really come for, I thought.

He turned to look at me with his pale-blue germanic eyes.

'I didn't know I was supposed to look for her,' I said.

'I sold her shortly before she ran away,' he said, 'but somehow I still felt responsible for her.'

'I did not see her,' I said laconically. 'I wasn't looking for her.'

'Sergeant Barbier.' He came right up to me, almost in the

131

manner of Petrus de Wet. 'You are aware, of course, of the severe penalty incurred by any man who assists in the escape of a slave?'

'I believe I am, Lieutenant.'

'Good.' He gave his enigmatic little smile. 'Good. I think we *do* understand each other after all.'

· 93 ·

I confess that after he left I took a bottle of arrack from the chest under my bed – the large sturdy chest of Burmese teak that had transported my possessions, and Jeanne, from Texel to Cabo two years before – and comforted myself from it. And I confess, too, that in the following months, as Allemann so relentlessly pursued his aims through me, my recourse to the bottle became both more frequent and more ample. On some occasions I had to be subdued and brought to my cubicle by my peers. I became touchy and ever ready to spoil for a fight. It was, I admit to my shame, because the only way to vent my frustration was to turn it against others; Allemann was too shrewd ever to risk an open confrontation. He knew how to push me, ever farther.

But there would come a day when it went too far.

· 94 ·

Have I ever told you the true story about my teak chest? On that long sea-trip, in that violent storm off the Gold Coast, when everyone believed we were going down, when even after abandoning our cargo of slaves to the turbulent sea, the captain assembled all of us on the stern to debate on what next to do.

In the course of our deliberations I became aware of the collective resentment of the crew against me: because I'd sided with the captain in the early mutiny attempt; because I'd been favoured with promotion to midshipman above some others; because I'd dared to intercede for the lives of the slaves; because – but this is conjecture – they had come to suspect Jeanne's presence and begrudged me her company (the nature of which they could not but have misapprehended). And from their murmurings arose a universal demand: that being a Jonah I should be cast into the waves. That, and nothing but that, their superstitious souls had come to believe, would save the bottom.

To cut a distressing story short, my chest was hauled to the deck, and I was forced into it (in their demented condition they did not discover Jeanne already huddling inside); and I was flung into the raging sea, landing with what has come to be described as a sickening thud.

Miraculously, this desperate action had an immediate effect. Instantly the waves became becalmed, saving both their lives and, separately, mine.

The currents of the ocean swept us apart in the night; when the sun came out there was no sign of *'t Huys te Rijnsburg*. But the chest had drifted close to the shore of a savage African land quite evidently unimpressed by human foot. Except possibly by aboriginals, but those were of no consequence – although I do wish to record, gratefully, that some of those we encountered, after their initial understandable caution, assisted us in fashioning from straight dried branches of light exotic wood two pairs of oars, for Jeanne and myself.

Having provided us also with food for a couple of days, they finally assisted us by pushing our crude vessel through the breakers into more placid waters; we took up the oars, and thus commenced our slow but steady progress in the teak chest down the long hazardous coast of Africa, stopping every few days to take in new supplies and obtain directions from whatever savages might show up (Jeanne addressed them in Latin), until at last, worn to the bone with exertion and constant worrying, and sick to boot, we beached at the Cape and I was transported to the hospital. With the rest you are by now familiar.

· 95 ·

This fascinates me: how each story displaces others, yet without denying or ever entirely effacing them.

· 96 ·

Halfway through January, in the midst of the Cape's summer frenzy as everybody prepared for the arrival of the homeward-bound fleet, Herr Allemann approached me with a specific request. It was the time of the year when the new *pasgangers* were withdrawn from their companies to undertake their private occupations.

'How many *pasgangers* are there in this company, Sergeant?' he wanted to know.

'Nine,' I informed him, having just brought the muster rolls up to date.

'You will be handling their service money, I presume?'

'Yes, Lieutenant.'

'There is no need to record the receipt of *dienstgeld* from more than five or six.'

'The soldiers are paid a pittance, Lieutenant,' I reminded him. 'They need the extra money.'

'Nine-something guilders for each *pasganger*, divided among more than sixty men, Sergeant: you really think that makes a difference?'

'To them it does.'

'You will bring all the *dienstgeld* to me at the end of every month, Barbier,' he said, with more than a hint of irritation, 'From now on I shall handle the distribution myself.'

'I understand it has always been the duty of the company sergeant,' I said.

'Then it will just have to change, won't it?' he replied.

'You will *have* to do something now,' said Jeanne. 'If you let him get away with this you have lost your first true opportunity of making your mark. Isn't this what you've been waiting for?'

'The man is powerful, Jeanne.'

'The man is a dog's prick.'

'A powerful dog's prick.'

'There are people more powerful than him. Why don't you go directly to the Governor?'

'De la Fontaine? I cannot just present myself to him! I have never even met him. Besides, from what Charles told me de la Fontaine himself is corrupt. Van Kervel, the Secunde, seems to be the only honest man at the top.'

'Then go to him.'

'Allemann is a friend of his.'

She turned on me in anger. 'Well, do *something*, Estienne!'

'Even if it's hopeless?'

'When I faced the English army at Orléans, don't you think it looked hopeless? They thought I was mad.'

'You had the trust of the king.'

'Even after he withdrew his trust I continued to fight.'

'And lost. And was burned.'

'In the end I was vindicated. Through my death my cause became stronger.'

'You want me to die?'

'I want you to try.'

'This isn't the right moment.'

'Moments never come by themselves, Estienne. One *makes* them.'

'When you made your moment the freedom of your country was at stake. Here it concerns a matter of a few stuyvers.'

'It's a matter of whether the strong should have their way simply because they're strong. Even if it means taking away from the weak and the poor. *Someone* must start by saying no.'

'Not if it's madness.'

'On the contrary: most especially if others call it madness.'

· *98* ·

Not only Jeanne's exhortations or the sporadic vexations of Allemann, but the sheer monotony of my life as a soldier at Cabo – those predictable days so uniformly demarcated by the sounding bell – began to erode my tolerance. The only person, during those many months, in whom I dared confide was the drummer Nic Wijs, perhaps because he, too, had been on that expedition with Allemann and had shared some of those early disillusionments with me. He, too, had come to Cabo in search of a dream; he, too, had left behind a family; he, too, was wondering whether it was all to end in drudgery. His only remedy was drink; and I'm afraid our mutual inspiration in this respect did neither of us much good.

After a bout with Nic Wijs it was even harder than otherwise to face the monotony of our bell-invaded days and nights. What had become of the dreams and images first aroused by the tales of the Couvrets – *la fille du Cap de Bonne-Espérance*! – and nourished over so many years? So much for taming a wild continent – repulsing the threat of savagery – the triumph of the forces of good and of order – living doubly in the flame of danger . . . What had become of the defiant *No!* I had shouted across the Loire that long-ago dawn when Jeanne had first spoken to me?

Desultorily paging through my book in sleepless nights was no compensation for the lack of action and significance by day.

And there were sufficient reminders of that other life, the one I had come in search of, to keep me in a state of agitation. Hunters returning from the frontiers with reports of arid or fertile regions, of new species of game witnessed and killed (never any testimony of another unicorn, a fleeting hippogryph). Tousle-bearded farmers arriving with wagons to sell their wares and lodge interminable complaints about hottentot or Bushmen depredations. Occasionally small bands of hottentots arriving at the Castle with their tribute of eggs and feathers and foul-smelling skins, perhaps a prize ox, a few sheep with tails so fat and long that they dragged along in the dust; perhaps a tusk or two of ivory – and bearing with them names and tales from an unknown world beyond our most distant frontiers, ever rekindling the possibility of Monomotapa. Rumours of clashes and wars among remote tribes and peoples. Reports of upheavals caused by that turbulent colony (never yet set eyes on by anyone from here) of exiles, vagabonds and runaways beyond the river our people call the Great and theirs the Gariep, and reviving every time the belief that you may still be there, alive, ready, waiting; a gasp and choking in the throat. Rosette!

Yet amid all these flickering stories our deadly routine persisted. A soldier's life in an exotic far-flung colony, this?

· 99 ·

There was one brief respite during the following months when I found myself – for what reason, and on whose instructions, I didn't know – in a small detachment of soldiers accompanying Hendrik Swellengrebel to the Tygerberg and Stellenbosch. All I knew about him at the time was that he was one of the Senior Merchants of the Company and an influential member of the Council of Policy, hence his right to the escort. It was a short outing, just over a week, on which he'd been sent by the Council to investigate some complaints from the local Landdrost about problems he'd been having with farmers in his district.

In spite of the fact that I had by this time developed an uneasiness about officials, this Swellengrebel appeared different from most of the others I'd encountered before. I found him direct to the point of bluntness: this, as much as the fact that he was born in the colony and not, like almost all the other officials, in Holland or Batavia, probably accounted for the diffidence – if not open hostility – with which some of his peers were said to regard him. Large-boned, strong, with big hands and huge feet, he seemed very much a man of the country; and for the high position he'd reached (all the more surprising for an Afrikaner) he was refreshingly young, only in his late thirties; like myself. What especially commended him in my view was the intelligence, spread by some of the soldiers in the group who'd known him for some time, that the Fiscal couldn't stomach Hendrik Swellengrebel. And it wasn't difficult to surmise the reason: in the devious and affected, powdered, powerful world of Daniel van den Henghel, this disarmingly straightforward man must have seemed particularly ill-placed.

At the Tygerberg we stopped over on the farm of Izak Nieuwoudt, an old friend of Swellengrebel's; having been alerted to our visit in time he had prepared a huge feast of many kinds of meat – mutton, veal, poultry, venison – and we were all invited to partake. Since, as I had found out only too painfully, not all colonists are well disposed towards soldiers of the Company, this hearty welcome made quite an impression on me.

The following day we rode on to Stellenbosch. In the meeting between Swellengrebel and Landdrost Pieter Lourens I sensed, even from the distance at which the rest of us placed ourselves during their deliberations, a tense undertone. The Landdrost had clearly anticipated immediate action against the farmers he'd reported for their unwillingness to respond to a call-up for commando duty; and he did not take kindly to Swellengrebel's insistence that the men concerned be interviewed first to establish the legitimacy of their grounds for refusal. Lourens raved and gesticulated. He was a short fleshy man with a wig like a moth-eaten merkin quite out of place on his blunt head that looked curiously like the glans of a penis on which someone had attempted, not very successfully, to draw a face; and in his anger his whole head (or whatever was visible of it) turned purple, which in the circumstances seemed particularly appropriate. But Swellengrebel was not to be moved, and Lourens was forced to concede. Even then he tried to insist that the farmers be summoned to be interviewed in the drostdy, whereas Swellengrebel preferred to visit them on their farms.

'They'll be much more impressed with the weight of our authority if they're forced to come here,' said Lourens. 'Besides, once we've summoned them, if anyone fails to turn up we immediately have reason to arrest him and make an example of him.'

'If I'm not mistaken, this is the time for harvesting the grapes,' said Swellengrebel. 'It may cause unnecessary hardship for them to leave their farms at such a time. Reason invariably works better than force.'

'You don't know these people,' said Lourens, piqued. 'They lose all respect for you if you don't act forcefully.'

'I *do* know them,' said Hendrik Swellengrebel. 'I grew up among them.' He smiled. 'Just like you.'

The Landdrost glowered like a full-fledged erection. 'They'll think you're a weakling,' he said. 'But go ahead if you insist. Only don't say I didn't warn you.'

We rode off at a brisk pace: there were six farms to be visited, three of them quite distant.

It was no easy task. On the second day, especially, violence was very narrowly avoided on the farm of Jan la Grange, whom I immediately recognised as one of my assailants from the previous October.

'Get off my farm or I'll shoot!' he shouted as we approached, coming towards us with a gun in his hands. Barely two paces behind him came a young boy carrying another, and a girl with two small leather bags; it wasn't difficult to guess that they contained lead and powder.

'You don't even know what we've come for,' called Swellengrebel.

'I've seen enough of soldiers to know that they only mean trouble. And that one especially!' He pointed the gun at me.

'I've had dealings with this man before,' I said to Swellengrebel. 'He means what he says.'

Before I'd finished the first shot exploded, throwing up earth and stones not more than a few paces in front of us, clearly intended as a warning.

Some of the horses reared up; one bolted. The soldiers drew their pistols.

In the background, I saw, la Grange switched guns with the boy, who immediately proceeded to reload the first from his sister's bags.

'This is too dangerous,' called Swellengrebel. 'We don't want bloodshed. There are children. Let us go back.'

'Let me try to talk to him,' I proposed.

'No. Someone will get shot.'

There was no time to argue: the desperate farmer might fire again, this time not in warning. I slid from my horse pulling out my two pistols as I landed on my feet, and throwing them to the ground. Raising my arms to show that I was unarmed I began to approach the man and his children, very slowly.

'Stay where you are!' shouted la Grange.

'I have no weapons. I've come to talk to you.'

As I moved another step closer, a figure appeared round the corner of the homestead, to the right. It was a woman; she also had a gun. There was no way I could turn back now.

There were confused sounds behind me. I half-turned round. The men were preparing to do battle.

'Stay where you are!' I called at the soldiers. 'Leave this to me.'

I took another step towards la Grange. As I passed through the gate into the farmyard in its encircling white wall it felt like stepping, deliberately, into a lion's den.

'Don't come any nearer,' he warned. I could see perspiration on his dark-tanned face. 'No one is going to take me to the Dark Hole!' he said. 'I'd rather kill myself. But first I'll shoot you.'

'Why should anyone want to take you to the Dark Hole?'

'Don't pretend you don't know. You've come back to take revenge for last year's beating.'

'That was between ourselves,' I said, trying my best to keep my voice steady. 'And I deserved it. I've told no one else about it.'

'You think I believe that?'

'If I wanted to take revenge I wouldn't have waited six months.'

I could see him waver.

'Be careful, Jan!' the woman shouted. 'You know you can't trust these bastards.'

'If it wasn't the beating that brought you back, then what are you doing here?' he asked cautiously.

'Mijnheer Swellengrebel wants to discuss the military call-up. The Landdrost reported a number of farmers. We've been to three other places already. Lood Putter, Sybrand van Dyk, Gert Campher. Swellengrebel has deferred the call-up for two of them, and Campher was exempted altogether because he is his mother's sole support.'

'Is that Swellengrebel over there?' he asked, wavering (it seemed) between suspicion and reassurance.

'It is.'

'I've heard he's better than the rest.'

'Talk to him yourself if you wish.'

'And you're sure you didn't report us?'

'I give you my word.'

He sneered. 'How the hell do I know that's worth anything?'

'I'm talking to you unarmed.'

'But *they* are just waiting to shoot.'

I turned away to face Swellengrebel again. 'Tell the men to put all their guns on the ground, and stand aside,' I called. And to la Grange I said, 'Your wife can stand guard over the guns if you want to, while we talk.'

'Don't trust them, Jan,' she said again.

But he seemed to find the proposition acceptable. Some of the men appeared reluctant; Swellengrebel himself looked none too happy to comply, but after another look at the two children (nothing innocent about them, I confess: two evil-looking smelly dirty brats if ever there were) he decided to risk it.

The end of the matter was that we were all invited in for a *bol* of coffee; and as we rode off again, two hours afterwards, it seemed to me that relations between officials and colonists had never been so good.

'By rights you should be punished, Barbier,' said Swellengrebel. But he was smiling. 'It was an unpardonable risk you took today. But if it hadn't been for you there might have been a tragedy.'

Our last visit, as it turned out, was to Hendrik Ras. And with four able-bodied sons around – the youngest still at home, the others on neighbouring farms – to bring in the harvest while he did his tour of duty with the burgher militia, it seemed unlikely that Ras would be granted a deferral. To make matters worse the sons were all present when our detachment arrived on the farm; and faced by that solid phalanx of bone and muscle another explosive situation was threatening.

However, after obtaining leave from Swellengrebel to talk to Ras alone I was able to report back that he would be only too happy to respond, provided Landdrost Lourens paid him the three rix-dollars due to him for his previous round of duty, the year before. The money for all the called-up farmers, it now transpired, had been dispatched from Cabo to the Landdrost, but only a handful of them had actually received their compensation.

I knew Hendrik Ras would never in his life obey a call-up order; neither would his oak-sturdy sons. But I also knew it would take a long time for the matter of the money to be sorted out between Cabo and Stellenbosch; and by then, hopefully, the farmers would have found another reason to initiate a whole new round of discussions.

Also, the burly farmer was carrying in his arms his frail, limp little rag-doll of a daughter: and I knew by now that, swamped as I'd heard he was at home by a locust-swarm of small children of his own, Swellengrebel would be unlikely to resort to drastic measures against this prolific tender-hearted paterfamilias.

I drank too much again once we were back. One night as I returned from a watch-round – summoned by that clanging bell – to retrieve another bottle from my magnanimous chest, I rediscovered among the bottles something hard with a jagged edge. My hand shot back as if it had touched a serpent. But I returned to the object, knowing it was futile to pretend it wasn't there. In my hands I held again that heavy metal ring I'd severed from your leg. Rosette, Rosette. What have I done, what was I going to do?

On Tuesday 30 April I received, as usual, the *dienstgeld* of the nine *pasgangers* in our company. Instead of turning it over to Lieutenant Allemann as I'd done in previous months, on his instruction, I distributed the full amount among the soldiers doing duty.

I knew it wouldn't be long before it drew reaction.

Late on the Saturday afternoon I am summoned to Allemann. He is waiting outside the Castle gate, on the great pure-white stallion he's recently imported from Batavia; the most beautiful horse in the colony, unabashedly coveted by all the top officials. (Van den Hengel especially, I've heard said, is apoplectic with envy.) On its back even the rotund little Allemann strikes an uncommonly impressive figure in his fashionable long claret coat (unbuttoned to display the richly ornamented waistcoat), the dark velvet breeches fitting to below the knee where they meet the white gartered stockings; and on his extravagant powdered wig the *tricorne* trimmed with a narrow feather edging.

In front of him, holding the horse, stands a recently appointed young sergeant of his company whom I know by sight only, Louis Panhard.

'Sergeant Barbier,' Allemann says from on high, 'I've been waiting for you all week.'

'I was not aware that you summoned me, Lieutenant.'

'We have an arrangement.'

'I obey all legitimate orders, Lieutenant,' I retort. 'I know of no arrangements.'

'At the end of every month you are to bring the service money of the *pasgangers* to me.'

'I have already distributed all the money among the soldiers. They were very grateful for the extra stuyvers.'

'My orders were very clear, were they not?'

'I've made enquiries, Lieutenant, and it seems I was right: it's the sergeants who are responsible for the *dienstgeld*.'

'You deliberately disobeyed an order?'

'I obeyed the instructions of the Lords Seventeen.'

'Are you looking for trouble, Barbier?'

'No, Lieutenant.'

He pulls himself up. 'At the end of this month you will bring the money to me as before. I have nothing more to say to you.'

'I'm sorry but I won't,' I say.

His face turns a deep claret, matching his coat, and from the way he fidgets with the reins it seems his pudgy hands are sweaty. 'This is insubordination!' he exclaims.

'I won't be a party to dishonesty any longer, Lieutenant.'

'Be careful, man,' Sergeant Panhard says under his breath.

'You call me dishonest to my face?' asks Allemann.

'Yes,' I reply; my blood is now on the boil. 'If you continue to steal the soldiers' money.'

Allemann is gasping for words like a just-landed fish. Finding none, he kicks his spurs into the white flanks of the horse. It rears and whinnies. Suddenly overcome by his rage Allemann leans over and starts striking down at me with his riding-crop. Momentarily blinded by the first stinging blow that cuts across my left eye and cheek, I soon recover to grasp the end of the crop and pluck him from his high horse. As he lands in a small cloud of dust Panhard turns tail and runs away. The horse, surprisingly, remains standing patiently as if he's witnessed it all before.

Even as he falls Allemann reaches for his sword. But I snatch it from his grasp. Not for nothing was I one of the most renowned swordsmen in my native France (all those irate husbands): without ever touching the skin, in a series of deft thrusts and swipes I disrobe him, cutting every item of clothing from his body until only his buckled shoes with their tall tongues remain. Crouching to protect his vulnerable parts he starts whimpering for mercy. But I pay no heed at all; I've had too much of him and his kind. With the broadside of the sword I belabour his miserable white body, leaving blackening bruises across the length of his rounded back and buttocks.

He starts cursing me in the foulest language imaginable. This, I'm afraid, drives me really mad. Hurling away the sword I lay into him with fists and feet until he lies blubbering in the dust. This is the time to stop; but I am by now so incensed I can no longer control myself. Grabbing him by the balls I begin to drag him to the Castle gate, and across the flagstones of the entrance hall, and then up the roughly hewn stone stairs to the small bell-tower above. The whole place is curiously deserted; not a soul in sight.

By the time we reach the top of the tower his scrotum has stretched so far that I can hoist him aloft by it to tie him to the bell-rope where each movement causes the great brass bell to boom. His weight causes his body to tear away, and he scampers off more dead than alive – abandoning his poor male pride to the pursuit of its independent musical career. I return to mount the waiting white horse and gallop off in search of you.

This is how it should have been. How much of what followed could have been avoided had I not been restrained – by what? Was it something to be proud of, or ashamed?

What happened was that when I grasped the end of the riding-crop before it struck my face, Allemann was momentarily pulled off balance, toppling over precariously, but then managed to right himself.

'After all I've done for you!' he gasped, beside himself. 'Barbier, you're – you're an ingrate!'

Then, without waiting for an answer, he cantered off at speed, losing only his *tricorne* in the race against himself.

For a moment it was very quiet at the Castle gate.

Then, smirking, Panhard said, 'Now you've done it.'

'At last,' whispered Jeanne, who'd witnessed the whole scene.

There is a peculiar satisfaction in communicating with you like this, through an imagined letter. I wrote so many letters during my long months as a fugitive (after I'd been declared, as they call it here, 'bird-free', which meant that anyone had the right to kill or capture me: what a weird notion of freedom). Some of them, as will be the case with this one, never reached a destination. But they were still *written*, in ink, each representing a laborious struggle with pen on paper, with the intricacies of grammar and the obscurities of a tongue not my own. Here in my mind it flows freely, unhampered; I need not stop to tease out meaning from a verb, a pronoun or a Latin phrase, to do battle with singular and plural forms. Both you and I, previously shackled in a language in which we stuttered and groped, can now converse without a single impediment. I do not write, you cannot read; the flow is perfect – as free indeed as the loops and sentences inscribed by a bird in flight on the parchment of the sky.

· 108 ·

That fateful Sunday evening, 5 May. I must tell you that I'd been drinking steadily, from the moment I returned to my cubicle – known commonly, in these parts, by the Dutch word *cagie* or cage – after the altercation with Herr Allemann. Throughout the night and most of the following day, expecting at any moment to be sent for.

Yet all day nothing happened. In retrospect I realised that it could not have been otherwise: it was, after all, the Sabbath, and Allemann and his wife, good Pharisees, believe that religion should not only be practised but be seen to be practised.

Jeanne had gone off to Mass in the early morning and stayed away for an unconscionably long time; I, too, felt an uncustomary need of Mass, but in this colony it is of course not allowed and like all the rest I pass for a Protestant. Even now that I have need of absolution, and of extreme unction, I must do without. No matter; it is sobering to have nothing but oneself to fall back on.

My mind is wandering; I must return to my discourse.

When the eight o'clock bell was rung I went on guard duty. I remember being surprised, and gratified, that the clanging of my enemy's balls against the brass should produce such an extraordinary volume of sound reverberating in my head. By that time I must have been far gone. And for my present recollection of the night I must rely on the testimony of others, including – regrettably – Allemann's eloquent submission to the court, in his demand for 'serious and extraordinary punishment', supported by affidavits of (who else?) Sergeant Godfried Lodewyk Kok, Sergeant Frans Hagen and Corporal Frederik

Willem Courthijm (*vide* Grotius *Dutch Jurisprudence* Lib 3 Part 35 No 2 en part; 36 No 3, and Simon van Leeuwen *Roman-Dutch Law* Lib 5 Part 19 No 18).

I can remember patrolling the front courtyard on hands and knees in search of Allemann's scrotum. And deciding to pay a visit to the Governor, but losing my way and lying down to rest supine for a while, in which position I began to sing with an abandon I had not experienced for some time.

It would seem that in due course my good friend, the renowned cunt-starer, sheep thief and murderer Godfried Lode-wyk Kok, deposited me at some unidentified hour of the night in my cage in the Katzenellenbogen Bastion, and then most uncivilly left me to my own devices. But within minutes I made my appearance in the adjacent cubicle where I found Kok and Sergeant Hagen (he'd been promoted from corporal during my absence as a *pasganger*) at dinner. In the passage I must have passed Corporal Courthijm who was on sentry duty, but the little shit presumably slunk away to avoid meeting me. Ever since I had taken his place on Allemann's cursed expedition inland eighteen months before there had not been much love lost between us.

I know I meant to knock, but somehow misjudged the distance to the door and fell against it; it swung open and I entered on all fours, greeting them with great enthusiasm. The two men looked up from the table and somewhat coolly invited me to join them. The food I declined, but I indicated that a glass of wine would be most welcome.

'You've already had too much,' said Kok.

'Then I'll fetch my own,' I replied, deeply offended, I may tell you.

It took some time to find my way back to my own abode; and even longer to fit the key into the heavy lock of my teak chest. After some random unpacking – items of clothing, my precious companion book of many voyages across the face of the earth, more clothing, a broken iron band which I confess took a while

149

to identify – I found a bottle, which unfortunately broke on the stone floor. The second remained whole. I stowed my possessions, locked the chest, and set out with the bottle. Unfortunately I must have lost my way, because my next recollection is of finding myself in a suddenly sobering cold gust of wind on the bastion outside, high above the waves breaking on the dark rocks, surrounded by the soldiers of the guard.

'What are you staring at?' I asked. Whereupon someone proposed that a *sopie* of my liquor would be most welcome. 'You can have the whole bottle,' I offered in a wave of compassion and generosity towards the poor creatures condemned to spend such an inclement night on the cold point.

The bottle was gratefully passed from hand to hand; but at a given moment I realised that Corporal Courthijm was also among the men, and waiting to take his turn.

'Oh no,' I said, grasping the bottle away from him just as it was passed to him. 'This is for the soldiers only, not for officers.'

Muttering something, he withdrew; and the bottle made another round.

When it was empty I returned inside. I presume I paid another visit to my cage, because at some stage, carrying a new bottle, I found myself back in Sergeant Hagen's room where I seated myself – not without some difficulty – at the table with them and proceeded to pour myself some wine.

Did Courthijm enter with me? He must have, because the next I remember was Hagen grasping the bottle from my hand and passing it to Courthijm with the instruction to 'put it away'.

The dirty swine! Criminals and thieves, the lot of them. Depriving a man of his own drink.

I must have started talking in a rather unrestrained fashion, because at a given moment I heard Hagen reprimanding me that I was saying things I could not substantiate.

'Substantiate?' I flew at him, stammering with anger. 'Well, let me tell you, the whole bloody lot of you, from Allemann all the way down, are thieves and scoundrels.'

'Leave Allemann out of this,' Kok said warningly. (They were all, of course, as you might have guessed, members of the Lieutenant's company.)

I wasn't going to be shut up by a turd like him. 'Allemann is a *canaille*,' I said, unrepentant. 'A *canaille* and a dog's prick. I told him so to his face, yesterday. You can ask Panhard, he was there too. And let me tell you another thing . . .'

But the cowards would not let me finish. All three of them, in a state of great agitation, were on their feet by now; and among them they forced me to the door, from where Courthijm escorted me home. If my legs were not so unsteady, I tell you, he would have had a hard time.

In the passage, seeing the two of us alone, I warmed to him. 'Come and have a nightcap with me,' I invited him. 'I'd like to tell you all about that whited sepulchre Allemann.'

'I don't want to hear,' he said.

'You've *got* to listen, Frederik,' I insisted. '*Someone*'s got to listen to me tonight.'

'You've already said too much, man. You can't prove a thing.'

'Just you listen to me,' I repeated. 'Now come on, Frederik. What's to become of you, trying to defend Allemann? You think crawling up his arse is going to make you big and strong? Think again. I tell you, you'll end up just such a *canaille* as he is.'

He pushed my door open; he appeared to be considering my invitation.

At that moment the Castle bell sounded again, striking – what ungodly hour was it? – eleven? – twelve? – I missed the count.

'You hear that?' I asked him. 'Those are Allemann's balls clanging away. Quite a pair of *couilles* that man's got.'

My words prompted an unexpectedly brusque reaction. Courthijm shoved me violently into the room and slammed the door behind me. I stumbled against my wooden chest and collapsed; and there I must have fallen asleep.

· 109 ·

Early on Tuesday morning, 7 May, when I'd finally slept off the awful after-effects of the weekend, I was with one of the soldiers, trying to fill in the lacunes in my memory of the Sunday night. The youngster, Kremer, saw it all as a priceless joke. He'd been on the bastion that evening; and having suffered, like most of the soldiers, under Courthijm's viciousness before, he'd been delighted by the way I'd snatched the bottle from the corporal right in front of them. In retrospect it began to seem funny to me too, and we were still sharing a laugh about it when none other than Sergeant Kok came into the small bare room.

'Ah here you are, you bastard!' he called out, his eyes lit up in venomous glee. 'I've been looking for you.'

'To what do I owe the honour?' I asked, winking at Kremer.

Kremer sniggered and was immediately called to order. Suddenly scared, he became deadly quiet in the background.

'State your business, man,' I said, impatient.

'I've just come to tell you that your loose talk has been reported to Lieutenant Allemann.'

'Now who could have been so eager to carry gossip?'

'Courthijm and Hagen themselves, if you must know.'

'Not you too?'

'That has nothing to do with you.'

'Of course not.' I looked straight at him. 'And is that all you've come tell me? That you three little boys have run to Papa?'

'No, there's much more. I thought you might like to know that Mijnheer van den Henghel himself has decided to take up the matter. He's asked us to come in for formal statements.

We'll be making an appointment to see the secretary of the Council of Justice later this week. Josephus de Grandpreez.'

'I'm surprised that the Fiscal should find time to investigate some loose chattering among drunken soldiers.'

'It may be more important than you think. You know what they say, A drunken mouth speaks truth.'

'*In vino veritas.*'

'What's that? Look, if you think you can insult me too . . .'

'I won't bother,' I said. 'If ever I do deign to take someone like you to court it will be for much more serious business.'

'Like what?'

'I think you know exactly what I mean. We were together on that journey with Allemann, were we not?'

'Barbier.' He was breathing heavily. In the background Kremer stared with wide eyes. 'One word from you – '

'You go to van den Henghel,' I said, 'and you'll have that one word.'

· *110* ·

I honestly thought I'd called his bluff; I honestly thought such a trivial matter could not possibly interest the mighty men of Cabo. If Allemann had himself reported our altercation of the previous Saturday, yes; but surely not the little vulgarities of the Sunday night.

I had underestimated his devious thinking. For himself to bring up our confrontation, I realised too late, would humiliate him in public; but to use some petty officers to salvage his chestnuts from the fire might be much more effective in the long run – *and* would keep his honour untainted.

Only hours after Kok's irruption into Kremer's room I was arrested in front of the bakery by a detachment from the garrison and taken to Captain Rhenius, the commanding officer of the Castle. Pending investigation and a possible trial, I was curtly informed by the dapper captain (without even being allowed to speak in my defence), I would be subjected to what at the Cape of Good Hope is termed 'internal banishment'. Translated into practical terms, it meant quite simply that, relieved of guard duties and of all privileges, but not excused from menial work, I would be confined to the precincts of the Castle; most of the time to my cage.

· *III* ·

Old Lieutenant Cochius was distressed when I appealed to him to intercede.

'My hands are tied,' he said. 'Once a process of this nature has begun it has to run its course.'

'But you're Allemann's senior,' I reminded him.

He wheezed unhappily. 'Unfortunately the order for your detention comes from higher up. From Captain Rhenius himself. And if the Fiscal is involved as well, it would be most unwise to intervene in any way.' He shook his head. 'Most, most unwise.'

'You're the only one who can help me,' I said.

'This is much too difficult, my boy.' Again that asthmatic wheeze. 'I really can't afford, at my age, to be drawn into the squabbles of the powerful.'

· *112* ·

'Try Hendrik Swellengrebel,' Jeanne proposed. I tried. But when I petitioned Captain Rhenius for permission to leave the Castle for an hour to set up such a meeting (unlike the other high officials, Swellengrebel did not live in the Castle but in his own house in the settlement) it was turned down without ceremony.

'This will not be viewed kindly by the Council of Justice, Barbier,' the old Captain reprimanded me, in a voice unexpectedly voluminous for his thin dried-biltong body. 'Swellengrebel is a member of the Council. To seek an interview with him will be interpreted quite rightly as an attempt to influence your judges in advance.'

'But if I'm just allowed to explain my situation the matter will probably never even come before the Council at all.'

'What do you know about the way justice is administered in this place?' he asked.

'It is clear that I know very little about it,' I said heatedly.

He preferred not to respond to that; but the narrowing of his eyes was expressive enough. All he said, very brusquely, was, 'In any event, you'll have all the time in the world to address the Council once your case comes up.'

'*When* will it come up?'

'How can I tell? It's not an important matter, you know. It will have to bide its turn.'

'But in the meantime I am treated as a criminal.'

'Justice will run its course. Now go, Barbier. You're wasting my time.'

· *113* ·

It will have to bide its turn. Which was four months. What kept me going was the thought of you, who now had to be free for both of us; what kept me going was reading my book; what kept me going was Jeanne.

'It's the uncertainty,' I told her. 'They haven't even told me what I'm accused of. And it's taking months.'

'I waited nine months in one dungeon after the other, Estienne, from the day that Picard archer plucked me from my horse below the walls of Compiègne, until they finally tried me,' she said quietly. 'First in Noyon, then in the castle of Beaulieu, then Beaurevoir, and Arras, and Drugny, and Crotoy, and Vimeu, and Saint-Valéry, and Eu, and then Rouen. Waiting, waiting all the time. Waiting and suffering.' She spoke in that low passionate voice, the voice that kindled armies into action and made her the most revered commander in France, the voice that in the end was her undoing because it was too eloquent for the interrogators of the monstrous Bishop Cauchon. 'You still have an easy life, Estienne,' she went on. 'You can still come and go within the Castle. I was fettered. In Rouen, in the tower by the Porte Cauchoise, I was kept like an animal in a metal cage. For two months, chained by my neck, my hands, my feet, I was forced to remain standing. And it was only because they feared I would die that I was then allowed to lie down at night, my fetters fastened to a chain over the foot of my bed, and that in turn to a heavy beam, six feet long.'

Chastised, I could not reply. She, too, was silent for very long. And then, so softly I could barely hear her, she said, 'But all of that I could bear. What was almost unbearable was being abandoned. Only my voices remained with me.'

'How can you ever forgive them?' I ask.

'I can forgive,' she said. 'But I cannot understand. The people I thought of as my friends not only forsook me but betrayed me. I fought, not only against the English who occupied my country, but against the French who didn't want to recognise the dauphin. And then, once I'd helped him to be crowned at Rheims, he lost interest in me. No one stood by me. Not even my only true friend, the gentle priest Jean Pasquerel who with a single testimony could have turned my whole trial against my enemies.'

I bowed my head. I cherished her closeness. In the end I said, 'At least you knew you were fighting for something worth while, the freedom of France, of your people. What am *I* fighting for? There's no one here I can even think of as "my people". It's a petty, personal thing. It's humiliating.'

'Don't you think it was humiliating to me to be tried for

witchcraft? Whatever they plan to accuse you of it won't be sorcery.' A brief ironic silence. 'And they won't burn you.'

'There is enough they can do.'

But then I stopped. How dare I argue with her? She had borne so much more than I ever could. She; you. You, the women.

'You must keep faith, Estienne,' said Jeanne. 'This is not the real battle. It's only a preliminary test of strength. If you pass this one, you can face the real ordeal.'

'Which is?'

'You'll recognise it when it comes.'

· *114* ·

It was around this time that I first espied the smooth, smiling, ruddy-complexioned presence of Herr Otto Friedrich Mentzel within the precincts of the Castle. He had ostensibly been appointed as comptroller in the Company's wood-shed (at an exorbitant salary, rumour had it). Don't tell me this was coincidence. At all times of the day, and sometimes at night, he could be found prowling along the corridors of the barracks in the top floor of the courtine along the waterfront, or hovering around the stores, or in the front courtyard near the guardroom at the entrance, or about the arms court and the stables at the back.

· *115* ·

Countless hours, days, nights, all marked by the clanging of Herr Allemann's balls.

There came a most unexpected respite in the maddening uncertainty of waiting for the trial to be announced, the indictment to be specified. The first hint of a change in the political climate of the Cape was when the news spread among the garrison in the Castle that Governor de la Fontaine was to retire. If the account was to be believed, he'd put in a request for retirement fully a year before; and in June a favourable reply from the Lords Seventeen was received at last. Two months later the old man moved from the Castle, back to his private house, and Secunde van Kervel was sworn in as the new Governor. Much more important for my own prospects was the news that Hendrik Swellengrebel was promoted to Secunde.

I began to loiter in the forecourt of the Castle whenever I could do so unobserved; and on Monday 2 September I saw Swellengrebel enter through the gate, presumably to pay a visit to the new Governor. He was, of course, escorted; and his men made every effort to keep me at a distance. But he recognised me and gestured at me to approach. It was immediately obvious, as I had anticipated, that he had no idea of my present circumstances. And without any ado he undertook to investigate.

The following morning I was summoned by old Captain Rhenius who was in a foul mood; and he dispatched his business as if there was an evil smell attached to it. I had been granted a reprieve from my arrest, he announced; I was free to resume my normal duties, and free, too, to leave the precincts of the Castle.

The very next day I was informed that at the forthcoming session of the Council of Justice, on Thursday 5 September, my case would be heard.

'If my experience is anything to go by, don't expect it to go fast,' Jeanne had warned me. Even so the first session of the Council in which, at last, Allemann and I faced one another (although he mostly kept his eyes averted), was an anticlimax. The Fiscal, with a great display of indignation, informed the Council that Lieutenant Alleman wished to enact civil proceedings for 'blatant libel', on account of 'disorder, disrespect and even contempt' demonstrated by the accused Estienne Barbier. Thereupon Allemann requested permission to have an act of accusation and three statements drawn up for submission to their excellencies. And that, for the moment, was that. I was still in the dark about the exact ature of the accusations against me.

It was two days later, in the evening, and I was on my way back from the female quarters of the Slave Lodge where I had gone to find some sexual release from all the tension (a remedy, I may add, from which I was deriving less and less satisfaction as every encounter merely served to confirm my shameful memories of you), when I was stopped by a small bow-legged man who had approached sideways, like a crab, from one of the side streets near the hospital.

'Estienne Barbier?' he asked, looking about him nervously.

'Yes. Who are you?'

'My name is Christian Petzold. I've heard that Siegfried Allemann is bringing a case against you and I think I can help you.'

'How can you help?' I asked warily.

'Perhaps I can't do much. But if you don't know how justice

works in this colony it is very easy for them to get you quite entangled, and I know all about documents. I work as a notary, you see.'

'I don't have money to pay you.'

'I won't be doing it for the money. I've been waiting for a long time to get my hands around that Allemann's throat.'

'What has he done to you?'

It transpired that Petzold had come to Cabo many years before; the only post the Company could offer him was that of baker. He'd had some legal training in Holland, but his father had been a baker, so he wasn't altogether out of his depth. He soon discovered, however, that he could get nowhere without official patronage: Allemann insisted that he himself be Petzold's sole supplier of wood (brought to Cabo from the Company's outposts in the interior), for which he then asked such an exorbitant price that the baker fell ever more deeply into his debt. After some years Petzold had the good fortune to marry a widow with some money, most of which was used to buy himself out of the Company's service. Now he was making a meagre living by assisting colonists with legal problems.

'You mark my word, Mijnheer Barbier, there aren't many citizens in this colony who get through life without sooner or later falling foul of the law. The only trouble is that so few of them can pay more than a stuyver or two.'

'My case is very simple,' I told him. 'And I have right on my side.'

'Most of the colonists have right on their side. But I'm afraid that counts for very little.'

'I assure you – '

'What happened at your first hearing?' he asked, ignoring my protestation.

'Allemann asked for permission to submit some documents. As soon as he does that I can start defending myself.'

'How?'

'What do you mean? I'll simply go ahead and tell the Council . . .'

'With due respect, that will be a grave mistake, Mijnheer Barbier,' he said.

'Why?'

'Because you cannot beat them at their game unless you address them in the only language they heed.'

'I know Dutch,' I said, offended.

'I'm not talking about Dutch, Mijnheer Barbier. I'm talking about *documents*. Those people don't listen: they only read. And they only read what is written in legal language with lots of Latin thrown in. Forgive me if I am mistaken, but I doubt that you can handle that on your own.'

'Thank you for the offer,' I said. 'But I'm sure I can manage quite well. I even know some Latin.'

'Church Latin, I daresay?' he ventured. 'That is not what will be needed here at all, if you will pardon my saying so.'

I began to walk on, but he stopped me with a hand on my sleeve. 'Excuse me,' he said. 'In case you change your mind, I live up there, to the right of the Gardens. Don't forget my name: Christian Petzold.' He raised his hat almost obsequiously and scuttled off into the night like a spider with several broken legs.

· *119* ·

At the next session Allemann's long act of accusation was read to the Council by a very tall, very lean man whose name, I gathered, was Tiemmendorf. He had, it transpired, been appointed by Allemann as his legal representative. I understood very little of what he read in his dry monotonous voice. Interspersed with innumerable Latin expressions there were phrases like 'most grievously violated in his honour', 'assaulting the law and order of the colony', 'shameful libel', etc. etc. Much of the recitation was devoted to various demands for restitution and 'serious, yea extraordinary measures of punishment'. What Allemann demanded, I gathered, was a full and public apology, 'with open doors and ringing of bells *facie ecclesia et coram judice*, the accused to be bareheaded and on his bare knees, confessing his malicious slander' – followed by such grave punishment as the Council might decide to impose, plus all costs, 'imploring in all this the *nobile atque benignum officium* something'.

There followed an intoning, in much the same kind of language, of the three statement by Kok, Hagen and Courthijm, all pertaining to the events on the infamous night of 5 May.

'Estienne Barbier, what say you to this?' asked the Fiscal, formidable in his great powdered wig and his most imposing attire.

'Is that all?' I asked, apprehensive about the omission of all reference to my altercation with the man on his white horse.

'It is sufficient for this Council to regard the matter in the most serious light.' His voice, though hoarse and rather high-pitched, reverberated through the room. 'And if you have nothing further to say . . .'

And then I remembered my nocturnal encounter with Christian Petzold; and I said, 'I beg leave to be furnished with copies of the documents submitted to the Council, to which I shall duly respond in writing eight days hence.'

There was a sudden deep silence. Was it my imagination or did Hendrik Swellengrebel smile very slightly in my direction; or that Governor van Kervel nodded in agreement? That van den Henghel was taken aback was quite obvious. I had no idea whether my request was justified, or outrageous.

But after a moment, in an indignant tone of voice, the Fiscal slammed down his papers and said, 'So be it. We are adjourned.'

Christian Petzold lived in a very small, uncomfortable house urgently in need of whitewash and repair. I was introduced, briefly, to his wife Johanna, her thirteen-year-old daughter Maria, and three smaller girls playing about like mice. Then the womenfolk withdrew very pointedly to leave us alone in the shoddily furnished *voorkamer*. It was only ten or so in the morning, yet Petzold was already reeking of liquor; this, it soon became obvious, was the harmless little man's only defence against the world.

Together, we prepared what to me seemed a most impressive response. Following Petzold's advice I then presented myself at the office of Josephus de Grandpreez (a curiously shapeless man looking for all the world like a parcel badly tied up for dispatch; and as pompous as his name), the secretary of the Council of Justice, from whom I demanded writing materials in order to commit to paper the document we had prepared. In this composition I offered an exposition of the real reason behind Allemann's offensive, namely our continuing tussle about the service money of the *pasgangers* which the lieutenant had appropriated for himself; and I indicated that this had been the subject of a confrontation between us on Saturday 4 May.

It had been Petzold's idea to offer no further particulars, believing that Allemann, too ashamed to be faced with the full truth, might prefer at this stage to back down before more damage was done to his reputation.

'And if he refuses to use this back door for a quick escape,' he said, 'we have the leeway to throw the whole book at him.'

As you will readily appreciate, it was with considerable new peace of mind that I awaited the next session of the Council, on Thursday 19 September.

And then fate intervened. Jeanne believed it was God's will, but I assured her God would never promote the cause of evil in that way. ('He allowed my adversaries to triumph over me, even to kill me,' she reminded me. 'What they did was surely evil, yes. But you cannot impute that to God. There are things we are not meant to question, Estienne.' 'That is where we differ,' I said, 'I shall never stop asking questions.')

Early on the very morning for which the next session of the Council had been scheduled, Governor Adriaan van Kervel died.

The governor had never been a strong man, yet no one, least of all himself, had ever suspected his frailty to be serious. That in itself was a shocking event. But its consequences were disastrous.

What I know about it comes from the gossip in the barracks; but two of the men had been on sentry duty inside the Council chamber, so I have reason to believe the truth of their report. And even if that report were amiss in some small detail the outcome was there for all to see.

On Friday 20 September the Council of Policy met for what should have been a mere formality: the nomination of Hendrik Swellengrebel as Acting Governor. But at the very moment when, their brief business concluded, the councillors prepared to leave, who but the Fiscal should jump to his feet in apoplectic fury to shout in his shrill voice that this decision was out of order. He, van den Henghel, had calculated the respective periods of service of Hendrik Swellengrebel and himself at the rank of senior merchant, and had found that he had a few weeks more to his credit; as a result of which he claimed the acting governorship.

There was pandemonium in the chamber, the sentries reported subsequently. Swellengrebel's brother-in-law, Rijk Tulbagh, himself a highly respected citizen, argued that it had always been the policy of the Company for a Secunde to succeed his Governor; but van den Henghel, in great agitation, shouted at Tulbagh to shut up as he had no right to promote the cause of a relative, whether by blood or by marriage. After heated debate the matter was resolved and Tulbagh was allowed to vote. There were four votes for Swellengrebel, and four for van den Henghel.

At this point someone proposed that the retired Governor, old Jan de la Fontaine, be approached to act until a successor could be named by the Lords Seventeen in the Netherlands. This was opposed by van den Henghel, and defeated.

The tone of the deliberations grew more and more frenzied. In the end the only resolution that could be thought of was – can you believe it? – to draw lots.

And Daniel van den Henghel won.

The very next morning I was summoned by the Captain of the Castle and informed that my internal banishment had been reimposed.

Back to that infernal monotony. Interminable conversations with Jeanne. Countless hours of reading in my heavy book with the imprint of the missile it once deflected to save my life; often I don't even read but simply sit staring at the pages. Increasing agitation about *you*: but why on earth? As you recede in time your presence in so many respects becomes more compulsive.

Occasionally, in great secrecy, whenever we can avoid the skulking Mentzel, I have consultations with Christian Petzold who meets me surreptitiously in odd corners of the Castle – in the bakery behind the Dolphin Court, in the stables along the back courtine between the bastions of Nassau and Oranje, in the storeroom between Buuren and Katzenellenbogen.

At night great insects come flying in through the open window and elaborately kill themselves in the flame of my lamp: not the customary moths or mosquitoes or gnats I know from Europe, but vicious-looking creatures with venom in their tails or snouts, with whirring scaly wings and many feet, miniature dragons that come from the mysterious night outside – a night with strange exciting or oppressive smells, of droughts, and dust, and unnamed aromatic herbs from distant plains and mountains. I stare into the dark space from which they hurl themselves at me, and try to probe beyond the rivers and ridges and ranges I have seen; beyond, still beyond; a land ancient travellers called Monomotapa, a land I call Africa. Yet what is the meaning of these syllables that both lure and intimidate me?

'Get out of this place,' Jeanne keeps urging me. 'While you have time and opportunity: go.'

'If I run away I vindicate that evil man and all he represents. I *must* see this through.'

Wading through the never-ending stream of paper was a tortuous and disheartening process deprived of all sense of progress. But Christian Petzold urged me on. For the first time since I'd met him his pale insect features were suffused with a glow not caused by alcohol. He seemed to derive genuine satisfaction, even a kind of fulfilment, from preparing my statements, running my errands, collecting the evidence he believed I required.

'I'm a poor man,' he said. 'But they're not going to have the satisfaction of seeing me prostrate. This means as much to me as to you. If we win against Allemann I can start charging people a decent fee. Then I can begin to repay Johanna all she's lent me. It's been a steep decline, Estienne' – we were soon on first-name terms – 'from the days I had my own house and everything. Now I'm renting that miserable hovel from a free-black. How low can one sink? And even that I can't afford, we'll have to take in a lodger. I loathe the idea, I tell you. A stranger about one's feet all the time, expecting one's wife to serve him. But what can a man do? We've *got* to win this one, Estienne.'

Sometimes it seems to me I *must* be mad, thinking that justice is possible.

On Thursday 26 September my response was submitted to the Council, where van den Henghel was now both my prosecutor and my judge. On Allemann's behalf Tiemmendorf requested eight days to prepare a response.

On 3 October he proffered his reply. There was little substance to it. Most of the verbose text was devoted to accusing me of 'phantasms and chimerae'; no attempt at all was made to refute what I had said about his dishonest appropriation of service money. I requested time to compose a *duplique*. But as Petzold had warned me that our next step might be costly, I also asked permission to have statements in my defence collected *pro deo*. Van den Henghel turned it down; but Swellengrebel interrupted and pointed out that in the interests of justice I should be allowed full opportunity to defend myself.

I was accorded two weeks.

Inside, I was jubilant, although I took care to keep a straight face. What I was planning, I believed, with Petzold's help, was nothing less than a *coup de grâce*.

· *129* ·

Allemann's immediate response was unexpected, and had nothing to do with the court proceedings. I learned of it through Petzold, when on the Saturday after the latest session he came round, in his furtive mousy way, to discuss strategy below the Katzenellenbogen stairs.

'Estienne, have you heard? The whole Cabo is talking about it.'

'What?'

'You know that white horse of Allemann's?'

'I know it only too well. What about it?'

'He's given it to van den Henghel as a present.'

'But they're not even friends.'

'Exactly. And it seems Swellengrebel is furious. I believe *he*'s been coveting that horse himself. Like everybody else, of course.'

What we had in mind for our next move was to collect as many statements as possible from people who'd been at the receiving end of Allemann's dubious transactions. Confronted with such a mass of evidence, we believed, he would have to withdraw from the battle.

I sent Petzold to the tanner Willem Meyer who'd turned me away the year before when I'd delivered to him the wood and bark from Hendrik Ras; I gave him the names of the others I'd come across on the same visit.

It turned out to be a task more arduous than we had anticipated: the people hated Allemann, no doubt about that, but they were afraid of him; and if he were now in league with van den Henghel that was all the more reason for them to be reluctant about testifying against the man.

'We'll need money,' said Petzold. 'I'm sorry, Estienne. But this is not going to be cheap.'

I gave him some of my clothes to sell; I had but little of value.

At the session of 17 October I was able to submit my *duplique* in reply to Allemann's previous reaction, as well as three statements from soldiers of the guard to support my account of what had happened on the evening of 5 May. But my most important statements, about Allemann's corrupt practices, were not yet ready; I had to request another week's postponement. It was granted, if only reluctantly. On the 24th I submitted statements from no fewer than seven victims of Allemann's extortion. (There was even a statement by Petzold himself, about the pigs and firewood he'd been forced to buy, in his time as Company baker, from Allemann.) If these didn't prove that I'd been justified in what I'd said of him, nothing would.

One thing, however, I hadn't counted on. The moment after I'd submitted my statements (which, unlike Allemann's, were not read out aloud: the Council, van den Henghel said, 'would keep them under advisement until such time as they have been perused'), Herr Tiemmendorf rose.

'I have here,' he said with his skeletal grimace, 'three more statements collected on behalf of Herr Allemann.' They had been compiled in great haste, I subsequently learned, only the day before; the reason presumably being that at the eleventh hour Allemann had got wind – through the eavesdropping Mentzel? – of my *démarche*.

'What is their bearing on the act of accusation?' asked Swellengrebel.

'There is no direct bearing, Mijnheer,' said Tiemmendorf.

'In that case we cannot entertain them.'

'But they do present a more specific image of the generally disreputable character of the accused,' added Tiemmendorf.

'Then we shall look at them,' announced the Acting Governor. 'Herr Tiemmendorf, would you like to read them out to us?'

'I protest,' said Swellengrebel. 'We have decided to peruse the accused's submissions at our leisure. We can do the same with these.'

'We can better judge their relevance if we hear them without delay,' argued van den Henghel.

'Then we must hear the others too.'

A vote was taken. The ballots were collected by an orderly and submitted to van den Henghel who quickly glanced through them and announced that Tiemmendorf's statements could be read.

They were read by Corporal Willem Willemse, the petty officer in charge of the guardsmen who had brought me home, drunk, that distant night, Rosette, when I'd come home to you; and by two of the soldiers in his company.

There were some details of little consequence, and in these the statements differed slightly: I'd often been seen drunk on duty; I had upon occasion supplied liquor to my convicts; I had even, one evening (and this was news to me), locked up one of the deponents, the hunter Harmen Croon, with the convicts.

But the substance of the statements concerned a single incident, and in their account of it all three were couched in suspiciously identical words.

On the night of 20 October 1735 the accused, Estienne Barbier, had harboured in his quarters in the Water Castle an escaped slave woman known as Rosette; the following day he had locked up said *meid* in the convicts' cage; twenty-four hours later he had aided and abetted her escape from Cabo de Bonne-Espérance to a destination unknown.

· *132* ·

They have found the one spot in my underbelly for which I have no protection. This is what it has always been about: but your name has not been spoken before. It may not be uttered again. It won't be necessary. We know now what is at stake. And it is more than *cherchez la femme*. Now there is nothing, I realise, they will not stoop to. What I am fighting for here is not my honour as a soldier. It is my life.

· *133* ·

My lamp is doused; there is still a fluttering of insect wings against the walls. But apart from that it is very quiet, a deadly stillness that conspires with a darkness within to render sleep impossible.

Rosette, my God, Rosette: what have we done, what have I done, and to what avail?

That devastating night. Your nakedness. (*This is the sign of my freedom: when I was cut loose from my mother.*) How I abused you. Woman, woman.

Jeanne is here too, in the dark, but she is silent. It isn't necessary for her to speak. I remember so well what she told me, once only, when I'd driven her to it. She was always reticent about herself, but in this regard even more stubbornly so than usual. Except for that single occasion.

'You are a man, Estienne. Can you ever understand? That there were times I was defiled by them and that those attempts sometimes seemed to me worse even than, afterwards, the fire.'

'You mean they raped you?'

'There are many ways to rape a woman.'

'I don't understand.'

'There was the first time: when, after travelling more than three hundred miles, a virgin in man's clothing surrounded by men, I was finally summoned to the Dauphin in the castle of Chinon. As I entered through the gate a horseman spied me and called loudly, "Is that the Maid?" And when someone told him that indeed it was, with a coarse laugh, he said, "Just give me a night with her and she'll be one no more!"'

'What did you do?' I asked her.

'Does it matter?'

'Yes, it does.'

'If you must know: I turned to the man and asked, "How can you offend God so if your death is so close?" And an hour later he was drowned.'

'How could you foretell that?'

'I had my voices.'

'And then there were other occasions?'

'When I arrived at Orléans, the English gleefully called me "the whore from Armagnac". You know, that must have been one of the few times I actually cried.'

'But you were never – physically – '

'In the dungeon in Rouen I was locked up with three guards chosen from the *houspilleurs* of the army. That's the lowest and toughest of the soldiers. Criminals, most of them. And there's no doubt that they were chosen to rape me.'

'But they didn't?'

'They tried. My God, how they tried. Day and night. I still find it unbelievable that I could fight back so viciously that Cochon's butchers were forced to retreat. Later, when I was ill and near to death so that I couldn't resist, rude doctors forcibly examined me and found me, indeed, intact. And that was almost as humiliating as the assaults of the wardens.'

'And no one ever tried to help you?'

'One woman did. It was, of all people, the Duke of Bedford's wife. You see, there were good ones even among the English.'

'What did she do?'

'She couldn't bear to hear of my constant humiliation. So she insisted that I should be better treated and that female clothing should be made for me.' A brief bitter laugh. 'And then the tailor sent to take my measurements used the opportunity to fondle my breasts. He even had the audacity to proclaim them "perfectly formed".'

'Which they are.'

'Don't say that, Estienne.'

'I am a man.'

'Yes.' A very long silence. 'Yes, you are a man. Regrettably.'

'And now you won't continue to tell me of your humiliation at the hands of men?'

'The last was the worst,' she said, as if oblivious of my presence. 'When at the stake my shameful whimpering – the pain was so bad – and my last cry had died away, the executioner came running up the scaffold to kick aside the flaming logs. He wanted to offer the crowd the ultimate evidence of my death and of my sex. And so he revealed to them the nakedness of my charred body from which all the clothes had been burnt; and all those things in a woman which are, and should be, secret were exposed, just so that their vulgar doubts might be set at rest.'

Jeanne, Jeanne; Rosette.

What I did to you that night, if it confirmed – horrendously – the eternal assault of the male upon the female, is perhaps more damnable than any other thing I have done. And when I hacked that heavy shackle from your festering leg it was Jeanne I tried, on behalf of all of us who are guilty, to liberate; it was myself I needed to set free.

There was so much I had still to learn.

· 134 ·

What is this shameful reasoning? Because you are a maid you must be a whore. Because you are a woman you must be a whore. Because I can defile you you must be a whore. Because I despise myself you must be a whore. Because I am a man you must be a whore.

Everything in this world is so diverse, so contrary, so obscure, that assuredly we cannot be confident of any truth.

· 135 ·

I was expecting some sign of progress – perhaps even, at long last, a verdict? – from the meeting of the Council of Justice on 31 October. However, there was not the slightest indication that anyone had taken the trouble of studying – of even glancing at – my previous depositions. More and more cynically they were showing the scaffolding of their edifice; more and more I refused to acknowledge what was happening. Because if I did that, I think I knew, I would be lost.

The only stated concern of the Council during the session

was to have two of Allemann's earlier documents – by Willem Hagen and Godfried Kok – officially certified. Through some inexplicable oversight they had not been sworn before.

The two statements were laboriously read out by secretary de Grandpreez, whereupon van den Henghel enquired, *pro forma*, whether I had any objection to either.

I had, most certainly.

'How can the court accept a sworn statement from a dishonest man?' I asked.

'Who are you referring to?' enquired the great man.

'Godfried Kok, of course.'

'Barbier,' said van den Henghel, meticulously touching his wig in what I'd come to recognise as a signal of alert, 'I must warn you to take great care in everything you say. As it is, your appearance before this Council is the result of slanderous attacks on a superior.'

'*Alleged* slanderous attacks,' said Swellengrebel quietly.

Van den Henghel's face flushed for a moment. Without looking at his Secunde he inclined his bulky frame in my direction. 'And what, if I may ask, do you have against Sergeant Kok?'

'He is a thief,' I said.

This caused quite a disturbance.

'It is a serious allegation,' said the Fiscal.

'That is why I'm making it,' I replied. 'And as in the Lieutenant's case I can prove it.'

'You haven't proved very much in the Allemann case,' van den Henghel snapped.

'Isn't that for the Council to decide?'

'For a man already in deep trouble you are very free with your mouth,' he remarked sharply.

(Jeanne, I thought, you must help me now, otherwise I may explode. Stay calm, she said, stay calm. You can win this, but only if you remain patient.)

'If the Council will allow me time to obtain such statements as I will require,' I said as evenly as I could, 'I have no doubt at all that I shall prove my case.'

'How much time?'

'At least two weeks. Possibly more.'

'One week is ample.'

'I need to go to the district of Stellenbosch.'

'You are not allowed to leave the Castle.'

'I can send a messenger.'

He gave me a smouldering look, shifting his great weight on his two short legs. 'All right then. Two weeks. But not a day more.'

I looked towards Swellengrebel, but he was drawing flourishes on the paper in front of him; perhaps he was practising a more elaborate signature.

· *136* ·

'I know,' I said to Jeanne, 'when the time comes, Swellengrebel will take my side.'

'When it really matters he will do what is best for himself. That is what everybody did who could have come to *my* aid when I needed them. Even the king himself.'

'Swellengrebel is an honest man.'

'He's a man in search of power. He has already chosen sides.'

'No! Jeanne, he's not like van den Henghel, not like all those officials from Holland or Batavia. He was *born* here. His concern is with this place.'

'His concern is with power, Estienne.'

'We'll see.'

'Indeed,' she said. 'We shall see.'

Christian Petzold's mission to Stellenbosch met with mixed success. He had found the widow Joubert – that formidable 'defenceless woman' – in great form, and more than ready to make a statement about the sixteen sheep she'd sold, in 1731, to Sergeant Godfried Kok. Petzold's difficulties, in several interviews with the widow, lay not in any reluctance on her part to impart information, nor in any deficiency of memory (her recollections, apart from an inability, six years after the event, to recall the day or month of the transaction, were in fact most dramatic in their vividness); but in her lack of restraint. It was only with the utmost effort, he assured me when we conferred near the Buren Bastion soon after his return, that he'd managed to compress her statement into four pages.

('You tell that poor Monsieur Barbier from me that I'll do anything I can to help him get that godless thief drawn and quartered,' she had enthusiastically told him. 'I'll personally come to Cabo if he wants me to, and I'll bring my hippopotamus-hide sjambok with me to flay the lot of them.')

But with Petrus de Wet, her feckless son-in-law, he'd had no success. The morose man had listened to Petzold's account in silence, his pale eyes staring fixedly at the notary's left shoulder; to each paragraph from his mother-in-law's statement read out to him he'd nodded his head in sad approval. But he'd doggedly refused to make a statement of his own.

'I don't want to get mixed up in the affairs of the big men of Cabo,' he'd replied to each of Petzold's urgently repeated pleas.

'But you did give Kok the sixty-four *guldens* to pay for the sheep?'

'Of course I did. You think I'd try to cheat my mother-in-law?'

The mere thought, admittedly, was preposterous.

'So he stole the money from you?'

'Yes. I heard later he spent it all at Jacob Cuijles'.'

'On what?'

'On drink, and for the use of one of Cuijles's slave girls, I was told.'

'Sixty-four *guldens*!'

'Well, I heard he used her many times, you see. And when he was finished with her she was in no state to work any more. But that is mostly hearsay. I didn't see the girl myself. So I can't tell for certain.'

'But you are sure about giving him the money?'

'Of course. I had a whole argument with Liesbet about it. That's my wife. And she told her mother. And – well . . .'

'What did you say to Kok?'

'I just told him to go.'

'Even if it meant losing the money?'

'I first tried to reason with him, but then he threatened me. He's a strong man. And look at me. He would have killed me. So what could I do? I sent him back to Cabo even though his time was not yet up. And then my mother-in-law took back all the sheep anyway, so I was the only one who lost out.'

'If you make a statement we may get your money back.'

'I told you I don't want trouble.'

'Estienne Barbier needs your statement.'

A shrug.

'Please, Mijnheer de Wet!'

The man's eyes, a mere hand's breadth away from Petzold's shoulder, barely flickered.

· *138* ·

I had to ask for another postponement. Frustration was burning up my insides. For a whole desperate week there was no sign of Petzold. One evening an almost illegibly scribbled note was pushed under my door. He could no longer visit me, he wrote; there were men following him about wherever he went.

The only way we can continue to work together now is for you to get me an official appointment as your procurator, he wrote.

Rather to my surprise this application was granted on 21 November. But at the same session of the Council of Justice I was informed that Godfried Kok had now also instituted legal proceedings against me, and that this matter, having arisen from the Allemann case, would have to be resolved before the other could proceed.

At least Christian could now openly visit me; I was even given permission occasionally to consult him at his house. And once or twice I did so, in spite of the annoyance of having to be escorted there and back, like a bloody prisoner, by an armed guard. But those were depressing meetings. Christian's fear had by then been realised and they'd been forced to take in a lodger, a large boorish lump of a man called Michiel Forster, who spent most of his time sitting in the *voorhuis* smoking or drinking, and ogling the comings and goings of Christian's wife and stepdaughter. This meant that it was impossible for us to consult in private.

We took to perambulating discussions, wandering along the lanes and *sentiers* of the Company Gardens; but there was a disquieting sense of *dépaysement* in these experiences, as if it was not I walking about among those exotic trees and shrubs, but an empty shell. I no longer had a natural right to be there (had I ever had such a 'right'?). Coming from my most aptly named *cagie* in the Castle, I was a stranger among those – even the slaves! – who could wander about so freely that they need not even remember they were there: I *knew* I was there, and knew, as if I were the bearer of some invisible but damning mark, that I no longer belonged among them. I came from elsewhere. And even what that elsewhere was I had no means of defining: not my *cagie*, surely, and not abroad, in Middelburg or Amsterdam, not even in France, in Orléans or Bazoches: only 'elsewhere'.

And soon the discomfort of this knowledge turned to irremediable anguish.

· 139 ·

Emerging from the Gardens, we would be met, every time, by that glittering inscription above the entrance to the hospital which has so long fascinated me and which Petzold now translated for me. *Belga tuum nomen populis fatale domandis – Horreat et leges Africa terra tuas*. And the African earth shudders at your laws. How true this had become; and how had it been turned inside-out for me.

· 140 ·

Even in purely practical terms our promenades were frustrating. The omnipresence of my guards was unnerving, and the incessant stares and snickering of passers-by turned our excursions into an ordeal. Moreover, Christian himself was labouring under increasing pressure, especially after an unknown slave had one night delivered to his house an unsigned message warning him to desist from further involvement in my case, *or you and your family may rue the day*.

'Then this must be the end for you,' I said. 'I can take care of myself. I can no longer involve you in my business.'

'It's my business as much as yours, Estienne,' he answered, as angry as a buzzing beetle, 'I've told you before, I've also been a victim of their practices. Who hasn't? We're not doing this for ourselves alone, man. Do you know how much talk this case has already stirred up? The whole of Cabo is waiting with bated breath, I tell you.'

That, it seemed to me, was a fantastic exaggeration. What perturbed me was precisely the impression that no one could

care a damn; that what was happening was no more than a
petty personal vendetta which concerned but a handful of us,
ignored by everybody else. But I was loth to hurt the poor
sincere little man; and all I said was, 'I can't let you risk your
safety, Christian. And especially not your family's.'

'Leave that to me to worry about,' He grabbed me by the
frayed front of my shirt. 'For God's sake, Estienne, we can't
give up now. The very fact that they're reacting like this proves
that what we're doing is important.'

'But we *aren't* doing anything!' I protested. 'We're getting
nowhere.'

'I'm going to Stellenbosch again tomorrow. This time, I
promise you, I'll badger de Wet until he signs that statement.'

He went. And returned again with empty hands. On 28
November I had to ask, yet another time, for a postponement.
On this occasion I detected signs of annoyance even in Hendrik
Swellengrebel.

· *141* ·

Life was becoming impossible.

'Impossible?' This was Jeanne, in one of her most passionate
outbursts. 'Don't use that word so lightly, Estienne. Do you
know, one of the things that offended me most deeply in my life
was when that one-eyed monster Jean de Luxembourg, after
he'd sold me to the English, chose for himself a new coat of
arms, a camel collapsing under its load, with the motto *Nemo ad
impossibile tenetur. 'No man shall be held bound by the impossible.'*
What did he know about the impossible? All he'd done was to
demonstrate the terrible confines of the possible: how low it is
possible to sink, what darkness of betrayal is possible to a man.
This is the sin of all of them, all these men who turn to politics
as a game to be played, a game of the possible. They become
powerful because they fetter the imagination. That is the very

source of their power. They forbid us to remember what is truly impossible. And by concentrating only on the possible, I tell you, they have made the world an impossible place to live in.'

'Then how do we get out of this *impasse* again?'

'We need someone who will again open our eyes to the impossible, Estienne. Only that will change the world into a place where life can be once more possible.'

· *142* ·

Tedious, endless days, waiting for news from Christian Petzold, weighed down by the possibilities of the present, the impossibility of the future. Hemmed in by the stern stone walls of the Castle, and even more so by the deadly semblance of certainty in mere routine. I find that I dwell more and more on memories of what I have seen beyond these confines. That endless land that once unfolded before the plodding progress of our oxen as we lumbered into the interior. That unremarkable muddy trickle of water that separated the known from the unknown. That forbidden space. Beyond, beyond.

Monomotapa.

I remember a broken man huddled in an orchard laid waste by a freak storm, surrounded by what had once been apples, pears, branches, leaves; a man swept out of his very mind, even out of language – those stuttered words, *The wind was blow* – so devastated as to be oblivious of the ruins of the house he'd abandoned to the injured woman sitting there, clutching to her breast her dead child.

And I wonder whether in a way even that man might not have been more fortunate than I: exposed utterly to the vagaries of nature, one *expects* the unexpected, the impossible becomes indeed possible; there is a cosmic dimension to experience. But here, enclosed in my cage like a trapped animal, I am surrounded only by the small, the meaningless, the ludicrous. (There was a monkey, once, in a cage at the fair in Orléans, where we also saw the lion, tormented by the crowd, its thumbs chopped off, its fur caked and mangy; and all it could do was chatter and whimper, covering its eyes as it cowered, or clutching at the pointed prodding sticks that assailed it from all sides.)

There is no *sense* in this. I am no longer sure of what is real. All that reaches me here are echoes from a distant and mostly incomprehensible world: rumours and gossip, stories told by soldiers (who often fall silent at my approach), the rare reports from Christian Petzold. Nothing I can grasp, clutch, examine, understand. Not even the sticks that prod me are real: I cannot believe in them.

Hence this curious, disturbing sensation of being at odds with myself, even when I am working on the documents for my defence: not of writing but of being written; not of observing, but of being observed – and from a great distance, a distance both of time and of space, from a century as yet undawned. And what would such a one know of this *me* enclosed in this space where I don't belong?

· *143* ·

I have often wondered, Rosette, how *you*, without anyone to help you, without a map, without any clear plan (as far as I know), how *you* effected your escape after I'd set you on your way that night?

We did have that one final meeting in the wilderness, of course. But then there were other, more urgent, things to talk about. And *they* will never believe it anyway.

· *144* ·

'In the beginning there was only,' you said in the course of that unreal night of tales, 'a Storyteller, and she was a woman. What kind of woman? you may ask. And I can only answer: a Woman, any Woman. Slowly, as time and more time went by, this Storyteller continued to tell tales to fill her loneliness, and spoke a world into being, a world of plains and mountains and rivers and dry places, and of forests and succulents and grass, and of birds and animals of all kinds; and in the end, because she was still aching with the need to be heard, and herself to hear another voice, she spoke into being a man and a woman.

'For a time that at first seemed endless they told her their new stories, and she listened in wonder and admiration. But in the end they began to forget that it was the Woman who had given them life through her stories, and they began to tell their stories to each other only, stories of children and cities and farms and ships and money, and of hunger and cruelty and slavery. And the forgotten Storyteller fell asleep into a deep sleep of ages, because they no longer seemed to need her. And when at last they remembered about her again they tried to find the story that would awaken her, but no one could tell them what that story was. And all the stories people have been telling since that time have been their attempts to find the one that would cause the Storyteller to wake up from her sleep again and restore the world to the happiness it surely knew in the beginning.'

· *145* ·

Do you find it strange that through those dreary months I maintained a measure of equanimity? I cannot pretend that I was not, often, dejected, even close to despair; or rebellious, and given to bouts of rage, which more often than not drove me back to drink. But you must remember that, on the whole, desperately and deliberately ignoring signs of impending disaster, I still clung urgently to my belief in ultimate victory. I could not believe that justice would not vindicate itself. Each postponement, even if it extended the process and the frustration of waiting and waiting, was also, perhaps perversely, a small battle gained over those who thought they could summarily crush me.

Jeanne was the one who would not let go. 'You must get out while you can,' she insisted, night after night. 'There are battles one cannot win in open warfare. Survival is more important. And to survive you must escape.'

'Escape means defeat,' I countered every time, as I had done before.

'It is just your male pride that keeps you here. There is no merit in mere stubbornness, Estienne.'

'I shall prevail.'

'*Listen* to me, Estienne! I'm warning you.'

'I know what I am doing.'

'I hope to God you do.'

· *146* ·

A bizarre event from one of my uneasy promenades with Christian Petzold: as we emerged from the Gardens in the late afternoon there was the slow rhythmic sound of a drum in the distance; and when we proceeded in that direction we saw, several blocks away, the bulky figure of a man on a tall white horse, preceded by a drummer. There could be no doubt about it: the rider was van den Henghel: the stirrups had evidently been adjusted especially to accommodate his short legs. And as he passed – we ourselves refrained from drawing any closer –

185

all the people on the way, attracted by the sound of the great drum, bowed in reverence.

About this event, as about so many others at the time, there was the unreality of an apparition.

It was, we learned afterwards, a new procedure introduced by the Acting Governor (that is, the *Gezachthebber*, or 'Ruler' as he insisted on being called) to mark his movements through the town. The full military band was required to be constantly in attendance at the Castle gate to sound a fanfare whenever he made a sortie or returned to his abode, no matter if that occurred once or twenty times a day; but the drummer – Nic Wijs, the only man on that early journey into the interior who had believed my account of the unicorn – actually had to accompany him on foot on each and every round through the town. (The only exceptions were those regular private visits the Ruler chose to pay to the women's quarters of the Slave Lodge after dark.)

· *147* ·

On 5 December the case came close to an untimely end. Once again, Petzold having been unable to obtain a statement from Petrus de Wet, I had no choice but to ask for an extension.

Van den Henghel rose to his feet, impressive as always.

'The patience of this Council has been sorely tested,' he said in that voice so curiously shrill for a man of his bulk. 'We shall not be trifled with any further. It is clear that, having no evidence to substantiate the wild allegations made in this very chamber against Sergeant Kok, you are now indulging in irritating little ploys merely to postpone what must be, to all here present, a most obvious conclusion.'

'We already have one sworn statement to establish a *prima facie* case,' replied Christian Petzold on my behalf. 'And we have a second, crucial witness. But the man is fearful of testifying of his own free will. On behalf of the defendant I request that the judicial means to constrain him to testify be placed at our disposal.'

'What would that entail?' asked Captain Rhenius, emerging from one of his brief naps.

'A small detachment of soldiers to accompany me to the witness's farm in the district of Stellenbosch, Your Excellency.'

'This Council has already borne the expenses of *pro deo* representation for the defendant,' van den Henghel reminded him. 'The cost of sending armed soldiers to Stellenbosch is out of proportion to the seriousness of the matter.'

'For my client it is indeed a very serious matter, Your Excellency. His good name is at stake.'

'I am more concerned about the good name of the plaintiff,' snapped van den Henghel. 'This Estienne Barbier has been attacking the reputation of one respectable citizen after another. First Lieutenant Allemann, now Sergeant Kok – who is to be next? I myself perhaps?'

'I don't think any honest man has anything to fear from Sergeant Barbier, Your Excellency.'

'What exactly is that supposed to mean?'

'Let him have two soldiers,' said Hendrik Swellengrebel, scribbling on the paper in front of him. He sounded irritable. Then he looked up, straight at me. 'But there can be no further extension. Is that clear?'

I nodded.

'And since the defendant is so eager to pursue a matter we all regard as a waste of time,' said van den Henghel, 'it seems to me only fair that henceforth he should be personally responsible for the cost of the exercise.'

To my relief Swellengrebel proposed a compromise: if, after obtaining de Wet's sworn statement, the Council found in my favour, Kok would be required to pay my expenses; should I lose, it would be my responsibility.

But at that stage I was so confident of success that I had no qualms about offering Petzold my last precious possession (apart from my leather-bound book, but that I believe was valuable only to me, alas, not to others), my father's watch. He was to pawn it; within a week, I believed, we would be able to retrieve it. At last the end of my ridiculous ordeal was in sight.

· *148* ·

In the course of that week (if only he had timed it better) Nic Wijs took his revenge on van den Henghel. Driven beyond endurance by the Ruler's demand that he be available day and night, the drummer had finally reached the end of his tether. It came after an evening out when van den Henghel had caroused with friends until after midnight, requiring Wijs to stand by all the while in order to escort him back to the Castle and wake up the whole town with his drumming. The very next evening Nic Wijs – by no means a young man any more – lay in wait; and when van den Henghel emerged, furtively, from the Slave Lodge, his breeches in fact still undone, the drummer fell into step right behind him thundering away on his huge drum as if it was the Last Judgement. From everywhere in the neighbourhood, as was their wont, good citizens appeared to survey the progress of the great man, who could do nothing to obscure his corpulent mass from their eyes (as Wijs had taken care to bring with him a torch-bearing slave).

Early the following morning Nic Wijs was placed, with me, under orders of internal banishment. Only, in his case it was unlikely that a charge would ever be officially brought against him as that would compound van den Henghel's embarrassment. It seemed that he might have to spend the rest of his natural life within the confines of the Castle without ever being brought to trial.

It also meant that our common enemy was in the foulest

temper imaginable when on Thursday 12 December my own case finally came to trial.

· 149 ·

It made my triumph all the sweeter.

Petzold was in great form, reading out our two damning statements to the full Council. Normally at least one or two members missed a session owing to more pressing – more lucrative – business elsewhere; but on this exceptional occasion not a soul was absent.

There was little discussion.

Kok, when asked to comment, merely shook his head and mumbled a promise to make reparation to the wronged widow and her son-in-law.

Rhenius read out the verdict, which was at that stage a mere formality. Kok was to ask my pardon in a public ceremony at the Castle gate, in front of all the dignitaries and all the assembled troops; he had to bear the full cost of the proceedings; and in addition he was instructed to pay me damages for my offended honour to the extent of two hundred and fifty *guldens*.

Immediately after the decision had been pronounced Tiemmendorf rose to his feet to announce that Allemann was withdrawing his libel suit, and offered to assume all the costs incurred by my defence.

The sweetest, the most cherished moment of all was when van den Henghel himself rose in solemn silence, removed his wig to expose his almost-bare skull glowing an angry pink through the remaining sparse blonde hairs, and offered me his unconditional abject apology.

'There is,' said Swellengrebel as soon as van den Henghel had finished, 'an additional compensation traditionally at the disposal of a defendant in such circumstances as here obtain, should he wish to avail himself of it.' One could hear a feather flutter in the ensuing silence while Swellengrebel exposed the terms of the tradition.

'What do you say to this?' enquired Rhenius.

'I accept,' I said.

Whereupon van den Henghel advanced across the floor in my direction until he'd reached the very centre. There he stopped, hesitated, his large face now an admirable and more rare purple, turned his back to me, elaborately unbuttoned his breeches, and descended into a kneeling position to offer me his voluminous posterior, sufficiently raised to be most readily accessible. Below the bulging globes dangled, like late-summer figs, in a rich colour outdoing even that of his visage, his miserable privates.

Taking my time, following strictly the procedure the Secunde had explained to me, I advanced, took careful aim, and planted, straight forward and up, the most ferocious kick I was capable of – expressing in it all the accumulated rage and frustration of those many months – right in that ample target.

· *150* ·

All night long, Rosette, you fended off my assaults – the next night theirs – by telling stories. Why? That was what I had to know. And I asked you as much: but if perhaps I did not ask, at least I seriously intended to (only I was too dazed with alcohol).

It was, as I remember (either that night or another), in Jeanne's voice that you replied.

'In confession, when I was small,' you said, Jeanne said, 'I used to tell the priest everything, everything. I even invented sins in order to suffer more, to be more worthy in his eyes of penitence and redemption. But it was humiliating too. Then one day, I think it was after I'd first put on a man's clothes, I realised that my whole life, the whole of *me*, existed for the priest only in the words of my confession. I could literally invent myself through what I chose to tell. I could cancel myself by remaining silent. Or I could create whole multitudes of me through different stories. From that moment I had control over my destiny.'

· *151* ·

I'll tell you this: it was a dismal day, that 12 December. Petzold had come back from Stellenbosch with his escort barely an hour before the session was due to begin; there was no time for him even to change his clothes, and although he did have the long-awaited affidavit from Petrus de Wet he was so nervous that it was at times difficult to follow his reading.

Even so our case, I felt assured, was unassailable. And from the subsequent interrogation of Kok by the members of the Council it seemed clear that the man had overplayed his hand in bringing his charges.

Swellengrebel himself mounted the attack. 'Do you have anything to say to these statements, Sergeant?' he asked.

'No sir, I'm sorry, sir,' said Kok, *bouche bée*.

'That's bad enough,' said the Secunde.

'Yes, sir.'

'And you have nothing to say against Barbier?'

'No sir. Except that he's being too harsh with me.'

'You admit that you never paid for the sixteen sheep?'

'I'll do my best to repay the widow, sir. As soon as I have the money. I've been in some difficulties recently.'

'But the money has been owing for these six years?'

'I know, sir. But I really intend to pay her back. Just give me time. I promise.'

'So you agree it is not unfair at this stage to accuse you of having taking possession of the sheep without payment?'

'No, sir.'

'And that this may be construed as theft?'

The tide was clearly turning. But my contentment was short-lived.

Van den Henghel cast an angry glance at Rhenius. With surprising alacrity the old Captain rose to his feet. 'Sergeant Kok,' he said, 'tell me, at the time of acquiring the sheep, did you intend to pay for them?'

'Absolutely, sir. I'd never do a thing like that without meaning to pay. I'm an honest man.'

'I thought as much,' said Rhenius. 'So you can confirm that only poverty and bad luck has made it impossible for you to repay the widow?'

'I swear to that,' said Kok.

'*Six years*, Sergeant?' Swellengrebel interposed.

'Surely the fact of poverty cannot serve as an excuse for anyone to call this transaction theft?' asked van den Henghel, crossing his hands on his broad stomach.

'It is an insult to my character, sir,' said Kok.

'We know the sergeant to be irreproachable in all other respects,' continued van den Henghel. 'I have personal knowledge of him as a most trustworthy soldier and an exemplary officer. Don't you agree, Captain Rhenius?'

'Most heartily, Your Excellency.'

'In that case it seems we can conclude this unfortunate business.'

Thereupon Swellengrebel intervened: it was turning more and more overtly into a struggle between the great men of Cabo; soon I might be only incidental to it. 'I'm afraid we have not yet heard the full story,' said the Secunde.

'Mijnheer Swellengrebel,' van den Henghel struck back, 'you have already questioned Sergeant Kok extensively. We have heard the statements made against him, both by inhabitants of this colony not here present and, may I say, typical in their attitude against those of us more privileged than themselves in that we had the good fortune to be born in Patria and not among the lower classes of this African territory.'

'Mijnheer van den Henghel!' Swellengrebel seemed ready to explode.

'Consequently,' continued van den Henghel, 'we cannot attach too much weight to their declarations. Sergeant Kok, on the other hand, born in the Netherlands and according to all evidence an honourable man, has given the admirable undertaking to pay the widow Joubert in full, which intention he has solemnly cherished since the day of the transaction. And in the circumstances the Council has no choice but to find against Estienne Barbier, a man already sorely compromised in other respects. I may add that any vote against Kok cannot but be regarded as a vote against my own integrity.' He paused. On his stomach the intricately woven gold chain of his pendulous watch caught the light from a tall window. 'Any opinions to the contrary?'

There was silence in the chamber.

I stared at Swellengrebel; he was drawing his interminable flourishes. One day, I felt sure, he should have the most flamboyant signature in the whole of Cabo.

'In that case,' concluded van den Henghel, 'we find Barbier guilty of malicious slander against an honourable man, Godfried Lodewikus Kok. The defendant will be required to make public reparation for the wrong he has done an honest man against whom nothing can be imputed. He will also pay the costs of both parties in the process.'

'Your Excellency!' Petzold was on his feet, trembling with anger.

'The case is closed,' said van den Henghel. 'Sit down, Petzold, or you will be held in contempt yourself. It is bad enough that you have sided with a disreputable slanderer like this Barbier.'

And then, all of a sudden, I saw myself standing too; heard myself shouting. I was transported with rage. How could I be expected to contain myself? And yet it was a strange experience, as if – again, and more disconcertingly than before – it wasn't *I* who was standing there, but someone else who looked like me and spoke like me; and from a great distance I observed myself, saw myself being written into a part I had no wish to play yet couldn't resist.

'You can condemn me until you're blue in the face!' I shouted. (Oh for a kick into that white rump, those purple figs: that they might clang and clang for months like those of Allemann.) 'Do to me what you wish: I'll never – you hear me? never! – I'll never as long as I live apologise to the *mécréant*! He's a bloody thief and he knows it and has admitted it right here in front of you all. He stole the widow's sheep and he stole the money his employer gave him to pay for them. You can send me to the stake if you wish, I stand by every word I've said about him. And worse. He's a murderer too! Of course no one will believe me, but I know what I am talking about. I have seen him, and so has Allemann. Birds of a feather, now they flock together, but if there was any justice in this colony *they* would be the guilty ones today. I know I have the whole populace of Cabo behind me. But who will bother to consult them? I tell you, I'd rather be damned for all eternity than apologise to that thief and murderer Kok. Just as Mordechai refused to bow to the traitor Haman I refuse to bow to this man.' Pointing at Captain Rhenius, and from him to all the others in the assembly, I shouted, 'Now it is clear for all to see what to expect from you!'

Swellengrebel interrupted. 'Do you accuse me, too, of being unjust?'

I was sorely tempted to confirm it; how could he condone what had been done to me? Yet even in my rage I realised that he was perhaps my only hope for the future. 'I'm talking about these others,' I said, still shaking. 'Can't you see what this man has done? And I tell you there's a lot more. Why don't you ask Kok about what happened at the Backeley Plaats!'

'How dare you!' shouted Kok, kicking over his chair and coming towards me.

'You want to kill me too, the way you murdered that hottentot Ruyter?' I asked.

And then there were orderlies all over the place and we were restrained – I was still shouting and ranting, I know, I could hear myself, nearly incoherent with rage, mouthing, 'The lot of you – The lot of you – !' – and at last order, or some semblance of it, was restored, and I was hauled away by four soldiers for a week in the Dark Hole.

· *152* ·

It is the worst that can happen to one in this place, I think. After some time in the stench, the gnawing hunger, the utter solitude of this space confined by its high walls, far below the Nassau Bastion, even death assumes an aspect of relief. There is an air-vent obliquely above the door through which one is first flung inside, but during the day it is blocked up; only at night it allows some (but not much) of the fetid air to escape. This means that it is always pitch dark; and within hours one loses all sense of orientation, missing even the corner one first selects to urinate and defecate. A nose serves no purpose, the smell pervades everything. There are only sounds. The rustling of vermin in the straw that covers the earth floor (it is supposed to be changed once a week, but in practice it hardly ever happens). A distant washing of waves against the wall, deepening to an awful boom in a storm. From the correction chamber outside the door there are, from time to time, the thud and sibilance of lashes applied to the back of a recalcitrant soldier, in series of forty; and the grunts, whimpers, screams of the victim. Occasionally barked commands from officers overseeing the exercises of the garrison in the Arms Court. Once a day, either before daybreak or after sunset, one cannot be sure, for it is always dark, the door groans and a mug of water and a morsel of mouldy bread are shoved inside. These are the only events of the day. For the rest, nothing. Silence, stench, hunger, thirst. You can break your fists or shins against the walls in fear or rage; there is no issue. Mounting terror. Because, having so soon lost count of time, you believe they have forgotten about you; an hour may be a year. There is a madness that rises in one. And this they call justice.

· *153* ·

Justice? But what justice do I deserve? This is the real madness: the rising horror about what I am, have been, can never be. And the madness bears your name, and only your name. Rosette. No matter that you told them stories; no matter that you seemed to emerge unscathed: in *my* actions I stand condemned forever. I am a man who flung a naked woman into a cage of wild starved animals because I could not bear the shame of my own guilt. I once thought that the most inhuman thing I had ever witnessed in my whole life was on the ship to Cabo when the slaves were flung into the sea during the storm. But what I did was worse. If this were the only wrong I had ever committed, if in all other respects I were a saint, it would still be sufficient to condemn me to hell.

· *154* ·

It was not all. I stole my father's watch from my dying mother's hands and left that helpless one-legged man to his fate when he most needed me. I betrayed women who loved me, and maimed or killed the men who tried to avenge them. I abandoned a pregnant wife and her sickly children at a moment when they could not fend for themselves. Since then I have lied and cheated my way through the world. In all things I have subjected myself – body, mind, history, created in the image of God – to the impetuosities and vagaries of six inches of sometimes drooping sometimes rearing flesh. I stand accused. *Meum peccatum contra me est semper.* There is no sentence to be pronounced on me that I do not deserve. *Homo sum et nihil humanum alienum mihi est.* That is the word I could not think of before. *Alienum.*

· *155* ·

Jeanne was – can you believe it? – amused. Sympathetic, and understanding; but mostly amused.

'What else could you have expected of them?'

'Kok is as guilty as hell.'

'Of course. But that's not the point, Estienne. You threaten everything they represent. How can they *not* act to break you?'

'But Swellengrebel?'

'He means well. But one day he may be governor. He has his whole future to protect.'

'He's an honest man.'

'Estienne, Estienne. There was a time when I, too, reasoned like that. But I was not yet nineteen, remember. You are almost forty. You ought to know better. It doesn't work like that, believe me. What they are concerned with – what they *have* to be concerned with – isn't honesty but power.'

'There must be justice somewhere.'

'With God.'

'I mean *here*. While we're still alive. And I won't stop before I've seen it done.'

'Then you still have some distance to go.'

'I'll go anywhere, to any lengths.'

I closed my eyes. I could feel the brush of her hair against my face.

'Do you really know how far that is?'

'I'm prepared for anything.'

'You have no idea at all what you're talking about.' And once again, as so many times before, she urged, 'You must escape, Estienne.'

'From this dungeon?'

'They said it would be only for a week.'

'And just as well. On this diet of bread and water I'll soon be too weak to move. And you can be sure, once they let me out I'll be under surveillance night and day.'

'One finds strength when one needs it. When I jumped from that tower in Beaurevoir – even after my voices had told me not to – I nearly died. But I've told you before: it is only when one accepts the impossible that life becomes worth living. There is so much you still have to learn.'

· *156* ·

On the Thursday when I was to be released from the Dark Hole, the secretary of the Council, Josephus de Grandpreez, appeared in the door. The light was too fierce for me to see properly. But through almost-closed eyes, peering through the fingers I'd frantically pressed against my face, I could make out the outline of his shapeless, unwieldy body, flanked by two guards.

'Enjoying your rest?' he asked.

'What do you want?' If the guards hadn't been there I might have done something irresponsible.

'The Council is in session. They're biding the honour of your company.'

'What more do they want of me?'

'The Allemann case is to be concluded today, didn't you know?'

'Then I'm more than ready.'

'Nothing like a week in this hole to teach one manners, is there?' My eyes still could not bear looking at him, but I imagined his nostrils delicately quivering. 'I presume you have now seen the folly of your attitude.'

'What do you mean?'

'You will be expected to offer your apologies to Sergeant Kok before the other case is wound up.'

'I'll never apologise to that bastard or to anyone else as long as I live.'

'You're making life unnecessarily difficult for yourself, Barbier.'

'Just take me to the Council and shut up.'

'I have instructions to escort you only on the express condition that you will first apologise to Kok.'

'Then go to hell!'

'I think you are likely to get there long before I do,' he said.

The heavy studded door swung shut. I was alone again in that stinking darkness.

· *157* ·

In my absence, de Grandpreez was happy to inform me, personally, afterwards, I had once again been found guilty, without any further discussion, and condemned to a public apology 'to God Almighty, the Council of Justice, and aforementioned Lieutenant Rudolf Siegfried Allemann', with costs. It had also been decided that I should spend another fourteen days on bread and water in the Dark Hole.

· *158* ·

Today, back in the same darkness, and with the certainty of my death which must be imminent, there is, even while I rage, a sense of calm as well. I know what has happened, I know I am here, I know what is to come: all that remains is to imagine the real, to improve on what has seemed like truth, to find or invent the shaded meanings of it all. You will know, Rosette, storyteller that you are, that the truth is environed by the lie, accessible only through the adventures of trying to tell it.

It was different then, more painful, less readily acceptable. Most of the time – when Jeanne did not besiege me with the prospects and projects of escape, each plan more daring and extreme than the previous – my mind could occupy itself only with the most immediate, physical, minute facts of my incarceration: intolerable heat by day, cold nights, the scuttling vermin, the stench of my own excrement, hunger gnawing like a rat at my entrails. A sterile anger, futile raging, fastidious plots of revenge.

What would I do upon my release, if indeed my dogged refusal to apologise – for that I could not, would not, do, not ever, not if it cost my miserable life – did not result in my perpetual confinement? I had already sold most of my clothes; my father's watch. My only remaining possession, apart from my book, was the teak chest itself: and that, I knew, would probably have to go the moment I left the Dark Hole. What further recourse was there for me? This seemed the ultimate cul-de-sac.

· *159* ·

Often, during those three weeks of darkness, I revisited the wide land outside, of which I had once, so superficially, so frustratingly, explored some contours. Its dazzling light, almost unimaginable in this darkness. A unicorn heraldic against the setting sun. A hippogryph. An imagined girl in a sudden flare of the fire, exploding sparks, revealing the secret flesh which had centuries ago been mercilessly exposed – then charred, forever inaccessible – by an executioner to a jeering crowd.

You: the clothes torn from your body, flogged by a hysterical white woman; dark weals on your back.

The land, in spite of its light – or because of it? – unfathomable to me. I knew then, almost fatefully, that I would have to return to it, restore myself to it, however, whenever.

· *160* ·

Two days into the new year, 1738, I was released from the Dark Hole. I was unsteady on my legs from loss of weight; I was blinded by the unfamiliar light, and it was days before my sight was more or less restored; inside I was bitter, and seething with thoughts of revenge.

Not caring to ask anyone's permission, as soon as I could, after a fashion, see and walk again, I paid a visit to Christian Petzold, whom I found in poor shape. He'd taken to drink in an alarming way, seeing no hope at all for himself in the future. Having lost both my cases he stood little chance of an increase in the demand for his services. In fact, unmistakable signs of pressure from above had already scared off the one or two prospective clients who had come to enquire about his services. His wife Johanna had been forced to take in washing to supplement the family's needs. The two smallest girls were playing about in a state of near-nakedness, their small monkey-faces streaked with dirt, their hair dishevelled; even Christian's fourteen-year-old stepdaughter Maria had lost her sprightliness. Her large blue eyes seemed dull and resentful now, and her dress, presumably handed down from the mother who was twice her size, fitted badly and gaped in unmended tears to embarrass even me. A family sinking relentlessly into indigence.

Depressing, too, was the continuing presence of their lodger, the oafish Michiel Forster who was still sprawling on a *riempie* couch as if he hadn't moved his carcass since my previous visit well over a month before; smoking a long pipe, and drinking arrack from a bottle. Once we'd left the house on a small promenade to the Gardens – we had, after all, most urgent business to discuss – Christian divulged to me his now firm suspicion that the man had been 'planted' in their midst to spy on the family and keep the authorities informed of all comings and goings to and from the house.

'I followed him once when he went out to buy drink,' said Christian. 'I was curious, because I knew he had no money – at least that was what he'd told me the night before when I'd asked him for the rent. And he led me all the way to van den Henghel's residence in the Castle, where he was admitted. When he came out again he went straight to a tavern and bought several bottles.' A bitter grimace. 'Estienne, the Cape is the *anus mundi*.'

'But what can they possibly want from you?'

'I don't think they want anything,' he said simply. 'They're only doing this to intimidate me.'

'Isn't it enough that they've tried to squash me?'

'No.'

'Christian, from here I'm acting on my own. I'm not going to drag you further down with me.'

'There isn't much further to go, is there?' he asked. In spite of everything his eyes, I was surprised to see, were still twinkling. 'Enough about my miseries, Estienne. It's time to discuss strategy. You'll be back before the Council this coming Thursday, I presume?'

· *161* ·

They were no doubt expecting me, after my ordeal in the dungeon, to offer, at last, my humble apologies. For the first time in months Allemann himself was there, small and rotund and content, his tidy paws clutched; and Kok too, of course, his uniform ill-fitting on his large frame, the broad face surrounding the small deep-set eyes contorted in a scowl that might have been intended as a smile. Not a single councillor was absent. There was about the whole occasion a sense of smug anticipation.

After the opening formalities van den Henghel rose.

'Well, Barbier? We all trust that your most recent experience has had a salutary effect. What have you to say to this Council?'

'Your Excellency' – Petzold had warned me to be as correct as possible in my behaviour – 'I have considered your verdict in the two cases brought against me by Lieutenant Allemann and Sergeant Kok, and I request your permission to appeal to the Lords Seventeen.'

'This is preposterous!' he exploded.

I unfolded the paper Petzold had given me. (I had insisted that he stay at home to avoid, if possible, the continued intimidation of his family.)

'It is the right of any citizen of Cabo to appeal against a sentence by this Council.'

'In serious cases, surely, not in a matter of this nature!'

'I'm afraid,' intervened Swellengrebel, 'the defendant is right. If he insists on appealing to the Lords Seventeen we have no jurisdiction to stop him.'

'The Council shall take this matter under advisement,' said van den Henghel, his voice even more highly pitched than normal.

· *162* ·

At the following session the appeal was allowed – though not to Amsterdam, as I had requested, but to Batavia. A week later, on 23 January, Tiemmendorf, on behalf of Allemann, presented an eloquent and furious argument for the summary execution of the sentence, citing pages and pages of learned references in support. But for once – and I could only suspect that Swellengrebel had intervened in some manner in the *coulisses* – the Council could not be swayed.

De Grandpreez was instructed to make copies of all the documents in the case so that these could be forwarded, with my own extensive formulation of appeal, to Batavia.

· *163* ·

In the course of February, as I paid one visit after another to de Grandpreez's office to enquire after the progress of the transcription, it gradually became clear to me why the Council had appeared so co-operative.

The transcripts – for which I was forced to pay out of my own pocket, investing in the process every stuyver from the proceeds of the sale of my teak chest, and borrowing the balance from a sympathetic shopkeeper – were, quite simply, false.

I couldn't believe my eyes, Rosette, when on 20 February, having paid the 32 rix dollars and 3 shillings demanded by that unscrupulous *scélérat*, I perused the copies de Grandpreez had handed to me.

Much of my own evidence, including parts of the affidavits I had submitted, had been suppressed; the *compte rendu* of the crucial meetings had been tampered with. Van den Henghel's interrogation of Kok, for example, was quoted verbatim, but not a word of Swellengrebel's interventions, whereas my own references to Kok's murder were merely described as 'incoherent mumblings'. To Kok's replies had been added remarks (including a statement to the effect that after arriving at de Wet's farm with the sixteen sheep bought from the widow Joubert, he had sent the full amount to her place with a hottentot servant) which had never been made at the trial. The whole transcript was such a concoction of errors, omissions, additions and downright lies that I was beside myself.

I tell you, the moment after I had finished reading through the documents with Petzold (in a quiet spot among the densest shrubs in the Company Gardens, where there was little chance of either Forster or Mentzel disturbing us) I ran back to the secretary's office and threw the papers on his desk. I would have struck him had there not been three armed guards in the room with him. (Only afterwards it occurred to me that he might well have summoned them in anticipation of just such an event. Two of them I knew from sight, Manie Blankenberg and Adriaan van Schoor; they belonged to the type Jeanne had called the *houspilleurs*. The third was unknown to me, but there seemed little doubt that he was cut from the same coarse cloth.)

'Now what's all this about?' de Grandpreez asked, reclining in his chair. The guards, I noticed, had their hands on their swords.

'I'm going to prosecute you for fraud!' I shouted.

'Really? I should have expected more caution – let alone better manners – from you after your recent miserable failures in court.'

'Josephus de Grandpreez,' I said, trying my utmost to control myself, 'you are going to recopy these documents word for word until they represent exactly what happened in those two trials.'

'The copies are correct in every word,' he said calmly. Leaning forward, he pushed towards me a pile of documents that had been waiting at his left elbow. 'You can compare them for yourself if you wish.'

I turned a few random pages. I was too perturbed to concentrate. But what I saw was enough to make me realise, choking with the urge to vomit, that the two sets of documents indeed coincided perfectly.

Jeanne, too, I remembered with sudden sickening clarity, had told me how she'd once accused her accusers, 'You write down what is against me, but not what is for me.' How, then, could I expect to be treated differently?

'It means . . .' I took a deep breath. 'It means that you have falsified your records from the very beginning.'

'I should be very careful about making such accusations, Barbier.' The menace in his voice did not escape me.

And now, in an extremely painful recovery, I recalled the journal I myself had kept, for Allemann, on our journey into the interior: remembering not only how Oscar Mentzel had afterwards rewritten every page, but – this was the most disheartening – how I myself had shaped each day's events to Allemann's requirements.

Whoever puts pen to paper, it seems to me, lies.

De Grandpreez rose. He must have known he had already won.

'Get out of this office,' he said, very quietly. 'And if ever you set foot in here again it'll be back to the Dark Hole with you.'

'Monsieur de Grandpreez – '

'Out!' he screamed, banging on the table, spilling ink over some of the copies with which I'd littered his desk.

I glanced at the soldiers. And left.

· *164* ·

How is it possible, you will ask, that after this experience I waited another month – almost to the day – before I finally escaped? I admit it is difficult, in retrospect, to justify my delay. But I assure you – you must believe me! – it was not out of indecision, and even less out of pusillanimity. If anything, it was inspired by an ever more fierce determination to *force* justice: to ensure that no one would have the right afterwards to accuse me of having had recourse to extreme action without first exhausting all the more reasonable possibilities of a resolution.

If I did escape in the end it was in emulation of David fleeing from Saul.

But during that exacting month I tried, grimly – and angrily, yes, but lucidly, with a kind of perverse satisfaction – every avenue still open to me.

I visited Paul Slotsboo, the secretary of the Political Council. He received me, not cordially, but civilly. But when I asked him for advice on laying a charge against de Grandpreez, he rose very promptly. 'I'm sorry, Barbier, but I don't want to have anything to do with this business.'

It was to be expected, I know – de Grandpreez is his brother-in-law: how tightly knit the network of power at the Cape – but it was a necessary station on my way.

I waited a week to be accorded an interview with Captain Rhenius, who laconically informed me that he was not prepared to discuss the case as it was now *sub judice* to Batavia.

I went to Swellengrebel's house in the Berg Street, where I learned that the Secunde had left on a journey of inspection to the Company's victualling posts in the interior.

I had to wait another week for an appointment with van den Henghel. When I arrived at the Governor's house a slave came to the door – a very black slave in a very handsome suit, with a very white powdered wig, and barefoot – to inform me that the *Gezachthebber* was not prepared to see me after all.

The next day I was informed that the conditions of my internal arrest had been revised. I no longer had freedom of movement within the Castle, but was confined to my *cagie* until such time as a suitable ship from Europe anchored in the bay to transport me to Batavia.

I had no more money. Even old Mr Berg, the most benevolent shopkeeper in Cabo, who had always been prepared to extend my credit, would no longer allow me anything; not even a sheet of writing paper. I had nothing more to sell. I could no longer place Petzold at risk by sending him messages.

This was the end of that particular road.

'There is only one way open now,' said Jeanne, 'and that is escape. At last you must admit it. You can no longer resist me.'

'I still cannot bear the idea of running away.'

'There are times when escape is not running away,' she said. 'In Rouen, near the end, when I was in a very bad way, little more than a skeleton in man's clothing, close to death with exhaustion and pain, Cochon offered to have my fetters removed – for even in my dungeon, and with three gaolers in my cell, I was in double irons night and day – on the sole condition that I take an oath not to try and escape.'

'And you refused.'

'Of course I refused. You know why? Because that is the last dignity left to a prisoner. They can take everything else from you: they can insult you, and torture you, and humiliate you, and rape you, and degrade you. But they cannot take from you the will to escape, the will to be free. If you give that up, you accept your condition, you yield to your gaolers, you imply that they have the right to do whatever they are doing. Only by saying no can you stay human.'

'They killed you.'

'Yes. But they couldn't touch my freedom.'

· 166 ·

On the night of 24 March 1738 the drummer Nic Wijs and I escaped from the Castle. I had finally bowed to Jeanne's wisdom. I took as my example her own attempt in the castle of Beaulieu, when she'd slipped through a crevice in a wooden palisade (she was by then such an emaciated little wisp of a girl) and locked up her sentries in the guardroom, then calmly walked to the front gate. Had she not met the porter on her way out she would have been free.

What an uproar our escape caused. Over and over again, in the course of my last trial, they came back to it: how did we manage to scale those walls? and what about the moat? who helped? how did we get rid, afterwards, of the ropes or chains or whatever we'd used? Bloody fools. It is true that Nic had to use a disguise – a wig and coat and breeches stolen from Captain Rhenius's rooms – to slip out. But I marched out openly, I told them, simply by putting to good use my knowledge of military routine: with the single precaution of locking the ever-prowling Mentzel into a storeroom, I walked out coolly and calmly through the front entrance, directly under the bell-tower. I knew that just before the 10 o'clock bell the guard would set out from the room below the bell-tower on its rounds inside, while immediately after the bell the sentries at the gate marched, respectively, to the Leerdam and Buuren Bastions of the fortress; in those two or three dark minutes I strode out unchallenged and unobserved, hid behind one of the sentry posts until the coast was once again clear, and then went round the Castle to join Nic in Lieutenant Cochius's garden at the back. From there we went to the mouth of the Salt River where the drummer had previously arranged with a friend to secure a rowing boat from the *Padmos* on the beach; and under cover of darkness rowed to *'t Huys te Marquette* with which we planned to return to the Netherlands.

That was the version I offered to my judges. But as you may already have suspected, the true fashion of our escape was both more elaborate and more daring. It was indeed inspired by Jeanne: not her straightforward attempt at Beaulieu, but that amazing action at Beaurevoir, when she hurled herself from a seventy-foot tower, injuring herself so badly they feared for her life. Three hundred years later Héloïse met with even less luck in that jump from the steeple in which I failed to follow her. (Or was she really, all things considered, the more fortunate?)

Now, it occurred to me, if they had tried to fly, not jump, perhaps it would have worked. And that set me thinking.

In the course of a long series of deliberations with Nic Wijs I reluctantly abandoned the idea of devising our escape around my solid trustworthy teak chest; instead, we developed a strategy involving his great drum, which was much lighter and more manageable. To this instrument, secreted in a seldom-visited store on the middle floor of the seaward courtine, close to the Buuren Bastion, we meticulously attached an oblong canopy, extended on both sides into two enormous wings of ship's canvas richly bedecked with feathers. Using two cranks located inside the drum (having of course first removed the top vellum), it was possible to manipulate these wings in a flapping motion at variable speed. Below the machine we fitted two wheels from a small cannon brought from the Water Castle for repairs in the smithy some time before.

Ideally the apparatus should have been submitted to rigorous testing; this, however, was ruled out by our condition of internal banishment. For us there could be but one test: the final enterprise itself. Should that fail, we might well run the risk of dreadful punishment. And it was our consciousness of this risk which so protracted the preparations that it was approaching the end of March before we felt confident enough of proceeding to the act of escape itself.

We had to bide a windy day; and as in this season the days at the tip of Africa tend to be sublimely and transparently still, it took several weeks of impatient waiting for a favourable wind to spring up at last. That was, as I have said before, the night of 23 March.

Immediately after the 10 o'clock guard had set out on its round we dragged the elaborate machine to the Arms Court. Nic Wijs seated himself inside the drum; I began to push heavily, making use of the sweeping South-Easter from behind, and as the wings began to flap and the drum became airborne I jumped in beside him. Even with the help of the wind we were courting disaster, as there was so little space in which to rise sufficiently high to clear the walls. But with barely a foot to spare we succeeded, close to the Oranje Bastion. Below us, as we flew over the wall and the moat into Lieutenant Cochius's garden at the back, there was a cry – not of alert, however, but of amazement. Whoever had seen us must have taken the contraption for some giant exotic bird that had visited these shores from the most secret recesses of Africa. And by the time the truth was discovered we were already in the small fishing boat on our way through the black breakers towards 't Huys te Marquette where the men were making noisy preparations to set sail for Europe at the first glimmer of dawn.

We were free: birds in the wilderness.

· *170* ·

In a most important respect, I should point out, our evasion was not intended as escape at all; not in the usual sense of the word. What we meant to do was to stow away on a ship to Amsterdam, bypassing Batavia, in order personally to present our cases directly to the Lords Seventeen. I still believed in justice, you see. If I couldn't believe in that, what else would there be to live for?

(*You* had escaped; I'd helped you. You'd given up on human justice long before I did. Did it make anything more worth while for you? What happens when one gives up on justice? Tell me that. Tell me another of your stories.)

That still, dark, moonless night; the sound of the water slipping from our oars, resisting smoothly, blackly, our cautious progress from the mouth of the Salt River. The meagre lights of the town – so few of them, here and there a flickering in a window; torches on the lookout points of the Castle – fading into a mere glimmer. Behind, the looming presence of the mountain against the shimmering dust of the stars. Something infinitely reassuring about them. Orion striding across the sky. The Plough. The Great Bear. And that other constellation of these austral parts, the Southern Cross, right next to the blackest black – a Dark Hole – of the Coal Sack. Pointing resolutely – but to what?

Perhaps it was as well I didn't yet know.

At last the black hull of *'t Huys te Marquette*. The busy sounds above: men shifting cargo, checking ropes and sails, stowing, cleaning, packing; occasionally an eruption of laughter, a bout of cursing.

In three months the ship would dock at Texel. Back in Europe. Freedom. Then why was there no elation at the prospect, no rush of joy at leaving this unjust and cursed place? Why, instead, this near-reluctance at relinquishing what I couldn't even define? What was there about this land, the land itself – its spaces, shapes, the unknown clicking tongues of its interior, tracts of emptiness, rich voices of people, strange songs, untellable stories, droughts, pests, fear, exhilaration: Monomotapa the unknown, the ever unknowable – that suddenly appeared to restrain me?

Yet this was not the moment to hesitate. We were there, the ship was ready, the ladder hanging from the keel, exactly as Nic Wijs had assured me it would; after his many years at Cabo he had friends aboard practically every visiting vessel.

'You go first,' I said. 'You know your mates up there.'

'I'll tug at the ladder when you can follow. *Tot straks*, Estienne.'

'*A bientôt*, Nic.'

My real reason was senseless and sentimental: to be alone, for a last few minutes, with the darkness of this benighted adopted land. To stare at the mass of the mountain, black upon black, solid, threatening, reassuring. To savour the little I knew and the immensity of what I should have wished to know but which was now denied me.

Voices from above. A few shouts, muffled talk. I held my hand lightly to the coarse weave of the rope ladder, ready to react to the slightest movement; yet feeling, with increasing urgency, the pull of the land behind.

A single loud outcry – 'Nooooo!' – immediately drowned by other voices. Then silence.

Had it been Nic's voice?

Even today I do not know for sure what happened on that dark deck. How could anyone but Nic's trusted accomplices have known beforehand of our plans? I couldn't even tell for sure, then, that Nic Wijs *had* been captured aboard; but I didn't wait to find out more either. Straining, tugging, heaving, driven by fear – yet also inexplicably and unreasonably elated at the thought of going back (to prosecution, persecution, prison, the machinations of power?) – I rowed back through the slick black water. I was sure I could hear, behind me, the splash of oars following rapidly in my wake. But I did not wait, the moment my little boat scraped across the coarse broken shells of the beach, to investigate.

Blindly I stumbled from the water onto the land. The land that had rejected me; the land I now claimed.

I returned to the Castle. This I have not divulged to anyone before. How could I? No one would understand. Time and time again since they finally got hold of me again they have interrogated me about those events following my *cavale*. All I have told them was that after being separated from Nic Wijs I rowed to the shore and thence proceeded to the Roode Bloem, and the Tijgerberg, and finally to Drakenstein. But what I have omitted was that I first returned to my *cagie* in the Castle: and this would probably be judged, from the outside, as the most irresponsible, and the least reasonable, of my actions. Yet there was little risk, at that hour of the night. Knowing only too well the movements of the night guard it was not too difficult to re-enter through the main gate, and scuttle back to my quarters on the Katzenellenbogen Bastion to retrieve my book which was the only valuable possession I had left.

In order to scale the back wall on my way out it had been necessary to leave the weighty tome behind, albeit *à contrecoeur*. But the moment our original mission had gone awry – poor, poor Nic Wijs! – I'd told myself that having left behind the only true companion I'd had through those many years of wandering must have marked our enterprise; be it superstition or not, I knew I *had* to secure it first, otherwise everything else might go awry on the long journey ahead.

It was just before two in the morning, moments after the guard had left the front tower, that I slipped through the main gate into the unpredictable night and was gone, clutching to my body the book which had already saved my life once and might do so again.

Imagined readings from my book, the only possible escape from this dark confinement. I remember the story of the hidalgo's descent into the cave of Montesinos, and his subsequent account of the amazing encounter he'd had down there with the heroes of the Battle of Roncesvalles, three hundred years earlier – an account so astounding that the narrator of the history himself, Cidi Hamete Benengeli, is led to confess that he does not know what to make of it. 'I cannot persuade myself that all that is written in the previous chapter literally happened to the Knight of the Doleful Countenance,' he writes (or words to that effect). 'The reason is that all the previous adventures have all seemed more or less probable, but this one of the cave exceeds all reasonable limits. At the same time I cannot imagine that this most truthful knight could be lying. So I write it down without affirming either truth or falsehood, leaving it to you, wise reader, to judge for yourself.'

And then, many pages later, the hidalgo and his squire are blindfolded by the malicious Duke, and put on the back of a wooden horse called Clavileño, and dispatched on what may or may not be a journey through the heavens. On their return Don Quixote remains silent and pensive; but Sancho, who by now has entered into the spirit of their adventures, launches enthusiastically into an account of the miraculous things he has seen on the way. Don Quixote makes no comment, but after all the others have gone, he goes quietly to Sancho and whispers to him, 'Look, if you want me to believe what you say you saw in the sky, I wish you to accept my account of what I saw in the Cave of Montesinos. I say no more.'

And what more, I have often wondered, *can* be said? They have each other, to put it crudely, by the balls.

Perhaps all stories reach for the balls?

But then, what is there for me to reach for in this dungeon? There is only you, Rosette, and you are already a memory feeding on itself. And Jeanne, who was but a voice: indispensable and often inspiring, but breath only, a stirring of wind, a featherstroke from the beyond, a flutter of the impossible.

When Nic Wijs and I set out from the Castle it was with the intention, as I have made very clear, I trust, of pursuing justice abroad. It was, in other words, a continuation of the same processes I had been involved in prior to my evasion.

When I returned, a few hours later, to collect my book and set out again, everything had changed. The final opportunity of an appeal had been denied; and I myself had renounced the idea of finding justice within their system. In heading, not towards the sea, but inland, it was a different kind of choice altogether, and I a different person.

My first sortie on that tremendous night was no escape: it was merely another, if final, step along a way I had been following all along. But the second *was* escaping – not outward, but inward, into the heart of the land.

You might say, Rosette, that I had finally accepted, as you had done so long before, the challenge of my own navel.

And so I departed from the town in the dark on what was to be my second voyage of discovery, quite unobserved, and proceeded so far that night that at daybreak, when I approached the farm of Roode Bloem, I thought I was safe; and that even if anyone came out to search for me I should not be found.

Part the Second

There is occasion on a journey to look past beginning and beyond end. In that second journey I rediscover the first; and both are already informed by the third. And now I observe it all anew, moving across the invisible walls of my cell: ten wagons, ten men and a boy (and myself; and of course Jeanne), some slaves, numerous hottentot servants; grinding very slowly through kloofs and valleys – jagged mountain ranges to the right, the sea an improbable dark blue smudge on the left – and then through landscapes of bone and rock, on and on, to a river once presumed ultimate, and beyond, wandering like Israelites in a desert of scrub and shale; then following another course which gradually becomes wider and deeper, dark green, the river named by the ancients Vigiti Magna, until we read in the distance, inscribed on the white sky, the great walls, the arches and towers, of a city previously only dreamed, Monomotapa.

It is, we are soon to ascertain, a town of some fifteen thousand inhabitants, on the right bank of the magic river. In shape it is roughly rectangular, some twelve hundred yards in length, five hundred in width. The outer defences consist of a stone wall four feet thick, and from eighteen to thirty feet high, dropping sheer into a series of moats which draw their water directly from the river. There are no fewer than thirty-four flanking towers; and five gates, with two posterns. A stone bridge, with nineteen arches and lined with houses, spans the river to the south side. On the penultimate arch a small fort has been built, consisting of two towers linked by a vaulted entry. The last arch carries a drawbridge (itself protected by an earth redoubt) to isolate the stronghold.

'It looks like Orléans from afar,' whispers Jeanne, 'the way it was long ago, when I saw it the first time.'

· 177 ·

If at first we are apprehensive about drawing too close it soon becomes clear that we have nothing to fear from the inhabitants of Monomotapa. I can only assume that they have in some fashion been alerted to our approach, because while we are still deliberating, at a safe distance, about how best to proceed, the drawbridge on our side of the river is lowered and a detachment of warriors comes riding out towards us on what seem like immaculate white horses, each of them so perfect as to make the memory of Allemann's appear dun and paltry by comparison. It is only when they reach us that I realise their steeds are, in fact, unicorns. The men themselves are bedecked in gold, their shining helmets plumed with *panaches* of many colours; and as they approach, riding two abreast, they fan out on either side to form a splendid escort.

What most amazes me is that they address us in Latin, which immediately places me – even though my command of that dead tongue has always been deficient – in an enviable position among my even more uncouth companions. We are promptly assured of their peaceful intentions and invited inside their walls.

These men are all, I should specify, European in appearance, although in stature they are closer to that of the smaller natives.

A curiosity which cannot but impress me, both on our way through tortuous streets and inside the royal palace to which we are so graciously escorted, is that all the male persons we encounter are covered, from head to foot, in some or other form of gold – gold-spun cloth, gold-leafed breastplates and knee-high boots, golden gloves, golden tricornes – leaving only a portion of the visage uncovered. The females, on the other hand, from infant girls to old crones, are all stark naked, except for gold ornaments: outrageously elaborate, high-piled head-dresses, colliers, bracelets and ankle-rings (the number of which varies, as far as I can make out, according to age). What makes their nudity even more striking is that their smooth limbs, both underarm and groin, show no trace whatsoever of bodily hair, as if that were their natural state. This shows off to particular effect the plaited gold rings that pierce, in each of them, the left nipple and the left lip of the genital cleft.

We are escorted to the royal palace, a building set apart from the others in the middle of the town, not particularly tall, but of striking beauty and symmetry, covered over its full extent from ground to spire with finely hammered gold leaf.

In a hall of impressive proportions we are invited to seat ourselves on rich embroidered cushions on the gold-paved floor, and closely questioned by the leader of our escort as to the cause of our unprecedented venture into the deep interior. When he learns that we have come in search of sheep and cattle, but that the hottentots in the more accessible regions of the Colony have refused to supply in our needs, he waxes most generous (at least that is what I deduce from the numerous words ending in -*issima* he uses in his reply), and undertakes to furnish us with whatsoever we desire. But first, he insists, our appearance demonstrates to his discerning eyes other needs that require more urgent attention: and indeed we are in a dismal state after so many weeks in the desert.

I shall not bore you with details of the sumptuous reception that is offered us: a feast undulating and reverberating through at least twenty-one days and nights (you will soon appreciate the impossibility of *post facto* certainty in this regard), and presided over by the Queen herself – the only female, by the way, whose nakedness is fully covered: in green, I should specify, so wondrously and richly attired that she looks the very soul of stateliness. And certainly the most desirable – if also the most unapproachable – woman I have ever set eyes on. Tall and young, with long hair, red and bright as copper.

The variety of the food and entertainment, the constantly changing circumstances as we progress from one chamber to the next (since each new item of sensual delectation requires a displacement to another space, each more ravishing than the previous), are such as to bedazzle the senses.

A most piquant touch is provided by the custom of the place to alternate gastronomic and sexual degustation: after each course in the seemingly interminable banquet an *entr'acte* is offered involving some presentation to stimulate the sensibilities (a show of virgins and unicorns, a puppet performance depicting a story of knights and heathen Saracens and a beautiful girl named Melisendra, music, dancing, prestidigitation of every imaginable kind); and following each such presentation a drove of nubile girls appears with whom the guests are encouraged to dally and take their pleasure – one girl for each guest after the first course, two after the second, three after the third, et caetera – in consequence of which the intervals between courses grow ever longer. By the thirty-second course (which is as far as I am able to count), more than a day elapses between the servings, as you may well imagine.

After the reception my ten companions and I are shown to bedrooms and allowed to rest for what may well be a week or more. I cannot speak for the others here, as each is shown into a separate chamber; but when at last I awake it is to find myself most fastidiously and lasciviously attended by a whole flock of girls, the aim of which preparation only becomes clear when they at last disperse, leaving me in a state of inordinate carnal appetite, whereupon none other than the Queen herself – blessed by the mellifluous name of Altisidora – makes her appearance. For propriety's sake, and out of respect for my hostess, I cannot bring myself to divulge particulars of the ensuing scene, but which no doubt you can, at least *en gros*, imagine for yourself.

This is another kind of journey, which lasts for an eternity before I am allowed – weak-kneed, aching in every limb, drained of all moisture, body and mind suffused with bliss – to rejoin my companions. And when we reluctantly prepare to take our leave, we find to our elation a whole horde of sheep and cattle awaiting us; and a wagonload of gold ornaments; and service wagons piled high with fodder, and servants in attendance, to escort us as far as the frontier of our Colony where we left our own servants to bide our return.

· *178* ·

If you will not believe me, how can I persuade you of anything else I witnessed or experienced en route?

Is any one phenomenon in this world more amazing than any other?

· *179* ·

'As my trial neared its end,' Jeanne told me, 'the council had to take a vote on whether I should be tortured or not. Maître Aubert Morel, one of those who favoured the rack, said he thought it expedient to put me to the torture in order to discover, as he phrased it, "the truth of my lies". But they never did.'

We first set out, the ten farmers and I, and Jeanne, late in 1738, from their various farms scattered through the outlying districts, from Stellenbosch and Drakenstein to the Breede River and the Piquet Berg, and converged on the property of that poor man, Matthys Willemsz, whose very grammar had once been devastated by a storm.

In a sense our enterprise involved two different treks which just happened to coincide in time and space.

Hendrik Ras and the others, their wagons loaded to capacity with beads and tobacco, brandy, copper, items of clothing and the trinkets and baubles of barter, were heading for the land of the little Namaquas some distance beyond the Oliphants River; intending, if the circumstances proved propitious, to proceed even beyond the Gariep to the Great Namaquas, in what was reputed to be a region of numberless long-horned cattle and fat-tailed sheep.

My journey was different. I went in search of you: somewhere in that vast interior, I knew, you had found sanctuary, and as surely as I had unfettered you I should trace the invisible line of your flight and reclaim you.

You, and Monomotapa. These, too, had become identical. If I found you, of that I was convinced, I would have found the magic land. If ever I discovered Monomotapa you would be there.

Initially I had resisted Hendrik Ras's entreaties. He had been planning this journey ever since I'd first met him, and every time something had happened to prevent it. Most importantly, there had been the protracted illness of his little lame daughter

Marietjie who'd been wasting away over many months. And then Landdrost Lourens himself had got wind of the project and moved to abort it. 'You know this kind of bartering is illegal,' he'd told Hendrik. 'We can't let just anyone pack up and trek into the interior and create trouble with the hottentots. One of these days there'll be full-scale war and you people will be responsible.' 'Then on my head be it,' Ras had said. 'Now get off my farm or I'll set my dogs on you.' 'I'll be keeping a watch on you,' Lourens had warned him. 'One wrong move and I'll have the lot of you marched off to the Dark Hole.'

But during the winter of '38 the little girl had died; and in the early spring the Landdrost and most of his *heemraden* had gone off on commando towards the north-east where Bushmen marauders had killed a few farmers. Hannie Ras, finding the brooding presence of her husband too much to bear any longer, had urged him to get off his broad backside; and fleet-footed messengers, spurred on by dire threats of punishment, had rapidly moved to and fro among the farms of Hendrik's most trusted friends; and by late August we set out.

My own inclination was to stay out of it. No one in Cabo knew where I was; to the best of their knowledge I'd escaped to the Netherlands. That suited me. The less I ever had to do with that corrupt bunch again the better. And joining a trek of this nature was likely sooner or later to attract attention. I much preferred to remain in my *terroir* on Tante Louise's farm and help the generous old soul, taking off weekends to visit the farms of younger widows in the neighbourhood where, if I say so myself, my amorous attentions were soon in high demand. But Jeanne would have none of my remaining behind.

'You cannot avoid trouble forever, Estienne,' she said. 'It's better to get involved from the beginning.'

'I've had enough problems and what good has it done me?' I protested. 'What must happen will happen. There's no sense in forcing anything.'

'You're a disgrace to your own dreams.'

'No. I'm just not disposed to provoke unnecessary trouble. We can no more precipitate events than stop them.'

'If you don't, you're either a fool or a coward.'

'What happened when *you* tried to interfere with history?' Always this challenge of the last resort.

And, again as always, the reply, 'In the end it was worth it.'

'Not for you!'

'But I wasn't in it for myself. Nor should you be.'

'Tante Louise needs me.'

'She needed you before. Then you returned to Cabo.'

'She's worse now, she needs me more.'

'Is it this old widow you're concerned with or the younger ones you visit so regularly?'

'Do you reproach me for being a man?'

'No. But I reproach you for being a slave to your *vit*.' A humourless chuckle. 'Unless that means the same thing.'

'You have no respect for me, Jeanne!'

'That's true.'

Piqued, I was silent for a long time. Then I tried a new approach. 'I am too small for history, Jeanne.'

'Do you think it was different when I set out from Domrémy the first time, with my poor kind uncle Durand Laxart, for Vaucouleurs? I was seventeen. I couldn't even ride a horse, let alone command an army. But I went, because my voices told me. And now I'm telling *you*.'

'I must bide my time.'

'Chronology is our challenge,' she said. 'Break the chain, as you once broke Rosette's.'

'It would be mad, or foolish,' I persisted.

'I should hope so. And preferably both. Otherwise you'd have no chance at all.'

'You want me to go?'

'*You* must want to go.'

'What purpose can it possibly serve?'

'You must get to know your troops.'

'Troops? For what? I'm not at war.'

'Not yet.'

'Tell me what you mean.'

'I want you to be prepared, Estienne. For anything.'

'What preparation lies in bartering cheap beads and brandy and tobacco for some sheep or cattle?'

'That's not what you're going for.'

'For what then?'

'To find Rosette. To find Monomotapa. To interfere with history.'

'Do you have a sign for me so that I may believe what you're saying?'

'To believe without a sign is better.'

And so I went.

· *182* ·

'Depraved' was the word I had used, I think, in my superfluous journal on that first journey along the west coast, to describe the nature and the circumstances of those unfortunate colonists we'd encountered on their dismal farms, shorn of human contact and comfort and subsiding slowly, it had then seemed to me, into a state of abject lethargy and abysmal ignorance. Men like that angry creature Hendrik Kruger who'd tried to blast us off his farm; or the wretched Matthys Willemsz; or the many others whose existence showed no difference from that of their sullen cattle, yapping dogs or scratching fowls. And 'savages' was the word I'd used in my mind to designate the band of ruffians that had beaten me black and blue on my way back to Cabo after my months as a *pasganger*, remember?

Somehow I now began to see them in a different light (and not only because I was now as bearded and unkempt in my appearance as they were). Hendrik Ras had been the agent of my changed perception. I had taken a liking to him long before, as you know; but the long winter of '38, which I spent partly with Tante Louise at *Orléans* and partly with him on his farm in the Roodezands Kloof after he'd sent word of his child's decline, sealed the friendship. Seeing that great bull of a man grieve for his desperately ill child, was one of the most painful experiences of my life. Unable to find words for his suffering, huddled on a *riempie* chair beside his daughter's bed, filling the dusky space with his gloom, he would remain for hours in one position, moving only to fetch her a mug of water or to feel her forehead with a clumsy paw. When someone addressed him, he would look up with uncomprehending eyes, frowning or shaking his head, and then return, still silent, to his massive vigil.

When she died at the beginning of August – there was no specific moment to mark the event, she seemed simply to slip away across some indefinite threshold – he took the frail bundle in his arms and started wandering across the farm in the way he'd used to do before, when she'd still been alive. We all thought (his wife Hannie, his four sons, I) it was a kind of leavetaking, and that he would come back in due course to put her away in the grave already dug behind the house. But when he returned, it was to go to sleep with Marietjie's body still clutched to him; and the next day he set out on his wandering again.

I remembered what I had once seen, on that first journey with Allemann, in a flock of baboons whose antics we had observed on the bank of some dry river: among them had been an emaciated female carrying with her, wherever she went, the decayed and shrivelled corpse of a baby. It had been dead so long that the little skull was quite exposed, dry white bone that seemed as frail as a small calabash and made an eerie hollow scraping sound whenever it was briefly put down.

On the fourth day of Hendrik's mourning it became evident that something would have to be done. Hannie's admonishing and pleading was ignored as if he had not even heard her; the sons' attempts were brushed away. When I approached him, he merely looked at me, uttering an animal groan – but whether it was in pain, or meant as threat or warning, was impossible to tell – and moved away, still clutching the rag-doll child to his body.

On the morning of the fifth day Hannie took control. Moving cautiously, in obvious trepidation, the three older sons (the youngest was but a boy of twelve), following her stern command, set upon him, and brought him down, and tore the dilapidated little bundle from his arms, while all the time he bellowed like a cornered buffalo, and thrashed about and fought, and nearly overpowered his assailants; but they managed to hold him down while Hannie herself took the child to the ready grave – wrapped in a cloth, like a small loaf of bread – and rolled it in, and ordered me to fill in the hole with the rich red soil heaped up around it.

Only then did they let Hendrik go.

All day long he raged. We stayed well out of his way. He broke most of the furniture in the house, even smashed down the doors. In the shed, which two years earlier I'd helped him build, he attacked the bags of wheat stored there, and tossed them about, and set to his wagon and tore it apart, and broke all the spokes from the wheels. His fury still unquelled, he next marched to the huts of the slaves and servants. Having witnessed from a safe distance the ravages of his rage, they had all taken to their heels in time, scattering across the farm, except for one man who was ill and had crawled under a heap of old skins. But Hendrik, attracted by a moan of fear, plucked them away and hauled out the poor creature and strangled him, then hurled away the broken body as one might imagine a rhinoceros tossing in the air the carcass of a victim. And then he marched to the kraal and started killing the sheep. Fortunately they managed, in their panic, to break down the gate and most escaped.

In the late afternoon he came trudging home again, his clothes tattered and caked with dried blood; and striding right past the house he went to the grave where he dropped down on all fours, howling, and began to dig into the earth with his bare blood-stained hands.

That was when Hannie went to him. His sons and I stared in horror; one of them went inside to collect a gun. But it wasn't necessary. That small, thin wisp of a woman went up to him, placed her hand on his buttock-sized shoulder, and said quietly, 'Now that's enough, Hendrik. Let her be. She is at peace.'

He stopped, and looked up at her. Then nodded dumbly; and she helped him up and led him into the house. She boiled a great cauldron of water on the open hearth, and filled a barrel from it, and stripped the clothes from him, and bathed his huge body, meticulously scrubbing all the mud and dirt and dried blood from him, and then brought him a clean shirt and breeches.

The following day we all set to work repairing the damage. No one spoke Marietjie's name again. In all that time I never saw Hannie shed a tear. A week later she told Hendrik that it was time he went on the journey he'd been talking about for so long. 'The Landdrost is away, this is a good time. I've had enough of your brooding about the house.'

'You need me here.'

'I have our sons to take care of me,' she said, in her no-nonsense way. 'Take young Daniel with you. It will do him good. You need a change. And I need time to grieve. She was my child too.'

· *183* ·

All the men on our expedition were known to me from before. Apart from Hendrik Ras there were the irascible Hendrik Kruger, and poor Matthys Willemsz; the impetuous Jan la Grange who had threatened to blast us off his farm when I had visited him with Swellengrebel the year before; and Arnoldus

Basson, Sybrand van Dyk and Gert Campher, whose leave from military service Swellengrebel had assured on that same mission. Also Jan Olivier, Lood Putter and Koos Jansen, who had been party, two years earlier, to the attack on me when they'd thought me a representative of the government.

Those from the environs of Stellenbosch, and as far as the Roodezands Kloof and thereabouts, had less to complain of than the others, although they too had had problems with Landdrost Lourens, especially about badly timed call-ups for militia service and official intolerance of delays in the payment of quitrent. Olivier had the aggravating complaint that only a few months earlier Lourens had sent a detachment of armed hottentots to arrest him for debt; and when they couldn't find him – he'd been on a hunting trip to the Warm Springs and beyond – they had had the temerity to take his twelve-year-old son hostage. Had not some of his neighbours, including Putter and Basson, chanced upon the scene the consequences might well have been criminal. In the skirmish that followed two of the armed bandits were shot dead. This so infuriated the Landdrost that he threatened arrest and prosecution, but the farmers in the district, in a rare demonstration of solidarity, had managed to dissuade him by intimating the disclosures they would make should the case ever come to court; so for the time being a state of armed truce prevailed. But the situation was explosive enough.

The others on our expedition had much worse to report, and the outrageous nature of their tales was commensurate with the increasing distance of their abodes from Cabo. The same Hendrik Kruger who'd once acted with such rash violence now appeared almost meek in his response to Hendrik Ras's invitation. Six months earlier his farm – already ravaged by ostriches – had been attacked by Bushmen. His haystacks had been burned down, his wife and two of his children had been killed by poisoned arrows; and the other two had been carried off by the attackers. Kruger and his slaves (his hottentot labourers had all absconded after the attack) had rounded up helpers from the neighbouring farms to follow the Bushmen into the mountains, and several of the marauders had been killed in a series of small skirmishes, but the rest had disappeared like game into the wilderness. As usual. And when at last Kruger had returned to his farm, a shocked and solitary man, it was to find the place razed to the ground. House, sheds, shacks, fields, grazing, all reduced to blackness and ash. On a borrowed wagon he'd travelled to Cabo to lodge a complaint and request permission to barter cattle in the interior so that he could start anew, but this had been promptly turned down: by none other than Daniel van den Henghel. No wonder he decided to join us.

And then the desperate Matthys Willemsz. Somehow he'd managed to stagger to his feet again after that devastating hurricane. But by the time our wagons converged on his farm he appeared, if anything, even more abject than the previous time. His wife, we learned, had never fully recovered from the loss of her child in the storm. Hardly ever speaking a word either to him or the servants, as insignificant as a damp stain on a wall, she'd spent her days staring through the solitary small window in the *voorhuis*. Then she'd fallen pregnant again (the poor man seemed ashamed at having to admit this; and perhaps he had reason to be). But instead of being restored to life by the discovery she'd seemed to waste away even more rapidly. And one day she'd disappeared. Just vanished. Matthys had been out in the veld tracking down a leopard that had killed a lamb; and when he came home she was gone. No sign of her. Not even the slave woman in the house had seen her leave. For weeks Willemsz continued to ride in ever-widening circles around his farm, but she might as well have fluttered away into an empty sky.

In a way, one might say, each one of us on that expedition had joined for reasons of his own. We were all in it together; we all wanted to obtain cattle and sheep; the farms were in need of stock. But deep in his heart each man had set out on a private quest.

What mine was is no secret to you.

· 184 ·

I have no interest in offering you a chronology of our journey. When we got where, what we did when, how we, why we. (Why indeed?) The first time, three years earlier, I had tried to record, in a language not my own, our trajectory through a wilderness, forcing observation and dream into the shapes dictated by the requirements of others – an expedition leader, a governor, the seventeen stern shadows of our European over- lords. This time I was free – as I am free now – to devise the names, the latitudes and longitudes of experience without regard to the prescriptions of others. You will not censure me; you have no demands, not even expectations. (Is that part of the agony?) But it does not mean I was without constraint, or am without inhibition. That you are *there* is frightening enough. And what was that whole expedition if not an attempt at finding, circumscribing, possessing you? Not the 'you' I once desired or held or subjected to me: the woman of flesh and blood, the you of night and stories, of pain and eruption, of shackles and navel, that terrifying hollow, that absence, that silence. But the you now forever secreted in the empty hollow of the land.

Rosette, Rosette. Not even your name contains you. *Least* of all your name explains you.

· 185 ·

Violence our language. A land hostile, empty, strange: it does not talk back, remains inaccessible. Which forces this violence from us, its motive achingly pure. On and on we move through the ever more arid landscape, sowing destruction as we go, voiding the plains of animal life, the white stretched vellum of the sky inscribed with the slow loops of the vultures that survey our route. An orgy of blood, visiting on the creatures we encounter our rage for what eludes us. Likewise, we annihilate kraals and villages and settlements of hostile or indifferent natives, with the single purpose of leaving on that virgin barren place the scrawl of our progress. *We were here.* The curious satisfaction produced by this fundamental language on an ever more intractable parchment of stone and sand. Like the animals I have witnessed demarcating their territory – lion, leopard, buffalo, hippogryph – with piss, we stain the unknown with our presence. To acquire, to conquer, to have, to possess: I have therefore I am. Land, you are woman. Woman, you are mine. Is this not beautiful? I am drunk with the bared beauty of the place. I spill my seed upon the ground. I even begin to understand – if I cannot bring myself to forgive – the infamous Sergeant Kok. Violent death is ineluctable; the language of love. But my possession, if I dare say so, is purer than Kok's: he had anterior motive: what compels *me* is ulterior.

· *186* ·

It is curious to travel for three months and more without encountering a single human being. We had prolonged arguments about this at night round the fire. Some of those in our midst contended that it might be possible to regard the hottentots as human beings, descended probably from the ancient Jews (with whom they shared the custom of a form of circumcision, except that in the case of the hottentots it concerned the removal of a testicle rather than a prepuce) or the Troglodytes (who shared with them their manner of hunting, their habit of giving their children the names of favourite beasts, as of an ox

236

or a sheep, and their funeral ceremonies such as only too often we had occasion to observe). Others among us differed strongly, on various grounds. What suggested to me that the hottentots of this land may in fact be considered as much a species of fauna as, say, gazelle or ostrich or camelopard, was – firstly – their language, which (as I had occasion to remark earlier) has nothing of sound or articulation that is peculiar to man in it, but resembling, rather, the noise of irritated turkey-cocks or the chattering of magpies; and – secondly – their habit of bestowing upon any man who singly encounters and slays a lion, tiger, leopard, elephant, rhinoceros or eland, what I can only call the Order of the Piss. This takes the form of a ceremony in which the hero squats himself down on a mat, and all the men take up position around him. Joy sits flush in the faces of the hero and his friends; envy contracts the features of others, when up to the hero marches the oldest man in the community and proceeds to piss upon him from head to foot, followed by all the others; the more piss the more honour.

· *187* ·

In terms of belligerence or treacherousness, too, there often was little to choose between hottentots and other animals. I realise, Rosette, that you may hold strongly different opinions on this (and with Jeanne, too, I had many arguments on the matter during sleepless nights obsessed with stars and silence), but consider this:

Not many leagues from the stream which had marked the point of our return on the first journey we came, one morning, upon a whole herd of tuskless elephants (known among the colonists as *poeskop* elephants, a word derived, as far as I can make out, from a rude local designation of the female parts; the ancient fear of the *vagina dentata* must run deep in these regions).

We were led, on this particular outing, by a young man of

barely twenty, one Pieter de Bruyn, whom we had the good fortune to meet on our way to the Oliphants River: in spite of his tender age he'd already acquired a considerable reputation as an elephant hunter; barely a year earlier he had already ventured beyond the last frontier of the colony, returning with a greater load of ivory than had ever been brought home before. An impetuous youngster, I may add, unafraid of death itself; and Hendrik Ras in particular had taken a liking to him (among other things, I surmise, because Hendrik's own youngest son David, whom he'd brought with him on our expedition, was a rather nervous and effeminate boy, which fact led to many an unpleasant confrontation, in which I sometimes had to intervene). It was Hendrik's idea that we should invite this Pieter de Bruyn to guide us into those regions which he alone among us had visited before.

Now the young de Bruyn was particularly aggrieved by the discovery of the *poeskop* herd, as he had somehow staked his pride as an elephant hunter on guiding us to large-tusked specimens. And in some illogical way his agitation had communicated itself to the rest of us, so that in a kind of precipitate rage we had proceeded almost immediately to the annihilation of the entire herd, males, females and young. I mention this because, normally, the sole motive for killing elephants is of course their precious ivory. Yet in this instance it was the *absence* of tusks that propelled us into a fury of destruction – as if that abnormality most grievously insulted us. It went beyond the simplicity of frustration: it was a kind of vengeance we were compelled to visit upon animals that had attempted to evade our accepted definition of them. There was no sense of accomplishment, certainly no pride, in the contemplation of our action. It was simply something that had had to be done. And then we moved on.

What prompted an uneasy reconsideration of the event was the experience of the following night, when in the profound nocturnal peace, without the slightest sound of warning, not even the snapping of a twig, our camp was suddenly invaded by a horde of trumpeting elephants. In the eerie light of our fires (in the brief minutes before they were utterly stamped out) we could not but notice that every single elephant in this herd was fully tusked, probably the most magnificent display of ivory any of us had ever witnessed. But there was no time for leisurely observation; there was not even time to grab our guns and shoot as we all scrambled and scuttled for our lives to avoid the thundering herd of avenging beasts. The whole episode could not have lasted for more than five minutes. Then they were gone, and the thunder of their stampede rumbled off into the distance, followed by a most profound and chilling silence.

Fearful of their return we did not dare emerge from our hiding-places, some of them quite distant from the scene I assure you, before the sun was out. A scene of devastation met our incredulous eyes. Two hottentots, a slave, and one of the colonists (the lethargic Sybrand van Dyk) had been trampled, and their bleeding bodies lay scattered in weird distortions. Van Dyk, thank God, although badly injured (to this day he has a limp, and a useless arm), was not dead; but the three others had been reduced to small bundles of flesh and bone.

That was but one part of the devastation. Hardly a single wagon or tent had escaped the attack. Every object of any size – including barrels and kegs, boxes, wagon-chests, wheels – had been battered out of shape. Much of our precious bartering proviand was destroyed. Even guns and muskets lay scattered over a wide area, bent and broken by the great tusks and trunks and feet. The kraal of thornbushes we had erected for our cattle was quite flattened, the branches flung far and wide; the oxen and sheep had escaped in a panic.

Unable to move on, yet terrified of what might yet happen, we had no choice but to remain in that place for several weeks, burying the dead, tending the wounded Sybrand van Dyk, rounding up what had remained of the oxen (several had fallen prey to predators; others had simply run away so far that they

239

could not be found), laboriously repairing the wagons and *matériel*. We assured a constant watch by four of our men while the others toiled. But the elephants never returned. Nor could we find a trace of them once we had sufficiently restored our camp to risk a punitive expedition.

I should add that, apart from young Pieter de Bruyn who was anxious to get away as soon as possible and had to be restrained, with some unpleasant force, not one among us thought of turning back. More than ever we were resolved to proceed and conclude the business we had come for.

· *188* ·

And now consider this. Beyond the Oliphants River, in a region of drought worse than anything I could ever have imagined, among a tribe known – as far as human ear could make out – as the Kabobiquas, we encountered grave problems in our attempts at bartering. As you know, we'd already experienced difficulties in this regard on the first journey when the hottentots' reluctance to part with their cattle occasionally required quite an assertive approach; but as bartering had not been, then, an important consideration (the company requiring only such cattle or sheep as had to be slaughtered for our sustenance from day to day) we were not unduly discouraged or hindered. On this occasion, however, we really needed stock, and in sizeable quantities. At the same time we lacked, after the elephant stampede, such commodities as are most specifically known for their appeal to the indigenous tribes – notably brandy. This meant that at least a modicum of force was required to persuade some hottentots to part with their animals. We had already, among the Lesser Namaquas, encountered some resistance. Now, among the Kabobiquas, occurred a particularly unfortunate incident – all the more so as the negotiations began in what seemed to be a relaxed and even generous spirit. These negotiations were facilitated by the fact that two of the tame hottentots on our expedition were of Kabobiqua provenance and eager to impress us with their proficiency as interpreters.

My own coup, after some hundred sheep and more than fifty oxen had already been acquired, lay in persuading the chief of the tribe to part with an ox, the like of which I had never seen before: a magnificent animal of gigantic size, with two enormous horns curving symmetrically backward before bending forward again in perfect semicircles, the points no less than four feet and eight inches apart. You will appreciate the haggling and bargaining and argument it caused to persuade the chief to part with this animal. But in the end he could not resist the collection of articles offered in exchange: a tinderbox, several strings of brightly coloured glass beads, two copper bracelets, a number of iron nails, and my last few spans of rolled tobacco.

Triumphantly we moved off, having employed several of the Kabobiquas to drive the newly acquired sheep and cattle. However, when we woke up the following morning it was to find a number of the tribe, including the grizzled chief, approaching the camp. A great altercation broke out between them and our own attendants; and when at last, with considerable effort, we succeeded in securing the intervention of our interpreters it transpired that the tribe had decided to cancel the transactions, notably that involving my ox, and had come to repossess the stock.

We began by offering them more trinkets, and initially they appeared to be appeased by this munificence; but after half an hour of further argument, mainly among themselves and untranslated, they threw down all the articles we had already paid them (minus the tobacco which had presumably been consumed) and proceeded towards the kraals to reclaim the animals. Understandably, however much *à contrecoeur*, we brought some force to bear on the situation, and after a dozen or so of the negotiators had bitten the dust the others had the wisdom to flee – in such precipitation, I should add, that several even shed their karosses and the small aprons protecting their shameful parts, leaving them stark naked.

That, we presumed, settled the matter. But to make doubly sure we immediately broke camp and began to move on, further inland, covering an impressive distance in the course of the day and some hours into the night. We took the precaution of posting guards, but when for three successive nights nothing untoward occurred – except for the desertion of our two tame Kabobiquas – we became convinced that the event was now conclusively behind us. Which made the events of the fourth night all the more unexpected, and *lâche*.

Exactly as in the previous episode with the elephants our camp was treacherously overrun by the enemy horde, who tore open the kraals and drove out the cattle, set fire to the wagons, and let loose upon us a veritable hurricane of arrows. Miraculously, we lost only two of our number: David, the young son Hendrik Ras had brought with him, and a wild farmer, Koos Pretorius, who had joined the trek near the Snake River. Two more, Hendrik Kruger and Koos Jansen, were seriously wounded, but recovered after protracted agonies. Among our attendants three hottentots and a slave belonging to Gert Campher were also killed; the slave represented a particularly grave loss as Campher had paid no less than ninety rix dollars for him barely six months before.

What particularly shocked us was the discovery, in the light of the following day, after we had descended painfully from the thorn trees in which most of us had sought refuge, that in the attack the hottentots had killed a number of their own cattle, simply – it seemed – because they could not drive the animals back with them. Included in these losses was the majestic ox I had acquired at such expense.

We soon mounted an armed expedition to avenge the raid; but arriving at the site of the Kabobiqua settlement we found it totally deserted, as if the entire tribe had dissolved into the surrounding dun-coloured emptiness.

It took us another two full weeks to repair the damage and set forth once more, undaunted in our endeavours to succeed. After this experience I had the impression that few among us still persisted in the error of believing that hottentots were human.

· *189* ·

One useful result of the encounter was that we were now mentally and physically prepared to expect treachery from the natives; and thenceforth, on every occasion we came upon a tribal settlement, we took the precaution of first exterminating the hottentots (even those who treacherously pretended to be friendly) before appropriating whatever sheep and cattle could be rounded up in the environs. Never again would we be fooled by mere appearances.

· *190* ·

A significant consequence of these events was the emergence of a new spirit of unity among the members of our expedition. Previously, we had been a bunch of individuals united only by our common aversion to the authorities in Cabo, and the prospect of barter; bound together by the practicalities of the journey but otherwise independent to the point of idiosyncrasy; suspicion, arguments, altercations were a daily occurence; on several occasions there were even fist-fights, and a semblance of order was maintained largely by everybody's respect for Hendrik Ras's physical strength.

Now, increasingly, through the experience of a shared adversity, there was a consciousness of our common purpose, even, if

I dare say so, a sense of mission into, and in, Africa. Only the nature of that mission, to my regret, was hardly defined. And sometimes I wonder, sometimes I fear, that it went no further than the urge to survive.

· *191* ·

Occasionally this urge was itself translated in conflicting ways. For example, the devastating encounter with the Kabobiquas was curiously negated when one of the more unpredictable members of our group, Willem van Wyk, a man given as much to bouts of magnanimity as sudden rages, decided, upon our approach to the land of the Greater Namaquas, to take to himself a woman from that tribe.

This was how it happened: a few days this side of the Great River van Wyk and young Pieter de Bruyn were dispatched, on horseback, to reconnoitre the way ahead – a necessary precaution in view of our previous experiences. When they returned they brought tidings of a large and seemingly prosperous Namaqua settlement on the far bank of the river. Unlike some of the tribes encountered previously these natives, van Wyk and de Bruyn reported, seemed well-disposed towards the idea of our arrival. As a token of their hospitality the chief, known as Gal, had even invited Willem van Wyk to marry his own daughter. This in itself was not particularly unusual, and if Willem had availed himself of the opportunity, after so many weeks of sexual privation, to make as much use of the woman as he could or would before discarding her, no one would have given it a second thought; but what did take us by surprise was Willem's ready acceptance of the female not as chattel or as concubine but as his spouse.

'You might as well marry a baboon,' Hendrik Ras told him (in the presence of the woman in question; but it was of course

244

doubtful whether she understood anything). 'Do you have no shame?'

'She can do everything a white woman can,' van Wyk said airily, 'except talk back. That suits me. If any man here has anything more to say about it, then say it now or forever hold your peace.'

We held our peace; from what we had seen of him, and from the way he held his musket, we knew better than to provoke Willem van Wyk.

But as you can well imagine the event stirred up a hornet's nest of uncomfortable thoughts in me and provoked many an argument with Jeanne.

'The man is a disgrace to all of us. A hottentot woman!'

'Suppose you were mistaken about the hottentots?'

'I've seen enough of them to believe the evidence of my eyes.'

'Why *should* it disturb you so, Estienne? Have you yourself not allowed a slave woman to dictate much of the course and content of your life?'

'Rosette is different!'

'Perhaps Willem van Wyk thinks the same about this woman?'

· *192* ·

You may have noticed that I do not particularly like myself.

· *193* ·

The thing, I think, is this: that this land does not make it easy for a man to hold fixed opinions. There are so few certainties. Would that stones were only stones, and rivers wholly rivers and nothing but rivers, and the yellow puff-balls of thorntrees merely dust; that things had no meaning beyond themselves: existing, having as their only meaning themselves.

· 194 ·

In extremis. Now here; but then too, in those endless tracts beyond the last known river, landscapes of shimmering heat from which, for days on end, all signs of life had been burned away, clean, to the bone. The satisfaction of irreducible anatomy, but seared with the pure pain of consciousness. And yet we would not turn back. Ahead, I knew, lay Monomotapa. Beyond, always beyond. And you.

Wherever we came, whomever we encountered, I enquired about traces of your transit, on horseback or on foot; not once was there the merest rumour of your passage. At least, or so I furiously believed, you were still alive: had you died, surely there would have been a record of your end, a testimony of bones. The very fact that no one had seen you meant that you were there, your absence your most infallible guarantee.

And so I persevered; we persevered.

· 195 ·

Once again, the second time in months, Hendrik Ras had to bury a child. Behind much of the urgency that drove us on I had sensed his rage to forget about Marietjie; this, too, must have informed his unreasonable expectations of the young David he'd brought along. And his death brought back the full violence of Marietjie's loss as well, but a violence turned inward, not outward in the kind of destruction I had witnessed on the farm. He became more brooding, preoccupied, turned in upon the darknesses in himself. And this, too, contributed to the feeling that we were bound together in a gathering storm of which he was the dangerous eye. We moved through the sere land like an avenging host. Too late I have come to acknowledge that at the first sign of adversity, the elephant stampede, we should have turned back. The energies we accumulated in going on could not in the end but turn against ourselves.

· 196 ·

There was something insanely self-defeating, self-cancelling about this energy. We must have bartered enough sheep and cattle for our needs within days of crossing the Oliphants River: but there was the urge, since we'd come so far, first to find what lay ahead in regions of which only rumours had previously reached Cabo. Then, in going on, we had lost our stock through the elephant stampede, the rigours of the thirstland into which we had penetrated, and the attack of the Kabobiquas. Every time we acquired new sheep and cattle in the settlements we devastated, further and further apart; and every time we lost them again to the depredations of enemies or elements, which would then compel us to proceed still further – in the knowledge that behind us there was only emptiness. But in the knowledge, too, that even if we were to find new stock again it was almost inevitable that driving them back through the desert already traversed would assure their loss. And so we moved ever on, inspired by the fierce illogic of pride, through regions of elementary space and pure futurity, the shrill of cicadas our only accompaniment, absurdity our only certainty.

· 197 ·

From time to time, yes, the monotony was interrupted. Once or twice, wholly unexpectedly, we would come upon a trickling stream or a mud hole, which would cause such a stampede among the emaciated oxen that had survived to pull the wagons that inevitably some of them (or some of our diminishing number of servants) were gored or trampled, or smothered in mud, or – the supreme irony – drowned. A few times there were sudden storms: usually winds unleashed on us from the south-east with sufficient force, it seemed, to blow us from the face of the earth into the heart of hell; and once a thunderstorm that turned the sky into a sheet of fire, while the earth trembled underneath and torrents of rain came down as if to wash the whole of Africa into the distant sea.

Never any moderation; always the extremes of experience as of climate. A crude land, Africa; only the strongest can hope to survive.

· *198* ·

In the kraal of chief Gal of the Greater Namaqua, on the far bank of the Great River, that definitive if unimpressive orange-muddy *limes* between the colony and its beyond, we leave behind – with five of the wagons, a number of servants and a span of oxen – Willem van Wyk and his new wife; and Sybrand van Dyk who has still not fully recovered from the wounds sustained in the elephant stampede; and Gert Campher who has contracted a stomach disease. With the remaining farmers, and a hand-picked collection of hottentots and slaves, I can at last proceed more deeply into the interior, a land where almost no human foot has yet left an imprint. Our guide is still the impetuous young Pieter de Bruyn, the only one among us who has ever ventured beyond the Great River. Having now only five wagons, and – for the time being – ample oxen, we can move at a better pace, more suited to the impatience that drives me on, into that vast beyond where anything is possible.

From time to time small groups of nomads, invariably in a sorry state, and usually on their way from the deep interior to the far coast, would offer us reports – if they happened to speak a language one of our few remaining hottentots could interpret – of what lay ahead. Mostly it was discouraging. But sometimes there would be rumours of abundant pastures and prosperous tribes ahead; and that would set us off again, each wagon now drawn by barely half its normal complement of oxen.

But at last we reached a point where continuing became suicidal. Without even having to discuss it we simply knew that we'd reached the *nec plus ultra*. To drive the oxen any further would mean to kill them; and our own survival depended on them. Pieter de Bruyn did not prove to be of much help either; I was beginning to doubt whether he had really set foot beyond the Great River before. But our situation was so desperate that there was no sense even in reproaching the dejected youngster. (Sooner or later we are all overtaken by our own stories. Their survival may be more certain than ours.)

Then, on the morning we inspanned to turn back south-east, another dilapidated band of nomads, pale with dust, appeared from the vastness beyond with news of a white woman living with a tribe known (as far as I could make out) as the Houzouana, four days to the north.

'Just too bad,' said Hendrik Ras with a shrug. Even that powerful man's shoulders were drooping. 'We cannot go on.'

'But what if it is my wife?' exclaimed Matthys Willemsz in a state of great agitation.

'No woman could have trekked so far on her own.'

I knew better; but I held my tongue. It was hard enough for me to give up, yet what else could I do? I had no wagon of my own, I had to go where Hendrik went.

'I know it is Susanna,' persisted Willemsz. 'How can I

abandon her to this emptiness? Only four more days, Hendrik . . .'

'It will kill us all.'

'Then I'll go on alone.'

'Look at your oxen, man.'

'They can make it.'

'And if you die?'

'So be it.'

One of the others also joined in; soon we were all involved.

'Even if it is your wife, Matthys,' someone said, 'and we know that is impossible, how can you even think of taking her back?'

'Why not?'

'For a woman to come all this way on her own – she'll have lost her mind by now. She'll be raving mad.'

'Then she needs me even more.'

'But suppose . . .' Hendrik Kruger fell silent; even this rude man found it hard to say what had to be said. 'Suppose she's taken a new husband? One of those Houzouanas?'

We waited in trepidation for the outburst which, surely, was now inevitable.

Matthys Willemsz began to cry. We dared not look at the man.

At last he said, very softly, 'Even then I must go to her. Don't you understand?'

I was the first to say, 'I understand, Matthys. I'll go with you if you will.'

There was a murmuring among the others; but then Hendrik Ras said, 'We're all in this together. Let us go.'

· 200 ·

Leaving us behind to follow at the tedious pace that was all our oxen were capable of, Matthys Willemsz went ahead on his own, on the back of the most able ox in the herd. Soon he was a mere dust-devil in the distance.

What our informants had estimated as four days travelling took us over a week. Even though, to spare the oxen, we travelled mostly by night, resting by day in whatever ludicrously inadequate shelter we could find, that week was hell.

But by the fifth day signs of more promising vegetation were beginning to overtake the monochrome grey of the landscape. On the sixth day clouds began to gather. On the seventh day, in the early dawn, the rains came.

At first there were only the sounds of individual drops, increasing to a dull patter on the canvas of the wagon; and an overwhelming earthy smell emanated from the dust. We all crept from our shelters, standing in silence, faces upturned. The hottentots were the first to break into a dance. The rain increased to a steady downpour. One by one we also began to move, a tremor in the limbs that soon became uncontrollable, until we joined the hottentots. Possessed by an irrational exuberance, we stripped the heavy dirty clothes from our bodies. A real sight it must have been, this band of naked men dancing and whirling in the rain, faces and forearms blackened by the sun, the rest of our bodies a stark white. Had some passer-by observed us then there would have been reports in Cabo of an unknown mottled species of *homo sapiens* discovered in the deep heart of the land. Who knows what myths and legends might have been born from us in that pouring half-light as we cavorted and pranced and hunched up and sprang and kicked and danced, arms and legs flung wide, appendages swinging and bobbing comically to an inaudible music; until too exhausted to care we fell down on our backs in the mud, mouths wide open, to let the rain make violent insistent love to us and utterly soak us, as if in preparation for being dissolved into the liquid earth.

Love of parents, I know now, love of brothers and sisters, of family and friends and lovers, all this dies away: only the love of the earth remains.

It is an unnerving experience in that wilderness to meet the white woman who is still quite young, but weatherbeaten and unkempt; tall, with long hair, red and bright as copper, one of our own kind, yet going about near-naked like the hottentots among whom she appears indeed to occupy a place of honour.

No, it is not Matthys Willemsz's runaway wife. (Matthys lies in one of the huts under a bundle of filthy skins of divers origins; he is red-faced and delirious, mumbling incoherently, sitting up from time to time, clutching at invisible tormentors, attended by old women who administer concoctions too malodorous for European words. Whether his illness has been brought on by exhaustion, or by the shock of discovering that the white woman is not his, no one can tell.) This one is named Dora Bothma, and we learn that some years ago she and her husband, having lost their farm to the government's tax inspectors, trekked beyond the frontiers of the colony to settle among these Houzouana who received them hospitably. Because of his skills and the protection his muskets and ammunition offered against various traditional enemies (both animal and allegedly human) her husband soon rose to eminence among them and after the death of their old chief was universally accepted as that dignitary's successor. About a year ago he was bitten by a cobra and died; and after some time of deep soul-searching Dora decided to remain with the tribe.

And it is indeed, we cannot but acknowledge, a paradisiacal

place of tall green trees, abundant grazing, a proliferation of game (I catch glimpses of animals never yet imagined in our tradition, including, once, a small herd of wild horses with multicoloured stripes). The fifty or sixty huts of the settlement, some of them quite sumptuous by hottentot standards, are sprinkled around a large pool whose near-blackness suggests that it must be almost unfathomable, set like a dark shining eye in a fringe of vegetation, fed by a permanent spring and debouching in a stream running like a green snake into the wilderness.

Welcomed by the Houzouana as kinsmen of the white woman they have come to revere, we find ourselves overwhelmed by their hospitality – so unlike the reception we have come to expect from indigenous tribes. Sheep and cattle are slaughtered in our honour; and for what must be three weeks of nearly incessant festivities we are entertained like potentates from a distance kingdom. We are even presented with a troupe of young girls with whom to entertain ourselves in something of a sexual frenzy after the long enforced abstinence of our trek.

Yet I am not ashamed to admit to you that in each embrace the woman I discover is you.

· *203* ·

On the final night of our sojourn (the duration of which has been determined by the time required to restore Matthys Willemsz to sufficient health for the taxing journey home) I find myself, by choice, alone in a hut, contemplating time: past, present, future.

In spite of my meticulous interrogations not one member of this remote tribe has been able to provide me with information about Monomotapa. It remains as inaccessible as ever.

'That is no reason to lose faith in it,' says Jeanne quietly. 'Monomotapa is a city made of words.'

'Touché,' I say.

There is a sound at the entrance to the hut.

· *204* ·

It is the white woman, Dora Bothma. For the first time she is wearing proper clothes. It is a green dress, faded, crumpled, frayed; but it must have been, once, beautiful.

'It is the only dress from home I still have,' she explains, bashfully, her hands resting on her breasts in that immemorial gesture of protection, as if she has just divested herself of her last item of clothing.

'What are you doing here?' I ask.

'In this hut? Or in this place?'

'Both.'

She sits down beside me, folding her legs under her, tucking in the green dress. She seems not to have heard me. 'Tomorrow you are going away again,' she says.

'You must come home with us,' I say suddenly. And I feel a desire for her as I have not felt for a very long time: not the precipitate flush preceding the couplings I have known in recent years, but an ache I have grown unfamiliar with since my early hand-holdings with the girl Héloïse, or Neeltje in Middelburg.

'What shall I do there? I no longer belong there.'

'You can't be happy here,' I insist.

'Why not?'

'Among these . . .'

'What do you know of them?' she asks.

'After four years I still know nothing of this land,' I confess.

She looks hard at me. 'Take me,' she suddenly says, without flinching, her eyes unwavering, a green as clamant as her dress must once have been.

I stare at her. I see her hands undoing her bodice.

'Are you afraid of me?' she asks when she is naked.

254

'Yes,' I say.

'Why?'

'Because I'm not sure you are real.'

'It is easy to find out.'

In the *délices de la volupté* it is, again, your face I see. She is, after all, not real.

Mirages, a lurid flowering of the obsessions that spring from abstinence.

What the woman Dora Bothma came to me for (if my memory is to be trusted), demure in her tattered green dress, was to seek advice.

Should she stay there, secure and absurd in the wilderness – or go back to be a wife to Matthys Willemsz who, she confided, had asked her? During his weeks of delirium she had nursed him back to a semblance of life.

'Why do you come to *me*?' I asked, feeling my own peace of mind threatened, aware of my unruly desires.

'Because you're not one of them.'

'We're all together.'

'But you're a foreigner, you don't belong here, perhaps you can see more clearly than them.'

'How do we ever know where we belong?'

I must have sounded even more brusque than I'd intended, for her eyes became fearful and her manner apologetic. But how could I explain my own desperation to this strange, poor, freckled, sun-burnt creature whose body, now so primly concealed in the green dress, provoked me more than when she'd carelessly displayed her bare breasts among the crude Houzouana she had adopted as her tribe? Behind me the lengthening trail of people denied, causes abandoned.

'What do you know of Matthys?' she asked.

'Very little. He is a lonely man.'

She shrugged, impatient, as if that was beside the point.

'Do you *want* to share your life with him?' I pressed her.

'I'm not sure I want to share anyone's life. I have my own.'

'A woman needs a husband. A man needs a wife.'

'Why?'

'Life is too hard to bear alone.'

'You are alone.'

It was my turn to shrug.

'I have chosen to be alone,' I said after a while.

'Don't I have a choice?' she asked.

'May I say something?' asked Jeanne from the shadows behind me in the hut that smelled heavily of thornwood smoke, and of rancid grease, and acrid *buchu*.

The woman seemed unsurprised by her presence.

'The hardest, for me,' said Jeanne, 'was waiting until I was sure the thing I most wanted to do coincided with what I knew I must.'

'That was perhaps your luxury,' said the young woman, appearing from close by much older than she should have been. 'I came here with my husband. I never asked questions. Then he died. It was over a year ago. It was a very bad time, but in the end I made my choice. I was sure it was the right thing. Now you and your men have come, bringing back memories of everything I thought I'd given up for good.' For a long time she didn't say any more, staring down at her hands. Then she raised her head again. 'I have these people who care for me. In a sense I have everything, in a sense I have nothing. If I go back . . .?' She shook her head. 'Poor Matthys needs me. I think he will look after me. But I . . .'

'You can't be happy here!' I said.

'Does happiness enter into it?'

'But these – these hottentots: they're not – I mean . . .'

'They're not what?'

'They're not – like you, like us.'

256

'They've been good to me. They worship me.'

'But you cannot *live* with them.'

A brief reproachful grimace. 'You and the other men with you haven't thought twice about sleeping with some of the women of this tribe.'

'That's different.'

'Is it?'

'Some men alone on their farms *foutent* sheep or goats. That doesn't mean they live with them.'

'Estienne Barbier,' she said in a commiserating tone, 'how little you know about this land, these people.'

For a moment I was shamefaced – yes, I wanted to say, yes, how right you are; but how could I confess this, how yield to instruction from a woman? – then recovered sufficiently to move to the offensive again. 'You came here for help,' I reminded her, 'not to teach *me*.'

'Of course.' Her eyes of jade were inscrutable. 'I should have known better.'

'It isn't fitting that you should stay here,' I said, sensing submission in her attitude. 'Back home there's . . .'

'What?' she quietly asked.

'Everything,' I said laconically. 'You must have relatives . . .'

'They won't take me back. When I left with my husband they said it was the end. You see, they're rather important people at Cabo, and I was a disgrace to them.'

'Even so you can have a better life there, with Matthys.'

'Can I?'

'Why do you ask for advice if you challenge everything I say?'

She was worse, I thought, than Jeanne in one of her petulant, defiant moods.

'There is a problem, you see,' she said.

'What is it?'

'I am pregnant.'

'But isn't it too soon to tell?'

'Matthys hasn't touched me yet,' she said.

'You can't do a thing like this to him.'

'I have told him. He doesn't mind. It's other people I am concerned about.'

'You don't seem to care much for what others think anyway,' I said.

An unexpectedly frank smile. 'Thank you,' Dora Bothma said. 'You have helped me more than you may think.'

· 206 ·

Those we had left behind at Gal's kraal on the Great River had begun to despair about us, but they were still waiting, their encampment signalled from afar by the slow gyres of many vultures in the sky. The reason was soon apparent. Three of the oxen had been caught by predators, and having already lost a few others (two through drowning, one to a crocodile, some more to Bushmen raiders) van Dyk, Campher and van Wyk had undertaken wide-ranging raids around the Namaqua settlement to exterminate every living thing they chanced upon – elephants, lions, jackals, eland, kudu, springbok, even *dassies* and *meerkats*.

After the rains our journey back to the river had been relatively easy, though our progress was retarded by the large flocks of cattle and sheep we brought back from the Houzouana as their generous farewell gift to us and to Dora Bothma. The vast plains we crossed, such a forbidding desert on our way inland, had been miraculously transformed into a landscape recklessly stained with flowers of all imaginable colours. There was abundant grazing; there were watering-places. Even Matthys Willemsz's chronically sad face wore the hint of a smile.

We remained in chief Gal's kraal for another week, putting the final touches of repair and preparation to our wagons, equipping ourselves with new provisions for the road ahead, and exchanging – not without a degree of coercion – some of the weaker cattle we had brought from the Houzouana for some of the better specimens from the Greater Namaqua.

At last we set off on the first lap of the long return journey. Given the predilection towards effusive sentiment among these creatures of nature, the tribe was singularly unemotional in taking their leave of us; even chief Gal – an unsavoury speciment with long spindly legs and shifty eyes – appeared relieved rather than sad at seeing the last of his daughter. In the whole gathering of a hundred or so hottentots and our handful of Europeans this young woman – named Eva by Willem van Wyk, her aboriginal name being unpronounceable – was the only one to show signs of distress as she sat huddled in a little bundle in her kaross on the *wakis* of Willem's wagon, uttering small whimpering sounds, until her husband silenced her with a smack.

A turn of events initially surprising, but logical upon reflection, occurred a mere half-day's journey south from the Great River, where we made our first halt for a midday meal. Having absented myself for a while to obey a call of nature and having subsequently become absorbed in my trusted old book in which I was wont to seek entertainment while my bowels were otherwise occupied, I was not party to the deliberations my companions had meanwhile engaged in. Upon my return from the cluster of bushes where I had sought my relief I was informed that in my absence a unanimous decision had been taken to organise a raid upon the kraal of the Great Namaquas we had left that very morning.

Far from being conceived as an act of treachery, as one might be tempted at first sight to regard it, the design was rather admirable. Willem van Wyk, Hendrik Ras and some of the others had during the last few days of our sojourn with Gal's tribe detected increasing signs of resentment, *voire* open animosity, among our hosts; most notable among the grumblers had been the chief himself, who had in an unguarded moment threatened to report to the authorities in Cabo what he'd termed our 'thieving' and 'deceitful' nature (a reference, one could not but presume, to the coercive measures taken to persuade his people to part with some of their more cherished livestock).

'This we cannot allow,' said van Wyk. 'You all know what great care we've taken to exterminate all the tribes that could possibly give false reports of our expedition in Cabo. So how can we now run the risk of Gal's scoundrels betraying us? Van den Henghel and his henchmen loathe the Afrikaner colonists. They'll be only too eager to lend their ears to these savages.'

'How can we prevent it?'

'We've decided to get rid of Gal's tribe,' said van Wyk.

The plan was impressive in its simplicity. Our own hottentot attendants, armed with all the muskets, powder and lead required for a successful operation, would return immediately to the Great River; and that very night, under cover of darkness, they would overrun the place and exterminate men, women and children with the kind of efficacy in which we had previously set an example to them. In addition to eliminating the danger of traitors, they were certain to capture an impressive booty of cattle in which they would be invited to share – thereby successfully avoiding any possible future betrayal on their part. Nothing, van Wyk pointed out, would so ensure their dedication to us and our service on our tedious return journey as this prospect of sharing in the spoils of war.

If I admired, as a soldier, Willem van Wyk's genius as a strategist, I could not but marvel at his temerity in conceiving such a scheme against what, after all, was his own father-in-law, chief Gal. And I'm sure some of the others must have wondered about it too. But we had come to know Willem better than to ask.

There was an unexpected reluctance among our hottentots about executing the enterprise; and foremost among the protestors was Willem's own foreman, Swartbooi. But a number of well directed kicks and blows soon settled the matter; and as had been foreseen, the prospect of taking home a fair number of sheep and cattle of their own proved an uncommon incentive to these normally lethargic creatures. By mid-afternoon all twenty of our servants, heavily armed, set out on their expedition. Towards nightfall of the following day they were back, driving before them, as we had confidently expected, a herd of several hundred head of cattle and sheep.

There had been no survivors, Swartbooi personally assured us.

We were impressed by this demonstration of their aptitude to learn. Perhaps, Hendrik Ras reflected, they were on their way towards becoming human after all.

· 209 ·

And then it was all fucked up after all. Properly *foutu*.

· 210 ·

On the return journey the precarious unity of the group once again began to disintegrate; there was less talk around the camp fires at night; long before the final violent parting of the ways on Matthys Willemsz's farm, each man had again begun to withdraw into his own silence. It suited me. Seated on the back of Hendrik's wagon, or following a hundred yards behind, I held long conversations with Jeanne. In a sense we were restored to our first travels – that long peregrination across the face of France, taking our leave of the land before proceeding north in search of my still undefined 'fortune'.

Domrémy, a mere cluster of small houses in a melancholy valley of the Meuse, divided by the narrow rivulet of Les Trois Sources. Jeanne's long low home, dark under its massive slate roof: and beyond its yard the great Roman road along which passed the couriers of kings and dukes, even the emperor; and merchants and emissaries and clergymen to and from Flanders, Burgundy, Savoy, Italy. On the island in the Meuse where she tended her flocks, the small abandoned chapel where, sheltering from a sudden *averse*, she first heard the voice of the Archangel Michael.

From there we followed the road taken, one day in May, and again the following January, by Jeanne to Vaucouleurs when, after resisting for four years the urging of her voices, she persuaded the unsuspecting Durand Laxart to accompany her to Robert de Baudricourt in his castle high above the Meuse and its billowing grasslands.

'I heard afterwards,' she told me, 'that my father had said if he'd known where I was going he'd rather have drowned me.'

From there we followed the road she had taken to Chinon, resembling a young page-boy, having cut her black hair *à la soldade*, like an inverted Mambrino helmet perched on her cropped head (revealing the endearing *grain de beauté* behind her right ear); the underlinen of a man – a shirt without collar or cuffs, brief underdrawers – black hose, a doublet, a man's riding cloak, long boots. Skirting Berri, we entered the district of Blois, Fierbois with its tall church, and thence to Chinon where she'd met Charles VII.

Here had begun her road to glory. She described to me, her dark eyes radiant, her healthy face beaming – there were times, I assure you, when her presence was startlingly visual – the outfit she'd worn on that route to Orléans, and the disarming female touches she'd brought to that stern apparel: the kidskin girdle, the thick jerkin, the padded hose and leather shoes, the chain armour, the brief kilt, the spherical *salade* on her head, the heavy *chaperon*. (I tried to imagine her small figure in that outfit – her head reached barely to my nipple – and could not suppress a smile. If anything, she must have looked like a boy playing at war, preparing perhaps to charge at windmills or flocks of sheep: who could be blamed for not taking her seriously?)

We retraced her steps to Orléans, the town spilling – as it had done three centuries earlier – across the banks of the Loire, with the bridge between the two parts, the five gates, the two posterns. And then north to the battlefields of Auxerre, Troyes, Châlons, and the splendid cathedral town of Rheims. Back to Paris, the site of her first defeat, following the ignoble withdrawal of support by those on whom she'd most relied; to Melun, that sad place where her voices had first warned her about the capture that awaited her; then the battlements of Compiègne, where her new surcoat of scarlet and gold had attracted the attention of the enemy, resulting in her capture by the Picard bowman, and her surrender to the archer of the Bastard of Wandomme who'd delivered her to Jean de Luxembourg. The beginning of the end. And then that tortuous final *via dolorosa*, from castle to castle, dungeon to dungeon, leading inevitably to the Old Market in Rouen.

Her journey, which had originally covered two years, took us four months. Nothing, in all the time I'd known Jeanne, had weighed so heavily on her as that long leavetaking. Many times I tried to persuade her to terminate our wanderings. But she had a mind of flint. 'I have to do this, Estienne,' was her persistent response. 'If we are to leave France, never to come back, I need this pilgrimage. To make sure I have every step of the way – every battle, every triumph, every ache, every wound, every adversity – imprinted on my mind. I dare not forget it. And if you are serious about me you'll come with me. Only on this condition will I afterwards go with you.'

And so we went, league by league, inch by inch. And here, following this placid wagon on its way back from Ultima Thule to Cabo, we retraced it. In preparation for the long finale that still lay ahead and of which, mercifully perhaps, I as yet had no inkling.

· 211 ·

There was a hell of a fracas on the farm of Matthys Willemsz where, as had been agreed, we prepared to go our separate ways in order not to attract the attention of Landdrost Lourens – or anyone else for that matter – by trekking through more civilised parts with our new abundance of sheep and cattle. The *casus belli* was the distribution of the livestock our servants had captured from Willem van Wyk's unsavoury father-in-law, the chief Gal. Fifty head of cattle each was what the hottentots, led by van Wyk's foreman Swartbooi, demanded; and, to be fair, that was what had been agreed originally. But feeling more secure by now in the greater proximity of Cabo, and having put up with a fair deal of unpleasantness from those servants on the road back, Hendrik Ras, supported by most of the others, now summarily offered them nine head each, take it or leave it.

'That's not fair,' protested Swartbooi. 'We did all the fighting, there was a lot of trouble, two of our people were badly wounded, and you promised us fifty cattle each.'

'You're a bloody lazy bunch,' said Hendrik. 'You malingered most of the way here. Even nine cattle is too much, but you can have them because I'm a fair man. Only take them now and shut up.'

'I won't shut up,' said Swartbooi, supported by a menacing murmur from the others, clustered in a tight phalanx behind him. 'You said fifty.'

'I'm the baas here, and you're nothing but a slave. You'll take what I give you.'

'No baas, that's not right.'

'Are you telling me what is right and wrong?'

'I'm telling you what you told us.'

'Then for your cheek you can now have five cattle each and no more.'

Swartbooi's kierie struck Hendrik on the left shoulder. He'd aimed for the head, but Hendrik was too quick for him. In no time, in spite of the injured shoulder, he'd grabbed hold of the end of the heavy stick; Jan la Grange was already loading his gun. And then the whole band of hottentots came surging towards us, kieries flailing, bringing down the first few farmers among us.

Willem van Wyk did not bother to load his gun. Simply grabbing it by the barrel he started striking out at anything within reach. As he lunged forward I suddenly saw an expression in his eyes I'd never expected. Not rage, not hate, not a lust for blood and violence but, quite simply, fear. And in that brief instant, for the first time, I understood what impelled not only Willem van Wyk but all these men. I understood at last something of what I'd been living with those past months: this violence, this energy, this seeming exuberant cruelty, this need to subdue all adversaries real and imagined by brute force, this passion to destroy. All of it sprang not from exaggerated confidence, not even from hate, but from terror: the fear of this vast land, of its spaces, of its unmerciful light, of what lay lurking in this light, of its dark people.

All about me the battle was raging. The hottentots vastly outnumbered us; but the white men had guns. And when the first shots rang out there was, predictably, a great scramble among the servants to get away as quickly as possible.

However, in the mêlée preceding their flight, as momentarily I still marvelled at my discovery, one of the servants, having stealthily crept up behind me, dealt me such a blow on the head with his kierie that I fell forward, losing my musket; and as I sat crouching on the ground a rain of further blows battered me into near-unconsciousness. I was consequently in a desperate state by the time the traitors withdrew, taking with them not only my musket but those of several others among my companions felled in the unexpected onslaught.

It was a miracle that no one had been killed, although on both sides there was a number of quite seriously wounded. The uproar subsided as quickly as it had begun. But it left unresolved bad feelings on both sides. And the consequences were more distressing than anyone among us could have foreseen – for who would have thought that those normally docile creatures would all abscond from their employers, two, three, four at a time over the following weeks, and slink off to Cabo to report to the ever-alert van den Henghel exactly what he was most disposed to hear?

· *212* ·

Owing to the pain and discomfort I was suffering, those last few days on the back of Hendrik Ras's wagon, as he once again drove out of his way to deposit me at *Orléans*, seemed longer almost than the whole rest of the journey. I tried to take refuge in the shelter of my book, but the swaying motion of the wagon and the pain in my head made concentration difficult. Moving uneasily between consciousness and oblivion I conducted long conversations with Jeanne; and I presume I spoke aloud, for once or twice I was interrupted by Ras, who must have thought me mad.

On one occasion, showing distress at my condition, and trying rather awkwardly to establish the state of my mind, he enquired – to my surprise and annoyance, as you can imagine – whether I knew my name. (Perhaps, in retrospect, the question was not as extraordinary as it then seemed to me, because I'd been discussing with Jeanne one of her battles, from which Hendrik probably deduced that I thought I was someone else.)

In spite of my annoyance I smiled to set his mind at rest. 'Don't worry, Hendrik,' I told him. 'I'm all right. Of course I know who I am.' Adding, with a touch of provocation, 'And I also know that I'm capable of being much more than that.'

He sighed. 'Those blows on the head have done you great harm, Estienne,' he commiserated. 'But soon we'll be in Drakenstein, then the good widow can nurse you back to health. In the meantime, don't read so much. That book is not doing you any good.'

In the end it was not Louise Cellier who pulled me through, but an ancient hottentot woman who had been living on the farm for more than twenty years, much sought after in those parts for her remedies. In spite of her long association with civilised people she continued, in the manner of the savage tribes of the interior, to utter only the clicks and grunts which among them pass for speech; and she wore only a brief skin apron to cover her pudenda, leaving exposed her elongated empty dugs and, seen from behind, the disproportionately heavy buttocks that made her look like an unsuccessful clay sculpture. Her small triangular monkey-face was wizened, her tiny snake-eyes almost obscured among the myriad of deep wrinkles. Not a very promising physician to behold, I admit; but she brought me back from what at one stage had seemed to me imminent death. The open wounds she cured with what I subsequently learned was dried rhinoceros blood and powdered herbs; what the foul-tasting concoctions were which she forced me to drink I preferred not to enquire, but I'm sure there was curdled blood in some, and presumably animal or human urine, and sometimes it smelled nauseatingly like cattle dung or goat droppings. It was hard to refrain from vomiting it all up, but after I had a few times done just that, only to be force-fed more copious dosages, I gave up. I was in any case too weak to resist. And within four or five days, inasmuch as I was able to keep count of time, I had recovered.

The experience became a source of deep reflection to me. Having been persuaded, in the course of that long journey, of the lowly status of the hottentot race on the scale from animal to human, I was now obliged to interrogate myself anew. How could I despise the knowledge and the skill that had restored me to life? Perhaps the nature of this remote land itself necessitated other forms and ways of living, a different kind of reason? But it was not an easy question to resolve.

· *214* ·

'We have a way of recovering,' said Jeanne. And she reminded me how at Orléans she had been struck by an arrow that penetrated six inches into her body above her right breast. Those around her, including Jean de Gamache who had previously scorned her as a fainthearted girl, feared for her life. 'And I *was* terrified,' she confessed. 'I even shed tears. But in the end I pulled the missile from the wound myself. It took a long time before they could staunch the blood with bacon-fat and olive oil.'

And again, outside Paris, when she'd stood beside a ditch, sounding it with a pole to discover the depth of the water, she was struck in the foot by a bolt. ('The crossbowman shouted "Slut and whore!" as he let loose the missile. I think that hurt me more than the wound in my flesh.') In spite of losing a great amount of blood she stood her ground, lying with her back against the ridge between two ditches, and there she remained until nightfall when she was forcibly carried back to her camp by old Gaucourt and a Picard officer.

And then, of course, there was the jump from the tall tower at Beaurevoir, that nearly killed her.

'If you recover it means you still have work to do,' she said simply.

'What work could I possibly have? I can't even show my face in Cabo. They think I'm far away in Holland.'

'I don't think you will have long to wait,' she said.

· 215 ·

Back, then, in the deceptive tranquillity of the farm in Draken-stein that had first shaped my resolve to stay in this land and which, after my escape from the Castle, had provided me with sanctuary. It had become the closest to a home the colony had yet offered me, the half-blind and increasingly old widow a surrogate mother. But the tranquillity, I say, was deceptive, because even as I slipped into the reassuring routine of those last few summer months the future was gathering around me.

This was the same ease I had experienced following my flight from Cabo, after spending the first night hiding on the farm of Izak Nieuwoudt at the Tygerberg (Izak being absent, no one was aware of my presence) and the next few on the farm of a young widow near Stellenbosch, Anne Leriche.

There is, I soon discovered, an abundance of widows in this colony, the result no doubt of the precarious circumstances of existence in an untamed land. And I soon learned to appreciate the advantages of their availability. Lacking a male presence on the farm, these widows were invariably overjoyed to accept whatever assistance I could offer, dispatching accumulated work, returning undisciplined slaves or servants to order and obedience, restoring to the womenfolk their confidence in their own ability to cope. Secrecy was ensured by the resentment each one of them bore the authorities in Cabo, whose indifference or malevolence they had all experienced, in one way or another, following the loss of their late husbands.

Deprived for shorter or longer periods of the comfort of a male presence in their beds, they also had few scruples about expressing their indebtedness to me in a variety of ways infinitely gratifying to my own emotional and physical needs – all the more so if they (or their late husbands) were of French descent, however tenuous. There is a certain gallic touch, I believe (without any undue overestimation) I could bring to courting which revived not only their interest but their pride in their own amorous accomplishments.

Without exception, after barely a few days (and of course nights) on such a farm, I could count on the absolute discretion – and the devotion – of the mistress of the place, and on the farm itself as a secure asylum in case of future need. This was to stand me in good stead in the turbulent months to come.

There had been only one earlier period in my life comparable to this time in terms of satisfactory relations with a variety of women, if hardly in other respects, and that had been the last year or so of my life in France, before setting off with Jeanne to find my ever-elusive fortune. Then widows had not featured much in the pattern of my exploits – there was no need for them – but married women in some abundance, being as a rule less prudish than the unmarried variety, more generous, and not too anxious about possible consequences. My only rule in those days had been to ensure that the husband of a prospective *amie* was a big man, not a paltry fellow, as it was my experience that, if by some misfortune an *affaire* did come to light, a big man was more likely to beat you up, while a small man might have recourse to a gun and kill you. (On the duels resulting from such liaisons I have already made a few observations.) But in the present circumstances even this precaution was unnecessary; all that had to be ensured was that my true identity be kept secret from the labourers on the farm.

So there was Anne Leriche, a plump little blancmange of a woman who provided me with food, clothing of her late husband (which fitted me perfectly), a horse, and a small lace kerchief steeped in the pervasive scent of her *motte*.

And during the ensuing months, before we'd set off on our journey, there had also been the red-haired Constance Bevernage, and the sturdy Fransina Basson, and Leonie Burgert with black tresses down to her dimpled derrière, and Jeannette Gobregts, who could smother me between her munificent breasts. And of course Liesbet de Wet, strictly speaking the only non-widow among them, although she was a grass widow by then. You see, her monosyllabic husband Petrus – he of the fixed stare – had been so perturbed by the affidavit Petzold had forced him to make at my trial that he'd packed up and returned all by himself to the more distant farm at Breede River where they had lived long ago, at the time when Sergeant Kok had stolen his mother-in-law's sheep. It was Tante Louise herself who had first dispatched me to Liesbet's place to mend a broken wagon; and at last the promise of those looks she had once given me was fulfilled. I had the singular joy of introducing her to the pleasures of *gamahucher*. ('What does it mean?' she'd asked with eager curiosity when I'd first caressingly pronounced the term to her; and I'd replied, '*Ma chère*, if your lips can shape the word you'll know what it means.') And so she became, as it were, another bead on the not inconsiderable *chapelet d'amour* of my sojourn in the colony.

Now, upon my return, and having recovered through the administrations of the old hottentot woman from my wounds, I recommenced my work on Tante Louise's farm, and resumed also the dispensation of my services on the farms of a widening circle of beholden widows.

I shall not offend you with a catalogue of their charms, the unique aspects of each, so closely observed and intensely savoured – for those, as a man of honour, I discreetly keep to myself, at most to revisit nostalgically, foolishly, desperately, in this extremity of time and place.

Do not, I pray you, judge me too harshly. I am, I was, a man in need. I am a man of the flesh. And a sentimentalist, which is worse. But in a manner of speaking my sorties among the younger widows of the colony might be judged, in the words Jeanne herself had used before the journey, as a way of getting to know my troops.

The war was very close now.

· 216 ·

Besides, in the constant depression following that exhausting journey on which I had failed to find the merest trace of you, I was trying compulsively, believe me, to forget you; perhaps to replace you, to reconcile me to your absence. All in vain. In every ecstasy I still encountered you.

· 217 ·

Was it merely coincidence or was it, as Jeanne believed, a sign that on her birthday, 6 January, a fuming Hendrik Ras arrived at *Orléans*? I was just on my way from the shed which was being thatched to the fields where a motley band of labourers were harvesting beans, when the sound of furiously galloping hooves brought me to a standstill. Hendrik came thundering round the side of the *opstal* and across the yard, scattering squawking and cackling chickens, ducks and turkeys in all directions. The flanks of his great black horse were streaked with saltpetre. It was the first time I'd seen him since the expedition.

'Ah,' he said, jumping from the horse and wiping his brow

with a huge paw, 'I'm glad to see you up and about again. I need you.'

'What brings you here in such a hurry? That horse looks terrible.'

'Call me a slave to cool him down. We don't have time to waste.'

'Come in for coffee, then you can tell me everything. Is there trouble at home?'

'No problems there. Hannie took the news of David's death badly' – in a brief flickering image I recalled that elephant stampede – 'but she's a strong woman and she's better now. No, I want you to come with me to Matthys Willemsz's place.'

'His new wife?'

'She's all right, I think,' he said impatiently, letting fly with a kick to hurry up the slave who'd come to take his horse. 'It's Matthys himself. I don't know whether it's true, but I've heard they've thrown him into the Dark Hole in the Castle, can you believe it?'

'Why?'

As far as he'd been able to make out from a message sent by the woman Dora Bothma, a detachment of armed hottentots led by Carel Counitz and Jan Louw, assistants to Landdrost Lourens, had turned up on Willemsz's farm and driven off all the cattle they could find. Instructions of none other than Daniel van den Henghel himself. The same thing had apparently happened on other farms, including that of the impetuous young guide from our journey, the hunter Pieter de Bruyn. Presumably prompted by de Bruyn, Matthys had borrowed a horse on which he and his new wife had accompanied the raging young man to Stellenbosch; but Lourens had refused to see them, and so they had proceeded to Cabo. Upon presenting themselves at the Castle van den Henghel promptly had Matthys and Pieter arrested. Dora was warned that unless she left Cabo before nightfall she would be detained as well. Her first reaction was to stay with her husband; apart from anything else her now advanced pregnancy made riding difficult, if not hazardous. But in the end she'd returned home, realising there was more she could do for the two prisoners from the outside than from inside.

'We must find out as soon as possible if it's true,' said Hendrik. 'And if it is, something has to be done to get them out of that place and claim back their cattle.'

'But how can I help you?'

'I don't want to go alone, in case something happens on the way. With those bastards around one cannot take risks. Koos Jansen and Sybrand van Dyk are off hunting, so your place was the nearest. Do you have a spare horse for me? Come on, we're wasting time.'

I showed him to the stables while I went home to confer briefly with the womenfolk.

'Do you think I should go?' I asked Jeanne.

'You have no choice. This is the moment we have been waiting for, Estienne. I'm glad it's on my birthday.'

'Suppose it's just a rumour?'

'No, it isn't, Estienne.'

'How do you know?'

'I know.'

'Will you look after Tante Louise?'

'No. I'm going with you. She'll be all right.'

Tante Louise could not quite understand the urgency of our mission; but I promised to tell her everything in detail when we came back. In spite of Hendrik's protestations she insisted on our partaking of a meal first, while two female slaves prepared food for the journey. In less than an hour we were off.

· 218 ·

In spite of travelling most of the night and changing horses at the farm of one of Hendrik's friends along the way, it was past noon the following day before we reached Willemsz's place beyond the Piquet Berg.

As we approached across the slow undulations of the ochre landscape there was no sign of farming life, not a cow or a sheep; only a few ostriches in the distance. A few half-heartedly ploughed fields lay parched and untended closer to the small rectangular house; apart from some pumpkins dotting the garden most of the vegetables seemed scorched. The farmyard itself was ominously quiet, not even a scrounging chicken in sight; and the few labourers' huts were clearly deserted.

'Then it's true,' said Hendrik, his deeply sunburnt face showing up pale from the clenching of his wide jaws. Behind the unkempt black beard his eyes were small and ferocious, like an elephant's. 'But where is the woman?'

We found her unconscious in a bare bedroom, on a bed drenched with blood. But she had not been attacked, as we first surmised; the strain of the past few weeks had obviously been too much for her and she'd miscarried. It was half a day before we were able to learn more. Only after Hendrik had ridden off to the neighbouring farm, two hours distant, and brought back a woman with some knowledge of medicine, could Dora be revived; and then she was too weak to speak more than a few words. What she said confirmed the worst of the report Hendrik had heard. And more: during her illness all the remaining servants had absconded, taking with them whatever they could loot from the unprotected house.

Even in her miserable state Dora had little thought for herself. 'Poor Matthys,' she said. 'He was so eager to start again. He's been through so much. And it really was beginning to look good . . .'

'Shhhh,' said the neighbour, a large heavy woman who sat on the edge of the bed like a bag of wheat. 'You sleep now. It'll be all right.'

'We'll bring Matthys back,' Hendrik said in a low voice. 'That I promise you, hey?'

After returning to the neighbouring farm to arrange for Dora to be transported there and taken proper care of, we changed horses and set out on our return journey.

· 219 ·

We were too late. The Landdrost's agents must have been lying in wait for Hendrik Ras to turn his back: striking in our absence, the notorious band of armed hottentots led sometimes by Counitz and sometimes by Jan Louw had driven off most of Hendrik's livestock – not only the sizeable herd he'd brought back from the interior, but twenty or thirty of his own cattle as well. He was bellowing in rage, as much about the loss of his stock as about the underhand way in which the raid had been organised. For as Hannie reported the event, the hottentots had initially hidden themselves while Counitz had accosted her youngest remaining son Callie in the veld where he'd been tending the cattle. Forcing the youngster at gunpoint to abandon his herd, Counitz had then instructed his armed escort to round up whatever animals they could find, holding at bay Hannie and her two other sons by threatening to shoot Callie at the first hint of interference or pursuit. Only after they'd reached the safety of the drostdy in Stellenbosch did they callously release their young hostage to find his way back home on foot.

· 220 ·

Hendrik was all for assembling a commando among his neighbours and storming the drostdy forcibly to reclaim his cattle; and in the heat of the moment I was eager to accompany him. But Jeanne restrained me.

'Showing yourself openly to the enemy,' she reasoned, 'will

mean losing the one advantage you have at the moment: surprise. Everybody in Cabo thinks you are safely out of the way in Europe. A good soldier, I found out the hard way, is a good card player. Don't play that trump too soon. Open conflict is the surest way at this stage of losing the war. A lot of people on both sides will get killed, with nothing gained at all. No, Estienne, this is a time for more careful strategy.'

'Look, if you're too shit-scared to help me I'll do it on my own,' Hendrik said when I returned to reason with him.

'I want to be right beside you when the battle begins,' I told him. 'But if we rush in now we'll be running straight into their hands. Don't you think they're expecting us?'

'We can beat them,' he persisted stubbornly.

'Perhaps we can,' I said. 'But not without losing some of our men too. Remember, Counitz has the Landdrost with him. And behind the Landdrost is van den Henghel and the whole military might of the Cape. Do you think they'll ever leave us in peace again if we attack them now?'

'Let them come,' he said. 'We know the land, they don't. We can hide in the mountains, in dongas in the veld, everywhere, and strike at them as they come. We can go on for years.'

'Is that the sort of life you want your family to lead?' I asked. 'Don't you think Hannie has had a bad enough time as it is? Losing Marietjie, losing David, living in fear day after day about what may happen to you and to her sons?'

He stared at me with his feverish enraged eyes. 'So what can we do?' he asked in a tone of despair. 'We spent months on that journey, man. I lost my son. Do you expect me just to sit back and let that dog-prick Lourens steal all my cattle?'

'Of course not, Hendrik. But we must bide our time. And we must strike when they least expect it, and in ways that don't make it easy for them to wipe us out.'

'They can never wipe us out,' he flared up again.

'Look,' I said, 'they already have Matthys Willemsz and Pieter de Bruyn. Suppose we attack them openly now, what do you think they'll do? The first thing will be to hang those two. Or torture them to death. Van den Henghel is more than capable of that. You think you can face Dora Bothma with her husband's blood on your hands?'

'My God, man!' he said in desperation. 'Then what do we do?'

'First we must find out exactly what has been done so far. Whose cattle have been taken, how many from each, what methods have been used. Once we know that we can go into action. Our aim is not to shed more blood but to prevail.'

Jeanne, I should say, was satisfied with me.

Hendrik Ras did attempt a peaceful resolution, leading a group of five or six farmers from the Roodezand and Paarl to Landdrost Lourens's lair in Stellenbosch to demand the return of their stolen cattle. I was not in the group: feeling, perhaps, ashamed about embarking on the venture after he'd solemnly promised me not to seek confrontation, or accepting that my presence in the district had to be kept secret, he'd rounded up his men without giving me any forewarning. It was only afterwards that, like an overgrown shamefaced boy, he came round to tell me the story.

This visit came well over a fortnight after the event, because following the confrontation, I learned, Hendrik had felt obliged first to return to the Piquet Berg to visit Dora Bothma; and there he'd spent a full three days to restore some order to her farmyard and to comfort her, as it seemed she was still in a deep depression after what had happened, and was threatening wildly to pack up – as if there was anything left to be packed – and go back to that tribe of the Houzouana she persisted in referring to as 'my people'.

This time, it transpired, Pieter Lourens was wise enough not to avoid the petitioners as he had done with Matthys Willemsz and Pieter de Bruyn; but he took the precaution of meeting them in the presence of a strong armed guard. Counitz, the *poltron*, was not present; but Jan Louw was. Not quite as virulently loathed as Counitz, he was an unpleasant character all the same. A man of squat, almost square build, he had a notoriously short temper; having failed as a farmer (mainly because no worker lasted long in his employ), he was shrewd enough to marry Pieter Louren's sister, which landed him the cushioned appointment as a deputy to the Landdrost.

On this occasion Louw acted as the landdrost's *porte-parole*. They had undertaken an unauthorised journey into the interior, he brusquely informed Hendrik and his deputation; they had acquired a vast amount of cattle through illegal bartering; a further grievously aggravating circumstance was that they had attacked and killed a number of hottentots well disposed towards the authorities, thereby risking continuing unrest in the outlying areas. (Louw's information was distressingly detailed.) One further sign of insubordination or resistance and they could expect a drastic response from Cabo: as it was they already ran the risk of having their farms confiscated and of being hauled before the Council of Justice.

Lourens's own contribution to the monologue was no more than regular emphatic punctuations from the background where he hovered, looking more than ever like an erect penis, 'Yes – Yes – Yes . . .'

When Louw had finished, Lourens stepped forward and granted them five minutes to remove themselves from the drostdy.

'Man,' said Hendrik when he finally decided to come round and tell me about the encounter, 'I tell you, I was so bloody angry I could have throttled the turd with my bare hands, and damn the consequences. But then I remembered what you told me, and I thought about Hannie back home, and I swallowed my anger. But I tell you, this is not the end.'

It was indeed only the beginning. For in the course of the following weeks there was one report after the other about the Landdrost's men combing the district far and wide in search of contraband cattle. The farms of every single man who'd been on the expedition were visited and raided. (Once again it was obvious that the Landdrost's informers had been devastatingly thorough.) And as the resentment among the farmers increased Counitz, who remained in charge of the Landdrost's security force, became more and more high-handed.

Soon even farms of men who had not been with us were raided, presumably because Counitz suspected that our companions, having had wind of the raids, had begun to hide their cattle on neighbouring farms, in the folds and kloofs of mountains. All right, I admit that they were not altogether wrong in this suspicion: but can you expect those men, after all they'd gone through, to sit back and wait for the hard-won cattle to be confiscated again? And surely that was no excuse for driving off, in addition, cattle that had been on the farms for years?

Even these shameful thefts and raids were not the end. On Jan la Grange's farm, and on Gert Campher's, when Counitz couldn't find the cattle he was looking for (Jan and Gert having timeously made other arrangements), he bluntly ordered his hottentots – can you believe it? – to set fire to the sheds, destroying whatever was stored in them: bundles of skins, bags of wheat and rye and dried beans, all the produce accumulated over several months to be taken to Cabo and sold there as the farmers' sole means of subsistence.

And what about Koos Jansen? He was over at Gert Campher's to commiserate with his loss when Counitz and his band arrived at his farm, even though they'd already been there the week before. They obviously thought that Koos had thwarted them the previous time, secreting some of his stock, and now expected to surprise the family. But there were no cattle at all. And seeing that Koos himself was absent they started intimidating his wife Truida. In the end, fuming with frustration, Counitz got on his horse and rode away, leaving her to his hottentots.

I find it difficult to keep my composure, Rosette, as I tell you this. But those miscreants set upon her and took turns to violate her. When Koos came home – himself, remember, not yet fully recovered from the bad wound he'd sustained in the attack of the Kabobiqua savages – he found her whimpering in a corner of the shed, like a plucked chicken.

The worst of all, she told him (when at last she was able to speak coherently), was that during the assault her husband's own servants had been present, watching and even encouraging the bandits, not lifting a finger to save her from disgrace; and after that they'd absconded.

I should add that on every other farm visited by Counitz and his henchmen the raid was followed by the desertion, *en masse*, of all the local hottentots employed there; only the slaves remained, although even some of them attempted to decamp. (However, those were all apprehended again in due course, and subjected to the punishment they so amply deserved.)

From all over the more remote parts of the colony reports were now coming in of marauding bands of hottentots trekking this way and that, slaughtering and stealing cattle, setting fire to homes or barns or fields, terrorising women and children: some of these were clearly those rogues that had deserted their masters; others, judged by the clothing or lack of it they were described as wearing, appeared to have originated from the extremities of the colony and even beyond. It seemed as if a veritable war was brewing. And there we were, the near-defenceless colonists, caught between the high and mighty of Cabo and those scum of the earth.

No man of honour could any longer sit back and allow the storm to gather uninterrupted.

As always when I felt the pressure of the world weighing heavily on me I spent many hours immersed in the great book I knew so well yet in which I always came across something hitherto unnoticed. What struck me during one of those unbearably hot February nights, when sleep was impossible, was the knight's very first sortie. Having finally made up his mind that he must venture into the world to restore the noble principles of chivalry among people who have grown content with mediocrity, he cleans a suit of armour which once belonged to his ancestors, and has lain for ages forgotten in a corner, eaten with rust and covered with mould. But half of the visor is missing. So he starts working painstakingly on fashioning a new visor from cardboard; and after considerable pains he tests it with his sword. Inevitably, two cuts of the sword utterly destroy what has taken him a week to make. Taken aback, but undaunted, he sets to work again. And this time – how well I know the passage – 'not caring to make another trial of it, he accepts it as a fine jointed headpiece and puts it into commission.'

That, I believe, is the secret: knowing when to turn one's back to the ordinary reality of the world and move into that realm of action most people regard as madness.

'You told us to bide our time,' said Hendrik Ras. 'We did. You told us to gather all the facts. We have. Now we cannot wait any longer or we shall all be humiliated and destroyed.'

They had all come over to *Orléans*. For the first time since the expedition we were assembled again – all except Willem van Wyk who had retreated to his farm with his hottentot wife; and of course Matthys Willemsz and Pieter de Bruyn, from whom there was still no word.

'I'm afraid of what those two may tell van den Henghel's *geweldenaars*,' said Hendrik Kruger. 'If a man is put to the torture he may say anything. And they've now been held so long I'm sure that is what is happening.'

'Pieter won't say anything,' said Ras. 'No one will get a word out of him.'

'But Matthys is a weak man,' said Koos Jansen. 'And he may talk if that is what it takes to be allowed to go back to Dora.'

'What's the use?' asked Gert Campher, stroking his beard. 'She's already run away, back to where we found her. I only heard this morning.'

'But Matthys doesn't know it. The point is, whether they talk or not, every day we postpone there is more danger for us.'

'What more can they want from us?' asked Sybrand van Dyk, a bitter sneer on his freckled face. His left arm, still useless since the trampling by the elephants, hung limply by his side.

'They came back to *my* place,' Koos Jansen reminded him, struggling to check his voice. 'Look what they did to my wife.'

'Well, Estienne?' Hendrik Ras turned to me. 'You were the one who told us to wait.'

'I said we shouldn't try to face them head-on, Hendrik. And I still think that would be suicide. But I agree: it is time to start hitting back. Only, we must use the kind of weapons they don't expect from us.'

'And what is that?'

'The law.'

'Much good the law has done *you*,' said Hendrik.

'I was one man against all of them. This time it's different. We represent the whole colony. They'll think twice.'

'Then why don't we round up a commando and march on Cabo?'

'For one very good reason, Hendrik. We must take on the

Cape authorities without affronting the Lords Seventeen. *They* have no part in this injustice.'

'And how do you propose to do that?' asked Jan la Grange, a lean dark scowling presence in the shadows behind the others. 'Only people who care about the law can be scared by it.'

'There's one man among them who does care about the law,' I persisted. 'And he can't stand van den Henghel. If we do this right and we get him on our side, our case is half-won.'

'And who might that be?'

'You should know from experience. Hendrik Swellengrebel. Don't forget, he was born in the colony, like all of you. He hates the high-and-mighty Dutch.'

'Then what do you have in mind?'

'We must first draw up a petition. In proper legal terms. Setting out exactly what has happened, what Counitz has done, what Lourens has done. Then we present it to Swellengrebel.'

'What's the use?' Hendrik Ras said simply. 'Most of us can't write.'

A deep murmur of voices supported him.

'I can,' I said. 'I have even learned some Latin. But more important than that, I know a man who can help us.'

'Who's he?'

'His name is Christian Petzold. And he'll do anything to get back at van den Henghel for what that man has done to him.'

'But he's in Cabo, we're here.'

'I'll go and see him.'

'You can't. The moment you set foot in Cabo you'll be arrested.'

'It's unlikely that anyone will recognise me with this beard I've grown. And I won't show myself in the streets in daylight.'

'You can try.' Ras still sounded dubious. 'But it seems a very shaky way of hitting back.'

'Give me this one chance,' I said. 'If it doesn't work, there's no harm done. If it does, we will have averted bloodshed. I can go to Cabo tomorrow and be back within three days.'

To the Hon. Mr Hendrik Swellengrebel, President of the right honourable Council of Justice of this Government –

Your Worship, and Honourable Gentlemen –

Inasmuch as the Landdrost Pieter Lourens, supposedly acting in the best interests of the country but in fact revealing himself to be a crook and a fraud in wrongfully taking from those in his care their very possessions –

Therefore we the undersigned are constrained, like children deprived of sustenance, to turn to you, Your Worship, in the firm belief that we can expect justice from you –

And consequently, robbed shamefully of both our honour and our possessions, we respectfully request Your Worship to coerce the aforementioned Landdrost Pieter Lourens into the restitution of our to dato missing stolen cattle, or alternatively to demonstrabile ex qualibus motivis, rationibus jure quali –

In view of which we also respectfully beg Your Worship to summon on our behalf the aforementioned Petrus Lourens to appear before you in order to demonstrate ex partibus producturis the full extent of his heinous misdemeanour.

In a slight drizzle, very early the following morning, well before the first glimmering of light behind the forbidding granite cliffs of the Drakenstein mountains, I set out from *Orléans*. Before me, astride like a man, sat Jeanne; she was in her element. And throughout that long day she showed no sign of fatigue.

Across her thighs she carried a single elephant tusk, not very large but the heaviest we could transport in that manner; the only remuneration we could offer Christian Petzold.

It was well after dark when I reached the outskirts of Cabo.

I feel no reservation about admitting that it was an emotional moment after an absence of almost a year once again to see, against the star-strewn sky and illuminated by an uncommonly generous moon, the outline of that great flat-topped mountain flanked by the reclining Lion and the Devil's Peak.

Taking every possible precaution – to the extent of wearing a broad-brimmed hat, which must have seemed extraordinary at that hour – I rode along the cobbled Heerengracht, past the squat dark walls of the Castle, and turned into the potholed dirt streets towards the slope behind the Company Gardens where Petzold lived.

Even in that scant illumination the small narrow house seemed more dilapidated than I remembered it. But I did not dare approach the front door. How little it required for someone to become suspicious, to summon a guard, to have me returned to the Dark Hole which, I knew, would continue to haunt me in my dreams for as long as I lived.

Instead, I hovered a block away in the dark, moving out of sight only once when the night guard came past on its rounds; until a slave carrying a torch approached, shuffling along hastily on bare feet, obviously on an errand. I had been quite prepared to withdraw, after a futile hour or so, to a safe retreat higher up on the slope, and there bide the morning. But the arrival of the slave, which was really the best thing I had hoped for against hope, made everything so much easier. I handed him a few stuyvers of the small sum I had brought with me, together with a note written the previous night (which, needless to say, I had spent sleepless, alternately tossing about on my bed and paging desultorily through my book).

I had not signed the note, for fear it might fall into the wrong hands; but I had phrased it in such a manner that Petzold would make the right deduction from it. And within half an hour he arrived.

'My God!' he exclaimed, peering into my face. 'It really is you – I couldn't believe – and this wild beard . . .?'

'Shh,' I said. 'Look, this is neither the time nor the place to talk. Can you meet me in the Gardens tomorrow morning?'

'Do you realise . . .'

'Will you be there?' I urged.

'Of course,' he said.

· 227 ·

He was even thinner than before, looking more like a praying mantis than ever, his hair wispy; and his pale eyes had a scared look as he continued to glance this way and that on our uneasy promenade among the trees.

'It's becoming impossible, Estienne,' he said. 'They're watching me all the time. That awful man they've stationed in my house – Forster – you know, last week I actually caught him fondling my stepdaughter. She's only fourteen, Estienne. And what makes it worse, she doesn't see the harm.'

'Can't you tell him to go?'

'He just swears at me. Once he gave me a beating. In fact it isn't even my house any more. We haven't been able to pay the rent for months now, you see, and last month the free-black who rented it to me, Robbens Schot, told Forster he could now have it. We're living there on his sufferance. And after what's happened to you no one will give me work. Tell me, how on earth did you escape? And how did you come back?' With a spurt of pathetic eagerness: 'What happened to your case in Patria?'

'I never left the country, Christian.' His disappointment was almost too much to bear. 'But I've brought you something.' I took him to the shrubs in a secluded corner of the Gardens where I'd hidden the tusk in Jeanne's care.

His drab eyes lit up. 'Is that for me?'

'Yes. I need your help again, Christian. This time I know it will work out: we're sending a petition straight to Swellengrebel. And soon you'll be able to work again, I guarantee you.'

He glared at me suspiciously, like a mangy dog lured by a choice morsel but scared of being beaten if he takes it. 'What is it you want me to do?'

· *228* ·

I did not know, when I took my leave of him, the carefully folded sheet stowed inside my shirt, that this would be the last time I set eyes on him. Carved into my conscience I shall forever (but it can't be much longer now) bear that final image of the thin colourless man with the drooping shoulders, clutching the dirty tusk almost too heavy for his frail arms; and that unnatural new light of hope in his sad eyes.

· *229* ·

'And now,' I said, once Hendrik Kruger had laboriously transcribed our precious document (we could not take the risk of sending it to the Council of Justice in my handwriting, or for that matter in Petzold's) and two of the men had appended their signatures and the rest their spidery crosses, 'someone has to take it to Cabo.'

Several of the men volunteered.

But I could not allow it. 'They know too much about our journey already,' I said. 'The moment they set eyes on any of you he'll be thrown into the Dark Hole with Matthys and Pieter.'

'We can send one of our wives,' said Hendrik Ras. 'I know Hannie will be only too eager.'

'That, too, is dangerous.'

After much discussion it was agreed to dispatch Hendrik

Ras's brother Johannes, a harmless creature somewhat soft in the head, who farmed at Paarl, not an hour's ride from *Orléans*.

'He's never harmed a fly in his life,' said Hendrik. 'And everybody knows that. No one will lay a finger on him.'

No one did; but neither could anyone foresee the sorry turn the *démarche* was destined to take.

· *230* ·

The poor idiot. It is still not altogether clear what happened when he arrived inside the Castle on that morning of 26 February, between 8 o'clock and 9. His own report, when he returned to his farm where the rest of us were waiting, was rather incoherent. But from it, and from what transpired subsequently at my trial, it would seem that Johannes was wandering about aimlessly in the front courtyard, uncertain of where to go – although I had given him explicit directions – when he was accosted by the formidable Ruler himself.

'Come here, my man,' van den Henghel called in his high-pitched voice. 'What are you doing in this place?'

Johannes, overawed by the imperious figure, blurted out that he had come to deliver a petition from a group of aggrieved farmers.

'Let me look at it,' demanded van den Henghel.

'But it is addressed to Mijnheer Swellengrebel, Your Greatness.'

'Am I or am I not the Governor of this colony?'

'I believe you are the Acting Governor, Mijnheer.'

'Then I have a right to see this.'

'If you say so, Your Honour, but it is still meant for Mijnheer Swellengrebel.'

Still hesitant, Johannes had no choice but to hand over the letter. Van den Henghel spent a considerable time perusing the document (but the handwriting might have had something to do with it).

Finally, looking up, stammering with rage, all he could utter was, 'You farmers – you farmers . . .' adding after a while, 'You people have written more than you can ever prove in court.'

'Excuse me, Your Reverence,' said Joahnnes, 'but what must I do now?'

Without bothering to reply van den Henghel turned on his heel and went into his official residence, still clutching the document. Briefly changing his mind, he emerged again and shouted at a passing soldier from the guard to detain Ras. Thereupon he returned into his house, slamming the heavy door behind him.

Almost two hours passed before van den Henghel made his appearance in the guardroom where Johannes had been kept standing by his warden.

'What is your name?' demanded van den Henghel. He was sweating like a horse, Johannes told us, but whether it was from anger or from wearing those heavy brocade clothes and the voluminous wig in the intolerable February heat, he couldn't tell.

'Johannes Ras,' he replied.

'Not Hendrik Ras?'

'I am Johannes Ras.'

'You're not lying to me, are you?'

'You can ask anyone in the district of Stellenbosch, Your Grace. I was Johannes Ras when I left home and I'm still the same man, even though I'm very tired from standing.'

'You have the temerity to accuse Company officials of theft? Do you realise that it reflects on me personally?'

'It has nothing to do with you, Your Highness. It was Landdrost Lourens.'

'How can you waste my time with such arrant nonsense?'

'Your Excellency, you were not even supposed to see that paper, I told you it was meant for Mijnheer Swellengrebel.'

There were a few more exchanges before van den Henghel instructed the guard to escort Johannes to the Secunde's office.

Swellengrebel invited him to sit; he glanced at the letter, then looked up. 'So this is the request you first gave to Mijnheer van den Henghel?'

'You have seen it?'

'He showed it to me. Why didn't you bring it straight to me?'

'I didn't give it him, Mijnheer. He took it from me.'

Swellengrebel read it again, then sighed. 'I'm afraid my hands are tied now,' he said. 'I have been given strict instructions.'

'What must we do now, Mijnheer?'

'You can wait for tomorrow's session of the Council if you wish. But because of what has happened the decision is a forgone conclusion.'

'And what is that, Mijnheer?'

'You must raise the matter directly with the Landdrost of Stellenbosch.'

'But he's the one who stole our cattle. What justice can we expect from him?'

'I'm afraid it has been taken out of my hands.'

'Then I came all this way for nothing?'

Swellengrebel rose. He made no further comment, merely offered his hand.

When Johannes reached the front gate of the Castle two armed soldiers suddenly stepped in front of him, holding their swords to his chest. He jumped back in fright.

'What's this?' he asked.

'You are under arrest,' said one. 'You're not allowed to leave the Castle.'

'But I've finished my business!'

'Mijnheer van den Henghel is not yet finished with you.'

Johannes Ras had a slow temper, like a hardwood log that takes a long time to catch fire; but the moment of conflagration was approaching. Fortunately for him the volume of the altercation brought several spectators to the scene, including, at last, Swellengrebel.

'What is going on here?' he demanded.

'We have orders from His Excellency to detain this man in internal arrest, Mijnheer,' explained one of the soldiers.

'Then I order you to let him go.'

'But Mijnheer – '

'I tell you: let him go. I'll take this upon myself.'

The best came afterwards. Upon returning to his bureau Swellengrebel found van den Henghel waiting for him. They did not mince their words.

'What was that noise at the entrance?' asked the Acting Governor.

'The guard was trying to restrain the man Ras.'

'I hope you sent him straight to the Dark Hole?'

'I ordered them to let him go.'

'You dared to countermand my orders?'

'Yes. Because however much you misuse your power to frustrate the processes of law in this colony, as long as I am here at least a modicum of justice will be done.'

'This is insubordination, Swellengrebel!'

'And you're a turd, van den Henghel.'

The Acting Governor moved his bulk towards his Secunde, but he was too slow, too massive for Swellengrebel, who sent him staggering back with a single blow that dislodged his wig and caused him to overbalance on his short legs and sit down heavily on the floor. The look of stupefaction on his broad face gave way to humiliation, and covering his visage in his hands he began to blubber, smearing himself with snot and abject tears.

Would that it were really possible to ascertain what happened between the Acting Governor and his Secunde; but that part of the story never reached us. Which left each of us free to imagine what he wished.

Not that the brief exuberance of our imaginings availed much against the desperation with which we learned about the outcome of our attempt. Yet it was not without benefit. Within a mere few days the tidings spread through every district. Johannes, previously an object of commiseration in the district or the butt of gentle jokes, had become a hero. And even farmers who had previously berated us for having acted foolhardily in bringing those cattle back from the frontier, now joined our cause. The time had come for decisive action to forge something clear and unambiguous from the inchoate anger and the seething frustrations evident all around us.

It happened on Sunday morning, 1 March. The preceding few days had seen much frantic travelling from *Orléans* to Hendrik's farm, from his to Johannes's, from there to a dozen others, some as far as the Swartland and the Piquet Berg. On that particular morning nine of us – on horseback, except for Johannes who'd come on foot – gathered outside the little whitewashed church of Drakenstein while the service was in progress. Some of the men had been on the journey with us – Kruger, Campher, van Dyk, Olivier – but others were new converts to our cause: Peet

Booysen, for instance, and Daniel Walters. Booysen had recently been threatened that his farm would be confiscated unless he paid his arrears in rent; young Walters was annoyed because for three years he'd had to postpone his marriage, as the constraints within which the Company allowed him to farm made it impossible to accumulate the nest-egg needed to found a family.

I cannot imagine that you have ever visited this church, although – strangely – ever since that morning, for an inexplicable reason, I have often imagined to myself how on your flight from Cabo you might have arrived there and slept fitfully there overnight, before moving on towards your forever unknown destination. And this image has immeasurably endeared the drab little place to me. An inauspicious long narrow building, more like a barn than anything else, huddling very low, and covered with reeds. Inside, I knew from the few occasions when, masquerading as her *knecht*, I'd accompanied Tante Louise of a Sunday (it was always a propitious occasion for arranging a rendezvous with this young widow or that), there was nothing but the bare walls and the mouldering reeds, with a few plain forms to sit on, brought by some of the meaner sort, and the sorriest desk and pulpit that ever was seen. Yet this humble edifice was to witness the beginning of our great enterprise.

· 235 ·

I had spent most of the previous night recording painstakingly, on a large sheet of good stiff paper, all the grievances we had accumulated over the past months. It had been a daunting task, I assure you, doing battle with the intricacies of Dutch grammar in the light of an oil lamp alternately smoking and flaring, while all the men thronged around me offering advice, suggestions and demands at every turn of phrase. But in the end, if I say so myself, it was an impressive document – I had titled it *Avis of Great Importance* – and on that historic Sunday morning, as the people were disgorged from the humble building, Sybrand van Dyk called them to attention. As the good Christians approached in curiosity, I began to intone in a ringing voice what I had so conscientiously penned.

Item, that the government in Cabo, instead of promoting the interests of its subjects, had become oppressors of the people and destroyers of the country.

Item, that the annual quit-rent on a farm, 24 rix dollars, was prohibitive, and that the corruption among the authorities, who demanded payment for the meanest services, had become untenable.

Item, that the present government was flouting all the directives and ordonnances of the Lords Seventeen, contravening both the spirit and the letter of the proclamations issued for the good governance of the colony after the unfortunate conflict between colonists and governor over thirty years earlier.

Item, that the Acting Governor had himself become the enemy of all honest men, relying on his henchmen to extort and oppress those entrusted to their care.

Item, that hottentots and slaves were enjoying better treatment than us, the loyal colonists of Cabo.

Item, that it was intolerable for Landdrost Lourens, himself the king of rogues, and his accomplices to steal the livestock colonists had acquired by the sweat of their brow.

Item, that the obstacles placed in the way of young prospective farmers were making it impossible for young men and women to get married and contribute to the prosperity of the colony.

Item, that free trade had been ruled out by the practice among Company officials to reserve to themselves the right of bartering with hottentots and trade with passing ships.

Item, that having now reached a limit to what we were prepared to suffer, we called upon all farmers to stop paying any rents and taxes until we were relieved of the evil regime abusing us and our liberties.

There was, as you can imagine, a deep silence after I had finished.

I took my time to study the assembled faces of the good Sunday burghers before me. Then, discovering Charles Marais among them, whom I had (for obvious reasons) not seen since that early sojourn as a teacher on his farm, I went up to him and offered him the document.

'You are a *heemraad*, Charles,' I said. 'I want you to affix this to the door of the church where everyone can consult it.'

'I – I have nothing to attach it with,' he protested lamely.

'We brought glue which Hendrik's wife mixed from egg whites and flour.'

'I think it would carry more weight if you did it yourself,' he said in an uncommon state of agitation.

'Is there anyone among you,' I called out, 'who objects to this *Avis* being posted on your church door?'

Not a sound of protest. They were, I think, spellbound.

'Is there anything untrue in our statement?' I asked again.

Now there were confused shouts, and acclaim. 'No it's true!' 'Go ahead!' 'Put it on!' 'Bravo!'

'Does anyone deny that we are right in our grievances and that our adversaries in government are rogues and ruffians and blood-suckers?'

'True! True! True!' they shouted.

'Then give it to me, I'll affix it,' said Sybrand in his show booming voice, shouldering his way through the throng.

· *236* ·

There was a profound sense of occasion, almost of awe, as the congregation looked on; even the *predikant* was there, albeit in the background. No one had ever done this before. We knew very well that in the whole colony none but the officials of the Company had the right to affix notices in public. The previous night, even among those hardy and dedicated men surrounding me, there were some so struck by the enormity of the proposal to post our *Avis* on the church door, that they considered withdrawing from the enterprise. But I was prepared for that. 'I have written it,' I said. 'I shall take the blame.' For these were dire times. And it was necessary to impress on all present the solemnity of the occasion. This was our declaration of war. And this time I was not only openly associated with it, announcing as it were my return to public life: I was the author and agent of it. If anything went wrong I was prepared to assume the responsibility. *La faim fait sortir le loup du bois.*

· 237 ·

We proceeded to the farm of one of our associates, David Senekal, to review what had happened. You will understand that we were all slightly delirious. For a brief bright moment it seemed as if we had already won: there had been such enthusiasm among the congregation of Drakenstein that it was easy to imagine we had the whole land behind us. We were claiming Africa for the Afrikaners.

How far away Cabo now seemed, that *anus mundi* as Petzold had once described it: a huge inflamed arsehole with van den Henghel in its middle, a purple haemorrhoid. But here *we* were and we were real, a team of surgeons who would lance the boil. Yes, *this* was real, these men, these shouts, this ringing enthusiasm, this leaping faith in the future.

The most beautiful moment of a revolution, I can tell you now, is the instant of beginning: when everything seems possible; when nothing has really happened yet. (I warned you that I am a sentimentalist.)

So we rode to Senekal's place, and thence to another, and yet another, drinking and carousing and celebrating. And in the irresponsible glory of the moment – grant us that! – we did not even know what we learned later: that the same afternoon our *avis* was blown away by the wind (or so they said) and collected by the sexton Job Friek beyond the graveyard stream, and kept safely by him in the vestry of his blessed little church. Safely, that is, until it could be dispatched as *corpus delicti* to the Council of Policy in Cabo.

· *238* ·

The first we learned of the official reaction to our *défi* was when the council of Landdrost and Heemraden of Stellenbosch posted, on the church door and the front wall of the wheat mill, two copies of an ordonnance – known in these parts as a *plakkaat* – issued by the Council of Policy in Cabo, in terms of which I Estienne Barbier had been outlawed. (Once again that fiercely ironic phrase: *to be declared bird-free.*) The other 'mutineers' were granted a month in which to repent. So much for taking seriously the genuine grievances of colonists chafing at the yoke.

What made it even more distressing was a string of reports from Cabo about extraordinary measures taken simultaneously to appease the 'justly aggrieved' hottentots, in support of their struggle against the 'incorrigible' colonists.

What had we expected? Looking back, yes, we had been so naïve. But I ask you – not that I doubt your response! – was it really wrong or foolish of us to have hoped that a just cause in itself was sufficient reason to prevail?

We were learning, though. Oh, we were learning.

· *239* ·

Much was made at my trial of the fact that I had 'wilfully and wrongfully' torn the official notice from the church door. A new act of insubordination, of calculated provocation. But what else could I have done? It was necessary to take the document to the others – assembled once again in Johannes Ras's nondescript little hovel outside Paarl – where we could consider it in detail in order to plan our own response.

There was only one person outside the church to witness the incident: Job Friek the sexton, sinewy as biltong, vicious as a lizard – but he cowered against the wall when he saw my gun. After removing the notice I handed him the nails with which it had been hammered in place. 'You keep these,' I said. 'I'll be back.'

And I plead now, as I pleaded at my trial (without avail, of course), that the next day, true to the promise I had made to that little reptile, Friek, I did restore the notice to the church door. If my action might be construed by some, I concede, as plucking the lion by the beard – I knew I would be shot on sight if anyone more substantial than Friek discovered me; and I took pride in doing it in the blazing light of noon – it was also, wasn't it, a demonstration of good faith. Especially against the background of the main plan of action we had devised after absorbing the contents of that infamous document.

· *240* ·

There were, this time, between twenty and thirty of us gathered at Johannes Ras's place. The house was evidently too small to accommodate us all; but it was a balmy night, with the mildness of autumn in the air, the sky shimmering above the jagged outline of the mountains, and after partaking of a sheep roasted whole over a great bonfire we pursued our deliberations in the bare expanse of the farmyard. We were all sitting around the slowly dying fire which, from time to time, would explode in great showers of sparks accompanied by a roaring and crackling as of gunfire.

It was hard to keep my thoughts from wandering.

But the discussions were serious and vociferous. Most of the men were intent on forming a commando – ideally, a network of commandos throughout the colony – to storm the drostdy in Stellenbosch; and then to proceed, unstoppable, triumphant, across the plains to Cabo, and take the Castle (that garrison, I knew from experience, was so small, so ill-trained, so unprepared, a mere fifty or so of us could overrun it). How inspiring the vision in the flickering red core of the fire – of commanders and officers (Captain Rhenius, Lieutenant Allemann, Sergeant Kok, the whole evil brood) hurled from the walls, van den Henghel roasted on a spit on the parade ground at the front entrance . . .

For a while I indulged the men, stoked up their fantasies in feeding my own. But then it was time to proceed to serious planning, to temper our wishful thoughts with what could be done; above all to remain reasonable, to keep on the side of justice, to avoid descending to the level of the enemy.

And it was I who persuaded them once more to adopt the path of reason. First, I said, we should meet the *heemraden* of Stellenbosch. Even if they assisted the Landdrost, they had been chosen from among the colonists, people like us, who would understand our suffering and our urgency. Let us reason with them first, I proposed, and persuade them; for without their support the Landdrost would flounder, impotent; and from there our cause and the justness of it would spread throughout the land.

I volunteered to approach Charles Marais. But this was overridden by the others: even if he were a distant cousin, they argued, there was by now a price on my head and even a blood relation might be tempted by such a reward. I had become – this pleased me no end, I confess – indispensable to their cause. They would not sacrifice me to possible treachery. And so Hendrik Ras volunteered to go to a *heemraad* he knew, Schalk van der Merwe, and set up a meeting. To ensure his safety he would be accompanied by Sybrand van Dyk. They were to report back as soon as possible. In the meantime we would once again ride crisscross through the district to spread the word and hopefully to add to our numbers.

I betook myself to the region of the Piquet Berg, spending a night along the way at the widow Bevernage's to rest my horse. My destination was the farm of Willem van Wyk, the only member of our expedition from whom we had not yet had any reaction. It was a hard ride, the farm was far out of the way towards the Verlooren Vlei; but I was expecting a ready recruit to our cause, which should make the effort worth the while.

The first surprise, as I approached, was the abundance of cattle in the veld. Lucky man. Clearly, neither the Landdrost's official raiders nor any marauding band of hottentots had yet visited these parts. The only other place in the region where a farmer prospered was the huge tract of land belonging to the infamous whip-wielding Jan Cruywagen whom I remembered only too well from my first journey inland with Allemann.

Willem van Wyk was in great spirits, and he greeted me with a resounding blow between my shoulder blades.

'You seem to be having a good life?' I said, with some caution.

'And why shouldn't I?'

I told him about what had happened to the other members of the expedition. The news did not seem to surprise him. He merely smiled.

'The problem with those people is they always try to provoke the Landdrost. That is not the way to handle Pieter Lourens.'

'Surely he's not a friend of yours?'

'Not a friend, no. But not an enemy either. You must just know how.'

He turned to his hottentot wife who had been hovering in a

corner near the kitchen, visibly uneasy in the European clothes she was now wearing, a good silk bodice and a taffeta gown; but she was barefoot.

'What are you staring at, Eva?' he shouted. 'We want tea, man!'

Without answering she hastily shuffled out towards the kitchen.

'No, man,' he said expansively, sitting well back on the *riempie* bank. 'It's as you say, life is not a bad place to live in. But what brings you here?'

I explained to him the purpose of my visit.

'Ag no, Estienne,' he said emphatically, rising to look for his pipe; unable to find it he shouted at his wife to look for it. 'Now forgive me for saying this, but you're a stupid lot. Why run the risk of all the trouble, this whole dangerous business, if a few well-spent rix dollars can assure you a life without worries?'

'You mean you paid Lourens?' I asked, unable to believe my ears.

'I paid Lourens, I paid Counitz, I paid Jan Louw. I even travelled to Cabo to offer van den Henghel a gift of a few prize oxen. Now I can get on with my farming.'

'Sooner or later the hottentots will get you.'

'No they won't.' He took the pipe his wife brought to him, and gave her a pleasant slap on her backside which bulged provocatively under the skirt as she hurried back to the kitchen. 'They respect my wife. To them I'm a proven friend and an ally. I tell you, Estienne, this is the best of all possible lives.'

'How can you live with your conscience?'

'A conscience is a luxury of the rich,' he said easily. 'As I see it, I was born in this land and I've got to survive here. One of these days I'll start having children. Eva is pregnant already. Now do you think I want my sons to inherit war, or peace?'

'Is it really so easy, Willem?'

'Yes, it is. Or do you prefer me to start fighting back and end up where poor Matthys Willemsz is today?'

'We're going to get him out of that place.'

'And when he comes back, what will there be for him? Not a living creature on his farm. His house burned down. And his woman dead.'

'No!' I said. 'She isn't dead. She only went back to – to "her" people. He can fetch her again.'

'She is dead,' he said solemnly. 'There were some hottentots here last week on their way from the Great River to Cabo. They found her bones on the way.'

'I don't believe it.'

He shrugged and motioned to Eva, who had just entered, to serve me my tea.

'They recognised Dora from the clothes, Estienne. She was wearing that green dress, you know.'

I took my tea in silence, unable for a while to speak. It was not the bad news as such that had shaken me, although God knows that was shocking enough. (How blindingly I remembered that night she'd come to me: had it not been, at least in part, my doing that she had decided to accept Matthys Willemsz's offer and come back to the colony? If that night had gone differently, she might still be alive, and among 'her' people.) It was the terrifying thought that, somehow, her fate illuminated yours. You too had set out for that distant space beyond our frontiers. Something about her toughness, her unassailable independence, was disconcertingly like your own. True: she had been a woman of my kind; you were – different. But both of you, in the brief experience I'd had of you, had embodied something beyond the reach of my male definitions. A femininity so hard and bright, so sure of itself, defiant, serene, so unsurprised by the world, affirmative. This was, this is, your uncompromising beauty. Now, suddenly, she had been devoured – not by predators, but by the land. And this compromised you too. My own *raîson d'être* was, somehow, subverted by it.

'You all right?' asked Willem van Wyk. 'I mean, in a way it

was perhaps a good thing. What could a woman like her have done on her own?'

'She was not on her own, Willem.'

'Ja, but you know what I mean, man. Women really need us. She shouldn't have run away just like that. Must be something wrong with Matthys, you know. His first wife too. Hell, it's going to be a bad blow for him.'

'The wind was blow,' I said.

'What was that?'

'Just something I thought of.'

Early the following morning there was a slave messenger from Hendrik Ras. The meeting with the *heemraden* had been arranged. I was to ride back to Johannes's farm without delay. 'But be on the Lookout,' warned the note (written laboriously on his behalf, presumably by Hannie), 'for the Landdrost has sent out a commando of forty men to make War on us so make sure you bring Willem van Wyk with you we need every Man.'

'Not a damn,' Willem said cheerfully when I pressed him again. 'Why don't you stay here instead? We two can have a good time together. What do you say, we even find you a hottentot wife too?'

'My place is there with the others. They are looking up to me.'

'But you're not one of them. You'll never be one of them.'

'I am. For the first time in my life I believe I belong somewhere, Willem.'

'You're a bloody fool,' he said. 'Being a stranger is bad enough. But being a fool is worse.' He shrugged. 'But it's your choice, hey, every man for himself. Just let me get Eva to pack you some *padkos* for the road.'

On 17 March, towards noon, about twenty of us, bristling with arms, converged on the farm of Schalk van der Merwe. There had been no sign along the way of the Landdrost's commando; we learned later that those brave men had in fact not progressed farther than the first farm, where they had made a halt and requisitioned all the wine at the place, as a result of which they had become so drunk, and that for several days, that afterwards, ashamed of themselves and suffering most abominably, they had quietly disbanded.

On the way to van der Merwe's farm we had assembled briefly at Putter's place near by for some refreshment; like the Landdrost's troops we partook of a fair quantity of wine (but let me not detain you with that). Thereafter, as we chanced to pass by the mill, I once again tore van den Henghel's infamous *plakkaat* from the door, this time to lay it before the assembled *heemraden*. This drew loud cheers of encouragement from my troops.

We made a halt a hundred yards or so from van der Merwe's homestead, as Hendrik Ras was concerned lest the Landdrost had arranged an ambush. I sent Sybrand van Dyk ahead to invite the *heemraden* outside so that we could hold our deliberations in the open.

Five of them returned with him, among them Charles Marais, which somewhat reassured me. The presence of Jan Louw, on the other hand, augured no good. The very attitude of his square body was belligerent.

Although we had never met personally before, he immediately came up to me, stopping a mere foot away to stare intently into my face as if I were some rare animal.

'Estienne Barbier!' he exclaimed at last.

'What are you staring at?' I asked brusquely. 'Am I a unicorn? Or perhaps a hippogryph?'

'I never thought I'd find myself face to face with one like you,' he sneered. 'What are you doing here? Don't you know you're bird-free?'

'I know that very well,' I said, producing the large crumpled poster I had torn from the mill. 'I can read.'

'Do you realise what you're doing?' he asked. 'You're leading these poor misguided people to perdition.'

'Listen, poor misguided people!' I called. 'Do you agree that I'm leading you to perdition?'

'Look here, Jan Louw,' said Hendrik, coming forward. He towered above the *heemraad*'s squat figure. 'Estienne Barbier has opened our eyes to the truth. If he hadn't helped us your thieving Landdrost Lourens might have got away with murder.'

'There's your answer, *heemraad*,' I said. 'Now can we talk?'

'Let us all go inside,' urged Charles Marais.

Hendrik Ras had little inclination to accept. 'How do we know this isn't a trap?' he asked. 'There's no scheme too low and underhand for that sly fox Lourens.'

I held a brief consultation with Jeanne on the side.

'You are four to one,' she said. 'As long as you keep your arms at the ready it should be all right.'

Reassured, I turned back to the others. 'We can go in. But at the first sight of treachery we shoot. Is that understood?'

'I'm speaking on behalf of the Landdrost,' said Jan Louw. 'And I warn you – '

'You shut your trap, *canaille*!' I told him. 'There are twenty of us and five of you and you are going to do some listening today.'

Louw glowered at me, then turned round sharply and led the way into the house. Prompted by Jeanne, I insisted on first inspecting all the rooms (as befitted a *heemraad*, Schalk van der Merwe lived in a tall sprawling mansion, gabled and thatched, a cool and dignified interior, the floors gleaming the rich colour of honeycomb). Schalk's wife and daughters were in the large kitchen, surrounded by female slaves; the rest of the place was empty. For safety's sake I posted sentries at the front and back entrances before returning to the men assembled in the voorhuis.

It was once again Louw who went on to the attack, but his tone was now more studied, less abrasive. 'If you people are really so aggrieved,' he said, 'why didn't you first come to us, your *heemraden*, to discuss matters? I'm sure we could have solved it all amicably.'

'I wrote you several letters about all kinds of grievances over the last year,' said Sybrand van Dyk. 'And so did Lood Putter and others.'

'I know nothing about your letters,' said Louw. 'You know you can't trust messengers. Why didn't you come straight to me?'

'We were afraid you'd arrest us,' said Putter. 'You'd done that to others before us.'

'And we didn't send messengers either,' said van Dyk. 'We asked Charles Marais to give you the letters.'

'But I – ' began Jan Louw.

'I personally brought you letters from the farmers,' Charles said quickly. 'I can remember at least three occasions.'

'I swear – '

'Stuff your swearing up your *cul*,' I told him. 'We're not here to refresh your moth-eaten memory. We've come to discuss serious business.'

'I've yet to see a farmer discussing anything serious.'

A cuff, I thought, might be useful; but I restrained myself.

'I have just been outlawed by your miscreant masters in Cabo,' I said. 'There's a ransom on my head. Yet I am an honest man. All I've ever sought was ordinary decent justice. And at this very moment there are two of our comrades, good upright citizens, Pieter de Bruyn and Matthys Willemsz, rotting in a dungeon which could be put to much better use if it held a *con* like you. But let me warn you – all of you – unless you start doing the work you've been appointed for we'll see to it that you all end up on the gallows.'

'Now Estienne . . .' said Charles.

'Including you, my own cousin,' I said. 'You've done your share of underhand dealing, I'm afraid.'

'How can you say so?' he asked.

'You yourself told me you gave the governor – dear old Jan de la Fontaine – a hundred sheep to get the farm you wanted.'

'But *everybody* has to do it, Estienne!'

'And by doing it you keep the whole rotten system going!'

'Tell me what you people really want.'

And so I told them. About our cattle that had been stolen, our homes burned down, our wives raped, our farms overrun by hottentot *skelms*. About how we'd been driven to live and act like outlaws simply to survive, to ensure a decent life to our families, only to be denied and thwarted and threatened and persecuted at every turn by criminals like Landdrost Lourens, following the example of van den Henghel in Cabo who acted as if he were the king of the hottentots. ('Good,' Jeanne encouraged me, 'this is the kind of inspired rhetoric that should impress them. Now move on to your demands.')

'What we want, is for the *plakkaat* of the Council of Policy to be withdrawn.'

'You want a pardon?' asked Louw.

'No. How can we be pardoned if we have done no wrong? What we did we were driven to do. What we demand from you is three things. We want van den Henghel to apologise publicly for his *plakkaat* and to have the new *plakkaat* posted in all the places where the first one was displayed. We want Matthys Willemsz and Pieter de Bruyn to be released. We want to be compensated for every head of cattle illegally taken from us, eight rix dollar a piece.'

'Hit them hard,' whispered Jeanne. 'This is your last chance.'

'This is your last chance,' I told the assembled *heemraden*. 'Unless you persuade Landdrost Lourens and those criminals in Cabo to make reparation for the misery they have wrought, we shall carry the fire throughout this colony.'

Jan Louw sprang to his feet in anger; but before he could speak, one of his colleagues, Theuns Botha, pulled him back by the tail of his maroon coat and he sat down rather more abruptly than he could have anticipated.

'I think,' said Botha, looking at each of the *heemraden* in turn, then back to me, 'I can give you our word that we shall faithfully report your case to Landdrost Lourens.'

'To report it is not enough,' I said. 'We want you to support it. We want your assurance that you will intercede for us. If not, this land will go up in flames.'

'But what if Lourens cannot be persuaded?'

'You must take the responsibility for that,' I said.

'Ask them,' said Jeanne, 'if there was anything on your *Avis* on the church door they regard as false.'

'Was there anything in our *Avis* you thought wasn't true?' I demanded.

For a moment they all were silent; even Jan Louw sat with his blunt head bowed.

Then Charles Marais said, 'I can't speak for the others, but as for me, I agreed with every word.'

None spoke against him.

'How shameful then,' I said, 'that for those who speak the truth there is no shelter in this land.'

This was the end of our discussion. Jan Louw departed soon afterwards, no doubt to report to his superior; but the rest of us remained with the *heemraden*, in a spirit of increasing conviviality, as Schalk van der Merwe plied us with the choicest wine from his cellar and his wife and daughters brought in an endless *suite* of dishes.

It was very late by the time we staggered out to our horses. The meeting had been, we all believed, an eminent success. The *heemraden* had been wholly won over to our cause. War had been averted.

Only Jeanne said, 'Never trust the cunning of your enemy, Estienne.'

· 244 ·

The few weeks that followed constituted, I realised in retrospect, the best moment of our campaign. And if that was the best, I am now inclined to think, how dismal the rest must have been! Yet we were convinced that a great victory was approaching – and that without bloodshed.

Barely a week after our meeting with the *heemraden* there came news from the Council of Policy: Pieter de Bruyn and Matthys Willemsz had been released, and all the members of my commando were offered a full pardon. This was the good part of the tidings. The bad news was, of course, that in the eyes of van den Henghel's regime I remained an outlaw. Also, we learned about a proviso attached to the pardon offered: those who sought it had to pledge their active support for the government's continuing attempts to arrest me. This was met with such jeers among my people that for the time being it seemed our resistance had been strengthened rather than weakened by the stance of the Council of Policy.

Another week, and more news from Cabo – this time so unexpected and so positive that it appeared truly to signal the end of our problems. After an unconscionable delay of nearly eighteen months Swellengrebel had been officially appointed governor by the Lords Seventeen, his brother-in-law Rijk Tulbagh as Secunde; and Daniel van den Henghel, in a most humiliating move, instructed to return to his position as Fiscal.

What misery could have been averted had this happened sooner! With Swellengrebel in charge, Allemann and Kok would have lost their trumped-up cases against me; I would have been saved the horrors of the Dark Hole, the tribulations of my escape and over a year of wandering as a fugitive.

But there was no sense in indulging such thoughts. It was time to take action and strike this particular iron while it was aglow.

Without delay I composed a letter to Swellengrebel to resume anew all the particulars of my case and my sufferings and ask for his understanding, his indulgence, and his pardon. If I had done wrong, I reminded him, in escaping from arrest, surely that had been no more than the fugitive David had done when he'd stolen the altar loaves. How could I be reproached with what had been done under grave duress? Had my motive not consistently been the struggle to see justice done – a cause to which, surely, he was as devoted as I had been?

It was now, I was perfectly convinced, only a matter of time before I could return to Cabo a free man.

When after a week I had not yet received a reply, I composed a second, longer, letter. And after another fortnight a third.

Still no response. To this day I don't even know whether he ever received those missives. I prefer to believe that he is innocent. But it is hard to give it credence. And while I waited in increasing agitation there were other shocks and setbacks to contend with.

· 245 ·

The first came when, just after I had dispatched my first letter, I rode out to the Piquet Berg to visit Matthys Willemsz, believing that after his ordeal and the terrible discovery that would have awaited him upon his return, he might have need of company; of me.

Instead, as I approached the blackened ruin of his house he emerged from the gaping doorway, holding his musket in his hands, his eyes bloodshot and screwed up against the light (although it was April by then, and both heat and light had become attenuated in the mellowness of autumn).

'Matthys!' I called out, stopping at a safe distance, 'Don't shoot, it's me.'

'Go away, Estienne Barbier!' he shouted, raising the musket to his shoulder. 'You're a bad omen.'

'I've come to help you, Matthys,' I called, wondering whether his sojourn in the Black Hole had indeed impaired the sad soul's mind as it had his sight.

'I need nothing from you,' he said in a cold measured rage. 'Your very name is an abomination. Go away!'

'You need help, Matthys.'

I came a step nearer. He prepared to pull the trigger. Again I stopped.

'You listen to me, Barbier.' I could see his hand trembling. 'I gave them my word I'd shoot you or arrest you the moment you came near me again. I'm not going back to that hell-hole. It's all because of you.'

His words settled heavily in my stomach like an undigested lump of cold porridge. But I persisted in my reasoning. 'Swellengrebel is in charge now. I'm expecting a pardon every day. I've come to help you.'

'If it weren't for you my wife would still be alive, I'd still have my cattle, my farm, everything. Now look at me. I have nothing. Ever since the first day I met you you've brought me nothing but trouble. You're worse than any devil in hell.'

'Matthys, please, man – '

He moved his feet. There was a deafening report and a small cloud of red dust blew up some distance to my right. In the doorway Matthys was already reaching for another gun.

I did not wait for the second shot. With a heavy heart I turned and rode away. I knew that I really had nothing at all to do with his misfortunes, yet I could not escape a heavy feeling of guilt.

A single day after my return to *Orléans*, where I had again temporarily took up my abode, there was news that Matthys Willemsz had hanged himself.

There was worse to come. On Tuesday 13 April Hendrik Ras brought me the tidings that on the previous Friday Christian Petzold had been shot dead in his house by the agent Forster.

Van den Henghel had taken his last revenge on that innocent man. For how long had Petzold complained about that unwanted, evil presence under his roof? The timing of the dastardly act was eloquent in itself, a mere five days after van den Henghel had been forced to relinquish the post in which he'd always been a usurper. He must have known that Swellengrebel would soon start acting to dismantle the whole edifice of lies that had been my undoing; and in the process Petzold too was likely to be rehabilitated after the long persecution that had already ruined him and his family – and this could not but rebound on van den Henghel himself. Instructing Forster to kill the man (for what other explanation could there be for the event?) was a way of disposing of evidence that might prove uncomfortable; and at the same time it was very clearly a signal of warning to me.

And to Swellengrebel himself? Was that the reason why even my third long letter to the new governor remained unanswered?

And amid these developments, just before the middle of April, I celebrated – if that is indeed the word for an occasion that turned out so lugubrious – my fortieth birthday. Birthdays are not made much of in this colony; and as a child it had been my saint's day on 26 December rather than my birthday my parents had observed. But Tante Louise had set her mind on it.

'We must respect the stars that supervised your birth, Estienne,' she insisted.

'You shouldn't be so superstitious,' I reprimanded her.

'The world would have been a better place if people had spent more time heeding the signs of heaven, good or bad.'

'I assure you my signs are all positive.'

'You see?' she chuckled happily. 'That is exactly what your stars have foretold: you will claim to be true what you know to be untrue, simply because you wish it so.'

We were still arguing playfully when Hendrik Ras arrived; and that was how he learned about the birthday. It seemed to him a shrewd idea to turn it into a celebration to boost the morale of our troops.

For you must know, I had by then a hundred men under arms, and another two hundred prepared to respond to a summons within twenty-four hours. And several hundred more – it may not be exaggerated to say a thousand – who had already pledged themselves to my cause and could be called upon to join us when necessary.

A good number, possibly a hundred and fifty altogether, converged on Hendrik Ras's farm in the Roodezands Kloof a few days before the celebration. And the high spirits that fired him led to several impromptu exploits of great daring. These included riding to Landdrost Lourens's own farm outside Stellenbosch (which he managed in contravention of all the express instructions of the Lords Seventeen) and driving from it at least ten head of cattle, several of which were then slaughtered for our festivities.

There was so much pent-up energy among the men that a number of sporting events – running, wrestling, riding, shooting – were arranged to occupy them. Then, on the morning of my birthday, a great commando was assembled to ride through the district in the direction of the Bokkeveld, simply to demonstrate our presence and our readiness and to muster even more support for our cause.

In the circumstances what next happened was perhaps inevitable: yet no one, I am sure, had actually foreseen it.

Approaching the straits of the Gydo Kloof a small band of hottentots – no more than eighteen or twenty – was espied in the distance, coming towards us. A great roar went up among the men: undoubtedly this was one of those marauding bands that had been pestering the countryside these past few months, burning farms and stealing livestock and terrorising women. There was an immediate surge forward in our midst.

As the hottentots saw us coming they broke into what seemed like a war dance, waving and shouting. This was all that was still needed. Without bothering to wait for orders my men galloped towards the enemy. Such was the momentum of the charge that the horses stormed right over and past the hotten-tots, coming to a standstill a good hundred yards beyond them, where they reared and swung round for another charge. And it was hopeless to try and interrupt the manoeuvre, even when in thundering past we discovered that there were mainly women and children in the group.

'What does it matter?' asked Lood Putter afterwards. 'They're a nation of thieves and plunderers, aren't they? The women spawn more and more of them and the children grow up to be robbers and murderers in their turn.'

No one even thought of using a gun. There seemed to be a raw, urgent need for the immediacy of physical contact.

It was over very soon. Too soon for most of the men, I'm afraid. I saw some of them continuing the battle by charging at trees and bushes, at boulders and at the very clouds of dust sent churning into the air by the fury of the gallop. I saw Sybrand van Dyk taking his gun by the barrel in his remaining good arm and clubbing away at the stump of a tree until the whole butt was splintered to bits and the iron twisted into a useless mess.

Even then it was not the end. Some of the men took out their hunting knives and set upon the sprawling bodies to hack off heads or limbs which it seemed they wished to carry off as trophies. My shouting at last stopped some of them; and by then Hendrik and a few others had joined me to put an end to the gory activity. But some of the butchers were so transported by their own excesses that we actually had to subdue them with the butts of our guns to beat them to their senses.

'We can plant these heads on stakes all round the farmyard at tonight's feast,' said one of them, his eyes shining madly through the red dust and grime that covered the whole of his face.

'It's enough, I tell you!' I answered, with an unfamiliar sickness in my stomach. For this I had not foreseen. And even the previous massacres I had experienced in the interior had not prepared me for this: there we had relied on our guns, the killing had been done from afar; never on those occasions had such a frenzy, such a lunatic immediacy of slaughtering, manifested itself.

There was only one feature of the new attack I recognised from its precursors: once again I had witnessed, in the eyes of my men as they raged towards the enemy, the look of nameless terror. Yet what madness was this? And to what further madness would it yet drive us?

It took a long time to round them all up and return them to their horses. I think something of the horror of the atrocity had by then worked its way through to more and more among them – they were good decent Christian people after all! – because an uncomfortable silence began to settle on us.

As we prepared to ride off I noticed movement in a cluster of dense bushes a hundred or so yards to our left. With Hendrik at my side I rode to investigate. There were three small children hiding in the thicket, one wounded (a broken arm), the two others only half-dead with fear.

'We can't leave them here,' I said. 'We'd better take them back with us.'

'I can use a few more hands on my farm,' said Hendrik.

After several more hours, and only with the aid of a few slaps from Hendrik's redoubtable hands, we coaxed from the children (who like most of the tame hottentots in the colony spoke broken Dutch) the history of their wandering: they had come from high up in the Bokkeveld, it transpired, where their tribe had been attacked by a band of Bushmen who had raided all their cattle; as a result they had decided to trek to Cabo to lay their complaint before their white fathers (as they phrased it) and beseech the help of the Dutch from whom, they believed, they could expect protection.

And so there was an unnatural solemnity that night among us around the huge bonfires Hendrik had lit; and what should have been a celebration became an occasion of silence and shame.

· *249* ·

Before the evening had progressed very far I slipped away quietly on my own, and saddled my horse and rode off into the night. I swear I did not steer the horse; all by itself it found its way to the home of Liesbet van Wyk.

She had a fright when I knocked. Not having my father's watch any more I had no idea what time it was; but from the position of the stars I deduced it must be at least two o'clock in the morning. Her voice trembled as she asked through the heavy door who was there, and threatened to shoot at the slightest warning. But when she recognised me warmth insinuated itself into her voice, and she unbarred the door, wearing only her shift, to let me in and lead me to her bedroom with the tall canopied bedstead; she removed my clothes with the deftness of experience, and drew me to her in the soft recesses of the feather mattress.

I had never had the experience of finding myself unable to

bander. But that night, my birthday night, at what should have been the moment of entry, the rage of my need subsided suddenly, and limp and humiliated I turned away from her. She cradled me against her ample naked body, coaxing, soothing, cajoling; but as she resolutely took in her hand the object of my shame I began to cry. Still she held me, mumbling small wet words in my ear. But how could she comfort me if she didn't even know the reason for my anguish? And how could I communicate it to her if I could not find the words for it myself?

After some time I warded off her stupid and sincere approaches, and fumbled for my clothes, and left again, although by now *she* was in tears.

The cocks were crowing, but the first greyness of dawn had not yet begun to discolour the night when I reached *Orléans* and tiptoed to my room (Tante Louise was used by now to my untimely comings and goings, poor soul). At least there was the comfort of understanding which none but Jeanne could offer.

· *250* ·

'This was supposed to have been my day of glory,' I said bitterly. 'Now I am ashamed not only of my men but of myself.'

Jeanne did not reply; she knew when to let me go.

'My fortieth birthday,' I said. 'This is the time a man is supposed to have settled down, to have achieved something, to look back over the trajectory that has brought him where he is, to assess his life so that he can decide how best to spend the rest of it. But what do I have, I ask you? Not a *sol* in the world. Only a single book, damaged by a bullet from a man who was once my enemy and is now my friend: but is this the kind of friend I need? I have achieved nothing. All remains to be done. But today I feel useless. I'm a failure, Jeanne.' I sat up in the bedclothes, rumpled with my tossing and turning, and displayed to her the sign of my misery, a small wrinkled worthless animal. 'Tonight I could not even *foutre* Liesbet de Wet. Can you believe it? What is happening to me? At forty a man should have a wife and children. I have no one.'

'There are several craving widows who would be happy to accept you,' she said; the touch of malice did not escape me.

'There is no one I can conceive of sharing the rest of my life with.'

'Even before I first set out for Vaucouleurs,' she said, more gravely, 'there was a man from Toul I was engaged to. I don't think I've ever told you this?'

'You haven't.' I felt a strange stirring of jealousy in me.

'He later even sued me for breach of promise,' she continued, ignoring the edge to my voice. 'But that was one of the first things I had to put beside me when I accepted my vocation. I swore that I'd remain a virgin for as long as it pleased God. How ironical that at my trial I should have been reproached for acting "contrary to the honesty of womankind". How could I expect them to understand? There is a kind of struggle which demands total dedication. One has to forgo the easy pleasures of others.'

'I have enough easy pleasures, Jeanne! But can't you see? It is driving me to distraction. I *want* to be married, and raise a family. My only reason is that I cannot afford it. I have nothing.'

'You don't have to have anything to be something.'

'This time your aphorisms are not enough, Jeanne.'

'Then why have you not chosen a wife in this country?'

'Because my mind, inside, is otherwise occupied. I have you. I have Rosette.'

'You have neither of us. I am dead. She may be too, for all you know.'

'Even if she is she has never let go of me.' I was almost pleading now; I needed her understanding so desperately. 'When I am with one of my widows it is different: a moment's pleasure, a trifle, then shame, then disgust. What are they to me? Women reduced to a collection of *cons*, all pleasing in different ways, intriguing, but trifles still.'

'Was Rosette any different?'

'That disgraceful night – ' I was silent. 'But that is not what she has since become. Do you know that I'm not even sure what she looked like any more. I wake up at night and try to conjure up her image which I thought was indelible in my mind. But it has gone. Sometimes I remember her breasts. Not even of that can I be sure. I only imagine them. And yet she is involved in everything I do, and wish for, and am. When I think of her she merges with the land, with its tit-hills and empty stretches, it's light, its kloofs and thickets, its secret depths. Is that not as insulting as it is to those others to be reduced to a single sheath of experience? I want a *woman*, Jeanne! Yet tonight I have nothing.'

'It is not night any more,' she said quietly. 'Listen to the birds. Look at the light beginning.'

I ignored her reminder; it was not relevant. 'Surely I'm not too old to expect the comfort and happiness of a woman at my side?'

A brief, mischievous chuckle from Jeanne. 'You are more than twice as old as I ever was,' she said.

'So I have nothing to hope for?' I asked in a rush of bitterness.

'No need to wallow in it,' she said sharply. Then, after a pause. 'In spite of everything *I* believe in you, Estienne.'

'You must be the only one.'

'On many, many occasions I, too, had nothing but my voices to support me.'

· *251* ·

I reflected for a long time before I said, 'You are right. I should take heart. If you think of it, I have a few hundred men devoted to my cause.'

'Ah but look at what they have done today. On your behalf.'

A moment ago she'd been exhorting me; the change in approach unsettled me. But I'd known her long enough to realise what she was doing, playing the devil's advocate. How else could she force me to see clearly, without prejudice or wishful thinking?

'You must look behind what they did,' I argued, 'at the reasons they had for their action.'

'What reasons?'

'Fear. I saw it in their eyes even as they went about their slaughtering. They saw into themselves today. I think they will be more reliable in future.'

'No,' she said. 'They have already begun to waver. That was perhaps part of their fear, as it is part of your despondency tonight.'

'They stand united with me.'

'I tell you they are wavering. Even if they themselves are not yet conscious of it.'

'Why should they waver? They are dedicated to me.'

'They waver because the best news you have had in years may strangely turn out to be the worst.'

'What is that?'

'Swellengrebel.'

'How can you say that?' I was both angry and alarmed.

'To fight against van den Henghel and his brood fires the purpose of your men. They will not fight against Swellengrebel who is an Afrikaner like them.'

'But that is the point. They *need* not fight him. He will resolve everything.'

'Has he replied to your letters?'

'He will. I have faith in him. Any day now I shall have his full pardon. He may even invite me to the Castle.'

'He is now the most powerful man in the colony. He has other interests to look after. I have warned you before.'

'I won't give up.'

'That was what I wanted to hear, Estienne. To go on fighting because your cause is just. Even if you know you will lose.'

'I am not going to lose.'

'Estienne.' How well I knew that tone of voice: quiet, gentle, almost sorrowful. 'Under the walls of Melun, after the defeat at Paris, but while I was still riding high and had every reason to believe in success, my voices spoke to me. "Jeanne," they said, "you will be taken before St John's day. This needs must be. Do not be astonished. Take all with a willing heart."'

'Did you believe them?'

'How could I not believe them? They had never lied to me. All I asked of them was that I might die quickly. I could not face a long ordeal. Like you, I was scared of physical pain.'

'And now you are telling me that I, too, will lose?'

'You will be taken, you will die. But whether you will lose is your own choice.'

'How can one go on if the end is certain?'

'The end is always certain. Losing is not. And that, I should think, is more important.'

'How did you prevail?'

'I was contrary enough.' Her small sad smile – in the slowly gathering light of dawn she was now visible – as she said, '*Aide-toi, Dieu t'aidera.*'

· *252* ·

I knew what I was looking for in my book. It had never failed me, neither did it on this occasion. The episode I recalled was the encounter with the Yanguesans, on the hidalgo's road to the inn which he was to mistake for a castle. While he and his loyal squire are resting in a pleasant spot, a group of carriers from the town of Yanguas join them there; but then Don Quixote's miserable old hack Rocinante is suddenly taken, quite unexpectedly, with desire for the Yanguesans' frisky mares. The men come running up to protect the honour of their lady horses and beat Rocinante to the ground. Whereupon Don Quixote and Sancho intercede – only, predictably, to be battered senseless and abandoned in what the storyteller describes, as far as I remember, as an evil plight and a worse humour. When at last they come round again the hero is hard put to offer Sancho an acceptable explanation for this new adversity. The actual reason he provides is obvious: he should not have drawn his sword on men who were not knights. But the truly illuminating moment of the encounter, to me, is his admission: 'For myself, I can see no end to our present plight. But I take the blame for everything upon myself.'

· 253 ·

My death is very close now, Rosette. With every line I address to you I feel myself written closer to it. Those outside have already written me off. The spectacle of my execution will be a last reminder: but even there I shall be essentially absent. What they will witness at the stake will not be the last sight of Estienne Barbier, but a mere body strangled and hacked to pieces like any carcass. I no longer exist. I am a *trépassé*, I have crossed the last frontier.

And I am scared of pain.

· 254 ·

Listen to me, Rosette. Listen well. I am speaking against accepted history, against that version van den Henghel so elaborately formulated in his Act of Accusation, which is the only version the world will know. If they even bother to look it up a hundred, or two or three hundred years from now. *You* must know the inside: because you are *there*: outside: free.

That month of April was indeed the turning-point: the culmin-ation of our rebellious action, and the beginning of the ebb. And Jeanne had been right. Swellengrebel was my downfall. This man on whom, from the very beginning, I had pinned my hopes, now became the agent of my undoing. And the worst of all to bear was that he did not effect this by acting against me but simply by cutting all the solid ground from under my feet. Even that, I believe, was no calculation on his part; it was not particularly shrewd. He merely did what circumstances dic-tated; what came natural to him.

At the end of April he announced a vast campaign (to be led by Jan Cruywagen) against the hottentots: to rid the colony of their menace and return them to the periphery. At the first signs of unrest van den Henghel, the foreigner, had chosen to support the hottentots in their clamouring against the colonists. But Hendrik Swellengrebel, the native son, sided by instinct with the farmers. It was so much easier to expel the hottentots and ensure the goodwill of those colonists on whom the continuing prosperity of the land depended. It was not a matter of seeking justice. (How ironical to reflect now, in the illuminat-ing darkness of my dungeon, that despite his prejudice and viciousness van den Henghel might have been, ultimately, more just – even though he himself was surely oblivious of it.)

What Swellengrebel proposed to do was exactly what my men had been demanding all along: to rid us of the pest of native marauders and restore to us the cattle confiscated from us. No wonder the farmers began to peel and flake away from me like chalk from a badly whitewashed wall. Why run the risk of persecution if they could obtain the same by joining forces with the government? Each of my followers who proclaimed himself willing to sign up was accorded a full and unconditional pardon; that they signalled perforce, at the same time, their readiness to track me down and hand me over and bring me, as the phrase goes, to justice – *that* was what rankled.

· *256* ·

The hour-long, night-long, endless arguments with Hendrik Ras, hitherto my staunchest ally. One I remember particularly well. He'd come to my hiding-place, which at that moment (I never stayed more than two or three days at any farm) was Fransina Basson's. She had brought us coffee, briefly laid a strong hand on my shoulder – a small, intimate, proprietorial gesture that both comforted and alarmed me – then left us alone.

'The men are weary, Estienne,' said Hendrik. 'They have farms and wives and children. Their danger comes from the hottentots, not Cabo. How can you blame them for joining Swellengrebel's commando?'

'It's a trick,' I stormed at him, 'and they're all falling for it.'

'Yesterday morning,' he said calmly, 'a bunch of hottentots in the employ of Landdrost Lourens came to my place and brought back to me every head of cattle Counitz had taken from me in January.'

'What!' This truly was beyond belief.

'I have made enquiries, Estienne, and as far as I can make out all the stolen cattle are being given back to the farmers. Swellengrebel's orders. This is a victory for you, man. Everybody's shouting with happiness. I tell you, I was at Koos Jansen's place. He wept for joy. Now we can all begin again.'

'You are being bought, Hendrik. This is just to force you into joining their commando against the hottentots.'

'What's wrong with that? They bloody well need to be taught a lesson.'

'And at the same time the men are now betraying me? Barely a month after they all pledged their loyalty to my cause.'

'But now your cause is the same as the government's, man. And there is so much more reward, supporting Swellengrebel. Who has always been your friend.'

I did not answer.

'He *is* your friend, isn't he, Estienne?'

'I thought he was. I'm not sure of anything any more. How many letters have I written to him? And I'm still an outlaw, any man who kills me can claim the price on my head.'

'Perhaps the letters did not reach him.'

'I'll write again. I'll keep on writing. But the least I expect of my men is to stay with me until my own safety has been assured.'

'They are under pressure, man. If they don't sign up they can all be jailed.'

'The government does not have enough space in prison for them all. It's an idle threat. And I need their loyalty, more than ever.'

'Don't doubt their loyalty, Estienne. One thing I can assure you: whatever they promise the government, not one of them will ever betray you. They're deeply grateful: if it hadn't been for you they wouldn't have got their cattle back. It's a hell of a blow to Landdrost Lourens, I can tell you.'

'And what about *me*, Hendrik? I'm a man too, not an animal. I don't want to be hunted to the end of my days. I need to live like others, settle down, have some peace.'

'By joining forces with the government against the hottentot enemies we can bring that peace closer for us all. Including you, in the end.'

'Hendrik, Hendrik.' I shook my head wearily. 'You have it all wrong, man. You keep on talking about the hottentots as our enemies. The enemy that first threatened me, the enemy I'm still fighting, is in Cabo: it's officialdom, corruption, power. The hottentots are powerless.'

'This thing is beginning to affect your head,' he said. 'You have seen yourself the destruction those creatures have caused . . .'

'Yes. Because we took their cattle and attacked their settlements.'

'Are you blaming *us* now?!'

'I don't know. Although that thing that happened on my birthday still keeps me awake at night. But if we were not to blame then we did what we did because the government pushed us and made it impossible for us to lead a decent life. Not so?'

'But the government has changed.'

'No, Hendrik. There is another man in the Governor's house now, true. And I believe he is a good man. But the *government* has not changed. The government, and its power, and its abuse of that power, is still as much of a threat to our freedom as ever before. That is what our war is about.'

'Will you resist Swellengrebel's commando?'

'First of all,' I said, 'it is not Swellengrebel's commando. If it was, it might have been different – although even of that I'm not sure any more. But this is Jan Cruywagen's commando. And Cruywagen is a *chienlit* and a joke. No one knows that better than you.'

· 257 ·

Do you remember the whip-man, that unctuous and obnoxious fool Jan Cruywagen, Rosette? But you may not have witnessed it when we stayed over on his farm on that first journey, with Allemann. After all, you were one of the servants; a slave. We must have been all alike to you. A sobering thought.

I remember, though. The way he cringed and smirked, even though he was lord and master of a farm that stretched from horizon to horizon: how he ingratiated himself with Allemann, inviting the lieutenant and his whining wife to do him the great honour of spending their nights in the *opstal* while we slept outside (and it was raining too, remember?). He slaughtered sheep and cattle to entertain us; he organised a hunt, sending his flocks of slaves and hottentots (all provided by the Company in exchange for 'services rendered') to round up springbok and hartebeest and zebra and even five camelopards so that the lieutenant could kill to his heart's content without much exertion; even Madame showed her mettle by bringing down a camelopard – although it took a dozen shots, and even then the poor animal refused to die. And when we skinned it – for naturally she wanted the skin returned to Cabo to be cured as a trophy to display to guests from abroad – we found a calf inside her, whose tender pale barely blotched skin was then also flayed. (This, I am sure, you must remember; if I recall correctly, she ordered you to bring a basin of warm water and wash her fat white feet while she sat watching the activity. Oh how I hate that couple, the authors of all my misfortune!)

To every utterance of Allemann's, however unremarkable – and most were profoundly unremarkable – Jan Cruywagen beamed, and rubbed his hands, and repeated endlessly, 'Yes-yes, indeed-indeed, isn't it just – isn't it just, if you say so, Mijnheer Allemann, if you say so – ' That man, I tell you, should have gone on the stage – I twice attended performances in Orléans, I'll have you know – he is a born comedian. Only, comedians are harmless, their gestures come to an end at the conclusion of their brief make-believe; but Cruywagen is dangerous. Through his intimacy with Allemann, with van den Henghel himself, with the whole brood of power-mongers at the Cape, he has the run of the outlying district. The men had spoken much about him on that journey into the interior, the second journey I mean: and that was when I learned about his nature. If he didn't like someone, a brief message to Cabo was enough to see that man's farm licence withdrawn; once or twice small detachments of soldiers had even been dispatched by van den Henghel to turn such hapless people from what had been their property. If he needed more cattle, he commandeered them from his neighbours; if he wanted more land he simply annexed it. If he took a liking to you you prospered; if not, you might as well pack up and seek refuge elsewhere in the colony.

A small fat man, more wide than tall; ruddy of complexion (not from the sun, I believe, but from ample acquaintance with arrack), with a high-pitched voice as if he'd jumped over a hedge in his youth. And I remember he had difficulty, on that hunt he'd arranged – and which involved no more than a few hundred yards on horseback, at an easy trot – to stay in the saddle.

With a mixture of revulsion and fascination I recall his dexterity with that long whip: how he'd belaboured me with it; and how he'd flicked a snake from the inside of a weaver's nest to demonstrate his skill; even more astounding, how he'd taken us to his fields where swarms of finches rose in clouds at our approach, and how he would invite us, to the accompaniment of Madame Abbetje's shrieks of delight, to point out a specific bird, which he would then – I swear to God – pluck from the sky with a single crack of that murderous instrument. (Would there still be birds in those nests, I wonder?)

And this, I tell you, was now the commandant of the Governor's *platteland* forces sent out to rid the land of hottentots. Do you blame me for responding with bitterness to the tidings brought by Hendrik Ras?

· 258 ·

I was not in a position, of course, to follow closely the vicissitudes of the Cruywagen commando: not only because reports were hard to come by, and slow in travelling; but because I myself had to be constantly on the move – a night or two at *Orléans*, then a few with the flame-haired Constance Bevernage, then the little *boule de suif* Anne Leriche, or Leonie Burgert with the long black tresses; then resolutely forward to the strong arms of Fransina Basson, or the blue-eyed wiles of Liesbet de Wet. (Yes, if you must know, I did return to her after a period of absence; and this time there were no problems with my performance, she even thought it had improved, which, if I say so myself, was quite a compliment.)

But the dangers were increasing. I was reassured, after some time, that Hendrik had been right: my own men, even those who had been lured into joining the Cruywagen menagerie, would not betray me for anything. And in a torrent of urgent letters I continued to dispatch from my widows' houses scattered throughout the colony, I continued to exhort them (*Oh my Afrikaner brethren, for God's sake, and in the name of the Lords Seventeen!*) to keep faith, not to be duped, not to accept new treacherous forms of enslavement to the thieves and scoundrels who had always sucked their blood. But beyond the tight circle of my immediate companions there were others less dependable who might well be tempted by the price on my head; in addition, and these were more dangerous, there were lowly functionaries in Cabo or attached to the drostdy in Stellenbosch, eager to prove their worth and buy promotion by finding me; there were paid hottentots and vagrants ever ready to earn an easy *skilling*.

Usually it was not too difficult to evade them. In the houses where I stayed most often the loyalty of the servants was assured, through ample gifts from their mistresses. Still, one never knew. Once, when I was with Fransina Basson, an agent from the Landdrost, a particularly persevering bastard called Witstock, having obviously received intelligence of my whereabouts, arrived so early in the morning that we were still in bed; I had to dive, naked, into the small space between the bed and the back wall when he irrupted unannounced. I had made it in the nick of time, and the widow, as strong as any woman among these peasant folk, belaboured him most energetically with a fire-iron before he managed, in a very bad state, to escape.

On another occasion, enjoying a post-coital cup of tea in the voorhuis of Leonie Burgert we were actually surprised by a *knecht* from the drostdy. But he seemed even more taken aback by his unexpected good luck, which gave me time to grab my pistol and give him such a whack over the head with it that I thought I'd broken his skull. We spent some time bringing him round with several pails of water; then, as he staggered dizzily to his feet, I offered him my pistol and invited him to shoot me, which offer he however declined. He was only interested in getting away as quickly as he could.

On yet a third occasion I was pursued, from the farm of Jeannette Gobregts (how often in this darkness my thoughts still dwell on my nights with that magnanimous body in my arms), by a whole detachment of soldiers commanded by Counitz himself. They tried to corner me against the Berg River; but capering along the bank I managed to reach just in time the primitive ferry operated by Hendrik Coetsee who, oblivious of my own interests, was himself at the time a suitor of the widow Gobregts. He had just sat down to breakfast and was in no mood to interrupt that serious business; but promising him that I had a message from the young widow which I would divulge to him on the other bank I succeeded in arousing the eager man's most passionate interest. We were but ten yards or so from the bank when my pursuers arrived, shouting at Coetsee to turn back. 'These are dangerous men,' I warned him. 'I have just lured them away from Jeannette Gobregts's place where they were preparing serious harm against her.' This caused him to redouble his efforts. Two of my pursuers charged into the river on their horses. One fell off. The other, Counitz himself – most certainly not out of bravery, the *poltron*, but only because his horse had bolted – reached the ferry, but I grabbed an oar and cracked him over the head; then, with Coetsee's help, I dragged him out, still dazed, on the rough boards of our craft, and shouted at the assembled men on the bank to desist or our hostage would be killed.

In this manner we reached the opposite bank, where we summarily stripped Counitz of his clothes – how it diminishes, in shape and size and dignity, a man of power and authority, now reduced to crouching pathetically to hide his privates, and blubbering for mercy – and ordered him back into the river.

'Now you must wait here until they have gone,' I told Coetsee.

'And the message?' he asked in great agitation.

'Jeannette wants you to come over tonight,' I said. 'Then, if she is still in the same mind, she will tell you herself.'

'Is that all?'

'Is that not enough?' I asked. 'Most men would sacrifice their right hand, if not a *couille*, to have a message like this from a woman like her.'

'But what do you think it *means*?' he asked.

'You have all day to ponder the possibilities,' I told him.

If there was a measure of merriment in such occasions as these (there were three or four others as well, with which I shall not try your patience), they also brought me profound unease – not only because of the danger I found myself in, but even more pertinently because of the danger my survival was increasingly causing others. The satisfaction of still being able to outwit, outrun or outmanoeuvre my persecutors became ever less than the malaise about the mere sense of my survival.

· 259 ·

Then, late in June, in a bitter cold spell that capped the Drakenstein mountains with snow for over a week, Tante Louise fell ill with what seemed to be pneumonia. I watched by her bedside for two days. Her mind was rambling most of the time. There were moments when she addressed me as her late husband; others when she mistook me for her brother, Paul Couvret, who had first brought her out to Africa. Towards the second evening there was a spell of lucidity and she began to talk again of my future, of her wish that I should take over the farm.

'We can discuss such things later, when you're feeling better,' I said as gently as I could, driven into an unexpected panic by the fear that she might really die. I still needed her too much, not just because of the haven she offered me, but because she stood between me and too many questions I was not yet prepared to face.

'We must talk now,' she persisted. 'You are always so busy, running here and there. We must use this occasion.'

'Not now, Tante Louise. You need to rest first. Sleep.'

I thought she'd drifted off. But after a few minutes she opened her almost-blind eyes again and said, 'There is one thing I have never told you. I don't know why. I feel guilty about it. When you first came here to *Orléans* as a *pasganger* you asked me about a slave woman you said you'd sent to me.'

My stomach contracted. 'What do you know about her?' I asked, grabbing her hand. 'Did you see her? Was she here?'

'It has continued to bother me,' she said. 'I suppose I reproached you for what I suspected was a reprehensible involvement with a slave woman. We French should set an example.'

'What do you know about her, Tante Louise?' I demanded.

She gasped a little from the rough way I was shaking her; I let go.

'I'm tired, Estienne,' she sighed. 'Let us talk about it tomorrow.'

In the morning she was dead. She must have gone very quietly during the few minutes in the night when I dozed off beside the bed.

I am travelling on horseback below the Paarl Mountain, on my way from *Orléans* to the drostdy of Stellenbosch; a few paces behind me follows a detachment of my troops, those last intrepid companions who will be faithful unto death. A rumbling sound from above alerts me. As I glance up I see those two smooth enormous boulders lodged in a wedge of the mountain trembling, balanced for a moment on the edge of the slope, before they come rolling down towards us with the thundering sound of an earthquake. It is too late to move; this is the end. We can only stare as they hurl themselves down the slope towards us, faster and faster. As they approach, I notice to my horror that they are not boulders after all, but two huge heads severed from what must have been truly colossal bodies. Hottentot heads, yellowish-brown in colour, with curiously protruding staring eyes. From what remains of the necks black-red blood is spouting in deep dark torrents, coming down the slope like a river of gore, engulfing us.

I wake up with the sound of my own terrified shouting in my ears. A woman is holding me, rocking me gently, uttering scared but soothing meaningless words. 'Now, now, Estienne, now, now, it was only a dream, man . . .'

I don't even know who the woman is.

Or this: I wander across a wide bare plain marked with innumerable small cairns; as I pass by them, the stones on each begin to heave and move and roll away, exposing grave after grave from which the bodies of dead and maimed hottentots emerge. There are men, women and children among them, all besmirched most gruesomely with blood and dirt; and they utter a collective wail that trembles right through my bones. In a frenzy I start working to put them back into their graves and shovel new earth over them; but each time, as I turn to another grave, the corpse behind me begins to claw its way back to the surface.

Again I wake from the sound of my own scream, to find a woman desperately comforting me.

· 262 ·

The scenes change from night to night; so does the voice, and the clinging shape of the woman. But the dreams recur, in many forms, each more hideous than the rest. I, who have almost never had my sleep disturbed by dreams before, am now racked by these nightmares. If I do not fall victim, soon, to the preying emissaries of the government with their guns and pistols and knives, these enemies from within will engulf me. No, it is not an easy time.

· 263 ·

There is only one remedy for these terrors which are all caused by enforced inaction. I cannot go on like this, a general with no troops; a mere fugitive, an outlaw hunted like a fox across the face of Africa, rolling through the desolation of the plains like a tumbleweed in the west wind. Even if it is the last desperate resort, what remains of my army must move into action, at least to leave behind the kind of memory future generations can draw inspiration from.

I ride to the place of Hendrik Ras to communicate my plan; he is, as I knew he would be, enthusiastic. Together, we visit his brother's place. Then the three of us proceed into the remote Bokkeveld, secluded among its high mountains capped with snow in this harsh winter; and in a wide curve towards the sea, the region of the Four-and-twenty Rivers, the Swartland, Piquet Berg, and back to the lush and more populated regions of Drakenstein and Paarl and Stellenbosch. As we proceed, the army grows. It is amazing how, now that we have decided to move into action and end the inertia, more and more men recover their initial passion for the cause.

Yes, yes, they agree: our true enemies are those in Cabo. We have been temporarily lulled into false security; thank God you have shaken us back to our senses. *Vive Estienne Barbier! Vive* the cause of justice and freedom!

I ride on ahead of them, Jeanne beside me, both of us swathed in great cloaks of gold and scarlet; then follow the Ras brothers with my standard, displaying what once was Jeanne's coat of arms, but which I have now appropriated for myself: azure, a sword argent huilted and supporting on its point a crown between two fleurs de lys. Further behind follows the rest of the army, now so innumerable that they cover the full extent of the Cape Flats.

The garrison at Cabo has been warned of our approach, but their defence is hopelessly inadequate (as I warned them years ago), and what there is is trained towards the sea. Their first volley, obviously triggered in too much haste, falls short; the second, after precipitate reloading, swishes harmlessly overhead. And before they can load for the third we are among them, overrunning their positions with the sheer momentum of our charge.

The Castle gate has been closed against us, but with one of the cannon we have swept along with us from the first redoubt, which I had built myself, we break right through it and what soldiers remain inside hurl away their arms and fall on hands and knees to surrender. Even the guards in front of van den Henghel's residence lose courage; in a single motion, as if rehearsed in advance, they draw their pistols and shoot themselves.

My companions hesitate in a throng on the threshold, intimidated by the sudden realisation of where we are. A solitary bland man confronts me there, armed only with a large green book. It is Herr Otto Friedrich Mentzel. I pluck the tome from his frightened hands and beat him down, then crush his skull with it as if he were a spider or a worm. Much more serious business awaits me. With drawn sword I rush through the house, from one high-ceilinged dark-beamed elegant room to the next until I am stopped by a trembling guard upstairs in front of a tall closed door. Even before I strike at him he drops to his knees and starts crawling away, shaking with fear. I kick the door open.

An unappetising sight awaits me as I stumble upon the van den Henghels in amorous embrace. All that is visible from my vantage point is the Fiscal's huge white rear, rising and plunging, balls dangling, the cyclops eye of his anus gawking at me. Into the heart of this target I plunge my long sword. He screams like a stuck pig. The violence of his contortions causes his wife to break through the barriers of the ultimate ecstasy as her small fat white feet kick frantically in the air above his raised posterior. Where I get the strength from is beyond me; but straining with both arms I raise the great squirming squealing body still impaled on my sword and carry him, like a standard, triumphantly through the house, across the front courtyard, and up the stone staircase into the bell-tower, my cheering army following in our wake. At the very top of the tower I plant the handle of the sword into a socket intended for a torch on festive nights; and there I leave the pink monster to bellow his agony across the length and breadth of the town, only a few feet away from the great bell from which Allemann's long-dried balls, like two withered prunes, still tinkle faintly in the breeze.

As we descend, Hendrik Swellengrebel arrives from his house in the Berg Street, prostrates himself before us, and promises in future to govern by the will of the people.

It is the final victory. The effort, the suffering, the sacrifice, has not been in vain. The people shall govern.

Vive Estienne Barbier!

· *264* ·

There was the sound of galloping in the farmyard. I grabbed my pistol and dived into an armoire in the voorhuis while Anne Leriche, calmly wiping her plump hands on her apron, went to the door. But a moment later she returned to call me: it was only Hendrik Ras. As usual, he had to stoop to get his huge body through the front door.

Normally a direct man, this morning he took his time to broach the subject he'd come to discuss. He was clearly most uncomfortable.

But at last he came out with it.

'Estienne, this is not an easy thing to say. We've come together a hell of a long way.'

I waited in silence; I felt what was coming, but I'd be damned if I made it easier for him.

'Hannie is pregnant again,' he said, grinning foolishly.

'That's good news.'

'Yes. Very. I hope it is a girl.'

'You deserve one.'

'Yes. Well.' He fiddled with his pipe. 'This means she will now need me around the house.'

'It is safe now, isn't it? Cruywagen's commando has expelled all the unwanted elements. They said we can relax now. Not me, of course; but the rest of you.'

'Estienne, there's no sense in it any more,' he suddenly blurted out. 'This thing can't work out. We'll all remain true to you. But there can be no more war.'

'There never was.'

'We tried.' A sudden boyish grin. 'Hell, man, those were good days in the beginning. Especially the day we met the *heemraden*.'

'Yes.'

'But a man's got to know when to stop.'

'For me, unfortunately, it is not so easy. I have no choice. I'm on the run.'

'Soon they will grow tired of it and give it up.'

'No they won't, Hendrik. I have challenged what was most dear to them. They can never forget or forgive that.'

'I tell you, in another year it will be over. One day we'll sit together on your stoep with our grandchildren playing around our feet, and tell them about these times. Hey?' He reached out to give me a tremendous blow between the shoulders.

'You mean this is really the end for us?'

'For me it is. And I've spoken to the others too.' He rose. 'Well, my good friend Estienne . . .'

'Good-bye, Hendrik.'

At last I was quite alone. How suddenly, how easily, it had come about. Life is not really very dramatic.

· *265* ·

Hiding in the houses of my widows after the death of Tante Louise, with *Orléans* no longer a protected haven, throughout that bitter cold month of July, I wrote Swellengrebel one last letter. It was too long, really, to be called a letter. A book, more likely, a book in three parts, recapitulating everything I had told him before, and more; rewriting my whole history. There was a curious deep satisfaction about it, as if it were my testament.

I did not really expect him to reply to it. Why should he, this time? But it was necessary for my own peace of mind to know that I had exhausted every possibility.

With the women, too, I was approaching the end. It began with
Liesbet de Wet, although it was not really her fault. Her
formidable mother, Elizabeth Joubert, was overcome by a
stroke while she was correcting a slave; for three days she lay
motionless, speechless, uttering only desperate moans and
rolling her eyes, at last truly poor and defenceless. Petrus de
Wet came all the way from the Breede River. True to his nature
he did not say much; but whatever he said must have been
persuasive enough for Liesbet to decide to transport her helpless
mother to his farm, and herself to pack up and follow, a dutiful
wife restored to her domestic responsibilities by an unmistake-
able sign from above.

'I hope you'll understand, Estienne,' she came to tell me
behind the shed where she had given me a furtive final
rendezvous. 'But I have to go, I need Petrus, he needs me.'

'You don't love that half-dead man, do you?'

She hung her head but said nothing.

'Look at me,' I said.

She raised her eyes.

With my mouth I shaped the word, '*Gamahucher*.'

She blushed a deep carmine, then turned and hurried away.

Jeannette Gobregts, shaking her bright straw-coloured hair,
said, 'Forgive me, Estienne. But I can't go on in this manner.
You come and go, I'm never sure whether I'll ever see you
again. I have to start thinking of my future, you know. There
are other men interested in me, but while you are around
they're all scared of approaching me. So I need to know, today,
what your intentions are with me.'

'You know I cannot marry anyone now, Jeannette.'

'Then you must go and not come back.'

'Is there someone in particular?'

'Yes.' She wasn't looking at me.

'Is it Hendrik Coetsee?'

She nodded fiercely.

'I hope you will be happy with him. He's a good man.'

'I know he is.'

She was crying; to tell you the truth, I too was close to tears. Around me even the small ramshackle temporary world was collapsing.

· *268* ·

And Leonie Burgert. 'There was a time when it was an adventure to be with you, Estienne. You came and went like a whirlwind. There was always excitement, you made the impossible seem possible. But now – you're just a man on the run, a vagabond, a hunted creature. There is no joy in it any more, only fear, and sometimes irritation. And sometimes – contempt. Do you understand?'

'I understand.'

I did not wait for the others. It was not necessary.

This was an end, it had to be accepted. Once again I had come to a frontier; once again it had to be crossed. Once again I had to go beyond.

Part the Third

Once upon a time on a faraway island there was a girl who had been born from an egg. This was something that happened from time to time, but very rarely. You must know that a woman born from an egg has a charmed life. It is given to her that if she finds herself in great trouble she can fly away. But this can happen only once in her life, and if she chooses the wrong moment her flight ends in disaster and she falls to her death. So she must be very very careful in choosing that moment, otherwise her whole life will have been in vain.

Now when this girl had grown up into a young woman the village in which she lived with her people was raided by strangers from the north of the island and all the young men and women were taken away to the Bay of Antongil.

'You must take special care of this one,' the village elders pleaded with the strangers before they left, 'for she has been born from an egg.' But the strangers merely laughed and threw stones at the elders, for they would not believe such a tale. And the young woman was treated just as badly as the others.

When they reached the Bay of Antongil the captives were sold as slaves to traders from the sea. Sometimes two, sometimes three women were exchanged for one gun; others were sold for knives, brandy, mirrors, beads. First they were carefully inspected to ensure that they were well equipped to procreate. This young woman was so beautiful in her parts that she alone was sold for a silver pistol inlaid with mother-of-pearl.

Those chosen to be taken away first had to be baptised forcibly. This killed the names they had been born with and gave them new names, stupid meaningless names like Apollo, Cupido or Achilles for the men, and Susanna, Catarina, Sabina or Rosette for the women. I shall not tell you the name this woman who had been born from an egg was given, it is too disgraceful. This was so humiliating to her that she considered flying away, but she thought: Perhaps this is not the worst that can happen, I must wait.

Once baptised, they were all loaded into the belly of a ship, the women near the back where they were kept at the disposal of the officers. Many committed suicide, some by beating their heads against the sides of the boat, some by fasting, some by holding their breath. And again the young woman who had been born from an egg believed she should fly away, but again she desisted, thinking that perhaps there was worse to come.

Once a week all the slaves were brought up to the deck where bucketfuls of seawater and vinegar were flung over their bodies to cleanse them. They were ordered to dance. Those who refused because they were too weak were thrown overboard. The woman who had been born from an egg was among those who refused, not because she was too weak but because she was stubborn. So she was beaten terribly, and once again she wondered whether the moment had come to fly away, but she stayed; and she survived.

In a distant land called Bonne-Espérance they were sold to new masters. The young woman who had been hatched from an egg fetched the highest price and she was taken to live with a rich man and his wife, and they treated her reasonably well because they had paid so much money for her. Nevertheless she was made to work all hours of the day and night, but she did not complain. Only when her master, who was an officer in the army, came to her sleeping-mat at night to force her to lie with him, did she resist. He was furious and reported to the authorities that she had been insubordinate and insolent, so she was bound to the stake in front of the Castle of that place and stripped naked and flogged by the torturers of the Governor, known as the *geweldenaars*. She was in so much pain that she thought: Surely this is the moment to fly away. But again she repressed the urge.

However, her mistress suspected that the real reason for her husband's anger was that he desired the body of the slave woman, who was indeed very beautiful. So the mistress hid one of her brooches among the things of the woman and reported to the authorities that someone had stolen it. When it was found, the woman was once again taken to the stake, this time to be branded with an iron. Now this, surely, must be the worst moment of my life, thought the woman who had been hatched from an egg: this time I have the right to fly away. But again she found the courage to resist the desire.

Soon afterwards, because the mistress could still not contain her jealousy, she forced her husband to sell the slave woman to a man notorious throughout that land for his cruelty. It was known that he had already beaten some of his slaves to death. To avoid this fate the woman who had been born from an egg ran away in the night. But she was caught and brought back. This time her punishment was atrocious, and a heavy iron was riveted to her leg, so tight that it bit into her flesh.

'Now you are truly a slave,' said her new master when she was brought back to his home, 'and I shall have my way with you whenever I please and in whichever way I please. Tonight your previous master will come to visit me and the two of us shall enjoy you, even if it kills you.'

And this time the woman who had been born from an egg thought: This must be the moment I have been waiting for.

That night, as the two men approached her, she stood up before them and began to beat her arms against her sides, and they turned to wings. And to the great dismay of the masters she changed into a bird, and flew away, and not even the heavy shackle on her leg could restrain her. Away she flew, through the night, and through many days and nights, back towards the island where she came from.

· 270 ·

'Did she get back safely?' I asked. 'Or did she fall to her death?'
'That is not for you to know,' you answered.

· 271 ·

I read in my heavy book. There are two ways by which men can come to honour. One is the way of Letters; the other the way of Arms. For myself I have more arms than learning, and my inclination is to Arms, for I was born, as Tante Louise assured me, under the influence of the planet Mars. So I am almost compelled to follow that road, and must pursue it despite the whole world.

It is night as I set out from the dark house of one of the last remaining widows on this my third journey. The farmyard is silent; there is no sound from the labourers' huts. They are all sleeping like logs. I feel a tinge of regret about having to leave like this, in stealth, like a thief in the night. But it is the only way: in my search for woman I cannot now be detained by any woman.

That long-ago first journey was a reconnaissance, exploring the territory, drawing its map in a journal subsequently removed from me. On the second I went in search of Monomotapa, which I found and didn't find. It, too, was taken from me. This one, Rosette, is yours. And I must find you even if I no longer remember what you look like. Will I even recognise you? This land may have enchanted you beyond recognition.

348

No, I shall recognise you. I know you by now better than I have known myself.

Darkness is your element. It was night when you set out; it is night for me too. Somewhere I shall discover you.

No matter what obstacles are placed between me and you, I shall not return without you, or without news of you. At last I shall know all. Nothing will remain unsolved. There is a remedy for everything, you know, except death.

· 272 ·

This time I am on foot, and (excepting Jeanne) alone. It is a daunting journey but I have all the time in the world.

For the third time I retrace the trajectory already drawn twice before across the dusty surface of the land. It is tempting, I admit, to follow a different route altogether – not having found you before might well suggest that you have gone another way – but Jeanne compels me to repeat what has been done before. And so, in this letter which is drawing to a close, I write myself into another quest for you. Hardly: I said in the beginning, didn't I, that this shall never have been written; not by me. I have not even pen or paper. (What a relief. That last long three-part letter/book I addressed to Swellengrebel had to be written on so many different kinds of paper, borrowed from so many different people.) I have become my own imagining. As I close my eyes to write, and in writing to travel once more towards you across this land of space and miracles, I am inscribed as it were by another pen into my journey. It is strangely comforting to feel that my own story now determines me as much as I have been inventing it.

Each life is a writing. What a pity most of us write so badly.

Slow, slow, this progress, if progress there is. One sees so much more, and much more intensely, travelling like this, having renounced the motion of horse or wagon. Part of the landscape, drawn into it with every step. A satisfying reflection in the execution of the most elementary motion: raising or lowering of foot, tensing of muscles in buttock, thigh or calf, inclination of torso, rhythm of arm and lightly clenched hand. When someone approaches – a wagon, a horse, a herdsman with his flock – I hide away or make a long detour to avoid them. I am sufficient unto myself. On my back a linen bag (taken from my last woman), strained only by the weight of my heavy book. Nothing else, not even food. The journey provides me with what I need. So little.

· *273* ·

I can read, eat, shit, piss, sing. I look, smell, taste, touch, listen as I go. I am being looked at, listened to, smelled, touched, tasted. I am perhaps free. Estienne Barbier: whatever I am due to be I am becoming fast.

· *274* ·

On my first journey I came in the name of the Company. *Belga tuum nomen populis fatale domandis/ Horreat et leges Africa terra tuas.* Remember? My God, how distant now. On the second journey I travelled with the colonists. This is the third. Only you know my mission. It is a kind of pilgrimage. I am in need of absolution. A necessary journey to redeem myself. For this I have to reach those we expelled, and scattered, and attacked, and insulted. Above all I have to find you.

I no longer know the names of the places I pass by. All the earlier names are now inadequate. I possess nothing. I have to learn anew, not their names but *them*. The stoneness of a stone, the ridgeness of a ridge, the thorniness of a thorntree, the silence of silence.

I am dying of thirst. Lying in the dust, resigned to absolute space, I prepare to relinquish all. But a small band of wandering hottentots – approaching from afar like a little cloud of dust, a humble cloud the size of a man's hand – come upon me and revive me with curdled milk from a calabash, and fermented honey-beer in the shell of such an egg as women are sometimes born from. They drag me to a place of meagre shade and tend me there, clucking like birds. Some among them can speak Dutch.

What are you doing here? I ask them. Are you not afraid the people will attack you again?

No one can drive us away, they say. Can you drive away the wind or the dust? We are here.

Indeed, it dawns on me, indeed: the misery and the magic of this land. One thinks, as a soldier, that you have power to solve the problems. It is not so. Our error is not that we deny solutions, or attempt the wrong ones. Our error is thinking in terms of solutions as such. The government is here and its soldiers are here, the colonists are here, these natives are here, the earth and dust and scrub and light are here. They are not problems to be solved. They are here, that's all. They can be loved, I suppose.

'Forgive me,' I say to them. I prostrate myself in the dust before them and clutch their gnarled feet and say, 'Forgive me.'

'There is no forgiveness to be asked,' says an old man. 'Why do you want it?'

'Because I am here,' I say. 'Because you are here.'

'You need nothing from us.'

'We need everything from each other. I was present at too many killings. Without forgiveness it cannot end.'

'What are you doing here on your own?' asks the old man. 'Where are you going?'

'I am looking for a woman. She has run away.' I try to describe the indescribable.

'Yes,' he says suddenly, and it comes to me like rain after a drought. (I have lived that; I know what it means, I have danced its ecstasies.) 'It is possible that she has passed by this place. There are many runaways beyond the Gariep.'

'I have been beyond that river,' I say, 'but saw no sign of her. Or any other runaways for that matter.'

'You looked in the wrong place.'

'How will I ever find the right place?'

'We can send someone with you if you wish.'

'I cannot pay. I have nothing.'

'But if we send someone with you to guide you we shall need something of you to keep in trust.'

'I told you, I really have nothing at all.'

'What is it you have in that bag?'

'A book,' I say. 'It was my father's.' I take it out and show it to them. They are dumbfounded.

'What is this thing you call a book?'

'It is a man's life.'

'You can eat it?'

'You can do nothing with it.'

'Then you will give it to us?'

'I can't. It has saved my life.' I show them the mark of the shot. 'Without it I may die.'

'Where you go you will not need it. It is too heavy.'

It occurs to me that they are right. What means most to me of this book I already have in my head; perhaps that is why my brains feel shrivelled-up and dried in my skull. With a smile of resignation I hand it over to the old man. 'Take it,' I say. 'Cherish it. Perhaps it will save your life too.'

'Is it magic?'

'Yes, it is.'

'Then we shall keep it carefully. And when you bring back the man we send with you to that place, you may have it again.'

'So be it.'

· 278 ·

Gaunt old man from La Mancha: I too am torn between the temptations of self-destruction and recklessness. I too must learn to be meek.

· 279 ·

This emptiness. Within four years I have seen the plains change. The first time there were herds and herds of game in abundance. Now it is difficult to find anything. There are no unicorns left. Perhaps even the hippogryphs have disappeared. It is a sad, sad land.

Beside a small fire we sit together in the dark, Jeanne, I, and the young hottentot. I check Jeanne's crotch.

The man's name is Khoib. It means 'man'. A strange name to give a man. In the beginning I find it quite unsettling, but one grows accustomed to it. He has begun to teach me the sounds of his language. Already I can produce a not unimpressive series of clicks. I am amazed at the intricacies of his speech. It can convey shades of meaning that don't even exist in my mother tongue. There are thirteen different words for smells, he teaches me. And there is no genitive. One does not say, *My hat* or *My sheep*, but *The hat by me* or *The sheep by me*. There is at most contiguity, not possession.

There are tongues even more subtle and complicated in the deep interior, Khoib tells me. In one of those tongues a man would greet you, if he sees you again after a long absence, by saying, '*Unqabe okwe thamsanqa.*' It means, he says, 'You are as scarce as happiness.' The clicks are beautiful.

I am ready to weep. There is so much to be learned.

It is easier now to travel through a drought-stricken barren regions. Following invisible beacons, unintelligible landmarks, Khoib knows exactly where to go: at easy half-day distances from each other there are ostrich eggs buried in the hard-baked earth, sealed, containing water. He smells or remembers or invents them. A small twig stuck in the egg protrudes above ground, that is all. He sees it from afar. In other places he kneels on all fours in what he calls a *goreh*, a shallow dry ditch, and starts digging with his hands; invariably, within at most a foot he strikes water. Alternatively he digs up tubers or hidden melons, *tsammas*, whose slightly acrid juice is incredibly refreshing. The forbidden land is beginning to yield its secrets, revealing itself generous, profound, miraculous. I am ashamed. When again we meet a small wandering band beside a trickle of a stream, I amaze them all – 'This man is undoubtedly mad,' one of them tells Khoib, not knowing that I can now understand his words – by insisting on washing their feet.

· 282 ·

'I think you're overdoing it,' says Jeanne that night beside the fading coals; Khoib has already turned on his side, drawn up his knees, and is fast asleep.

'I have only begun,' I say.

'You think one man can cancel the accumulated guilt of a generation?'

'One young girl, not even seventeen, defied the greatest armies of her time to do what was right,' I challenge her. '*You* have taught me to start with the impossible.'

'This solitary crusade – is this the right way?'

'I think it is the only way.'

'Are you sure you're not only looking for a woman, Estienne?'

'Rosette is no longer a woman,' I say. 'Rosette is now the name of everything I have to do.'

'You need rest.'

'I have renounced sleep until I find her.'

'You're doing penance?'

'I suppose so. Do not mock me.'

'I'm not. But sometimes the old uncertain, blustering Estienne was easier to handle.'

'You also have your sanctimonious side, Jeanne.'

'I know. But I've had three hundred years of experience. And seeing each generation blundering into the same error, the same violence, the same injustice, the same misunderstanding, is not conducive to equanimity.'

'Go to sleep,' I say, annoyed.

'I won't,' she says. 'We'll sit it through together.'

· 283 ·

'This woman we are going to,' says Khoib, 'what is her name?'

'She has no name,' I say, and of course it is true.

'This woman without a name,' he continues, 'she must be a great storyteller.'

'She is the greatest storyteller I have heard,' I assure him. 'But how do you know?'

'We are getting closer to her,' he says, 'for we are beginning to see her stories.'

'I don't understand.'

'Don't you see?' he says, describing a sweeping gesture with his arm, covering a broad range of landscape from horizon to horizon. 'These rocks, this sand, those mountains, everything you can see, these are the stories she has told, that is why they are here.'

We are standing together on an outcrop. I stare at the contours of the landscape, flowing about me like a narrative without end. On the last journey, I remember, I thought that these hard clear things contained her; but of course that was my uninformed guess, confirming the inadequacies of my language. Now I see it as it is, in this light: and I know that, of course, what he says is simple truth. This is indeed your visible language.

Then why am I terrified?

The terror lies in knowing I have no tongue in which to reply. I can say *buttes* or *rocher* or *plaine*, or in the language of this land *heuwels, rots, veld*: but these remain empty sounds drifting on the wind, as inconsequential as the brittle shiverings

356

of grass. How different is this, *your* language, the world you are speaking into being as I gaze at it: hard sediment, languorous contours, deceptive distances, space, space.

· *284* ·

To test the limits of the sayable? To confirm the limits of the said. To live the limits of the self.

· *285* ·

It takes some time to study, and reflect on, all the different storylines running from this outcrop on which we find ourselves, and then to select the one that appears most promising, a subterranean course marked only by slight differentiations in colour above, ever deeper and more dramatic, until it breaks out in a violent current, visible and abundant, an affirmation of resistance overcome. If it were not a story it would be taking months.

'Are you sure of the way you must go now?' asks Khoib.

'Yes, I can see it. Why do you ask?'

'Because from here you must go alone. I can no longer help you.'

I tremble, not so much from fear as from the awareness of the daunting responsibility I must now assume. But I know he is right; and I have Jeanne.

'I shall find my way,' I say.

We embrace. I watch him as he goes back from where we have come, growing smaller and smaller, a shadow, a speck.

I follow the storyline, your story, as it runs through the shimmering land.

I encounter many people on the way. Some I recognise, others not. They belong to all the tribes and settlements decimated by us a year ago, and as they approach their lamentations ring against the up-ended white bowl of the sky. To all of them I kneel and ask forgiveness; I wash and kiss their feet. I call them by their own name now, Khoikhoin, People-of-people, no longer by that derisive white word 'hottentot'.

Among them, more and more often, are men, women and children I recognise as dead. The chief Gal and members of his settlement. Others from the Kabobiquas and the many tribes we have annihilated on our raids. The members of the small party encountered on my birthday. They, too, stop to have their feet washed, to exact homage from me.

I harangue them as they surround me in the sun. 'In the name of my race,' I say ('Noble rhetoric again,' whispers Jeanne), 'I address yours, with whom we have had a prolonged experience of pain. Let us share our humanity instead. Let us share hope. We have seen you look back in horror and sorrow at the tragedy of your past. Let us now break, for heaven's sake, for this earth's sake, the cycle of hate and vengeance.'

Many of the people, living and dead, are touched by my words and my actions, content to see me humble and prostrate, prepared to extend forgiveness. Others are not so easily satisfied and demand punishment. Day after day I am stripped and beaten with thongs, with kieries, with thorn branches; I am forced to lie outstretched for them to trample and kick me and drive their meagre cattle over me. I am covered in blood and dung. Even that is not the end. Men and women take turns to squat over my abused body and defecate on me. Children hurl scorpions at me and spit at me.

All this I undergo, encouraged by Jeanne, without complaint.

I accept every blow, every kick, every turd, every gob of mucus. Because I know it is the only way to redeem myself.

Every time I rise after such an encounter and prepare to proceed along the course of your harsh narrative, another group arrives and exacts its tribute and its retribution.

I am buried in sand, I am smothered in excrement, I am suspended from trees, my ears and nose and tongue pierced with spiky white thorns. It is a terrible *via dolorosa*, yet I exult. This is my necessary purging on behalf of all of us who have invaded this space to subjugate it with our presumption and visit it with our devastation.

· *287* ·

Other experiences accompany these physical exertions, the suffering. I'm learning, learning all the time. I learn their multifarious languages, I learn from them how the world was made, how this land was told into existence; they teach me their remedies, their stories, their secrets of hunting and gathering and caring for the cattle, the long-tailed sheep, caring for our mutual deep mother, the earth. I learn to recognise her voice, to breathe in her breath, to attune myself to her arcane rhythms in profound incestuous couplings. Then more, still more. I learn the intricate sign-languages of trees and rocks and water, of dust-devils and the rain; I learn to dance the dance of the sun, of the moon, of the hills and plains.

This, I acknowledge, is now my madness. To have sided with what used to be the enemy, to have forsaken the privileges and comforts of my own position. At last I have escaped from the redoubt I once built on a gull-ridden beach. I have renounced protection or shelter of all kind. *J'ai passé outre.*

And all the time I progress along the meanderings of your narrative: upstream, upstream all the time, closer and closer to the source, to you. Some days we cover miles. On many others our progress – depending on the kind of the encounters along the way, the extent of the demands made on me, the compass of the pain inflicted on me or exacted from me – can be measured in feet, *voire* in inches. But every inch, I assure you, is earned in joy and pain, filth, fatigue, bliss, bliss.

Mea culpa, mea culpa, mea maxima culpa.

· *288* ·

In this confessional rage, let me add my betrayal of the poor drummer, Nic Wijs. It was so easy really. A message with a callow recruit (two stuyvers) to the captain of '*t Huys te Marquette* on the day before our cavale. Only by drawing all the attention to him could I establish the space for myself to make my own escape. It was the only way, I swear, and I was desperate.

· *289* ·

Do you really believe me?

· *290* ·

I am willing to acknowledge that I may have been mistaken about the unicorn. The sun was right behind it, in my eyes, when I first saw it; and when I reached the carcass it was getting dark. And the next morning I set out before sunrise. It might have been – I cannot say for sure: anything is possible – a one-horned oryx.

I have given up clothes. Exposed to the sun I see and feel my body toughened, hardened, shrivelled, stripped of excess. I am bone and leather-skin and beard. My penis is shrivelled and brown like an old turd. I have sacrificed one of my balls to emulate those I once despised and now do homage to. I renounce food, and drink only small quantities of water. Soon I shall give up shitting and pissing. My life is purified. I am feeling the onset of transparency; in good time the sun will shine right through me and cancel my shadow.

But the hippogryph, I swear, was real. You saw it with me.

And then there is, on the last night, just before I reach you, the rocky hill, curiously conical and tall, very steep and bare, and scaly like the petrified skin of some vast animal older than history, yet covered on the very top with brittle grass. This promontory I mount painfully, and there, ascended to the cold gleaming top where the coarse grass grows, I discover very plainly that the moon is not so far from earth as the astronomers assert; for as the planet passes at this time over my head, the night being very still and clear, I can plainly perceive the grass there to wave and wave, and have the noise of its motion in my ears.

The earth about me is heaving. New hills are thrust, as I watch, towards the inverted sky. The sun has gone down. There is the moon, the breeze of its passage still about me. It is night, but a night so luminous that I can read mountains and scrub and earth by it. I know you must be near and this must be the source of your stories: a hollow high up against a bare mountainside, a shallow cave, an indentation like a navel.

I *entame* the last incline. But Jeanne restrains me.

'From here you must go on alone, Estienne,' she says. '*She* awaits you, whatever the outcome of your meeting, in sickness or in health, for richer or poorer, life or death.'

'I cannot go without you,' I say, in the clutch of panic.

'Of course you can. We have covered enough ground together.'

'How can you abandon me?'

'This is not abandonment, Estienne,' she says in my ear. 'I must leave you to face the rest on your own. I cannot be an alibi for you any more.'

Gravely I ask, 'Are you satisfied with me?'

'No,' she replies quietly, in her disarmingly direct manner.

I bow my head.

'But then, I haven't been satisfied with myself either,' she adds. 'We have to learn, I suppose, not only to accept judgement or forgiveness from others, but to forgive ourselves.'

'Where will you go now?'

'I must find someone new. Who feels the urge to say no, yet still lacks the courage.'

'Can you never rest?'

'Of course not.'

'The burden of immortality?'

'What *you* need to assume now is the burden of mortality. Both to acquiesce in it and resist it. I know how hard that is.

Towards the end, those last months in Rouen especially, when they daily tormented me with their inquisition, I began sometimes to long for death. I'd seen by then too much of evil, of horror, of lies and violence: all I wanted was the fire. To be consumed and turned to ashes. But the urge is ignoble. Even though futurity is our nature one should not try to bypass the present.'

'I shall try to remember.'

'Adieu, Estienne Barbier.'

· *295* ·

So many years ago: the first time she came to me. On the tall stone bridge of Orléans. I was – what? – seventeen, I think. Papa had sent me to town on my own on the rickety one-horse cart to deliver to a customer on the Route d'Autun a heavy armoire we had just finished. Previously, too proud of his handiwork to miss a delivery, he'd always done it himself. But this time, in the first chill of autumn – it was mid-October – his amputated leg was aching and Maman had persuaded him to let me go alone. 'He is no longer a child,' she said. After delivering the cupboard and securing in my knotted handkerchief the ninety-five livres (barely the price of a horse) I had received for it, I proceeded in a flush of recklessness to a tavern to celebrate the heady feeling of having accomplished some obscure rites of passage. A man I met there, Louis, talked me into going with him to a dance where, he assured me, the prettiest girls of Orléans would be in attendance. At first, bearing in mind the admonitions of my parents, I made some attempts at protesting; but as I gradually succumbed to his lurid imagery and the effects of the wine which he continued to coax me into buying (depleting quite rapidly the proceeds of my sale), the idea became irresistible.

My memories of the night are still confused. Confused and

inexpressibly sad. Not so much because, in the course of it, I spent – or was robbed of – every *sol* of my earnings (representing more than a month's work), as because of the nature of the event itself. The exuberance of peasant folk released, briefly, from toil; drinking and dancing and celebrating, in a frenzy of merrymaking, to forget for those few hours, for a night, the hard labour in the fields or in some exacting landlord's service; or sentry-duty at some castle; or shoeing horses; long hours in a smithy, a carpentry shop or tannery; whatever. To forget the aggravations of a nagging wife, an abusive husband, sick children, unrelenting creditors, court cases, imprisonment, branding irons, the stake on the village square. A brief respite – and then, come the dawn, back. Back, as always; every one of them.

I could not bear it any more. Leaving behind the last revellers (my newly found friend had disappeared long before, as soon as my last coins had gone), I ran away. I was racked by sobs. About betraying the trust of my parents, about losing my money, about a night wasted; but above all about that terrifying discovery of what I would be going back to.

Despite the cold I crossed the Loire, and stopped halfway on the bridge, where I leaned on the parapet and stared at the dark grey water. My breath made small white plumes in the half-dark. And suddenly I was beset by an anger and a terror more desperate, more absolute, than I'd ever known. An endless dreary future seemed to be closing in on me, suffocating me. In spite of the cold I was sweating.

I heard myself cry out aloud, 'No! No, I won't! I tell you, I won't ever accept it!'

'Why not?' a young girl's voice asked.

I swung round, my cheeks stinging. It was a stranger, a small dark peasant girl with an unusually short haircut that rather disfigured her attractive features. What struck me above all was her eyes, their blackness, their passion, their light.

'Who are you?' I asked in a rush of aggressiveness.

'Jeanne d'Arc,' she said.

'What are you doing here?'

'I heard you shouting "No". It sounded like a battle cry. I thought we could have a talk.'

Only now did her words penetrate my consciousness. 'Jeanne d'Arc? You must be bloody mad. Or do you take *me* for a madman?'

'I'll go with you if you like,' she said.

'Go where? Back to Bazoches?'

'To the ends of the earth if you wish,' she said, and smiled.

· *296* ·

Here at last I face you, in the navel of the mountain. It is darker in here than outside, as dark as that cage of criminals to which I once condemned you and where I later found you miraculously alive. There are people huddled about you. I think they are people: but they are so still they may be boulders. They are listening, entranced. And you are telling them stories. From where you sit a spring breaks from the earth – I can hear it burble with your voice – and flows outside, down the slope, finding its many-fingered way across the plains of the dry land.

'So you have come,' you say, breaking off in the middle of your story.

'For years I have looked for you. The search has consumed everything. But now nothing else matters. You are here. I have found you, Rosette.'

'That is not my name.'

'I know. But it is the only sound I can call you by.'

'Don't call me anything.'

'I love you.'

'What do you know of love, Estienne Barbier?'

'I am learning.'

'If you have really learned to love, you must let me be.'

'I can't. I have searched for you for too long. Look at me: there is almost nothing left of me.'

'That is as it should be.'

'I want to remain here with you.'

It is hard to make out your gesture in the dark, but you seem to beckon me. And I approach. I see your eyes, your woman's eyes, dark with everything you have witnessed in your life, the undisclosed horror and the triumph of it.

Those people – rocks? – around us still don't move.

'You must not touch me.'

I pay no heed; I cannot have come all this way and not embrace you. Even if it means my death: in this instant my desire for you *is* my desire for extinction. Body against body we shall be consumed.

In my mind I see again our single giant shadow on the walls and ceiling of my room.

Yes. Now I embrace you. It is not the flesh I once knew, its pliant smoothness, its hardness sustained by bone. You are like an ancient paper-thin dry leaf to my touch; as my fingers brush you I feel you disintegrate. In a slight sifting of ashes – whirring wings – you disappear.

This, too, then, will have been inevitable.

You must go back, you tell me in a voice that is no longer a voice, and face whatever awaits you. Your story is reaching for its end.

· 297 ·

I no longer recall where I wandered, alone and on foot, during the month or more since I left my last widow. A network of lines across the far reaches of the colony. Perhaps beyond, who knows? Avoiding all human contact; suffering; abandoning my last possession, the book, my father's book. At some stage, this I do know, I decided to return. It was the one remaining necessary act: not to wait for them to find me but to deliver myself – consciously, freely – to their justice.

· 298 ·

Somewhere along the way a wagon passed me from behind, with a solitary man, spindly and bearded, on the front seat. He seemed singularly placid; not even my sun-scorched unkempt appearance or my nakedness seemed to surprise him. For all I could tell he had been passing many such subhuman creatures on his way.

His name, he said, was Stefaans. I'm not sure about the surname. Joubert? Fouché? Malherbe? A Huguenot name, was all I grasped. Good.

I know I was amused – detachedly, distantly – as I said, 'I am Estienne. It's the same name as yours. Perhaps we *are* the same person.'

It provoked neither smile nor frown. Imperturbable, morose, he raised his eyes at me, then stared ahead of him again.

'Estienne Barbier,' I said.

Still no sign of recognition.

'I'm on my way to Cabo.'

'I can take you as far as Stellenbosch.'

'You can hand me over to the Landdrost then, if you wish,' I said. 'There's a price on my head. You can claim it.'

He just stared at me, the way a small child stares at a moving object.

'Jean de Luxembourg got a good reward for handing Jeanne d'Arc over to the Bishop of Beauvais.'

He sniffed; not, I think, to express any sentiment, only because he had a runny nose.

'Where have you been?' I asked.

He looked at me again as if the world was weighing too heavily on him. After a while he said, 'I don't want trouble.'

367

'There won't be trouble for you.'

'I'm just going my way, I'm not bothering anyone.'

'Good for you.'

He sighed.

'The wind,' I said, 'was blow.'

'Yes,' he answered, as if he knew exactly what I meant.

Most of the rest of the road we travelled in silence.

· *299* ·

My only regret on that tedious journey with the taciturn Stefaans was the absence of my book; though even to that I was now resigned, contenting myself with efforts to recollect what I had read so many times. Among the passages with which I thus entertained myself was the rather disturbing one that occurs on Don Quixote's final return to his village when a hare, fleeing in terror from a number of greyhounds and hunters, seeks refuge beneath the feet of Sancho's donkey. Sancho picks up the little creature and presents her to his master who, however, cries out in horror, '*Malum signum! Malum signum!*' reading it as a token that Dulcinea will now not appear to him. Sancho reasons that if the hare indeed represents Dulcinea, then saving her from the hunt and placing her for safekeeping in Don Quixote's caressing hands can be nothing but a good omen. But the hidalgo, having already renounced knight-errantry, refuses to be consoled. 'All Christians who heed omens are fools,' he says. And when the hunters arrive and demand their hare, he calmly hands her over to them.

· *300* ·

I am much more at peace with myself now than I was when I embarked on this long letter to you, my love. I have discovered a strange sense of freedom within this small dark fetid hole from which my thoughts can wander freely across the bright expanse of this wide land to which I came a stranger and with whose fate I am now singularly bound up. Adversity is a greater challenge to the imagination than contentment.

Both the living and the dead have accompanied me on this journey. But sometimes the dead appear more real than the living, who after all have their own lives, and part of whose existence must needs always remain secret unto themselves; while one assumes within oneself the dead.

My own death is now very close. The *predikant* has just been to visit me. I sent him away.

Shall I tell you about the trial? About the outrageous pleasure Landdrost Lourens took in sending me, bound and shackled, to Cabo, accompanied by a large detachment of soldiers carrying a message in which he related extensively – he had read it out to me – the circumstances in which 'the fugitive Barbier' had at last been captured and at what tremendous risk to himself? The weeks – months? I told you I have no grasp on time any more – I was kept in the Dark Hole before my interrogation began, day after day after day after day. And then the trial itself, Daniel van den Henghel in great form, perspiring under his noble wig, his huge face ruddy with effort and with malignant joy; Swellengrebel proud and powerful, studiously avoiding my eyes. The impressive and sickening turning of the wheels of injustice. And then – *Ite, missa est* – the culmination of the sentence.

—bound to a cross, his right hand and his head severed from the body, subsequently to be drawn and quartered, the head and hand to be placed on a stake in the Roodezands Kloof, and the four remaining quarters to be displayed in four different places alongside the most frequented highways of the Settlement as prey to the air and the birds from heaven—

I remember Jeanne telling me about her own trial; how one day she'd told Bishop Pierre of Beauvais: 'You say you are my judge: take good heed not to judge me ill, because you would put yourself in great peril.'

Not one of those who had ridden with me was there. Not even Hendrik Ras. No one had offered to speak up in my defence. And the only one who might yet have risked doing so, Christian Petzold, was dead.

The ones who were there, and who will undoubtedly – today? tomorrow? soon – attend my execution, were my enemies. Lieutenant Allemann in full uniform, clutching his small hands in satisfaction. The scribe Mentzel, thinlipped and correct and disapproving. Sergeant Kok, grinning with accomplishment, his small red eyes aglint with malice. Even the doddering old Captain Rhenius. Their wives will also attend the spectacle. One has to be seen on such occasion, it is a high point on the social calendar. Mejuffrouw van den Henghel, puffed up and strutting like a pigeon. Madame Abbetje, flushed and short of breath. If she had not flogged you that day, if I had not interfered, we both might have survived. If I had not angered Allemann – if I had not refused to be silent about his petty thefts – if I had not spoken against Kok – If, if: what's the use?

I am here. And I do not regret it.

What I do regret is my terrible misjudgement, my blindness, my arrogant misreading of what really had to be done. It was right that I should accuse the criminals in power. It was right that I should call up the exploited colonists. But how unforgivable it is that I should not have recognised our true allies, the people of this land, who suffer everything. In this blindness I insulted *you*: even in setting you free I was being merely selfish; I did not think about *you*, woman, slave.

They have sentenced me to death for what I have done. I now accept that sentence for what I have *not* done, for what I have failed to do. Even if no one knows it. *I* know my true guilt. I acknowledge it. I assume it. And in writing it here to you today – Rosette, Rosette: I still have no other name to invoke you by – I must try to ensure that my confession reaches others beyond you. There is no guarantee at all: I am dead, you cannot read; I have said it before. But the attempt is worth it. For this alone, perhaps, Jeanne has accepted to be my companion for so long. I never understood. Do I even now? I can but hope.

That night I removed the shackle from your leg I did not realise it meant assuming for myself a burden for the rest of my life: my responsibility to you, to all those who remain shackled. I bow to that knowledge now.

· *301* ·

There are sounds outside. The beating of a drum. (Nic Wijs? No, no, he has flown away long ago.) Marching feet. It is a big company. They are coming for me.

Once I was myself part of such a group. There were then seven runaway slaves, two of them women, awaiting the end in this same place. As we led them out one of the men defecated in his breeches. It was repulsive and earned him a kick from our commander.

God forbid that this should happen to me. You know I have always feared physical pain, however ill this becomes a soldier. But a modicum of dignity to the end is what I most fervently hope for.

They have come to a standstill outside. There is a clinking of keys.

In a moment the light will stab me in the eyes.

They will escort me to the double flight of stairs that leads to the Governor's residence, and thence to the parade ground where the full garrison will be assembled, and all the dignitaries; and behind them the motley festive populace. Perhaps a holiday will have been declared. It is, after all, a great menace to the whole colony that is being averted today.

Afterwards my body will be torn asunder and the parts

371

distributed far and wide, along the roads I have travelled so often these past few years. My head not far from Hendrik Ras's place. His daughter must be due soon. I hope she is a healthy peasant girl, worthy of her parents.

My rump? My legs? My arms? One part perhaps on the road to the Bokkeveld. Another on the road from Stellenbosch to Drakenstein, not far I hope from Tante Louise's grave at *Orléans*. With some luck a portion of me will be displayed on the road across the Berg River: and perhaps a *reconnaissant* Hendrik Coetsee may feel obliged to take it down and offer it burning or burial to celebrate the consummation of his love for Jeannette Gobregts?

Undoubtedly one of my limbs will be nailed up along the West Coast, the road that leads to the Piquet Berg and beyond, the Oliphants River, the parched land of the Little Namaqua, the insignificant frontier of the Gariep.

Will they reserve something – my paltry penis, perhaps, much abused and guilty of abusing many – for the road to that imaginary necessary land of Monomotapa where a woman in green once entertained me?

I wish there were something to be sent abroad, entrails, in a small keg of bad brandy, to the muddy path that runs from Bazoches to Orléans, or the outskirts of Domrémy. But this is too much to hope for.

I should have been an octopus, there are so many places I should wish to retain in my ultimate grasp. But I am but a man, and that is not much; although I have dreamed much and imagined much. I have led a contrary life. My lies condemn me yet. But perhaps even a lie is not to be scorned.

The key is turning now. The heavy door really needs oiling.

A voice is calling my name.

Estienne Barbier. Yes, I am here.

Here comes the piercing light.

Let us go gently from here, for there are no birds this year in last year's nests.

—Concluding herewith, and persisting in the same, imploring the nobile benignum officium judicis, exhibitum in juditio,

Estienne Barbier

Acknowledgements

Nigel Penn of the Department of History at the University of Cape Town first kindled my interest in the exploits of Estienne Barbier, particularly through his article 'Estienne Barbier: An Eighteenth Century Cape Social Bandit?' (Social Dynamics *14(1) 1988); and once this interest became more focused, I relied on the enthusiastic help of Roy Pheiffer, whose thesis on the broken Dutch spoken by French speakers at the Cape in the first half of the 18th century, published by Academica, Cape Town etc, 1980, contains the fullest account to date of Barbier's life. The State Archives in Cape Town made available to me, with great efficiency, all the documents surrounding Barbier's trials.*

I made grateful use of Jeanne d'Arc *by Lucien Fabre (English edition translated by Gerard Hopkins, London: Odham's Press, 1954) and* The Trial of Jeanne d'Arc *by W. P. Barrett (London: George Routledge & Sons, 1931). Among other things, Fabre's description of Orleans informed Barbier's vision of Monomotapa.*

Cervantes was, of course, indispensable, both in the original and in J. M. Cohen's English Penguin translation; and a brief passage in Chapter 134 ('Everything in this world is so diverse . . .' etc.) comes from Erasmus's In Praise of Folly. *The suspicion that madness may reside in the belief 'that justice is possible' (Chapter 127) is inspired by Carlos Fuentes's wonderful essay 'Cervantes, or the Critique of Reading' (in* Myself With Others, *New York: Farrar, Straus & Giroux, 1988).*

A number of descriptive passages on the Cape, its hinterland, its peoples and its fauna in the 18th century are quoted, either verbatim or in

some adaptation, from Peter Kolb's The Present State of the Cape
of Good Hope *(1724); others are plundered from, or inspired by, the
journals of Johannes Tobias Rhenius (1724), François Valentyn (1726),
Jacobus Coetsé (1760), Carl Frederik Brink (1761–1762), Carl Peter
Thunberg (1772–1775) etc. (all published by the Van Riebeeck Society,
Cape Town), or from François le Vaillant's several* Voyages *(1783,
1784 and 1785). Some exquisite curiosa, including the effect of the female
pudenda on a lion, originate from Olfert Dapper's account of Africa
(1686). Most of the biographical details on Lieutenant Allemann, and
much information on the Cape of his time, come from two books by Otto
Friedrich Mentzel:* Life at the Cape in the Mid-Eighteenth
Century; Being the Biography of Rudolf Siegfried Allemann
(1781), and Complete and Authentic Geographical and Topographical Description of the Famous and (All Things Considered) Remarkable Cape of Good Hope *(1785), both published
by the Van Riebeeck Society.*

*The description of the mouthless people comes from Pomponius
Mela.*

The idea of a woman born from an egg first surfaced in my novella
The First Life of Adamastor, *written in 1985; subsequently I
discovered the episode of an egg caught in a trap in an unpublished story
'The Beginning of Tax' by Lynot Damalekani Masuku from Malawi,
submitted for the SABC Short Story Competition in 1992.*

*Part of Barbier's address to the Khoikhoin on his last voyage is
adapted from an appeal by Hanan Mikhail-Ashrawi of the Palestinian
Liberation Organisation to the Israeli delegation during their peace
negotiations in 1991.*

*I am indebted to Jacques Derrida for his introductory sentence to the
essay 'Outwork' in* Dissemination *(translated by Barbara Johnson, and
published by The Athlone Press, London, 1981) which has been incorpo-
rated in my own first line; and for his well-known reference to 'this
dangerous supplement' in* Of Grammatology *(translated by Gayatri
Chakravorty Spivak and published by The Johns Hopkins University
Press, Baltimore & London, 1976), which features in my second chapter.*

A few lines from Fernando Pessoa ('Thank God that stones are only

stones/ And rivers nothing but rivers/ And flowers only flowers (. . .)
Things have no meaning: they exist./ Things are the only hidden meanings
of things') have been adapted in my Chapter 193.

Most of the rest, I think, is invention. But one never knows.

André Brink
Cape Town, May – December 1992